FOUR MORE
YOU SAY WHICH WAY
ADVENTURES

❖ DINOSAUR CANYON

❖ DEADLINE DELIVERY

❖ DRAGONS REALM

❖ CREEPY HOUSE

Published by:
The Fairytale Factory Ltd.
Wellington, New Zealand.

YouSayWhichWay.com

ISBN-13: 978-1523672783
ISBN-10:1523672781

How These Books Work

In these stories YOU are the main character.

At the end of each chapter, you say which way the story goes by selecting the link that matches your choice. For example, **P233** means turn to page 233.

There are many possible paths through each story, and many different endings – some will surprise you! Once you get to an ending, you can go back to the beginning and try other paths, or you can go to the List of Choices for more options.

Your first decision is which book to read. After that it gets trickier.

Oh... and watch out for alligator pits, hungry dinosaurs, haunted washing machines, monsters, leaky rafts and cannibals.

FOUR MORE YOU SAY WHICH WAY ADVENTURES

List of Books

Dinosaur Canyon – Are you ready to meet T. Rex? This book is packed with prehistoric possibilities. While on a field trip to Montana, you spot a meteorite falling from the sky. Heading out to find the space rock starts a chain of adventures, including a trip back in time. Will you tell your teacher where you've been? Will you take him back to prove it? **P1**

Deadline Delivery – You're just a poor kid living in the flooded under-city after the waters rose. Life is hard, especially for a courier like you, delivering packages to the under-city's most dangerous neighborhoods, while dodging pirate gangs, wild animals and security robots. But today is no normal day – today, you might end up as an explorer, or a froggy, or a trainee manager. Or dead. Or worse. **P105**

Dragons Realm – Escaping the school bullies you stumble into a world of magic and dragons. A voice that only you can hear calls out for help. Will you answer? Who should you trust? Are the bullies behind you? Luckily you packed a good picnic lunch for your adventure in Dragons Realm. **P199**

Creepy House – Your cat disappears through the window of a creepy old house. Do you go and rescue her? Will you get out again? Shhh! What was that noise? There is only one way to find out, so get reading! **P347**

List of Choices P376

FOUR MORE YOU SAY WHICH WAY ADVENTURES

DINOSAUR CANYON

by Blair Polly

At the campsite

A meteorite streaks across a cloudless Montana sky and disappears behind a hill, not far away.

"Anyone see that?" you say to your classmates as you point towards the horizon.

Inside the bus, a couple of students look up from their phones. "What? Huh?"

"The meteorite. Did you see it?"

"Meteor what?" the kid sitting next to you asks.

"Never mind." You shake your head and wonder if you're the only one who's really interested in this fieldtrip.

"I saw it," Paulie Smith says from a seat near the back. "That was amazing!"

As you and Paulie search the sky for more meteorites, the bus turns off the main road and passes an old wooden sign.

WELCOME TO GABRIEL'S GULCH.

"Right," Mister Jackson says, as the bus comes to a stop. "Once your tents are set up, you've got the afternoon to go exploring. So get to it. And remember, take notes on what you see and hear. You *will* be tested."

You're hoping to find some fossils. You might even get lucky and stumble across a piece of that meteorite. That would be awesome.

After locating a level patch of ground near a clump of saltbush, you set up your dome tent and toss your sleeping bag and air mattress inside with the rest of your gear. Then you grab your daypack and water bottle. You'd never think of going for a hike without taking water with you. They don't call this area the *Badlands* without good reason.

A couple of energy bars, an apple, compass, box of matches, waterproof flashlight, folding army shovel and some warm clothing go into your daypack as well, just in case.

Mister Jackson is drinking coffee with some parents who've come along to help. They've set up the kitchen near the junction of a couple of old stone walls as protection from the wind and are laughing and telling tales of other camping trips.

"My tent's up Mister J, so I'm off to look around."

He nods. "Make sure you fill in the logbook with your intentions. Oh, and who're you teaming up with? Remember our talk on safety — you're not allowed to go wandering about alone. And watch out for rattlesnakes."

You look at the chaos around camp. Rather than being interested in dinosaur fossils, which is the main reason for this trip, most of your fellow students are puzzling over how their borrowed tents work or complaining about the cell phone reception. Camping equipment is strewn everywhere. Apart from you, Paulie is the only one who's managed to get his tent up so far.

"Hey, Paulie. I'm heading out. Want to tag along?"

Paulie points to his chest. "Who? Me?"

Paulie's not really a friend. He's a year behind you at school, but at least he seems interested in being here. He's even got a flag with a picture of a T. Rex working at the front counter of a burger joint, flying over his tent. Chuckling, you ponder the silliness of a short-armed dinosaur flipping burgers

"Yeah, you, get a move on." You walk over and write in the camp's log book. *Going west towards hills with Paulie. Back in time for dinner.*

"What are we going to do?" Paulie asks.

"Explore those hills," you say, pointing off into the west. "Quick, grab your pack and let's go, before Mr. J or one of the parents decides to come along."

As Paulie shoves a few supplies in his bag, you look across the scrubland towards the badly-eroded hills in the distance. It's ideal country for finding fossils. Erosion is the fossil hunter's best friend. Who knows what the recent rains have uncovered for a sharp-eyed collector like yourself.

"Did you know they've found Tyrannosaurus Rex bones around here?" Paulie says as the two of you head out of camp.

You pull the *Pocket Guide to the Montana Badlands* out of your back pocket and hold it up. "I've been reading up too."

"But did you know scientists reckon T. Rex had arms about the same length as man's but would have been strong enough to bench press over 400 pounds?"

"Yeah?" you say, remembering Paulie's love of obscure facts and how he drives everyone at school crazy with them. "Well according to this book, there's been more dinosaur fossils found in Montana than anywhere else in the country."

Paulie nods. "I want to find an Ankylosaurus. They're built like a tank with armor and everything. They had horns sticking out of the sides of their heads and a mean looking club on the end of their tails!"

That would be pretty awesome. "A tank eh? Maybe we'll find one of its scales embedded in the rock, or a horn sticking out of a cliff. Anything's possible when fossil hunting, that's what makes it so exciting."

You both stride off across the prairie with big smiles and high hopes. Fifteen minutes later, when you look back, the camp is nothing but a cluster of dots barely visible through the sagebrush.

"Where to from here?" Paulie asks.

"There's a couple of options. We could search for that meteorite. It

4

must have come down somewhere around here."

"Maybe it landed in that canyon?" Paulie says, indicating a gap between two hills. "Could be all sorts of neat stuff in there."

"That's Gabriel's Gulch," you say, referring to the map in your guide. "Or we could look for fossils in those hills," you say, pointing to your right. "According to the guide, there's an abandoned mine over there too."

Your adventure is about to begin. It's time to make your first decision. Do you:

Go left into Gabriel's Gulch? **P5**

Or

Go right towards the eroded hills? **P9**

You have decided to go left into Gabriel's Gulch

The canyon is narrow with a dried creek bed running down its centre. Wind and rain have sculpted the sandstone cliffs on either side into unusual shapes. You've followed the creek up for about a mile when you see a graceful sandstone arch sitting on a narrow ridge high above the canyon's floor.

"Wow," Paulie says. "Look at that." He pulls out his cell phone to take a picture.

"Let's climb up and get a closer look," you say. "We can take some shots of us standing beside it."

Paulie likes your idea and hurries along the gully spouting facts as he goes. "Did you know sandstone dates back to the Late Cretaceous period?"

You shake your head. "Do you live on Google, Paulie?"

"But–but that was the time of the dinosaurs. Everyone knows that!"

You're not sure that everyone does, but you do remember reading something in your guide book about this place. "It says here that Gabriel's Arch was named after the man who discovered it in 1802. It also says he died after being bitten by a rattlesnake a week later."

"Don't rattlesnakes rattle if you get near them?" Paulie asks.

"Unless you sneak up on 'em," you say. "Then they strike first and rattle later."

"Oh no!" Paulie says in mock terror, flapping his hands in exaggerated fashion and whipping his head back and forth faster than spectators at a tennis match.

"Don't give yourself whiplash," you say, trying not to crack up at his antics.

Paulie giggles. "I'm not afraid of snakes. Snakes are awesome. Our friends even. They get rid of the vermin. Besides, they're more afraid of you than you are of them."

He stops playing around and leads you up a washed out section of canyon wall and then up along a narrow ridge. Near the end of the ridge, a stone arch soars above you like a gateway to some mythical kingdom. Beyond the arch, the ridge comes to an abrupt end and a vertical cliff drops to the canyon floor. Across the canyon, in the distance, layered hills rise from a barren landscape to a clear blue sky.

As you walk towards the arch, you spot a fist-sized piece of rock that looks strangely out of place here in the Badlands. Rather than being ochre or tan – the colors usually associated with this part of the country – this rock is dark charcoal and covered in glassy specks and tiny holes. You wonder if it's volcanic in origin, but when you pick it up and feel its weight, you instantly know what you've found.

"Paulie, look. This could be that meteorite we saw."

Paulie looks down at the piece of rock in your hand. "How do you know?"

"See this blackish crust? This side would have taken all the heat as the rock burned its way through the atmosphere."

Paulie touches the pitted surface with his finger.

"And feel how heavy it is. Iron most likely."

Paulie tests the weight in his palm. "Wow, it is heavy!"

You can't wait to show this to Mister Jackson. With the hunk of rock in your hand, you walk towards the sandstone arch. "Take a photo of me in the arch with it, Paulie."

"I'll set the timer and get us both in the picture," Paulie says, placing the phone on a nearby boulder and adjusting its angle. "Right, get into position, we've got 10 seconds."

As you wait under the arch, the rock in your hand glows red and starts to vibrate, slowly at first, then faster and faster. A high-pitched hum gets louder and louder. You drop the lump and place your hands over your ears.

Paulie's eyes are scrunched closed and his hands are over his ears too. "Owwwwww!" he yells.

Then, with a bright flash, the sound stops.

Paulie looks at you in confusion. "Holy moly, what the heck was that?"

"I don't know, but it was awfully strange. Rocks don't normally make a—" And then you notice the landscape around you has changed. What was semi-desert is now lush and green with broad-leafed plants and ferns. The dry grasslands have turned into a steamy jungle.

Paulie's notices it too and stands there wide-eyed and trembling. "Wha–what's going on? Am I dreaming?"

"This is impossible," you say, looking through the arch into the canyon. "Where did all this water come from?" Blinking, you try to make the illusion go away. "I don't think you're dreaming, Paulie." You pinch your forearm. "Ouch! I'm not."

"It's a lot warmer too," Paulie says. "And humid, like in the tropics."

Along the ridge, ferns and other tropical plants crowd a narrow, muddy path. The soles of your boots sinks into the soft soil, leaving footprints as you walk down it.

"Wait for me," Paulie yells, scurrying after you.

"I see animal prints," you say.

Paulie looks down and sees the impressions left by your boots. "So do I. What happened to the heel of your boot, it looks all chewed up?"

"My dog took a bite out of it," you say as you crouch down. "The boots still work okay though. But that's not the prints I'm talking about."

You point at the strange shapes in the mud. It's like a huge chicken has just walked by. "This must be an ostrich, or maybe an emu."

Paulie's eyes are wide. "I don't th–think so. It's way too big for that."

Your speculation is cut short when a strange lizard, about six-feet-long and three-feet-tall, scuttles into view from further down the ridge.

The creature looks at you, flicks its tongue a couple times, hisses, then stretches its long neck in your direction. It hisses again, snaps its teeth and moves towards you.

"That doesn't look friendly," Paulie says.

8

You agree. "Quick, Paulie, run!"
It's time to make a very quick decision. Do you:
Run back and climb the arch. **P12**
Or
Head back down into the canyon. **P16**

You have decided to go right, towards the eroded hills

"Those hills look perfect for fossils," you tell Paulie. "Some may have washed out in the last rains."

"Now we just have to find them," Paulie says as the two of you veer right and pick up your pace.

As you walk, you scan the ground for rattlesnakes, just in case. Although rattlesnakes usually rattle when they sense a person coming, it never hurts to take a few extra precautions this far from medical help.

"Look there, Paulie," you say, pointing at a long S-shaped groove in the sandy ground. "That's a snake track if ever I saw one."

Paulie squats down and runs a finger along the groove. "Did you know there are 30 different species of rattlesnake in the world?"

"Really? That many?"

"But only one lives in Montana," he says with a smile. "So don't worry."

As you get closer to the hills, the layers of rock become more distinct. Like a cake with hundreds of thin layers ranging in color from light grey, to beige, tan, brown and even orange and pale yellow, they rise from the flatland around them. Some layers show the volcanic origins of this area, while others are fossilized sediments, laid down when the area was covered in a vast inland sea millions of years ago. Along with these sediments, the bones of many dinosaurs have been found.

After reaching the base of the hills, you stop briefly and refer to your guide. "There's meant to be a trail around here somewhere."

"There's a marker," Paulie says, pointing to a white post about 50 yards further along.

The track is narrow and leads up a dry watercourse between two hills. Very little plant life hangs on to these constantly eroding slopes, and deep ruts have been caused by rain and the runoff from melting snow.

"Looks like we've arrived on Mars," Paulie says.

You nod in agreement. "It's a strange landscape, all right."

The trail winds around one hill and then turns steeply uphill and runs along a broad ridge. "Look. There's the mine they mention in the guide."

Cut into the steep slope is a large hole framed by sturdy timbers. Near the entrance is an old pulley, some cable and other disused mining equipment. On its side is a beaten up wooden box with a steel undercarriage and wheels. Two railway tracks disappear into the hillside. To the left of the entrance, tumbling down the slope, is the pile of rubble discarded by the miners during their excavations.

"They must have used that railway to bring the dirt out," you say. "I wonder what they were searching for?"

Paulie pulls out his phone to take a picture. "Gold and silver most likely. Or maybe copper. There's also a lot of coal in Montana, but coal mines are usually big, ugly, open cast things, not underground mines like this."

"Where do you learn all this stuff, Paulie?" you say, amazed. "Do you spend all your time on the internet?"

"Not really," he says. "I just remember things. And, I did some research before we came on this trip. I enjoy places more when I learn a bit about them beforehand."

"So do you think there's any gold left down there?" you ask.

Paulie shakes his head. "Not that we'd be able to find without some major equipment."

"What about fossils?"

"That's more likely," he says. "The miners probably weren't interested in those. They might have left a few lying around."

This sounds more interesting. You walk over and poke your head inside. "This shaft doesn't look very safe. These timbers are pretty old."

Fine dust drifts down from the roof. A few of the uprights have fallen onto the floor. You pull the flashlight out of your daypack and

BLAIR POLLY

point it down the tunnel. About thirty yards in, you see a pile of huge bones.

Paulie sees them too. "Holy moly, are those dinosaur bones?"

You heart thumps with excitement. "Those bones are way too big to be anything else. Wow we've hit the mother lode."

"Wait," Paulie says, looking around nervously. "Who piled them up like that? Doesn't look like the work of miners."

"You're right. The miners would have dumped them outside with all the other rubble."

As you're thinking about this mystery, the scrunch of footsteps comes from further down the path. Then, from around a corner, two men appear.

"Hey you brats! What do you think you're doing?" yells the larger of the two men.

"I don't think they're happy to see us, Paulie."

Paulie gasps. "They must be fossil smugglers. Look! He's got a pistol!"

"You two stay right there!" the man shouts.

"What do we do?" Paulie whispers.

"I don't know, but I'm not hanging around here. Quick, run!"

But which way do you go? You can't go back the way you came, the men are blocking your way.

It looks like you only have two options. Do you:

Go into the deserted mine shaft? **P20**

Or

Follow the trail further up the hill? **P23**

12

You have decided to climb the arch

You and Paulie run back along the path and waste no time climbing up the sandstone arch. Thankfully, erosion caused by the wind and rain has provided you with plenty of handholds.

"What is that thing?" Paulie cries, his breath coming in short gasps as he climbs.

You're both puffing by the time you reach the top of the arch. As you catch your breath, you study the creature circling below. Its skin is a pale, scaly-green with tufts of red feathers on its elbows, head and tail. It walks on slim rear legs and has short forearms. Its big eyes look at you as if it thinks you'd make a nice lunch. The creature snaps up at you as it attempts to climb the arch, but its body isn't designed for climbing and despite the sharp talons on its hind legs, it skids back to the ground before making much upward progress.

Studying the beast, you pull out your guide book and flip through the pages. "I think it's a Troodon," you say. "But how could it be? They died out over 65 million years ago."

Paulie looks around and scratches his head. "Yeah I know. Only minutes ago, this place was almost desert. Now it's covered in plants and stuff. It's like we've traveled back to the Cretaceous period."

As bizarre as that sounds, how else could a dinosaur be pacing around beneath you? And how could so much of the Great Plains be covered in swampland?

Then you spot the meteorite lying on the ground far below and remember the strange humming. Could that have had something to do with all this? Did its vibrations open a portal to another dimension?

"This is so weird."

"It's a lot stranger than weird," Paulie says. "It's totally freaking me out."

The big lizard doesn't look like it's going anywhere. In fact, three of its friends have come to join it circling the arch. They look up at you, hiss, and make odd growling noises.

You sit down. "Well for the moment, I think I'll stay where I am. Those oversized reptiles look hungry. Look at the size of their teeth!"

"Did you know that Troodons were the smartest dinosaurs ever?" Paulie asks.

"How smart?" you ask nervously.

"A lot smarter than your average lizard, that's for sure. Dog smart maybe."

Thinking you may have quite a wait, you take off your daypack and pull out your water bottle. "Drink?" you say, offering the bottle to Paulie.

He shakes his head and sits down beside you. "How long do you think they'll hang around?"

"I don't know. More importantly, how long does it take an extremely smart lizard to learn how to climb?"

"Don't say that!" Paulie says, his eyes boring into yours.

Another hour passes. You and Paulie eat an energy bar each.

When Paulie reaches for a second, you grab his arm. "We need to ration our food in case our new friends stick around."

"Not my fr–friends," Paulie says. Then his eyes widen and he turns his head slightly. He raises a hand to cup his ear. "Do you hear that?"

You listen hard for a moment. Then you hear it too. A low rumbling is coming from somewhere further down the ridge. It sounds like a lion's growl, only deeper, followed by something that sounds like an angry bull elephant calling. The Troodons hear it too. They screech nervously at each other and run about in confusion.

When the massive head of the T. Rex appears, you nearly poop yourself. You grab Paulie's sleeve. "Do you see what I see?"

"Holy moly!" Paulie says. "What do we do?"

The Troodons scuttle around looking for some way to escape, but they're trapped at the end of the ridge with steep cliffs all around. The T. Rex has cut them off and is moving towards them, its jaws snapping viciously from side to side. Drool flies from its mouth in a large arc, like a sprinkler watering a lawn. A few drops splatter the front of you.'

"Yuck! Dinosaur slobber," Paulie says in disgust. "Gross."

"Quick, lie down and stay still," you say. "In the movie *Jurassic Park* they said a T. Rex can't see you if you don't move."

Although Paulie does as you say, he shakes his head. "I read somewhere that the movie got it wrong," he whispers.

"Thanks. Remind me to send Spielberg an email demanding an explanation if we get out of this."

"Did you know that Spielberg—"

"Paulie, be quiet! Let's just hope the T. Rex likes the taste of Troodon, better than people."

"But dinosaurs and humans didn't live in the same time period," Paulie says. "How would it know what people taste like?"

You shoot Paulie a scathing look and hold an index finger to your lips.

A growl from the T. Rex and another shower of drool makes you press yourselves down onto the rock of the arch. The dinosaur is bigger than you ever imagined. It stalks the Troodons, snapping left and right, as the much smaller, yet more agile dinosaurs try to sneak past it to safety. As one of the Troodon makes a desperate attempt to skitter past the T. Rex's position, the much bigger animal swivels its jaws and clamps on to the poor Troodon. A high-pitched screech echoes over the ridge.

As the T. Rex chews up the unlucky Troodon, the others take the opportunity to sprint past their unfortunate companion while the T. Rex's mouth is full. The last you see of them are their tails disappearing into the dense foliage.

With a swallow and a roar, the T. Rex spins around and takes off in pursuit.

"Do you think the T. Rex will come back?" Paulie asks, as if not quite believing what his eyes have witnessed. "Or should we make a run for it?"

Should you stay up on the arch or, like the Troodons, should you take this opportunity to get off the ridge?

It's time to make an important decision. Do you:

Stay on the arch? **P28**

Or

Get off the arch and off the ridge? **P33**

You have decided to go back into the canyon

You start to run, but the ridge is narrow and the big lizard is blocking the path you came up. Skirting along the edge of the cliff, you search for another track down, but the canyon walls are far too steep for climbing. And even if you could get down, the once-dry canyon is now filled with murky brown water.

Paulie panics beside you. "Let's jump into the water!"

"But how deep is it?" you ask. "And what else is in there?"

"I don't know," Paulie says. "But we'd better do something or we'll end up being lizard lunch."

You look one way, then the other. "Back to the arch!"

"Hurry!" Paulie yells. "He's right behind us."

As you rush through the arch, you skid to a stop and duck to the right, behind one stone pillar. Paulie nips left.

In its eagerness to sink its teeth into you, the slobbering lizard is going way too fast to stop. With a final snap of its jaws and a scrabbling of hard claws on even harder rock, it skids right past and plummets over the edge and into the water below.

"Phew, that was close," you say, peering over the cliff to where the lizard is kicking hard, trying to stay afloat.

Neither you, nor the struggling Troodon, see the huge Tylosaurus coming, until it busts out of the water with the Troodon clamped in its massive jaws. Then, with a splash and a gurgle, both creatures disappear below the surface, leaving nothing but a series of ripples.

"Just as well we didn't go swimming eh, Paulie?"

Paulie stares at the water below. His knees wobble. "Please tell me this is a bad dream."

"Okay, it's all a horrible reptilian nightmare. You happy now?"

Paulie looks up at you. A tear rolls down his face. "But it isn't. Is it?"

You shake your head and give Paulie a pat on the shoulder. "No. And we need to figure out a way to get back home. Hang in there, we'll be okay."

Paulie does a 360 degree turn, his eyes searching, trying to make sense of it all. He sees his phone lying on the ground. "I wonder if that shot I took came out?"

"Have a look," you say. "It might give us a clue about what is going on."

He picks the phone up and starts scrolling though the images. "Here it is. Holy moly, look at this!"

He holds up the phone so you can see the screen. "Look at the rock in your hand!"

You peer at the screen. "That's right, the rock went bright red."

"Did it feel hot?" Paulie asks.

You shake your head. "Not really. And then the thing started making that horrible noise."

Paulie's left hand cradles his chin as he thinks. His eyes roll skyward. "That rock must have created a rip in the fabric of space-time somehow," he says.

Your upper lip rises as your face contorts. "Huh? Space-time?"

"Got a better explanation?"

You shrug. "No… Not really. Do you think it'll work in reverse?"

"Worth a try," he says. "Just one problem."

"What's that?"

"Well, if we go back in time, earth may not be here when we arrive. Remember our planet is moving through space."

"But what other option have we got?"

Paulie shrugs. "None that I can think of. We'll just have to hope space and time look after themselves."

You shake your head. "Well I'm pleased we've got the technical difficulties sorted." You pick up the meteorite and hold it out, willing it to turn red.

After a minute Paulie sighs. Nothing's happening." He looks at the photo again and a smile crosses his face. "The arch. We need to stand directly under the arch!"

You both move under Gabriel's Arch and, once again, stand expectantly with the rock held out. But still nothing happens.

You kick the ground and look over at Paulie. "Why isn't it working?"

Paulie shrugs. "I don't know. I'm not a physicist. Give it another minute."

Two minutes later it becomes obvious Paulie's theory is not going to work.

You look around. "Well I don't know about you, but I'd like to get off this ridge. I feel a bit trapped up here."

Paulie nods his agreement and points to a narrow track leading between a patch of ferns. "Let's head down there, eh? I can't see another path, can you?"

After putting the meteorite into your daypack, you head off, pulling fronds aside as you work your way down the ridge. You can hear Paulie's footsteps right behind you. Every twenty yards or so, you stop and listen for danger.

Paulie has his phone out, taking pictures.

As your ears strain trying to hear approaching dinosaurs, you hear a funny vibration coming from your daypack. "What's that?"

A blinding FLASH leaves you seeing spots.

"Yikes!" Paulie cries. "What the heck caused that!"

When your vision clears the jungle is gone. Once again the terrain around you is barren. If the jungle has gone, maybe the dinosaurs have too.

"Ar—are we back?" Paulie asks.

"The water is gone," you say looking over the canyon rim. "But I don't think we're back."

"Why do you say that?"

And then Paulie sees what you've seen. Bison. Not just one or two. But tens of thousands of them.

"What's going on?" he asks. "And where did all these bison come from?"

"I'm more interested in what caused that flash," you say. "Do you think it was the meteorite again, or something else?"

Paulie scrunches up his face as he tries to fathom out what is happening. "It must be the meteorite, but what's triggering it to flash like that? We know it wasn't the arch so what else could it be?" He looks down at his phone.

"What are you doing?" you ask him.

"I felt my phone vibrate just before the flash. Do you think that might have something to do with it? That's so weird, my phone only vibrates when I receive a text, but there's nothing."

"I hardly think there were cell phone towers in the Cretaceous period, Paulie."

Paulie looks a little hurt. "Yeah, but–"

"But what? You think text messages are going to zap us back and forth in time?"

Paulie shrugs. "I don't know what I think."

He looks about ready to cry. You move closer and put your arm over his shoulder. "Don't worry, we'll get back somehow. Hey, look on the bright side. How many kids get to go back in time? Imagine the school report we'll be able to write about our adventures!"

Paulie tries hard to smile. "Yeah, I suppose."

But what do you do now? Do you:

Head back to where your school group set up camp? **P42**
Or

Go back into Gabriel's Gulch and keep exploring? **P46**

You have decided to go into the deserted mine shaft

"Quick Paulie, in here."

You jump over a fallen support near the entrance of the shaft and rush deeper into the mine. As you pass the pile of bones, you see a couple of picks lying on the ground.

"Grab a pick for protection," you say, snagging one as you pass.

"Still no service." Paulie shoves his phone into a side-pocket of his pack, and grabs a pick. "We must be too far from the tower."

"Being underground won't help either," you say as you continue on.

Holding the flashlight, you work your way further into the mine. As you do, the support timbers look even less stable. The tunnel twists and turns. Side shafts branch off every fifteen yards or so. Some of them only go in for a few yards, others disappear into a darkness the powerful beam of your flashlight can't penetrate.

"Looks like the miners were following veins of ore," Paulie says. "There are tunnels all over the place."

The air down here is much cooler than outside. When you reach a large side shaft you turn to Paulie. "Let's see where this goes."

Paulie looks up at the cracked support timbers and frowns. "You sure this is a good idea?"

"Would you rather get caught by those men?"

Paulie shrugs. "Okay, let's go. Just be careful."

The next bones you pass are human. A skeleton, still dressed in tattered clothes, lies near the shaft. From its size you can tell it's an adult.

"Holy moly," Paulie says. "Its skull is cracked."

"It must be pretty old. Look at what it's wearing."

The pants, shirt and coat look like something you've seen in old photographs. With a shudder, you grab Paulie's sleeve. "Come on. Let's keep moving."

"We're gonna find you brats!" a voice echoes from the darkness

BLAIR POLLY

21

behind you. The men sound quite a way back.

"Walk quietly," you whisper to Paulie. "We might be able to lose them."

The shaft slopes downward. You're careful not to trip over the rails running down the tunnel. But then, without warning, the rails disappear under a pile of rubble.

"There's be–been a cave-in," Paulie says. "Wha–what now?"

You shine your light over the pile of rubble. The roof has collapsed all right, but there is still a small gap between the pile and one of the walls. You feel a cool breeze.

"This tunnel must lead to the outside," you whisper. "I feel air coming through." You take your pick and start scraping at the loose rock. "Help me Paulie. We just need a hole big enough to squeeze through."

Unfortunately, it's hard to be quiet and dig at the same time.

"Work fast, they're bound to hear us," you say.

At least the rocks that have fallen are small enough to shift. In less than a minute the hole looks big enough to squeeze through.

You shine your light into the gap. "You first, Paulie. Quick! They're coming!"

When another shaft of light flashes on the wall beside you, Paulie wastes no time in diving into the hole. You toss your flashlight after him and squeeze through. It's a tight fit, but you just manage to get through with only a few minor scrapes and scratches.

The men are close now. The scrunch of gravel grinds under their boots.

"Look, fresh prints," one of them says. "They must have wiggled through this hole."

A big hairy arm pokes a flashlight through the hole and illuminates you and Paulie. Then both of the men start laughing.

You turn to Paulie. "Why are they laughing?"

"Don't worry Walter," a gruff voice says. "Those brats aren't going anywhere."

After a moment of silence, you hear thumping further back along the shaft. Then there's a splintering sound as one of the supports crashes onto the floor of the shaft.

Paulie grabs your arm. "I think they're trying to collapse the tunnel."

Paulie's suspicions are quickly confirmed when a low rumble shudders through the shaft and the sound of snapping timbers and a blast of dust and grit from falling rock shoots through the hole. When the cloud finally clears, you shine your light back towards the hole.

It's gone. All you can see is rubble.

"You okay, Paulie?" In the beam of the flashlight, damp lines run down Paulie's dirt-covered face. "Hey don't worry. Remember there was a breeze coming up this tunnel before those guys blocked it off. It must go back to the surface."

"It could be miles away. Maybe we should try to dig our way out. It could be dangerous going further in. What happens if our batteries run out while we're underground?"

Paulie has a point. Maybe digging your way out is the right plan. But then how are you to know how much rock has come down?

It's time to make a decision. Do you:

Go further down into the mine? **P76**

Or

Try to dig your way out? **P82**

You have decided to follow the trail further up the hill

"Quick, up here, Paulie!"

Without waiting for a reply, you start running up the track. When you look over your shoulder, Paulie is on your heels and the men are about 150 yards further down. There's a lot of loose rock on this part of the track. You try not to knock it down onto Paulie.

Uphill from your position, there's been a rock fall. A pile of stone lies across your path. Many of the stones are the size of softballs. You stop and heft one in your hand. It's heavy, with sharp edges.

Paulie stops beside you. "Are you thinking what I am?" he says, a grin crossing his face.

"Should give them second thoughts about chasing us," you say, flinging the rock down the slope towards the men.

Paulie picks up a rock and does the same.

As fast as you can, you throw rocks at the men.

"Hey you brats! I'm gonna–" The rest of his words are cut short as he dodges the missiles bouncing dangerously down the hill towards him.

Despite the men's curses, you and Paulie keep tossing rocks.

One of the men dodges left, then right, avoiding the rocks. His friend isn't so lucky and falls onto his back, clutching his leg and groaning. "Walter, help me. I think I've broken my leg."

"Let's go," you say. "I don't think they'll be following us anymore."

Paulie drops the rock in his hand. "So, what now?"

"We need to get back to camp and tell the park rangers there are smugglers up here."

Paulie looks down towards the men. "But they're on the path."

"We'll have to find another way," you say. "Come on, we don't want to be out here after dark."

Without further delay, you and Paulie head up the hill.

Once you've put a bit of distance between you and the smugglers, you stop climbing and pull out your guide. "This map isn't very detailed, but I think this trail leads around the hill to a spring at the head of another canyon."

Paulie pulls his water bottle out of his pack and takes a slug. "A spring, that's good. My water's getting low."

The ground is rugged. Eroded channels streak the hillside, cutting across the path in places. Rain has washed a lot of soil away. In the distance, pinnacles point towards the sky, all that is left of once-mighty hills.

"What the heck?" Paulie says as you come around a corner. He points towards a dusty old trailer, its hitch propped up on a lump of sandstone. "How did that get up here?"

You look around expecting to see a dirt track. But Paulie's right. There's no road, just the narrow track you're on. Outside the trailer sits an old lawn chair and a barbeque. Whisky bottles and tin cans litter the ground around the chair. As you survey the camp, you notice a big eye-ring bolted to each corner of the trailer's chassis. One still has a length of rusty chain attached to it. "It must have been lifted it in by helicopter. See those ring thingies?"

Paulie looks confused. "But why here?"

"I don't know. Survivalists maybe? Fossil hunters?"

"What if they're friends with those men?" Paulie asks.

You shrug. "I suppose it's possible… but this trailer looks like it's been here for years. I doubt the smugglers have been operating that long. Surely someone would have seen them."

The raggedy curtain in one of the windows twitches. You grab hold of Paulie's elbow, turn your back to the trailer, and pretend to look at the view. "Don't look now, Paulie," you whisper, "but someone's watching us."

"Wha–what do we do?" he asks

"They could be friendly."

"Or they could have a shotgun." Paulie shakes your hand off. "Let's get the heck out of here."

You're about to agree when the trailer door creaks open and an old-timer with a long white beard, flannel shirt and tattered trousers peers out at you. He steps down from inside clutching a walking stick in one hand.

"What're you two young'uns doing way up here? Not looking for gold I hope."

Deciding to play it cagey you don't mention the two smugglers. "Nah, we're on a school trip. Just out for a walk. The rest of the class should be along soon."

The old man scratches his chin. "Long as you don't do no prospecting. I've got claim to this here piece o' dirt."

Then you have an idea. "Have you seen any bones lying around?"

"Bones? Now why would I want bones? I'm looking for Bill Rafferty's hidden…" He scowls at you. "You sure you're not lookin' for Rafferty's treasure?"

Paulie suddenly takes an interest. "Is that the prospector that went missing in 1863?"

"So you are claim jumpers!" the old man yells.

Paulie shakes his head. "No, no, I just read about it on the internet. Didn't Rafferty strike it rich in Willard Creek?"

The old man seems unsure for a moment, then he looks you both up and down, realizes you're just harmless kids, and smiles, showing a gap in his front teeth. "Lewis and Clark named it Willard creek when they passed by in the early 1800s. But when a plague of grasshoppers came through in '62 they renamed it Grasshopper Creek."

"That's right," Paulie says. "Wasn't the gold unusually pure?"

The old man nods. "Ninety nine percent they reckon. You got a good memory there, kiddo. I've been lookin' for that gold nigh on forty years. Not found a single nugget. But I will, just you watch. Long as this wonky knee don't give out on me."

"Well good luck," you say. "I don't suppose you could point us towards the campsite at Gabriel's Gulch? We need to get back before dark and report some smugglers we saw further down."

"Smugglers eh?" the old man says. "Those varmints better stay off my patch, or I'll give 'em what for." The old man takes a few practice swings with his cane, pretending it's a sword, before pointing up the hill with it. "See that ridge. Well, over that is the top o' Long Canyon. It's narrow, but once you work your way along, you'll come to a spring, then you just need to follow the creek bed down to the flat. Should be able to see your camp from there."

"Thanks Mister," you say, grabbing Paulie's arm and dragging him along before he starts asking the man more questions.

"Oh and if you're interested," the old guy says, "there's some big bones near the bottom of Long Canyon. Look along the north wall. I ran across a paleontologist once a few years back, said they was an Eino ... um ... Eino something or other bones."

"Einiosaurus?" Paulie says.

The old man nods. "Yes'um, that's it."

Paulie smiles and turns to you. "They're like a Triceratops, only smaller."

"Those big ones with the three horns and bony collar?" you ask.

Paulie nods. "That's the one."

"Just a pile o' bones to me," the old man grumbles. "You're welcome to all the bones you like, just leave my gold alone or you'll have me to answer to."

You wave goodbye. "Hope your knee holds up, Mister. Good luck."

With that, you and Paulie continue your trudge uphill. At least the sun is lower in the sky and the heat of the day is lessening. When you finally reach the ridge, you stop and take in the view.

"Wow, look at that," Paulie says.

Far below, water has cut a deep scar across the landscape. Layers of red, brown, orange, tan and yellow strike through the hills. Pinnacles of harder sandstone have been left standing, and the wind and rain have carved many unusual shapes out what were once solid mountains.

There are a couple of ways down to the canyon floor from here. You could go along the ridge, which is more gently sloping. Or you could take a more direct route down one of the many watercourses.

It's time to make a decision. Do you:

Follow the ridge? **P38**

Or

Go down a watercourse? **P58**

28

You have decided to stay on the arch

A slight breeze blows across your sweaty skin as you sit atop the arch. "With so many dinosaurs around, maybe we should stay up here until dark," you say to Paulie. "We can't afford to be caught in the open."

Paulie looks like he's about to cry. His lower lip quivers and his eyes dart left and right as if expecting a new danger to show itself at any moment.

"Hey, don't worry," you say, trying not to expose your fear to your younger companion. "We'll make it out of this."

"Oh yeah. How is that?"

"Hey we've got bigger brains than those lizards. We just need to make a plan."

Paulie exhales a long slow breath, then sniffs. "I'm glad you're so confident." He pulls his knees in tight to his chest and wraps his arms around them before closing his eyes.

Paulie looks pale and his breathing is coming in rapid gasps as he rocks back and forth. You place your hand on his arm. His skin is cool and clammy despite the warmth of the afternoon. This does not look good.

"I think you're going into shock, Paulie. Lie down on your back and rest your feet on my lap."

Paulie opens his eyes and looks at you. His pupils are enlarged. Another bad sign. But at least he does as you say and lies on his back and elevates his feet. You pull your extra sweatshirt out of your daypack and lay it over him.

Down the valley, you hear the screech of Troodons and wonder if the T. Rex has cornered them.

The sun is getting low in the sky, and grey clouds are rolling in from the north. After twenty minutes or so, Paulie's breathing has settled and the color has returned to his face.

Further down the canyon you hear the sound of running water – a stream or waterfall perhaps. Every now and then there is a big splash, and you make a note not to go in the water without good reason. Who knows what creatures lurk below its surface?

Paulie opens his eyes. His pupils are back to normal. "I'm feeling better now," he says. "I thought I was going to puke there for a moment." He sits up and reaches for his water bottle. After a long drink and a look around he opens the front pouch of his daypack and pulls out a chocolate bar. "Want some?"

As the two of you munch on the chocolate, you discuss your options.

"We need to figure out what caused us to time-jump," Paulie says. "Then figure out how to do it again, but in reverse."

What he says makes sense.

"It's got to be that meteorite," you say. "What else could have caused it?"

Paulie pulls an ear as he thinks. "Maybe. But meteorites don't usually cause time travel so there must be something else to it as well. Some interaction we don't understand." Then, Paulie sees his phone still sitting on the rock where he put it to take the picture. "The phone … it must be the phone!"

"You think so?"

He clutches your arm. "One of us needs to climb down and get the meteorite and the phone."

You can see the fear in his eyes and the last thing you want is for him to go back into shock. "I'll go," you say. "But you keep watch. Call out the moment you see anything coming. Okay?"

Paulie nods enthusiastically. "Will do."

Climbing down is always trickier than climbing up because it's harder to see where to put your feet. Much of the time your feet are swinging in thin air trying to find the next hole. Your arms ache by the time you get to the bottom and sweat runs down your back in the hot, sticky air.

You walk quickly over to the phone and put it in your front pocket. Then you pick up the meteorite. The rock looks normal again. Not a hint of red anywhere. "Hmmm." You stuff it into your back pocket and look up towards Paulie on the arch.

When a large shadow moves across the ground in front of you, at first you think it's Paulie's. But then you realize the sun is in the wrong position for that to be the case. You swivel around and scan the sky. Then you see the flying lizard. It's a Pterodactyl.

The strange beast has a thin membrane of skin stretched between its elongated front arms and its rear legs to form a wingspan of about nine feet. Its head is like that of a deformed goose, with a long orange beak containing rows of small teeth.

"Watch out!" you yell.

Paulie sees the Pterodactyl just in time and ducks, but not before the creature has knocked him off balance. "Whooooa!" he yells, teetering on the edge.

Things happen in slow motion. Paulie is falling. Without thinking, you position yourself to catch him, stretching your arms out as his frame fills the sky above you.

"Umphhhh," you grunt as you hit the ground with Paulie on top of you.

"You okay, Paulie?" Untangling yourself, you sit up and check for injuries. A large graze down your leg oozes blood. Your ribs hurt. But otherwise, you've been lucky not to be more severely injured.

Paulie rubs his hip where he landed. He has a raw patch near his elbow, but as he gets up, you see he's okay.

Another shadow flashes across the ground, then another. This time you both know where it's coming from and scan the sky.

"Quick — under the arch," you say, scrambling to your feet.

Paulie wastes no time following you. When you look up again you see three Pterodactyls, circling above, like vultures.

"We need to get the heck out of here," Paulie says. "Quick — give me my phone. Let me see if I can work out what happened."

Pleased to see that the phone wasn't damaged in your tumble, you pass it over. "No rush, Paulie. Anytime in the next minute or so should be fine."

Your backside is a bit sore where you thumped down hard on the meteorite. You pull the rock out of your pocket as Paulie fiddles with his phone. Then unexpectedly, after Paulie has switched the phone off and then restarted it, the meteorite starts to vibrate and turn red.

"Something's happening!" you say, one eye on the rock and the other on the circling dinosaurs above.

Then, with a FLASH, the Pterodactyls are gone — and so is the jungle.

All seems normal again. "Hey, Paulie, I think we're back."

"Look again," Paulie says, his eyes wide as he looks through the arch towards the flatland beyond the canyon.

"But–" Then you see what Paulie is referring to. Along the base of the hills, in the distance, is a raised track. Running along that single rail is a sleek train moving at incredible speed.

"That certainly wasn't there when we came into the canyon," Paulie says. "It's like that fast train in Japan–"

"The bullet train?"

"Yeah, but look at it go! It must be doing five hundred miles an hour!"

You and Paulie sit down under the arch and look out over the landscape. Further down the valley are a pair of gleaming towers. As the train approaches them, it quickly slows, then stops altogether.

"Is that a train station?" Paulie asks.

"Dunno. Those towers must be 100 stories high."

"Maybe it's a town?"

You scratch your head. "Not like any town I've ever seen. But I suppose we should go and check it out. They might help us find a way home." After cleaning up your scrapes and scratches, you head towards the towers. It takes about an hour before you can see them more clearly.

"I see a sign," Paulie says, pulling a pair of binoculars out of his day pack.

"What's it say?"

Paulie starts laughing. "You're not going to believe this." He hands you the binoculars.

You hold them up to your eyes and peer through the lenses. Twiddling the dial, you bring the sign into focus. It reads:

WELCOME TO GABRIEL'S GULCH WORLD WILDLIFE HOTEL

"Looks like we jumped a bit too far," you say.

"Yeah, but won't it be interesting!" Paulie is bobbing up and down like a jack-in-the-box. "Did you know that Einstein said…"

You ignore Paulie's ramblings as you wander towards the hotel. The sky is crystal blue and cloudless. The air smells pure and clean. Maybe the people of earth finally got their act together and stopped the pollution and the damages due to climate change. Maybe things are different now. You sure hope so.

"Hey, Paulie," you say. "Can I borrow those binoculars again?"

He digs in his pack. "Sure."

Then you see what you're looking for. It's another sign just beside the entrance to the hotel. It reads:

FREE ICE CREAM FOR CHILDREN UNDER 18

"Hey, Paulie."

"Yeah?"

"I think we're going to like the future."

"You think so?"

You're grinning so hard your face hurts. "Yeah. I'm sure of it."

Congratulation you've finished this part of the story. What would you like to do now?

Go back to the beginning of the story and try a different path? **P1**

Or

Go to the great big list of choices and pick a chapter? **P376**

You have decided to get off the arch

"We've been up here long enough," you say. "We need to figure out how to get home."

"Did you know that Einstein predicted that man might be able to go forward in time, but never backward?"

"Well we've proven him wrong, haven't we? Remind me to write up the mathematical equation for it when we get back to camp."

Paulie looks puzzled. "The mathematical equation?"

You give him a smile. "I'm joking, numbskull."

"Oh," Paulie says, his face reddening.

You spin around onto your stomach and start climbing down the arch. "Now stop talking about Einstein and help me figure out a way to get home. Oh, and keep an eye out for those lizards."

Back on the ground, you pick up the meteorite. "This rock must have something to do with what happened. Did you see how it turned red and vibrated before it flashed?"

Paulie nods. "And the sound it made. What was that all about?"

You shrug. "Alien folk music?"

"Not funny," Paulie says rolling his eyes. He picks up his phone from the rock and slides it into his pocket. "So, what now?"

"Well normally if you get lost, you're meant to stay put and wait to be rescued. But I doubt anyone will even miss us for a few hours."

"Not to mention the 65 million year time difference," Paulie says.

"Yeah, and that."

Paulie sits on a rock and closes his eyes. It is a pose you've seen him take many times over the last couple of hours. His thinking pose. You've been doing a fair bit of thinking yourself. Trying to remember exactly how you found yourselves in this situation.

"Have you heard of meridians, Paulie?"

Paulie opens his eyes. "You mean spots on the earth that have some sort of mystical energy?"

"Yeah I remember reading about them somewhere. Could that be the cause of our jump?"

"It's possible," Paulie says. "It also possible that little green spacemen or the cookie monster did it. Extremely unlikely, but within the realm of possibility."

"Yes, but—"

"Have you heard of Occam's razor?" Paulie asks.

"What's shaving got to do with it?"

"No, it's nothing to do with shaving. It's just the principal that a simple explanation is more likely to be correct than a complicated one."

"Such as?"

"Like UFOs for example. A simple explanation for weird lights in the sky could be that it's something earth-based – a plane or balloon – or some unusual atmospheric condition."

You nod. "Okay."

"A complicated explanation would be that aliens have made a spacecraft capable of travelling hundreds, or millions of light years and they've managed to find earth amongst the millions of billions of planets out there in the universe. Oh, and then they leave again without bothering to say hello properly."

"I see what you mean. So simple is good."

"Yes."

"So, what's the simple explanation for us time jumping?"

"Well, let's just say, it's probably something less complicated than some wacky notion of invisible meridians that science has never detected."

You can see where Paulie is headed. "Okay, so the simplest explanation is that it's something to do with either the phone, the arch, or the meteorite?"

"Exactly." He pulls his phone out of his pocket and looks at it. "I can't see anything strange going on with my phone. Except that there's no reception."

"Well that's hardly surprising. I'd be pretty shocked to discover dinosaurs had cell phone towers."

But when Paulie's phone make a loud DING indicating he's just received a text, you both stare down at it.

"How is that possible?" you ask.

Paulie hits the key pad and peers at the screen.

You watch as Paulie's eyes widen and jaw drops. Then he brings the phone closer to his face, as if looking at it closer will change the message somehow. "Bu–but that's imposs–impossible."

"Come on. Tell me. What's it say?"

Paulie shudders like something's sent a chill through him. "It's a message from the future."

"From who?" you say, leaning forward, trying to catch a glimpse of the screen.

He holds up from the screen. "From me in 2060!"

The message reads:

MAY 2060: YOU CAN GET HOME BY REBOOTING YOUR PHONE WHILE HOLDING IT NEAR THE METEORITE. PAUL LEIGHTON SMITH.

"But that's over 40 years from now!"

Finding yourself back in the Cretaceous period with the dinosaurs was strange enough, but messages from the future? That's totally weird.

"Yeah, isn't it great?" Paulie has a big smile on his face. "Don't you see, for me to be sending messages from the future, we must survive!"

You think about what he's said for a moment, then turn and look directly at him. "We?" you say. "Is my name on the text too?"

The smile drops from his face. "Sorry, I just assumed..."

"Yeah well don't! Just get moving with the phone. I want to get home. Now would be good, before that hungry T. Rex returns!"

Paulie wastes no time turning off his phone. You hold out the meteorite in the palm of your hand as he turns his phone back on. Both of you stare at the screen as you wait for it to come to life.

The rock in your hand has just started to vibrate when there is crashing through the jungle nearby. It sounds like it's coming right towards you.

"Hurry up, phone!" you yell at the piece of plastic in Paulie's hand. "That sounds like Mister T. Rex, and he's moving fast!

The animal's massive head pokes above the nearby bushes and you nearly pee. The T. Rex growls, low and mean, then stretches its neck towards you just as the vibrating meteorite starts its high-pitched screeching. The T. Rex snaps its head back, raises it to the sky and lets out a massive roar.

"I don't think it likes that squeal," you yell to Paulie.

FLASH!

"Are we back?" Paulie says, looking around.

The jungle is gone and the much sparser scrubland of sagebrush, gumweed and various grasses is back. A lizard skitters along the ground. Thankfully, this one is only a few inches long.

"I think so," you say. "Come on, let's head back to camp and find out."

The two of you waste no time walking back down Gabriel's Gulch. A red-tailed hawk flies high overhead looking for prey. Then, as a jackrabbit darts across a bare patch of land a few yards away, the hawk dives, only to have the rabbit disappear down a hole moments before it can get its razor-sharp talons onto it. Life and death on the badlands goes on. Only the hunters have changed.

"Who'd want to be lunch eh, Paulie?"

"We nearly were!"

You have never been so pleased to see a clump of pup-tents in your life. "Phew, Paulie," you say with relief. "Looks like you're a hero."

"Me?" he says. "How do you figure that?"

"Not you now. You as an old man in 2060. You saved us from that T. Rex. If we hadn't got that text, we would have been eaten."

Paulie stands taller. His chest puffs out. "Yeah, I guess I am ... I mean will be. But how did that work without us having any cell phone reception?"

You shrug. "That, my friend, is a very good question."

Paulie turns to you and smiles. "I wonder if we're still friends in 2060? Maybe you and I work out how to time travel. You've still got that meteorite, don't you?"

It's then that you realize the meteorite is no longer in your hand. "Where is it?" You pat your pockets, looking around at the ground."

You are so focused on finding the piece of space rock that you jump when Paulie's phone goes off.

"Who's that?" you ask.

Paulie hits a button on his keypad and reads the message.

"It's from me again."

"Really? What's it say?"

Paulie laughs. "Here, read it yourself."

> MAY 2060: I HAVE HIDDEN THE METEORITE. YOU WON'T FIND IT UNTIL YOU ARE A FEW YEARS OLDER AND MORE RESPONSIBLE. IN THE MEANTIME, STUDY PHYSICS. YOU TWO ARE GOING TO BE FAMOUS … JUST NOT FOR A FEW YEARS YET. HAVE FUN IN THE MEANTIME. PAUL LEIGHTON SMITH PHD.

Congratulations: This part of your story is over. You and Paulie have survived an encounter with a T. Rex. And, it sounds like you both have a bright future.

So, what would you like to do now? Do you:

Go back to the start and read a different path? **P1**

Or

Go to the great big list of choices and pick a chapter? **P376**

You have decided to follow the ridge

"So, bones in the canyon eh?" Paulie says.

"That's what the old guy said. Assuming they're still there."

Paulie speeds up and takes the lead, "Only one way to find out."

Walking down the ridge is easy going. With all the amazing scenery to take in, it doesn't seem long before you're standing at the bottom. The canyon is wider here than further up, but the layers in the rock are still plainly visible.

"Now to find these bones." Paulie's head turns left, then right.

"But shouldn't we be getting back to camp to report those men?"

"Of course. Duh," Paulie says, smacking himself on the forehead. "I almost forgot about them."

You smile. "I suppose we can look as we go … can't do any harm, can it?"

"Sounds like a plan."

"If we pick a side of the canyon each, we can cover more ground," you say. "You take this side, and I'll go over and scout the other. But we can't waste too much time, so keep moving."

Paulie agrees. You walk the twenty yards or so to the other side of the canyon. The layers of rock are very interesting. Some are only a few inches thick, while others are a yard or more. Each layer represents a period of time. Now you just need to figure out which one is the right time for dinosaurs.

Across the canyon, Paulie is facing the rock wall as he walks. Every now and again, he stops and picks up a rock, or pokes at the rock face.

You're so busy watching your friend that you don't see the rotten timbers on the ground in front of you until it's too late and the planks are cracking under your feet.

"Yeowwwwww!" you yell as you crash through a trap door and start to fall.

Paulie's head snaps around just before you disappear.

Luckily, quite a bit of sand has drifted through the cracks over time and piled up at the bottom of the hole to break your fall. As you pick yourself up and dust yourself off, your eyes adjust to the gloom. Off the main pit, someone has dug a narrow chamber back into the rock under the canyon wall."

"You okay down there?" Paulie yells.

"Yeah, thanks to the sand." Then, through the gloom, you see an old wooden trunk. "There's something down here!"

"Not rattlesnakes, I hope."

You hadn't thought about snakes. You reach into your pack, pull out your flashlight and scan the hole for reptiles. Thankfully there are no snakes, just an old ladder leaning against the wall.

"No snakes," you yell up to Paulie. "But there is an old trunk."

Paulie's head pops over the edge and he peers down. "A treasure chest with Rafferty carved in its top, perhaps?"

"Not that I can see." You undo the clasp and lift the lid. "Here goes…"

"What's in it?" say Paulie. "Don't keep me in suspenders!"

"Nothing!" you grump. "Filthy thing's empty, apart from a piece of paper."

"Empty? You're joking."

Disappointed, you reach down and pick up the sheet of paper. It looks like a map, but you're not sure. You sigh and tuck the note into your back pocket. After climbing back up to the surface, you take the note out and hand it to Paulie. "Here, have a look."

Paulie looks at the paper, rotates it around and then starts laughing. "You know what this means don't you?"

"No. What?"

"It's a map to Rafferty's treasure! See here. X marks the spot. And this faded writing says William Rafferty."

"Okay, so it's his map. But where the heck is X?" you ask.

"Remember that old stone wall in the campground?"

"The one by the camp kitchen?"

Paulie and you stare at each other a moment. "Shaped like an X," the two of you say in unison.

You give Paulie a grin. "So we were camped right beside the treasure all along?"

"That's my guess," Paulie says. "Only one way to be sure."

And with that, you forget all about fossils and head back towards camp.

About halfway to camp, Paulie's phone beeps. He pulls it out of his pocket. "We must be back in range." He shades it from the sun so he can read the screen. "It's from a friend wishing me luck finding fossils."

"Hey, while you've got a signal. Call the police and tell them about the smugglers."

Half an hour later, after speaking to the police, and as the sun sets behind the hills, you stroll into camp. The old stone wall looks more like an X from this angle. Next to the wall, you find various parents sitting around the table, talking and preparing the evening meal. Mister Jackson looks up from chopping onions and gives you a funny look. "What are you two so happy about? You're grinning like you've won the lottery."

"Grab a shovel, Mister J, and we'll show you."

"Show me what?"

You shake your head. "Nah. I'm not going to say. That would spoil all the fun."

The next day, all the kids call you the "prairie dogs" as you dig around the old wall. It doesn't help that you haven't told them why. The first time you ask Mister Jackson to move the camp kitchen, he lightheartedly complies. The second time, he decides enough is enough.

Then, just as you're about to get a telling off, Paulie's shovel rings out against something metal.

"Holy moly," he says. "I think I've found it!"

Congratulations, that is the end of this part of your story. But have you followed all the different paths the story takes?

It's time to make another decision. Do you:

Go back to the beginning and try a different path? **P1**

Or

Go to the great big list of choices? **P376**

You have decided to head back to where your school group set up camp

"I think we should head back to camp," you say. "At least that way if there's another flash, we can tell if we're back in the right time or not."

Paulie nods. "Okay with me, assuming we don't spook the bison and start a stampede."

He has a point. There are so many animals out there, who knows how they'll react to seeing people.

You and Paulie follow the ridge until you get to a point where you can descend back into the canyon. From this vantage point you can see a long way. On the far side of the canyon the great plains stretch out for miles in all directions. Countless bison graze on the lush grassland.

Feeling more relaxed, you study the amazing sight. At least bison, being herbivores, aren't going to eat you.

Paulie looks less frightened too. "Hey," he says. "Did you know that there were more than 20 million bison grazing on the Great Plains at one time?"

Considering how many you can see right now, you're not at all surprised.

"And over 40 different bird species lived here."

Yup, Paulie's back to normal, all right.

"Come on," you say. "We'd better make tracks."

But Paulie's on a roll. "Oh and prairie dogs and pronghorn lived here too," he says. "Still do."

"Pronghorns?" you say over your shoulder. "What are they when they're at home?"

"Relatives of the antelope," he says. "They're the fastest land animal in all of North America and second fastest in the whole world, after the cheetah."

"You obviously haven't seen me being chased by that nasty dog that lives down my street."

"I doubt you hit 60 miles an hour, somehow," Paulie says with a grin. "Pronghorns run fast enough to merge with freeway traffic."

"Beep, beep!" you say, speeding up. "Just watch me!"

The canyon floor looks much the same as it did when you first arrived, before the episode with the Troodons and T. Rex. Still, you scan the area just to be sure there are no gigantic reptiles hanging around waiting for lunch to wander by.

Paulie sees your nervous looks. "Don't worry, dinosaurs were extinct well before the rise of big mammals like bison."

You feel a little better, but only for a second.

"But there might be mountain lions around," Paulie says, "so keep your eyes peeled."

High above you, on the ridge, you see the arch. The sun glints off its surface. It looks pretty much the same as before you were taken back to the Cretaceous era, maybe a little bigger and thicker, but not by much. You turn your back on the arch and start hoofing it back to where camp would be, if only you were in the right time, keeping an eye on the terrain around you as you go.

"So what do we do once we get to the campsite?" Paulie asks.

"We try to figure out what made us time jump."

"And if we can't figure it out?" Paulie's looking a bit agitated again. "How will we survive out here on our own?"

"I'm sure it won't come to that," you say, trying to sound confident. "Besides, there's a trillion bison burgers within a mile of where we're standing."

Paulie gives you a funny look. "Yeah, we'd just need to figure out how to catch them ... and make fire to cook them ... and grind wild wheat to make buns for them to go on."

You pull a box of matches from your daypack and give them a shake. "Would you like fries with that?"

But Paulie's having none of it, "Sorry, no potatoes around here. They originated in South America. Peru or Bolivia, I seem to recall."

"What about corn, then?" you say. "We could make tortillas."

Paulie shakes his head. "Corn comes from central Mexico. That's quite some walk from here, I'm afraid."

By the time Paulie stops telling you where all his favorite foods come from, you are out of Gabriel's Gulch and heading across the flat land towards where the campsite should have been.

Fifteen minutes later you stop. "I reckon this is the spot."

Paulie looks around. There is nothing but sagebrush. "Okay, now what?" he says, dumping his bag on the ground. "All that talk of food's made me hungry."

"We need to figure out what made us leap back in time," you say, pulling the meteorite out of your daypack. "It must have something to do with this rock."

Paulie's face is twisted in confusion. "But how?"

You've been mulling over this problem on the walk back. "Paulie, where's your phone?"

"My phone? What's that got to—"

You sigh and hold out your hand. "Just give it to me."

"Okay, okay. Don't blow a foo-foo valve." Paulie grabs his phone and passes it to you. "So what are you going to do?"

You turn the phone off. "I have an idea." Once it's powered down, you turn it on again while holding the rock nearby.

Paulie stares for a moment and then his eyes widen. "So you think something to do with the phone's electromagnetic radiation has reacted with the meteorite to alter the space time continuum? Seems a bit of a stretch."

"Got a better idea?"

He shrugs and shakes his head. "Where's a physicist when you need one, eh?"

You're not all that hopeful that the phone is the cause, but then, as the phone lights up, you feel a tingling in the palm of your hand. At first you think it's just the phone's vibrate function, but the rock is getting warm as well. "Something's happening!"

The rock starts to glow. A few moments later, it looks red hot, but you have no problem holding it in your hand.

"It's working!" Paulie says in excitement, but then he looks confused. "But how?"

"If I knew I'd tell you. Let's just hope it gets us back to the right time."

As the vibrations increase, Paulie inches away from you. His eyes are wide, with white showing all around his pupils. "Holy moly…"

"Move closer!" you say. "You don't want to be left behind do you?"

Just as Paulie takes a step in your direction, there is a blinding flash.

As the smoke clears you see tents and classmates.

"Where did you two sneak up from?" says Mr. Jackson from ten paces away. "And where did you get the fireworks? You know they're not allowed on school trips."

Paulie's in shock. His mouth is hanging open and there is a smudge of soot on his cheek.

Mr. Jackson's hands are on his hips. His eyes bore into you. "Well, are you going to answer me?"

But how do you explain what just happened? And would Mister Jackson believe you if you tried? You look at Paulie. He's lost for words, his mouth is moving, but nothing's coming out.

So what do you do? Do you:

Try to explain the time travel to Mister Jackson? **P52**

Or:

Keep the secret to yourself? **P63**

You have decided to go exploring in Gabriel's Gulch

When you reach the bottom of the gulch you see a fast-moving stream running through its center. The water looks clean and cool as it races through a narrow channel in the rock, worn smooth over time.

"We should fill up our water bottles," Paulie says. "Just in case we have to leave the canyon in a hurry."

You nod. "Good idea."

With bottles filled, you work your way further upstream. You can hear the sound of Bison grazing on the prairie above the canyon rim. Around one corner you come across a carcass lying on the floor of the canyon.

Paulie look up the steep canyon wall. "This bison's gone base jumping without a parachute." He kicks one of the huge horns protruding from the animal's head.

"Don't touch it," you say. "It'll have germs all over it."

Paulie crouches down and studies the dead bison. "I'm not worried about germs so much," he says, poking at some deep scratches in the animal's hide with his finger. "I–I'm worried about what's been eating this."

"What could it be?" you ask.

"Wolves maybe," he says, "or a mountain lion?"

"Maybe we should head back." A tingle of fear runs down your back. "I don't mind bison or pronghorns, but wolves…"

A deep snarl echoes through the canyon. Your stomach lurches as you scan for the animal that made it.

Paulie leaps up and looks around nervously. "You see it?"

Then you spot the big cat against the canyon wall. Its tawny coat blends in with the surroundings perfectly. Only the white patches on the cat's chest, cheeks and mouth stands out against the sandstone.

You lift an arm and point. "There."

"Uh oh." Paulie clutches your arm. "It must think we're after its meal."

You search for an escape route. "Back up slowly, Paulie. Angle towards the water."

Your eyes never leave the cat as it slowly creeps toward you. A dozen or so steps and you are on the edge of the quickly moving stream.

"I hope big cats don't like to swim," you say.

As the cat moves forward, you and Paulie walk backwards along the bank.

Then with a sudden rush, the mountain lion is sprinting flat out right at you! You hook your arm into Paulie's and leap.

In an instant you're sliding along the well-worn channel. You struggle to straighten up and point your feet downstream. The powerful current pushes into your back, moving you faster and faster along the slippery rock.

Paulie's arm tightens on yours.

You take a quick glance over your shoulder. The confused cat is almost fifty yards back, standing by the channel where you entered. The danger has passed. For now at least.

"Yippee! This is like a big slippery slide!" you yell.

But Paulie's face is twisted into a grimace rather than a smile.

"Come on, Paulie, enjoy the ride while it lasts."

Paulie grits his teeth and shakes his head. "Did you know that most fast moving streams end in waterfalls?" he says.

"You just made that up!" you shout over the sound of rushing water.

"So what's that then?" he says, pointing with his free arm.

Paulie's right. Thirty yards further down, the stream disappears over a lip.

"Yikes! How far will the drop be?" you ask.

"How should I know!"

You let go of Paulie's arm and try to climb up the channel walls, but it's useless. The rock is far too slick to get a hold on, and the force of the water is too strong to fight. You have no option. You're going over the edge whether you want to or not.

Paulie is doing windmills as he furiously back-paddles in a useless attempt to slow his progress towards the edge.

You fly over the lip of the falls and plunge towards a deep pool at the bottom. Thankfully, rather than there being rock, it's more like jumping off the high platform of your local pool.

With a SPLASH, you hit the water. You dogpaddle over to a low bank on one side, climb out of the water and up into a patch of sun. After slipping your daypack off, you look back towards your friend. "You okay, Paulie?"

Paulie is lying on the edge of the pool shivering. After a moment, he climbs up to join you. "Now I know why I prefer books. Real life is scary."

"Don't people say, what doesn't kill you makes you stronger?" you say, with a grin. "Wow, what a ride."

Paulie looks over and scowls. "Do you really believe that? I was nearly maimed. How would that have made me stronger?"

You start to reply, but then notice Paulie has taken his phone out and is giving it a shake.

"Is it still working?" you ask.

"It should be alright," he says. "I've got a waterproof cover on it. But there's only one way to find out. I'll be angry if I've lost all my photos."

As Paulie fiddles with his phone, you sit on the smooth sandstone and warm up. Steam rises from your clothes as they dry.

"Okay, here goes," Paulie says about to push the 'on' button.

"Hey, wait a minute," you say. "Look at that!"

Distracted from his phone, Paulie looks up to where you're pointing. The end of a large bone is poking out of the crumbling canyon wall. Paulie stares at the bone like he's trying to burn a hole in it with his eyes. Then, after a minute, he looks over at you. "Is that what I think it is?"

"Well, if you think it's a ginormous dinosaur bone, I think you're right. Look at the size of it!"

Both of you leap up and rush over to the bone protruding out of the cliff.

"That's huge," Paulie says rubbing his hand along fossil.

"If this were a chicken leg," you say tugging on one end it, "the chicken would have to have been twenty feet tall. Give me a hand, Paulie, it feels loose."

The next few minutes are spent wiggling the bone left then right, gradually working it out of its resting place for the last 65 million years or so.

"I don't think it's big enough to be a bone from a T. Rex," Paulie says, "but it's way too big to be a bison."

When the bone finally lets go, you lurch back and fall on your backside. The bone, all five feet of it, drops to the ground in front of you.

You wipe your sleeve across your forehead. "Phew, that was hard work."

"Holy moly," Paulie says, looking at the bone on the ground in front of him, "what a good score."

"Yeah, I can't wait to show Mister J…" you say before realizing you're still in another time.

"Let's take a picture," Paulie says. "Then when we get back home we can prove what we found. I'll set my camera for time delay so we can both be in the shot."

You're quick to agree with Paulie's logic. As he sets his camera on a rock, and lines it up for the shot, you brush as much dirt and sand off it as you can.

Paulie hits a button on his phone then rushes over to where you've hoisted your end of the bone off the ground. Ten seconds later, both of you are straining under its weight and smiling like it's Christmas morning.

With a FLASH you're knocked off your feet.

As you brush the dust from your clothes you look around. "Have we jumped again?"

Paulie scans the canyon. "We must have, the creek is dry."

Then you see the big bone. "Did that come with us?"

"It must have."

"Wow, we should carry it back to camp."

"Carry it? We can barely pick it up," Paulie says, scrunching his forehead and looking at you like you're a moron.

You look at the bone and scratch your head. The bone has a slight curve to it. "I bet we could drag it like a sledge," you say. "We just need some rope or something."

You can see Paulie's mind working as he tries to solve the problem. Then he smiles. "If you don't mind sacrificing some clothing, we could twists some strips of fabric into cord and hook it onto our backpacks. Then we can drag the bone to camp."

"I've got a spare sweatshirt in my pack. That might work."

Paulie nods. "I've got one too. That should be plenty."

You set about cutting your sweatshirts into thin strips and braiding them into lengths of rope, then tie them together into an elongated Y. You attach the base of the Y to the bone and then tie the other two ends to your packs.

Like horses in harness, you and Paulie try out your contraption. With only a couple of feet of bone dragging on the ground like a big spoon, the going isn't too bad.

"Hey, I think this is going to work." You grin. "I knew there was a reason I brought you along. Now, mush!"

And you really are pleased. You don't know how you would have gone if you'd been out here alone. Even though Paulie is younger, having company has made a big difference to your confidence.

"There's only one problem," you say, remembering what you read in the guidebook. "Aren't we meant to mark the location of fossils we find and report it to the rangers so the park paleontologists can check out the site first?"

"But that law is recent," Paulie says with an evil grin. "We collected this fossil millions of years before that law was passed. Heck, we collected it before Montana even existed, and brought it back to the present. Technically, I reckon we're okay."

You give him a sideways glance. "Proving that might be tricky."

"Ah, but I've got the photos! They'll show water in the canyon."

"Sounds good enough to me," you say. "Assuming we've got the strength to get it back to camp."

Paulie looks pleased with himself. "We could sing a song to help us," he says. "Help us get a good rhythm going."

You look back at your prize and then over at Paulie. "Okay. Why not?"

And with that, Paulie breaks out into song. "Yo, heave ho, yo heave ho ..."

By the time you're 100 yards from camp, a sea of amused faces is staring at you. But this only makes you and Paulie sing louder.

"Well you two seem pleased with yourselves," Mister Jackson says as he comes out to greet you. "Looks like you've got quite a prize there. How did you come across that?"

You sneak a knowing look at Paulie and grin. "It's a long story Mister J. A very long and interesting story."

Congratulations, this part of your story is over. Well done. You've found a big dinosaur bone and have survived a trip back in time. What would you like to do now? Do you:

Go to the beginning and read a different path? **P1**

Or

Go to the great big list of choices? **P376**

You have decided to try to explain the time travel to Mister J

The still-warm rock is in your right hand. Paulie's cell phone is in the other. "It wasn't fireworks, Mister J, it's this meteorite we found. It's causing us to jump back and forth in time."

"Funny. Ha, ha! Let me see that thing." Mister Jackson strides towards you with his arm outstretched.

You drop the rock into Mister Jackson's palm and wait for his reaction. "It certainly absorbs the heat from the sun. It's much warmer than I expected."

"It's been vibrating fast," Paulie says. "No wonder it's warm."

Your teacher ignores Paulie's comments and holds the rock up in front of his face, turning it from side to side. "Certainly looks like a meteorite. Where'd you find it?"

"Up near Gabriel's arch," you say. "We think it's reacting with Paulie's phone somehow. We got sent back to the Cretaceous era. There were dinosaurs and everything!"

"Yeah," Paulie says. "The climate changed too. The place was all swampy. We saw Troodons and a T. Rex!"

"Fossils?" Mister Jackson asks.

Paulie is hopping from foot to foot, getting more agitated by the minute. "No! Real ones! I swear Mister J. There were real dinosaurs!"

You nod your agreement, but the doubt in Mister J's expression is obvious. "You should have seen them Mister J. They were awesome!"

"They tried to eat us!" Paulie says.

"Very funny," Mister Jackson says. He tosses the meteorite towards you. "Now go and catalogue your find and stop this nonsense." And with that, Mister J turns and heads back to the other parents sitting around the makeshift camp kitchen.

You turn to Paulie. "Well that went well. Still, it's no wonder he thinks we're nuts."

"Wouldn't you?" Paulie says. "I'm having problems believing what happened myself, and I was there!"

"So, what now?" you say. "Do we take Mister J on a time jump so he'll believe us?"

"I don't think that's a very good idea."

You turn towards the setting sun. The sky is streaked orange and red. "Let's sleep on it, Paulie. We can decide what to do in the morning."

Paulie agrees, just as one of the parents rings the dinner bell.

The next morning, despite being warm and comfortable in your sleeping bag, you get up early and throw a few chunks of wood onto the embers of last night's bonfire. The morning air is crisp and cool, but you know once the sun gets up the day will get quite warm.

As the new logs begin to pop and crackle, you grab a folding chair and sit, staring into the flames. It's hard to take your mind off the events of the previous day and you're pleased the others are still asleep. You need time to think.

The sun creeps over the ridge to the east and the first rays of light hit the tents. People begin to stir. The first adult up is Mister J. After making himself a cup of instant coffee, he pulls up a folding chair and sits beside you.

"So, what's all this dinosaur stuff about?" he says. "You and Paulie aren't usually ones to tell tall tales. What's got in to you two?"

"It's not a story, I swear Mister J. It really happened. I just wish I could figure out some way to prove it to you."

"So, this isn't some elaborate joke? You're actually serious?"

You nod. "We really did see dinosaurs Mister J. Honest we did."

Mister Jackson shakes his head in confusion. "Well, today the whole class is going up to the arch and beyond. Why don't you show me exactly where this time jump happened. Then we'll see if we can make sense of it. Maybe there's a logical explanation for what you two experienced."

"Thanks Mister J." At least he hasn't discounted your story out of hand. "You're right. There must be a logical explanation."

And with that Mister Jackson gets up and walks over to the camp kitchen. Then he turns. "You weren't eating cactus were you?"

You shake your head, wondering what he's on about. Mister J shrugs and heads off to help organize breakfast.

An hour later, all fed and watered, Mister Jackson, thirty students, and three of the six parents are ready to hike off into the hills. The group will retrace your path up to Gabriel's arch and then move further into the canyon to a spot where fossils have been found before.

After packing your supplies for the day, you slot the meteorite into a side pocket of your daypack and walk towards Paulie's tent. His T. Rex flag hangs limp above its opening. "Don't forget your phone, Paulie," you say. "If we're going to reproduce the conditions for our time jump we'll need everything to be identical."

Paulie's head pop out. "Are you serious? You're actually considering going back in time again? Holy moly, you've got rocks in your head."

"Hey, this could be the biggest scientific breakthrough of the century. We could go down in history."

Paulie climbs out of his tent, dragging his pack behind him. "Or go down a T. Rex's throat. Don't you remember the close calls we had?"

"Yeah I know, but—"

Paulie hands you his cell phone. And then separately, its battery. "Here take it. Just tell me before you boot the thing up so I can get well away."

"But I thought you liked dinosaurs?"

"I like learning about them, not being eaten by them." He turns his back and wanders over to where the others are gathered.

You shrug, then slip the phone and battery into your pocket. At least Mister Jackson seems interested in getting to the bottom of this mystery.

"Okay everybody, listen up," Mister Jackson says. "The first thing we're going to do is buddy up. Everyone find a buddy. At each stage of our fieldtrip, you have to make sure your buddy is with you before moving on. We don't want to leave anyone behind."

"Should we buddy up?" Mister Jackson says, looking down at you.

Paulie's wandered off and is standing next to one of his classmates so you say, "Sure, Mister J. Why not?"

"Right, let's go. We've got a fair distance to walk today so keep together, and keep an eye on your buddy."

Mister Jackson stops along the way and tells you about the history of the Badlands. It isn't until you get to the ridge where Gabriel's arch is located that the group stops for a break.

While you wait for your chance to talk to Mister Jackson, you look around the area, trying to remember where the T. Rex had been standing. By imagining yourself up on top of the arch, you walk along the ridge to a spot that look about the right distance from the arch. Here there is a patch of low scrubby bushes. While keeping an eye out for snakes, you scrabble around pulling the bushes aside, and looking for telltale signs of prehistoric life. It's then that you see the animal print in the rock.

When you see a second footprint your eyes widen. "Hey Mister J! Hey Paulie! Come and look at this!"

Mister Jackson, wanders over. "What's so urgent?"

You pull a branch aside. "Look."

Now you've got his attention.

"It's an old fossilized animal print of some sort," Mister J says. "Well spotted."

"It looks like the one we saw when we time jumped," Paulie says. "It's a Troodon print."

"You still sticking to that story?" Mister Jackson says as he studies the footprint in the sandstone more closely. "You probably saw this yesterday and decided to dream up this hoax."

You point to the second print. "Okay then how do you explain that!"

"These can't be that old, this looks like a boot print ... people weren't here..." But then he realizes the boot print is set in stone.

While Mister Jackson studies the print, you take off your boot. "Here, try this for fit."

Mister Jackson looks confused at first. And then he sees the chunk of heel that is missing from the sole of your boot and the corresponding shape in the rock. He grabs the shoe and places it into the impression made in the sandstone.

It fits perfectly.

"But how?"

"Exactly," you say kneeling down beside the footprint. "Unless Paulie and I were telling the truth."

"Give me another look at that meteorite," Mister Jackson says.

You open your pack and take out the shiny black rock and place it gently in Mister Jackson's hand. Then you pull out Paulie's cell phone, slip the battery into the slot in its back and replace the cover.

"So should I turn the phone on and see if we time jump Mister J?"

"No!" Paulie says, scrabbling away from you with a look of terror in his eyes.

Mister J glances at Paulie, then at you, and then back down at the rock. His hands are trembling.

"There's more danger than just dinosaurs, you know!" Paulie yells from ten yards away. "We could end up in the future too," he says. "What if we jump so far forward the earth is no longer habitable? We'll never get back."

You can see Mister Jackson's mind ticking over. Before you can stop him, the teacher stands up and, grunting with effort, throws the meteorite as far as he can.

As the rock flies over the edge of the cliff and sails down into the dense scrub below, you wonder for a moment what opportunities you've missed and what dangers you've been spared. Then you turn to your teacher and look down at your finger hovering over the 'on' button on the Paulie's phone. "I guess that's a no then?"

"I think fossil hunting is exciting enough. Don't you?" Mister Jackson says with a look of relief in his eyes. "Besides, it probably wouldn't have worked a second time."

Now that the meteorite is gone, Paulie relaxes.

You shrug and give your teacher a smile "Yeah, you're probably right Mister J, you're probably right."

Congratulations, this part of your story is over. It's time to make another decision. Do you:

Go back to the start and read a different track? **P1**

Or

Go to the great big list of choices? **P376**

You have decided to follow a dry watercourse to the canyon floor

"Let's take the direct route," you say. "We'll end up in the top of the canyon that way."

Paulie peers down the slope. "It's pretty steep."

"We can always slide down on our butts if we have to."

With that, you inch your way over the edge, and with feet side-on to the hill, start slip-sliding your way down towards the canyon floor. Pebbles bounce past you as Paulie moves into the dry watercourse above you, adding loose stones to those already rolling like marbles underneath your feet.

A couple of times, you slip and fall on your backside, grazing your hand as you reach out for support, but for the most part progress is good.

Until you spot the rattlesnake.

With a sharp intake of breath, you dig in your heels and try to stop, but the pebbles under your feet have another idea. They roll off in front of you, bouncing down onto the snake, giving it a fright and causing it to coil up ready to strike.

"Snake!" you yell up to Paulie.

Rattle, rattle, rattle, rattle, rattle.

You're on your bottom now, doing your best to stop, but you're nearly upon the reptile. And it's not a small snake either!

Maybe you can kick it away?

The rattling is close now. The snake has a diamond shaped head and a thick body, bigger around than your arm. Coiled up, it's hard to say how long it is, but it must be at least five feet.

You dig your fingers into the soil, but still you slide towards the rattling snake. It's too late. You're moving too fast.

Rattle, rattle, rattle, rattle, rattle! STRIKE!

A sharp stabbing pain runs up your leg.

"Owwww!" You kick out wildly, sending the snake slithering off down the hillside. "He got me!"

More pebbles clatter past you. Then Paulie stops beside you.

"Are you okay?"

"I've just been bitten by a rattlesnake. What do you think?"

Lifting your knee towards your belly, you reach down and pull up the leg of your jeans. Half way between knee and ankle, are two puncture wounds. They are already red and inflamed.

"Okay keep calm," Paulie says. "I've read about snakebite and you're meant to keep quiet so you don't pump the poison around your system."

"I'm bleeding."

"Bleeding's good," Paulie says. "The blood will wash out some of the poison."

"Aren't you going to suck out the poison?"

Paulie shakes his head. "You've been watching too many old movies. That will just make me sick too. We'll let it bleed for a minute then wrap the wound up to keep it clean. Once we've done that I'll help you the rest of the way down. Then I'll run and get help."

As the blood seeps from the snakebite, a burning sensation surrounds the wound. "It hurts, Paulie."

"Don't be a baby," Paulie says as he rummages in his pack for something to put around your wound. "Did you know that over 8,000 people are bitten by poisonous snakes in North America each year. Guess how many die."

"2,000?"

"About eight," he says. "So stop worrying. You'll be okay."

You're not so sure. "Doesn't a big snake mean lots of poison?"

"What self respecting snake wants to waste all its poison up on you? You're not its lunch."

Paulie pulls a spare t-shirt out of his pack and starts ripping it into strips. He ties them loosely around your wound.

"Aren't you going to make a tourniquet?" you ask.

Paulie laughs. "No, that's from the movies too, silly. The poison from snake bites destroys tissue, it's better if it spreads a bit, it will be more diluted that way and cause less damage."

It's times like this you're pleased your companion is a nerd. "Just as well you know all this stuff. Remind me to recommend you for a medal when we get back."

Paulie gives you a smile as he finishes off a knot. "Okay, you're all bandaged up. Let's make a move. Just try to slide and not use your muscles any more than you have to. Lean on me."

You both make an awkward two-headed four-legged animal that half slides, half slips down the last of the hill to the canyon floor. Once there, Paulie props you up in the shade of a boulder.

"You're not supposed to eat or drink after being bitten by a rattlesnake. Just keep quiet and I'll be back as quickly as I can."

You look up at Paulie through vision that's going blurry. "Okay. Just hurry … and thanks."

"No prob."

Paulie jogs down the canyon towards camp. As his shape disappears around a corner, the throb in your leg increases. A burning sensation sears a path from the wound up into your thigh. You hope Paulie gets help in time.

You pull your pack over to use as a pillow. Now that the sound of Paulie's footsteps has gone, it's so quiet. All you can hear is the whistling wind as it comes up the canyon. Far above, a prairie falcon soars. You drift in and out of sleep. Then blackness takes you.

You're not sure how long you've been out, when you hear someone calling your name. It sounds like Paulie. Lifting yourself up on one elbow, you peer down the canyon. A number of blurry shapes appear. It's hard to see who they are, but at least someone is coming. Exhausted, you flop back down. Never before has your body ached so much. Then, as you're about to drift off again, hands lift you onto a stretcher.

"Hang on there, we've got you now," a man's voice you don't recognize says.

There is a sharp prick in your arm.

"That should make you feel better."

When you wake up, you're in a room with white walls. It smells of disinfectant and it's dark outside. Near the window, Paulie is asleep in a chair and the ward is reasonably quiet apart from the squeak of rubber shoes on hospital linoleum and the *beep, beep, beep* of a monitor somewhere.

Paulie is still wearing the same clothes but he's washed his face. You cough, and reach for a glass of water on the cabinet beside you.

"Oh you're awake," Paulie says, rubbing his eyes. "How do you feel?"

"I've been better, but I'm alive, thanks to you."

"You really scared me," Paulie says.

"I thought you said I'd be fine. That not many people died of snakebite."

"Yeah, well I didn't want to worry you. On the bright side, Doc says you'll be okay to leave tomorrow afternoon. You'll just have to take it easy for a few days."

"No more fossil hunting, eh?" you say, giving your friend a smile.

"Not this year. But there is some good news. They caught those fossil smugglers. I forgot all about them when you tangled with that rattler. But it seems you were talking in your sleep and one of the paramedics asked me if what you were saying was true or just a nightmare. I said it was true and told them about the men. They got on the radio and contacted the police."

"Wow, that's great," you say, resting your head back down on your pillow.

"It's been exciting alright. I got to give a statement to one of the policemen. Did you know that police capture over three thousand…"

You drift off to the sound of Paulie telling you all the facts he's learned about the police. It's quite comforting, almost like having someone read you a story.

This part of your story is over. But have you tried all the different paths? Have you found fossils? Have you found gold? Have you seen the T. Rex?

It's time to make a decision. Do you:

Go to the beginning and read a different track? **P1**

Or

Go to the great big list of choices? **P376**

You have decided to keep the secret to yourself

You pull Paulie aside. "Let's keep this to ourselves. They'll think we've gone crazy if we try to explain."

Paulie nods. "I'm still trying to convince myself it actually happened. Have you heard of mass hallucinations? Maybe we had one of those."

"I don't think that foul-breathed T. Rex was a hallucination." You pluck at your sleeve and take a sniff. "I can still smell his slobber on my clothes."

Paulie lifts the hem of his t-shirt and buries his nose in the fabric. "Yep, that's T. Rex all right."

"Besides, we may want to go back again," you say. "If we tell Mister J, he'll just stop us."

Paulie's eyes widen. "Are you serious? You want to go back?" He shakes his head slowly from side to side and whistles through his teeth. "Holy moly! You're nutzo!"

"But, what an opportunity. I thought you liked dinosaurs."

"I do," Paulie says." I like them in books and movies and museums where they belong."

"But to see really see them…. Where's your sense of adventure?"

"Where's *your* sense of self preservation? In case you've forgotten, we nearly got eaten back there. What happens if we end up right in the middle of them with nowhere to run? What then?"

Paulie does have a point.

"Well, let's sleep on it and decide in the morning. We just need to think of a safe place to time-jump from. Somewhere the dinosaurs won't be able to get at us. Please, think about it, Paulie. We could make history!"

Paulie scratches his head. "Okay I'll think on it. But no guarantees."

You're about to tell Paulie about the possibility of winning a Nobel Prize when the dinner bell rings and the camp erupts with screaming kids running towards the picnic tables.

After eating hotdogs and salad, your group sits around the campfire, singing songs and roasting marshmallows. Paulie avoids eye contact with you, so you give him time to think. Push too hard and he'll turn you down for sure.

Then, as a nearly full moon rises over the hills in the distance, Mister Jackson yawns loudly and stands up. "Okay everyone, time to hit the sack. We've got a busy day tomorrow."

The next morning you're one of the first up. Last night, it had taken you a while to get to sleep, and when you did, you'd dreamed of standing on Gabriel's arch looking at a T. Rex. In your dream, the massive dinosaur had ignored the Troodons and walked right up to you. And even though you were standing atop your rocky perch, its massive head was level with yours. The beast's teeth were long and sharp, and as it tilted its head sideways, one of its eyes, big as a softball, stared directly at you, its pupil black and glistening. You remember your frightened face reflecting back from the eyeball's shiny surface. Then, when you turned to find Paulie, he was nowhere to be seen.

The dream had been so real you'd startled yourself awake and then spent the next half hour staring at the nylon roof of your tent with every nerve in your body tingling. Even after the tremors had stopped, sleep would not return. Finally, after dawn's weak light penetrated the walls of your tent, you'd given up, climbed out of your sleeping bag, and gone outside to prod the campfire awake.

As you stir the embers and add small pieces of wood to them, you think about going back in time again. It's a scary idea, but despite the bad dream, the concept is both frightening and exciting. This could be the defining moment of your life. The one time that sets you apart from the crowd. Your one chance to become an internet sensation. You could start a science channel online, or write a book about your experiences. Or both!

Then you remember Paulie's words. He's right, the dinosaurs would eat you without a moment's hesitation. But is it worth the risk?

You're deep in thought when Paulie sits down beside you.

"How'd you sleep?" he asks.

"Not very good," you reply. "You?"

Paulie's yawns then looks up with bleary eyes. "I kept thinking about that T. Rex. It's a wonder anything survived with those things around."

"Yeah but–"

Paulie holds his hand up to stop you. "Look, I've decided. I'm not going back, but I won't stop you if you want to go." Paulie hands you his phone, and then its battery, which he's taken out. "Just give me enough time to stand clear if you decide to go for it. Okay?"

"But Paulie, I thought we were a team."

Paulie shakes his head. "No we're–"

"We are, Paulie! We're the only ones who have ever gone back in time. Do you know what that means?"

Paulie glares at you. "It means we're lucky to be alive."

"No, it means we've got a chance to make a difference. We can go back and take photographs so that scientists know exactly what these animals looked like. Remember the feathers we saw on the Troodons? Aren't the experts are still arguing about that sort of thing?"

Not being drawn in, Paulie closes his eyes. His hands fly up to cover his ears. He shakes his head and mumbles "No, no, no, no," under his breath.

You pull down one of his arms. "Come on, Paulie, please! You know you want to."

He stops rocking and looks up at you. "You should tell Mister Jackson what happened to us." Then he stands up and walks away.

You look down at the phone and the battery, then towards Paulie as he nears his tent.

It's time to make a decision. Do you:

Have a go at time jumping on your own? **P66**

Or

Tell Mister Jackson what happened? **P52**

You have decided to time jump on your own

"Okay, I'll do it myself!" you yell at Paulie's back.

After slotting the battery back into Paulie's phone, you take the meteorite and hold it out in your hand. You hold the phone over the rock and push the power button and wait.

"Who are you yelling at?" Mister Jackson says.

"Nobody Mister J." You inhale deeply trying to steady your nerves as you wait for the phone to power up. Then as the phone's screen turns on, the meteorite begins to glow. You can feel its vibrations pulsing through your arm.

"And what's that?"

"Nothing Mister J."

"Doesn't look like nothing to me," your teacher says, glaring at the rock in your hand. "What are you playing at?"

"I'd move back if I were you, Mister J." You stand up and take a few steps away from your teacher. "Watch out! This thing's about to go off!"

"What the—"

FLASH.

Mister Jackson is staring at you and waving the smoke away from his face. "What the heck was that?" Then he looks around at the steaming jungle.

You give your teacher a sheepish smile. "Welcome to the late Cretaceous, Mister J."

Mister Jackson's face is a mask of confusion. "Don't be ridiculous!" he says. "Time travel is imposs—"

The roar of the T. Rex is unmistakable. You and Mister Jackson spin around towards the sound. The beast is running towards you. It has two friends with it this time.

"My God! What have you done?"

Mister Jackson sprints off into the dense ferns, running for his life. You're about to take off after him, when your alarm buzzes and you spring upright in bed. Sweat drips off your forehead. Despite being in a familiar place you look around for signs of dinosaurs before realizing it's all a dream and today is the day you leave on your field trip to the Badlands of Montana to look for dinosaur fossils.

"Phew," you mumble as you swing your legs off the bed and start thinking about getting dressed for the field trip. "That was a little too real."

Quite a few hours later, on a bus in Montana, a meteorite streaks across a cloudless sky and disappears behind a hill not far away.

"Wow did you see that?" Paulie says, as he points towards the horizon.

A couple of students look up from their phones. "What? Huh?"

Paulie waves his hand excitedly. "The meteorite! Over there! Did you see it?"

"Yeah I saw it, Paulie," you say, remembering you dream. "But if you happen to stumble across it while out fossil hunting all I can say is leave it alone."

"What? Why?" He asks, giving you a strange look. "Are you okay?"

You shrug and give him a smile. "Do you believe in premonitions?"

Paulie shakes his head. "No. Don't be silly."

"What about time travel?" you ask.

Paulie smiles back. "Well now that's a different story. Did you know that Albert…"

You turn and look out the window, ignoring Paulie as he rambles on about the space-time continuum and Einstein's special theory of relativity. You admire the rugged beauty of the Badlands and wonder what adventures the next few days will bring. Whatever happens, there's one thing you do know for sure. You won't be picking up any meteorites this trip. Especially with all the cell phones around.

You have reached the end of this part of the story, but you still have decisions to make. Have you tried all the different paths?

68

It's time to make a decision. Do you:

Go back to the start and read a different track? **P1**

Or

Go to the great big list of choices? **P376**

You have decided to tell Mister Jackson what happened

Maybe Paulie is right. There are so many dangers involved with going back in time. Who knows which era you'd jump to if you went back a second time. And where would you land? Amongst a pack of Velociraptors? Without understanding how these jumps are happening and how to control things, there is just too much that could go wrong.

It would take a proper expedition, fitted out with modern equipment and some form of protection to have any chance of survival in such a hostile environment for any length of time. Unlike modern times, where humans are at the top of the food chain, during the age of the dinosaur, they were the top predators.

Having made your decision, you take the meteorite and Paulie's cell phone and go looking for Mister Jackson. When you find him, he's leaning against an old stone wall, drinking coffee at the camp kitchen with a couple of the other parents. You are so concerned about what you're going to say to him, you don't notice he is sending a text.

Startled, you jump back and look down at the meteorite expecting it to turn red at any moment. But nothing's happening. How can that be? Why would Paulie's phone make the meteorite send you back and forth in time, while Mister Jackson's doesn't? It just doesn't make sense. Is there some weird fault in Paulie's phone that is reacting with the meteorite?

"What's up with you?" Mister Jackson says. "You look like you've seen a ghost."

Again, you look at his phone and then at the rock in your hand. "I'm trying to understand—"

"Understand what?" Mister Jackson says, sliding his phone into his pocket and taking a step towards you. "Why are you acting so strange? And what's that in your hand?"

"It's a meteorite Paulie and I found when we went walking yesterday afternoon." You hold the rock up for Mister Jackson to see. "But it's got some strange properties we can't understand."

"Properties?" Mister Jackson asks. "What's that supposed to mean?"

"It's hard to explain, Mister J."

The teacher grabs your sleeve and leads you over to a couple folding chairs, away from the others. You and Mister Jackson sit face to face.

"Okay, tell me. What's going on?"

"It's hard to know where to start," you say.

Mister Jackson's eyes bore into you. "How about at the beginning. That usually works."

You watch his expression as you tell your story – about picking up the meteorite, standing under the arch, the T. Rex, the Troodons. Everything. By the time you reach the end, Mister Jackson is left with his mouth slightly ajar and a confused look on his face.

"Do you seriously expect me to believe that?" he says.

You shake your head. "No, I can barely believe it myself ... but it's true."

"Give me the meteorite and Paulie's phone," Mister Jackson says, holding out his hand.

You do as you're told.

"So this happened when you took a picture, and again when the phone booted up?"

You nod and feel yourself blush. Why you're embarrassed about telling the truth you're not quite sure. Maybe it's because the story sounds so far-fetched.

Without another word, Mister Jackson slots the battery into Paulie's phone. He holds his finger over the on button. "So you're saying if I turn this phone on I'm going to jump back in time?"

You stand up and take a few steps back. "I'd be careful if I were you Mister J. I swear I'm telling you the truth."

"Ha!" he scoffs. "What do you take me for? You kids and your silly stories." He pushes the button.

"Mister J!" You jump back a couple of steps back and stare at the meteorite. At first nothing happens, but then as the phone goes through its start-up sequence, the rock starts to glow.

"Look," you say. The rock glows brighter and brighter. "It's happening!"

Mister Jackson stares at the rock. His eyes widen. Then with a flash Mister Jackson disappears into thin air.

"Whoa!" You look around to see if anyone else saw what happened. But instead of gasping in shock at the disappearance of their teacher, the students are pouring cereal into bowls and toasting bread over the campfire, oblivious to what's just happened.

Now what do you do? You stand there looking at the spot where Mister Jackson used to be. You can still see his boot prints in the dirt. Hopefully, an idea will pop into your head.

You look up and see Paulie's T. Rex flag fluttering over his tent. Who else would believe what just happened? You race over and pull back the flap. "Hey, Paulie. You're not going to believe what just happened," you say, crawling in. "Mister J didn't believe me when I told him about going back in time and he turned on your phone. Now he's vanished!"

"Vanished?"

"Gone back in time! I tried to warn him."

Paulie cradles his head with both hands and closes his eyes. He rocks slowly back and forth mumbling under his breath.

"Don't zone out on me, Paulie. What are we going to do?"

His head snaps up and his eyes squint at you. "What can we do? Nothing. That's what."

"But surely we should tell someone."

Paulie laughs. "Like they're really going to believe us. They're more likely to think we've gone crazy, killed our teacher and buried him somewhere out in the desert."

"You've been watching too much T.V. Why would they think that?" you say. "We're just a couple of kids. I'm going to go tell one of the parents. Come on Paulie. Back me up. Surely they'll believe both of us."

Paulie sighs. You can sense his reluctance. "I don't know…"

"Paulie, come on, we have to tell someone!"

For a moment he sits in silence. A last he does a little shake, like a chill has run down his back, and then, on hands and knees, makes a move towards the entrance of the tent. "All right. Let's get it over with."

Once out of the tent, you start walking towards a group of parents. Suddenly there is a FLASH and a puff of smoke off to your left. Then, from behind a clump of sagebrush, his shirt in tatters, soot smudges on his face and gasping like he's been running, Mister Jackson appears.

You and Paulie rush over to him. "You okay, Mister J?"

His hand shakes as you take the phone and remove the battery. The meteorite, clenched tightly in his fist, you pry loose and drop into your pocket. Your teacher barely notices. Instead, he stares straight ahead, like a statue.

With the phone and meteorite tucked safely away, you grab Mister Jackson's arm and give it a shake. "Mister J? Can you hear me? Mister J?"

"He's in shock," Paulie says.

"A… Daspletosaurus… nearly… got… me." Mister Jackson says, a bubble of drool running down his lower lip.

You and Paulie lead Mister Jackson over to a seat by the fire where he sits trembling for a few minutes before turning to you.

The teacher wipes his mouth with his sleeve. "Sorry… I… didn't… believe—"

"Holy moly, Mister Jackson," Paulie says. "Sounds like you had a narrow escape."

Mister Jackson slowly moves his head up and down a few times, then slaps his cheeks lightly with his hands. A rush of air escapes his lungs and he looks over at Paulie. "It was… awful. Incredible, but awful at the same time. I can't believe…"

"Where did you end up?" Paulie asks.

"I'm not exactly sure. But as I was wandering around the jungle trying to figure out how to get back, I came upon a group of Daspletosaurs ripping some poor creature to bits."

"Must have been late Cretaceous then," Paulie says. "That's where we went too."

"Yeah, well one of the critters saw me and I had to run for it. Kept getting hooked up on branches as I ran through the jungle. I hid behind a tree and turned off the phone and then rebooted it. The thing took ages to get going again. I was nearly lunch."

"I did warn you Mister J," you say. "But I'm glad you made it back in one piece. We were just trying to work out how to break the bad news of your disappearance to the others when you reappeared."

"So what now?" Paulie asks. "Do we tell the others?"

"Or do we keep it secret," you suggest. "We could come back over summer and do some real exploring. What do you say Mister J, should we organize a proper expedition and come back? We'd be famous. Imagine all the exciting things we could discover."

"We should take the phone and meteorite to the Smithsonian, or some research institution," Mister Jackson says. "I certainly don't want you children getting in harm's way." He pats his pockets. "Where is the phone?"

You stab Paulie a look, then turn back to Mister Jackson. "Didn't you bring it back with you?" Your right hand moves over the lump of rock in your pocket, shielding it from Mister Jackson's view.

Confused, Mister Jackson searches his pockets. He finds nothing but a set of keys and a penknife. "I—I must have dropped it somewhere. He looks at the ground around his feet, then walks back around the sagebrush. "It's gone. What a shame."

Paulie scowls at you, but you raise a finger to your lips and signal him to remain silent.

"Well I'm going to go write my experience down in my notebook while everything is still fresh in my mind. You two should do the same. We still might be able to provide some information scientists can use, however vague it may be."

"Good idea Mister J," you say, dragging Paulie by the sleeve towards the tents.

"But I saw you take the phone and meteorite out of his hand," Paulie whispers. "Why are you lying?"

"I'm not lying. I'm protecting our discovery, Paulie. This is a once in a lifetime chance to—"

Paulie is looking over your shoulder. You stop talking and turn around. It's Mister Jackson. He's standing there with is hand held out.

"What?" you ask.

"Hand them over. Just as well my memory came back. Knowing you two, you'd probably rush off and get yourself killed."

"But Mister J," you say. "We're the ones who found—"

"Give them up," Paulie says. "Mister Jackson is right. It's too dangerous."

You shrug and dig the phone and meteorite out of your pockets. "No one is going to believe us, you know. They'll think we've gone crazy when you tell them what happened."

"Under normal circumstances I'd agree with you. Except that I took photos while I was back in time." In his excitement to show you his pictures, and still suffering from shock, Mister Jackson slots the battery into the phone and hits the on button. "Here have a look."

Before you have a chance to jump back, the meteorite glows red and there is a FLASH.

Suddenly it is hot and sticky and thick ferns and forest surrounds you. Strange flying reptiles soar overhead.

"Holy moly, Mister J!" Paulie yells. "Look at what you done!"

"Wow," you say. "Look over there, Pachycephalosaurs. They're butting heads."

The two animals are crashing through the jungle and slamming their horned heads together in some strange duel. Their screams are ear splitting as they rush towards each other.

Unfortunately, not one of you hear the two T. Rex's sneaking up behind you.

The T. Rex's look at each other and drool, as if to say "lunch is served."

You've reached the end of this part of the story. But have you tried all the different paths? It's time to make another decision. What would you like to do now?

Start the story over and try a different path? **P1**

Or

Go to the great big list of choices? **P376**

You have decided to go further into the mine

"There could be tons of rock, Paulie. Digging ourselves out could take hours … or days." You turn and shine your light further into the mine. Then you lick your finger and hold it up.

Paulie gives you a strange look. "What are you doing?"

"Testing for wind. It's faint, but I can still feel it. Come on, let's get moving before the flashlight runs out."

Paulie grins. "You sure you didn't fart?" he says, trying to make light of the situation.

You laugh. "Well if I did, even more reason to keep moving."

As you head deeper into the mine, there are many side shafts. Most only go back ten or fifteen yards before coming to a dead end. One of them holds a pile of old cable, lengths of chain and other rusty equipment.

The temperature gets colder as you descend deeper and deeper. You take a sweatshirt out of your pack and slip it on.

"This isn't looking very ho–hopeful," Paulie says nervously, pulling a sweater out of his pack. "How will we know which way leads to the surface?"

"Be quiet for a moment," you say. Then you lick your finger once more. As you stand quietly feeling for breeze you hear the faint trickle of water off in the distance.

Paulie cups a hand around one ear. "You hear that?"

"Come on, I can still feel a breeze, let's find out where it's coming from."

With more urgency, you and Paulie push forward. About five minutes later the floor of the tunnel starts showing signs of moisture. There are puddles on the floor, and rivulets running down the rock walls of the mine.

Then suddenly, the beam of your flashlight disappears into nothingness.

Throwing your arm out, you yell, "Stop!"

The ground in front of you is gone. When you shine the flashlight at your feet, you're standing near the edge of a vertical drop. How far down it goes is anyone's guess. But one thing for sure is that the breeze is blowing harder here.

Inching forward you shine the light into the void. "It's a huge cavern!"

"I've read about these," Paulie says. "Ground water eats away at the softer rock, and over thousands of years it leaves a cave system behind."

"Do you think there's a stream down there?"

"Makes sense," Paulie says. "The water has to go somewhere."

"Maybe it leads to the outside?"

He nods. "It's possible. But how do we get to it?"

On hands and knees you crawl to the edge and peer over. The beam from the flashlight is quite dim by the time it hits the water. "It's a stream alright," you say. "It's not that far, twenty-five feet or so."

"How deep is the water?"

"I can't tell," you say rising from your knees.

Paulie is shivering. "So what now?" he asks.

Then you remember the rusty cable you saw in one of the side tunnels. "Let's get some cable and climb down. We can follow the stream out of the mine."

"How long can you tread water?" Paulie asks.

"How long can you go without food and water?" you reply.

After dragging a length of cable back through the tunnel, you tie one end around one of the heavy support timbers and then drag the remainder to the edge of the drop off and toss it over the side. There is a satisfying splash from below as the cable hits the water.

"This isn't going to be easy to hang on to," Paulie says, looking at the cable. "It's going to be rough on our hands."

He's right. The cable isn't that big around either. It will be hard to hang on to something so skinny.

As you stand there trying to come up with a solution, Paulie reaches down and unbuckles one of the shoulder straps of his daypack. He wraps the strap around his hands and then grabs onto the cable and gives it a tug.

"I think this might work," he says. "It's not as good as a glove, but it's better than nothing."

"Okay," you say. "I'll give you some light while you climb down. Then I'll toss down our packs and climb down myself."

Paulie hands you the other strap from his pack and then gets on his hands and knees and slowly maneuvers his way back to the edge. With a grasp on the cable he lowers his legs over and then the rest of his body.

"Whooooah! I'm slippppppppppping!" he yells.

SPLASH!

You lean over the edge and sweep the beam of your flashlight back and forth. Then you see Paulie's head poking out of the water, his hand hanging onto the cable.

"You okay?"

"Yeah fine," he yells up. "The water's really deep and there's a current."

"Okay, well hold on to the cable. Here come the packs."

"Toss me the light too," Paulie say. "I'll light your way as you climb down."

When you drop the flashlight, you are cast into darkness. You wrap the strap of Paulie's pack around your hands and grip the cable, lowering yourself over the edge just as Paulie did. With your feet pressed against the wall of the cave you manage to half abseil, half slide down the cable.

"Brrrrr… Why didn't you tell me the water was so cold?"

"Yeah well, there wasn't anything I could do about that, so there wasn't any point."

Your pull as much of your body as possible out of the water and up onto your floating backpack. Thankfully, all the air trapped inside makes it quite buoyant. "At least we can float downstream," you say.

"Give me the light back. I'll lead the way."

So, with your head and shoulders out of the water, and kicking with your feet, you and Paulie head off into the unknown. You make good progress, but it doesn't take long for the chill from the water to seep into your bones. After fifteen minutes, your toes are numb.

Then, just as you're about to think you've made a terrible mistake, a pinpoint of light appears in the distance. "Paulie! Do you see it?" You turn the flashlight back onto Paulie and see him, grimly hanging on to his pack, his teeth chattering, lips turning blue. "Hang on. It's not far now."

When you finally pop out from under a rock ledge and into a shimmering pool, relief floods through your body. Never did you think that seeing the sky would give you such joy.

The pool is about ten yards wide and surrounded on three sides by smooth rock that rises up to create a natural bowl. The fourth side is open and the water from the pool trickles down a narrow watercourse.

Shivering, you and Paulie drag yourselves out of the water and flop down like seals basking in the sun.

The warm rock is the best thing you've ever felt, and before long, you can feel your toes again. Even the chattering of Paulie's teeth has stopped.

"You ready to head back to camp, Paulie?"

He rolls over, leaving a wet print of his body on the sandstone. "Let me toast the other side first."

You roll over onto your back and close your eyes. "Fine with me. It's no fun walking with wet clothes anyway."

Within twenty minutes, the sun has dried your clothes and warmed you through. You stand up and look down the watercourse. "I wonder where we are. Do you think this stream will lead us back towards camp?"

Paulie looks up at the position of the sun. "It should do. The sun is setting behind us. East is towards camp so…"

While Paulie reattaches the straps to his pack, you climb up the slope behind the pool to see if you can get your bearings. As you crest the ridge, you see a pickup truck parked behind a couple of boulders off to the north. The truck has chunky fat tires suitable for the sandy terrain. In the tray are what look like bones. Huge bones.

You squat down in case the smugglers are about and study the area. The truck has come along a rough track from the main road. They've parked as close as they can get to their stockpile of bones in the abandoned mine.

The camp is off in the distance. Paulie was right about the watercourse heading the right way.

You watch for a few minutes. There is no sign of the men, so you slide back down to Paulie. "I can see the smuggler's truck," you tell him. "It's just over the ridge, hidden from view."

"Any sign of them?" he asks.

You shake your head. "No, but we'll have to cross their path between the mine and the truck to get to camp."

Paulie looks worried. "We can't let them know we've escaped. They'll hightail it out of here before we can alert the authorities."

Then you have an idea. "Do you know how to hotwire a truck, Paulie?"

He starts shaking his head. "No ... and even if I could, I don't steal."

"Even from smugglers?"

"It's still theft." Paulie unzips the side pocket of his pack and pulls out his cell phone. He wipes the phone on his shirt. "It's still working, but there's no signal."

"Well, if we can't phone the authorities, and you don't want to take their truck, maybe we could disable it somehow?"

"Like let the air out of their tires?"

You smile. "That would do the trick."

"But what if they catch us? Wouldn't it be better to get to camp and phone the police?"

Calling the police makes sense, but what if the smugglers take the dinosaur bones and leave before the police arrive?

It's time to make a decision. What should you do? Do you:

Try to disable the smugglers' truck? **P86**

Or

Rush back to camp?**P93**

You have decided to dig your way out

"I think we should dig ourselves out," you say. "Hold the light while I dig. When I get tired, you can have a turn."

Paulie swallows hard and nods. "Okay, but hurry."

After five minutes, you realize the hopelessness of your task. The light is already starting to fade and you've made very little progress.

"Come on, Paulie, there's no way we're going to get through this lot." You throw down the pick in frustration and snatch the flashlight out of Paulie's hand. "Let's find that other exit."

Another couple of hundred yards into the hillside, the tunnel splits in two. Down one tunnel, water is running, so you take the other. The breeze feels stronger here.

There is a slight vibration in the rock beneath your feet. You stop and listen for a moment. You turn back to Paulie. "Can you hear that?"

Paulie cups his ear. "Sounds like a generator."

"What? Down here?"

Paulie nods. "My uncle has a generator up at his cabin that sounds like that..."

The two of you pick up your pace. Further along the tunnel, the putt, putt, putting of generator becomes louder.

"I smell fumes," Paulie says.

"That's not a good sign. We'll die of carbon monoxide poisoning if they get too strong."

Fifty yards further on, you come to another split in the passage. A large electrical cable runs up one tunnel and into the other. This time you take the one that goes away from the noise of the generator. Already you are beginning to cough. You need to get away from the fumes.

Three minutes down this side tunnel you both stop, not quite believing what you see.

"What is a door doing way down here?" Paulie asks.

"I don't know, but I hope it's not locked."

Paulie looks confused. "And why do they need electricity?"

The door is made of steel. It fits snugly into a rectangular hole cut into the side of the shaft. The cable runs through a conduit drilled into the rock beside the door. You reach for the handle and push down on the lever. The door swings open.

Neon lights flicker, then switch on. The room is full of stainless steel benches and laboratory equipment. On the far side of the lab is another door.

Paulie walks around inspecting the equipment. "This is a centrifuge," he says pointing a piece of equipment, the size of a microwave, sitting on one of the benches. "And this is a gel box. I've read about this stuff. It's used for extracting DNA."

"But why would anyone want–" Then you see the dinosaur bone on another table. It's been sliced down the center and the marrow has been scraped out and put into test tubes sitting in a rack beside it. "Paulie!"

"Wow," he says. "Someone's trying to clone dinosaurs!"

"Very clever," says the man in a lab coat as he comes through the door, carrying a big bottle of isopropyl alcohol "That's exactly what I'm doing."

"But why are you doing it down here?" Paulie asks.

The man laughs and sets the bottle on a bench. "Come, I'll show you." He walks back to the door and pulls it open. "Follow me."

You have second thoughts about going with the man, but he seems friendly and his story makes sense. Besides, it's not like you've got much choice if you're going to get out of here.

Through the door is a long corridor with doors running off it every ten yards or so. Each door has a glass panel in it, and when you look though them you see more people working on different projects.

"What is this place?" you ask.

"Well, as you probably guessed, it's a lab. It used to be a missile silo, but when it was decommissioned, the University of Montana took it over as a research centre."

"So you're not connected to those men who tried to kill us?" you ask.

"Kill you?" The man looks genuinely confused. "Which men?"

You and Paulie explain how you came to be in the mine. How the men collapsed the shaft, and how you found the door.

"And you say these men have a big pile of dinosaur bones?"

"Yes," you and Paulie say in unison.

"Well that's great news," the man says suddenly excited. "We're in need of some more bones. So far we've not been able to isolate any DNA. Too old, unfortunately. But if what you say is true, the pile those men have collected should give us a chance to find some."

"So you're going to bring the dinosaurs back?" asks Paulie.

"I know, you're thinking Jurassic Park. But no, we don't want that. We do, however, want to discover more about these creatures, and how they evolved."

You point to a phone hanging on the wall. "Well you'd better call the cops and get them to stop those men from getting away. Otherwise you'll be out of luck."

"Yes. And then, we'd better get you back to your school group," the man says. "They must be worried. Maybe you'd like to bring them back tomorrow for a tour of our facility?"

Paulie's eyes go wide. "Could we? That would be fantastic! Did you know that T. Rex was—"

"Hang on, Paulie," you say. "You can discuss all this tomorrow."

"Yes," the man says. "Tomorrow we'll have plenty of time to talk. Right now, I've got a call to make about those smugglers."

After his phone call, the man takes you along another corridor to a foyer with two elevators in it. The ride is quick. Once you're back on the surface, you see how well the complex is hidden from view. The only part visible is a concrete building covered in the local rock. It houses the machinery for the elevator. Outside, half a dozen cars sit in a dusty lot next to the park headquarters, a mile or so from the campground entrance on the main road.

"That's my blue pickup," the man says. "Jump in. I'll give you a ride back to your camp."

Mister Jackson stops what he's doing and looks up as the pickup pulls into the campground. "So what trouble did you two get into?" Mister Jackson asks as you get out of the Ford. "I hope you haven't embarrassed the school."

The man from the lab chuckles. "No, nothing like that. In fact, these two have been quite helpful." Then he explains the situation and repeats his invitation for the students to tour the dinosaur lab. "See you tomorrow at ten," the man says, getting back into his truck.

You and Paulie wave as he drives away.

Once the pickup is gone, Mister Jackson puts his hands on his hips and stares down at you. "Well it sounds like you two had quite an adventure."

Paulie is so excited about the lab visit, he can hardly contain himself. "Did you know that the lab used to be a missile silo and that there's all sorts of equipment they're using to extract DNA…"

You look at Mister Jackson. He raises an eyebrow and nods towards Paulie. Paulie hasn't noticed that the two of you have stopped listening. He's still rambling on about the lab.

When Mister Jackson starts laughing, you join in, unable to help yourself.

Paulie stops talking, looks first to you and then to your teacher. He seems confused. "Wha–what's going on? Did I say something funny?"

Congratulations, this part of your story is over. Now it's time to make another decision. Do you:

Go back to the beginning and read a different track? **P1**
Or
Go to the list of choices and pick another chapter? **P376**

86

You have decided to try to disable the truck

"I think we should sneak down to the truck and let their tires down," you say. "You don't want them to escape, do you?"

"No, but–"

"But what?"

"But we're just kids. And–and those guys have a gun."

You'd forgotten about the pistol. Maybe this isn't such a good idea after all. Then you have an idea. If you get Paulie to keep an eye out for the smugglers, he can warn you if they return. What other option is there?

"Come with me, Paulie." You lead him up the slope to where you first saw the truck. Off to the right is the track that leads up to the mine. To your left is the truck.

"See over there," you say pointing. "The smugglers will have to come along that track to get to where they've parked. You just need to sit up here and signal if you see them coming."

Paulie looks unsure. "How will I do that?"

From the depths of your pack, you pull out a bright orange t-shirt. "Here, wave this."

"Are you sure?"

You nod. "We can't let the bad guys get away, can we?"

"Okay, but be careful," Paulie says.

You take the pocketknife out of your pack. Then you grab your water bottle. You leave your pack behind in case you have to run for it.

"Back soon," you say.

The climb down to where the truck is parked takes you longer than expected. It's too steep to go in a straight line, especially with all the erosion and wash outs. Instead, you follow a ridge that runs off to the east for a quarter of a mile or so, before angling back.

About half way down the hill, you look back. Paulie is crouched on the ridge, the balled up t-shirt in his hand.

So far so good.

When you reach the truck, it is bigger than expected. It sits high off the ground on huge knobby tires. A spare is mounted on a steel rack over the cab in between a pair of spotlights. You'll need to deflate at least two tires to slow these guys down.

The small black cap over the air valve of the first tire comes off easily. You find a stick and use it to depress the metal pin on the valve. A hiss of air escapes. But a couple of minutes later, the tire is barely down. This is going to take ages.

You glance up at Paulie and feel your stomach lurch. He's on his feet waving the t-shirt frantically. Your heart races. "Rats! Time for plan B."

You put out your knife and open the longest blade. The blade looks tiny against the truck's big off-road tires. Still, it's your only hope. You stab the side of the tire a couple times. The sudden hiss of air sounds like an angry cobra as it escapes through the punctures. You move to the front of the vehicle and stab the left front tire too.

With the sabotage done, you run back towards the ridge keeping low and using what little scrub there is as cover.

You watch out for the men as you climb. Then, after gaining a bit of altitude, you see them. Both are carrying dinosaur bones over their shoulder. Thankfully, they are watching the ground as they walk, keeping an eye out for rattlers, perhaps. You sidle around the ridge, putting some rock between you and the men. No point in taking any chance of being spotted.

It's tougher climbing along the side of the ridge, and you have to watch your footing. But at least you're out of the men's sight.

By the time you reach Paulie, he is lying on his stomach, peering over the ridge, watching the men's progress. "They're nearly at the truck," he says.

You crouch down to watch. As they near the truck, one of them throws his bone on the ground and starts yelling. His curses float up on the breeze.

"He's not a happy camper," you say with a smirk.

"Aw... poor little smuggler."

The man is kicking the truck's tires, yelling and screaming at his companion who is looking around, trying to see who has done this. His face turns towards the ridge.

"Get down!" Paulie says, grabbing your arm and jerking you off balance.

You land flat on the ground. "Hey!"

"Sorry, but I think he saw you," Paulie says. "Let's get out of here."

"Yep. We need to make it to camp before they do. Otherwise who knows what they'll do."

With that, you skid back down to the pool, skirt around its cool water and head downstream. "Watch your footing, Paulie, some of these rocks are slippery."

The creek doesn't run far before it disappears into the sand. This makes it easier to rock hop down the gully. Before you know it, you're on the flat again, not far from the track leading up to the mine.

You tighten the shoulder straps on your backpack and then look at Paulie. "We need to get to camp as quickly as possible. Keep low. Use the scrub for cover. It's about two miles, I reckon."

Paulie swallows and cinches up his straps.

"Oh and listen out for rattlers!"

"Great," Paulie says. "If the smugglers don't get us the snakes will."

"You'll be fine, Paulie. Just follow me."

You take off in a half trot, dodging from bush to bush. You figure you've gone about half way to camp, when you hear the growl of a diesel motor in the distance. But how?

When you look through the scrub, the truck is coming across the flatland, leaning awkwardly to the left. The truck is making good speed, despite what you've done to it.

"Oh no!" Paulie cries.

You stop behind a big clump of saltbush. "Keep low, I don't think they've seen us yet."

From the direction the men are driving, it looks as though they are sticking to the track you saw from up the hill. Thankfully, this track goes to the main road, not directly to the camp. Once on the road however, there will be nothing stopping them from driving a mile or so down to the campground turnoff. As if to confirm your theory, the truck turns slightly away from you as the dirt road arcs around to avoid a dry wash.

"Come on," you say. "We've still got time." You slip off your pack and let it drop to the ground. "We can come back for these later. Right now, we need to run!"

Like a pair of jackrabbits, you and Paulie jink back and forth between clumps of saltbush as you head towards camp.

Off to your left, the truck's flattened tires kick up a cloud of dust. Luckily, the wind is blowing the cloud in your direction giving you some extra cover.

The truck has just reached the main road when you and Paulie skid exhausted into camp.

"Mister Jackson!" you pant, out of breath. "Smug–smugglers!"

Mister Jackson looks up. "What are you on about?"

"Fossil smugglers," you say. "Paulie and I caught them up at the old mine. They tried to bury us!"

Paulie points towards the road. "They're coming in that truck! And they have a pistol."

"What happened to their truck?" Mister Jackson says when he sees the funny lean on the truck.

"I stabbed their tires to slow them down," you say. "Maybe that wasn't such a good idea."

Mister Jackson gives you a hard look. "Because now they have to come to camp for more transport. What were you thinking!"

You look down at your feet. "We just…"

Mister Jackson shakes his head and then turns to the other students milling about. "Okay everyone listen up. I want everyone on the bus right now! Duck down below the windows and stay there until I say otherwise."

As you wait in line to climb aboard, Mister Jackson runs to a locker on the side of the bus and pull out a flare gun. From a small box he takes out a cartridge and slots it into the chamber before closing the gun up and slipping it into the back of his shorts, under his t-shirt.

Paulie's pushing you in the back, so you run up the step and duck down beside the driver's seat. The students, sitting on the floor further down the bus, chatter nervously.

"Shush everyone," you say.

The gravel crunches as the smuggler's truck roars into camp and skids to a stop about twenty yards from the bus.

"Quiet everyone! I want to hear what's going on."

A hush falls over the bus. You take a quick peek outside.

"Looks like you've had problems with your truck," Mister Jackson says as he approaches the men.

The men have thrown a tarp over the bones in the back of the truck. Neither of them look happy. They face Mister Jackson while the other parents stand back, unsure of what to do.

The men are covered in dust.

"Someone in your group has stabbed our tires. So we'll need to borrow your bus."

"I'm afraid that isn't an option," Mister Jackson says. Your teacher reaches into his pocket and pulls out his cell phone. However, I'll call for someone to come and tow you to town."

"You seem to have misunderstood me," the bigger of the two men says. "I wasn't really asking." The man pulls out his pistol and points it at Mister Jackson. "Now give me the keys and get those brats off the bus."

Mister Jackson raises his hands, palms out. "Whoaa… Steady there. We're not looking for any trouble here."

The man scowls. "Well then, do as I say!" He waves the gun towards the bus. "Now!"

"Okay, okay, take it easy." Mister Jackson walks to the bus and pokes his head through the door. "Everyone off the bus. Go sit on the picnic tables by the fire. Don't worry, everything's going to be fine."

The students do as they're told. A couple have been crying. You're about to join them outside when you hear rattling under the bus. You freeze. Then you hear the distinctive sound of the snake again. It seems to be moving towards the front steps.

You have an idea. Rather than getting off the bus, you duck back down.

You listen as Mister Jackson gives the man the keys.

"Now get out of my way," man says.

There is a scrunch of gravel as the men make their way to the bus. When you think they are about to climb aboard, you stand up and start down the steps, stopping at the bottom one.

You and the man are eye to eye.

"I said, get off!" he yells.

You wipe his spittle off your face with the back of your hand. You're about to climb down when the rattlesnake strikes.

"Yeow!" the man yells, throwing himself back.

But the snake is on the attack. It whips its head forward and strikes him again.

When the man grabs at his leg and falls to the ground, the pistol skids on the dirt. The second man moves to pick it up.

"I wouldn't do that if I were you," Mister Jackson says, leveling the flare gun at the man's face. "Now back up! Put your hands on your head!"

The snake backs off at the sound of Mister Jackson shouting and slithers off into the sagebrush. The second man does as he's told. You jump off the bus, pick up the pistol, and run behind Mister Jackson.

The man on the ground has his cuff pulled up and is staring at the puncture wounds in his calf. His face is twisted in pain and the area around the wounds is already red and swollen. "I need a hospital," he moans.

Mister Jackson takes the pistol from your shaking hand and sends you to sit with the other students.

"Tie them up," Mister Jackson says to the other parents. "I'll phone the police."

Once the men have been secured, and police phoned, Mister Jackson grabs a snakebite kit from the first aid box and moves towards the injured man. "Just take it easy, you'll live."

Paulie sidles up next to you. "Did you know the snake was there?" he asks.

You tell him about hearing the rattle just before you got off the bus and how you planned to get the man to stop by the steps in the hope that the rattler would strike.

"Who needs a gun when you have a prairie rattler to do your dirty work, eh?" Paulie says.

"Snakes are our friends," you say, quoting Paulie's words back to him. "Isn't it their job to clean up the vermin?"

"Yeah, I suppose it is." He gives you a huge grin. "Did you know that some vermin, especially rats, have teeth that can grow five inches in a single year? They wear them down by gnawing on things. And some carry plague ... and ... and..."

Paulie keeps waffling on about rats, but you're not really listening. Instead, you're thinking about the adventure you've had.

When you see the flashing lights of the police car and ambulance in the distance, you know that this time you've been lucky. What would have happened if you'd chosen differently?

Congratulations, this part of your story may be over, but now you can try another path and see what happens when you make different choices.

It's time to make a decision. Do you:

Go back to the start and read a different track? **P1**

Or

Go to the great big list of choices? **P376**

You have decided to rush back to camp

You and Paulie slide back down the rock and skirt the pool towards the watercourse.

"Watch your step, Paulie, these rocks are a bit slippery. The last thing we need is an injury."

But slippery rocks are only a problem for a short distance. Before long, most of the water has seeped into the sand and disappeared.

"The stream's gone underground again," Paulie says. "It must only run on the surface when it's raining."

"Which, by the look of the sky behind us, could be any moment."

Paulie looks back over his shoulder at the dark grey clouds billowing up like menacing waves. "Where did those come from?"

"I don't know, but if it rains higher up the hill there could be a flash flood. We'd better get out of the streambed just in case."

A bolt of lightning flashes towards the ground. Seconds later, a huge BOOM echoes across the sky.

"Whoaaa!" Paulie says. "That was a beauty."

Another bolt streaks towards the ground. FLASH! BOOM!

"Come on, Paulie. Let's keep moving. Those smugglers will probably head back to the truck before this storm hits."

You and Paulie move out of the streambed and pick up the pace. But the storm is gaining on you.

Fifteen minutes later, just as you hit the flat land of the prairie, the storm front hits. The wind gusts, and hailstones the size of walnuts, pelt down.

"Ouch!" Paulie yells. "That hurts!"

"Quick, over here, under this sagebrush. Hold your pack over your head," you say.

Rushing over to the nearest patch of scrub, you and Paulie cower under its thin branches, your packs held up as shields. The lumps of ice beating on your packs sound like some crazy drummer. Strong gusts fling fine particles of sand like miniature missiles, stinging your exposed skin.

"Holy moly," Paulie says, picking up a huge hailstone. "This is awesome!"

You're not sure 'awesome' is the word you'd use. But you have to admit that Paulie has a point. The storm has moved in so fast, and its power is so strong, it's taken you by surprise. The sky has gone so dark, it's like the sun has set.

Between two flashes of lightning, you see the smugglers running for their truck, their hands and arms held over their heads to protect them from the hail.

Unfortunately, straggly sagebrush isn't the greatest hiding place. And, you're directly in the smugglers' path.

"Down," you whisper. "Lay flat, maybe they won't see us."

It was a poor plan, one doomed to failure.

"Hey, Walter. Look! It's those two brats!"

"Well I'll be…" the other man says.

"What do we do?" Paulie squeaks.

"Leave the packs and run for it!"

Paulie takes off behind you. You've only got a hundred yards head start on the smugglers, but that's better than nothing. Unfortunately, because of the men in your path, the only way you can go is away from camp. You'll have to go in a big arc if you're to make it back without the men getting hold of you.

The storm strengthens. Hailstones pound the ground, kicking up little craters in the sand. Lightning strikes the ground a quarter of a mile to your right. The men are gaining on you.

Paulie gasps. "I can't run anymore. Can't breathe in this dust." He slows down.

It's then that you see the dark grey funnel dropping from the bottom of one of the clouds towards the ground.

Paulie looks up, his eyes wide. "Holy moly. A tornado!"

The men are only 60 yards away when the funnel picks them up and swirls them into the air. You're not sure if the high-pitched screams are the men or the wind. But the funnel is still coming right at you. Grabbing Paulie's arm, you throw yourself onto the ground and cover your head with your arms.

The edge of the funnel misses you by twenty feet, scattering sand and pebbles in its wake, then races on across the prairie.

"Phew," you say. "That was close!"

"You're telling me," he says.

"Those poor men."

"Yeah, even criminals don't deserve that. Still there have been cases of people being dropped safely some miles away after being picked up by a tornado."

"Really?" you ask.

Paulie nods. "There was this kid in Alabama who got sucked up out of his bunk bed and was dropped alive. He had a few cuts and bruises, but lived to tell the tale."

"Well let's hope those men get dropped into prison, that's where they belong."

You brush the dust and sand off your clothes, and watch as the dark mass of clouds moves further off to the north, its funnel touching the ground occasionally along the way.

"I hope the camp is okay," you say. "We'd better get going and find out."

You're about to walk off when you see a couple of strange looking lumps lying on the ground about 50 yards off to the north. "What're those?"

Paulie peers at the strange formations. "Let's go find out."

At first they look like rocks protruding out of the sand. But as you near, you see it is the two men. They look unconscious.

"Quick, let's tie them up before they wake up." you say.

"Tie them up with what?" Paulie asks.

You think a moment. Then notice the men's sturdy boots. "Use their bootlaces."

Kneeling down, you tie the man's wrists behind his back, watching for any sign that he's waking up. Paulie does the same with the other man. Once they're secure, you'll breathe easier.

"Right, that should do it," you say standing up. "They're not going anywhere."

"Now what?" Paulie asks, admiring his handiwork.

You look towards the camp. It's still at least a mile away. "We can't leave them here alone. They'll run away."

When you look back towards Paulie, he has a big grin on his face. "Not without shoes they won't."

"Now you're talking!"

You get the men's boots off, just as they begin to move.

"Good work, Paulie. Now, let's go get help."

Carrying the men's boots, the two of you jog towards camp.

"I just thought of something," you say. "It's not that far to their truck, what if they get loose and drive off?"

Paulie reaches into his pocket and pulls out of set of keys. "I took these while I was tying the guy up."

"Stole them, you mean?"

"I've borrowed them," Paulie says. "He can have them back once the police arrive."

And with that sorted, you head straight back to camp.

Congratulations, you've finished this part of your story. But there are more tracks you can read and more adventures to have. Maybe things won't end up so well next time if you make different choices.

It's time to make a decision. Do you:

Go back to the start and try a different path? **P1**

Or

Go to the list of choices and start reading another chapter? **P376**

Animal Facts

Rattlesnake facts:

Although there are many different types of rattlesnakes, the only rattlesnake that lives in Montana, where this story is set, is the prairie rattlesnake. Prairie rattlesnakes have a triangular head, narrow neck and a thickset body. Rattlesnakes swallow their prey whole.

The largest rattlesnake in the U.S. is the Eastern Diamondback which can grow to over 8 feet in length. Prairie rattlesnakes are smaller and only grow up to 5 feet or so. Their color varies, from light green to a blotchy brown.

Prairie rattlesnakes have heat sensors between their nostrils and eyes. Hollow fangs inject poison into their prey. More poison is injected in hunting bites than when striking defensively. (Why waste good poison?) At the end of a rattlesnake's tail is a rattle that warns predators of the snake's presence.

More than 8,000 people are bitten by venomous snakes in the US each year, but the average number of deaths from snakebite is under a dozen.

Rattlesnakes belong to a group of snakes called pit vipers. They have good vision both night and day.

Prairie Dog facts:

Prairie dogs can grow as long as three feet from head to tail and weigh from 1.5 to 3.3 pounds.

Sometimes they are mistaken for squirrels, but can be identified by their thicker body and shorter tail. Prairie dogs are herbivores and get their water from the plants they eat.

The animals live in burrows in flat open grassland. Colonies can cover quite a large area (twenty-five acres or more). Burrows can be as deep as 14 feet underground and run for 30 yards or more. A family group usually comprises a male and three or four females. Females give birth to 4 or more pups depending on conditions. After being born, pups stay underground for up to 8 weeks before appearing above ground in mid-May to early June.

The main predators for prairie dogs are ferrets, snakes, coyotes, badgers, and birds of prey.

Pronghorn facts:

Pronghorn antelope live in open sagebrush country and grasslands. They migrate south during harsh winters. Females breed in September and males shed their horns in November. Sometimes males will fight to the death for control of females.

Pronghorns are the fastest land animals in North America and can reach speeds of 55 miles per hour (but only over a short distance). They stand just over four feet tall and weigh approximately 140 pounds for males, and 105 pounds for females.

Bison facts:

Bison stand up to six and a half feet tall and can weigh over a ton. They are grazers, eating grass, herbs and shrubs. Like cows, they regurgitate their food and chew the cud before the food is fully digested.

Females are called cows, while males are known as bulls.

Bison once covered the Great Plains and were an important source of food and raw materials for the Plains Indians. It is estimated that settlers killed over 50 million of these animals.

Bison are speedy and can run at up to 45 miles per hour.

Dinosaur Facts

Tyrannosaurus Rex facts:

T. Rex were massive – nearly 40 feet long, over 13 feet tall and weighing six tons or more. They lived 68 - 66 million years ago in the upper Cretaceous Period. T. Rex were one of the biggest ever land-based carnivores. They had a massive heads and teeth the size of bananas. T. Rex's huge heads were balanced by a big strong tails and although their front arms were short, they were very powerful.

So far scientists have identified over 50 different Tyrannosaurus species. Some scientists believe that these animals had feathers on parts of their bodies.

Ankylosaurus facts:

Imagine a cross between a tank and a 30 foot lizard! Ankylosaurus were nearly 6 feet tall and 20 to 30 feet long with tough bone armor on their backs and a wicked looking club-shaped tails which they swung around in defense.

For added protection, rows of spikes ran down their body and horns grew from their heads. The only weakness was the animal's soft underbelly.

Because they weighed in at 3 to 4 tons, attacking an Ankylosaurus was no easy task, even for a T. Rex.

Ankylosaurus was a herbivore and ate large quantities of plant material each day. It lived 68 to 66 million years ago.

Troodon facts:

Troodons lived in the Cretaceous period, approximately 77 million years ago. They were small by dinosaur standards, growing about three feet tall and eight feet from their nose to the tips of their tails.

Troodons were slender with long hind limbs. This suggests they were able to run quite fast. They also had curved claws on their second toe (not so good for climbing sandstone arches).

Because of their large eyes, scientists think that Troodons may have been nocturnal. They are thought to be one of the most intelligent of the dinosaurs, with a large brain compared to their body size. Like many dinosaurs, Troodons laid eggs.

Tylosaurus facts:

Nothing was safe when a Tylosaurus was about. Tylosaurus (a type of mosasaurs) were the dominant predator of the western inland seaway in the late cretaceous period (85 - 80 million years ago). This seaway split what is now North America, from the Gulf of Mexico to Canada.

Tylosaurus reached lengths of 45 feet and weighed 7 tons or more. Tylosaurus had a long alligator-like snout, front and back flippers, and a broad powerful tail used for rapid acceleration.

Scientists believe that Tylosaurus used its snout as a battering ram. Once stunned, the Tylosaurus would clamp on to its prey with its powerful jaws and large cone-shaped teeth to keep the stunned prey from escaping. Once the Tylosaurus' prey was disabled, it would be swallowed whole.

The main diet for Tylosaurus was fish, sharks, plesiosaurs and other smaller mosasaurs.

Although not a true dinosaur Tylosaurus lived and became extinct at the same time. It's thought to be a relative of the monitor lizard. Dinosaurs and lizards (which are reptiles) are different. Many scientist believe dinosaurs were warm blooded (reptiles are cold blooded). Also their posture, skeleton, teeth etc are different. It's believed that many dinosaurs had feathers and were relatives to modern birds. Remember, turtles and snakes are reptiles yet quite different to a T. Rex.

Daspletosaurus facts:

Related to the T. Rex, Daspletosaurus lived 77 - 74 million years ago.

Although slightly smaller than the T. Rex, Daspletosaurus was an aggressive and formidable predator at the top of the food chain.

It walked on two hind legs and had small, yet powerful, front arms.

Its skull alone could reach 39 inches in length. Nose to tail, Daspletosaurus 25 - 30 feet in length weren't uncommon.

Daspletosaurus had teeth! Lots of teeth.

It's thought that Daspletosaurus lived in social groups, possibly hunting as a pack. Yikes!

Velociraptor facts:

Well known for their role in the movie *Jurassic Park*, Velociraptor, which lived 75 - 75 million years ago, were actually smaller than portrayed in the movie. In reality they were about the size of a turkey, with sickle-shaped claws on its feet and feathers over most of its body. They had wing-like arms, but couldn't fly (although some scientists believe they could climb trees using the sharp talons on their feet).

Full grown, Velociraptors could reach 6 feet in length and weigh over 30 pounds.

Velociraptors hunted and scavenged for food. They were fast on their feet, and capable of bringing down prey up to 50% larger than themselves.

Scientists believe modern birds evolved from dinosaurs similar to the Velociraptor.

Pachycephalosaurs facts

Estimated to be about 15 feet long and over 900 pounds, Pachycephalosaurs went extinct with the last of the dinosaurs about 65 million years ago. Pachycephalosaurs' most distinguishing features were the thick plate of bone on their head. Boney knobs surrounded this plate, with blunt horns protruding from the back of it. More boney bumps covered their snouts making them quite strange looking.

Scientists believe their diets were most probably leaves, seeds, insects and fruit, rather than tougher, more fibrous plants due to their small, serrated teeth.

Pterodactyl facts:

Not officially dinosaurs, Pterodactyls were flying reptiles that lived from the Jurassic period some 150 - 148 million years ago, to the time of their extinction by the late Cretaceous period 65 million years ago. They were the first vertebrates (animals with a backbone) known to have developed powered flight.

Their wings were made from skin and muscle stretched between their front fingers and hind legs and had a span from 3 to 35 feet, depending on species.

These animals had long thin heads with a crest made of soft tissue. Their mouths contained 90-or more cone-shaped teeth that got smaller as they went back into the animal's head.

With sharp eyesight and even sharper talons, they preyed on fish and other small animals.

Some of the larger species could have flown long distances.

Einiosaurus facts:

A dinosaur similar in appearance to Triceratops. Its name means 'buffalo lizard'. They grew to approx 20 feet in length and over 6 feet high.

Like the modern day rhino, Einiosaurus had a horn in the middle of its face, but Einiosaurus' horns slope forward and down like an old-fashion can opener.

Einiosaurus had teeth capable of eating the toughest plants, but they were also thought to have died in vast numbers during times of drought.

They lived in the late Cretaceous, approx 74 million years ago in the Montana region.

Triceratops facts:

Triceratops lived approximately 68 million years ago. That's 68,000,000 if you write it out in full.

With its boney frill (like a large collar) and three big horns (tri means three), Triceratops is estimated to have weighed from 13,000 to 26,000 pounds. One skull recovered was over 8 feet long, nearly a third of the animal's body length.

Because of unusual formations on the animal's skin, some scientists think Triceratops might have been covered in bristles, or similar.

One of the largest land animals ever, Triceratops was a herbivore that grazed on shrubs, and possibly, like modern day elephants, knocked over larger trees to feed.

Triceratops had a mouth full of teeth. Rows and rows of them, suggesting they were able to eat the toughest of plants.

Damage to skulls found show that triceratops used its head as a battering ram, possibly in combat with predators.

DEADLINE DELIVERY
by Peter Friend

Dispatch Office

Out of breath from climbing stairs, you finally reach Level 8 of Ivory Tower. Down the hallway, past a tattoo parlor, Deadline Delivery's neon sign glows red. The word Dead flickers as you approach.

It's two minutes past seven in the morning – is Deadline Delivery's dispatch office open yet? Yes, through the mesh-covered window in the steel door, Miss Betty is slouched behind her cluttered desk. You knock and smile as if you want to be here.

Miss Betty turns and scowls at you. Nothing personal – she scowls at everyone. She presses a button and the steel door squeaks and squeals open.

"Good morning, ma'am. Got any work for me today?" you ask.

She sighs, scratches her left armpit, and taps at her computer. Then she rummages through a long shelf of packages and hands you a plastic-wrapped box and two grimy dollar coins. "Urgent delivery," she says. "Pays ten bucks, plus toll fees."

Ten dollars is more than usual. Suspicious, you check the box's delivery label. "390 Brine Street? That's in the middle of pirate territory!"

She shrugs. "If you're too scared, there are plenty of other kids who'll do it."

Scared? You're terrified. But you both know she's right – if you don't take this job, someone else will. And you really need the money

– you have exactly three dollars in the whole world, and your last meal was lunch yesterday. "Thank you, Miss Betty."

"Uniform," she says, pointing to the box of Deadline Delivery caps. You pick up the least dirty cap. What's that stink? Has something died in it? You swap it for the second-least dirty one and put that on. You'd rather not wear any kind of uniform – sometimes it's better to not attract attention in public – but Miss Betty insists.

The steel door squeaks and starts to close, and you hurry out. Miss Betty doesn't say goodbye. She never does.

After stashing the package in your backpack and the toll coins in your pocket, you hurry down the stairs to the food court on Level 5. Time to grab a quick breakfast. This might be your last meal ever, and there's no sense in dying hungry. This early in the morning, only Deep-Fried Stuff and Mac's Greasy Spoon are open, so there's not a lot of choice.

In Mac's Greasy Spoon, Mac himself cuts you a nice thick slice of meatloaf for a dollar, and you smile and thank him, even though his meatloaf is always terrible. If there's any meat in it, you don't want to know what kind. At least it's cheap and filling. After a few bites, you wrap the rest in a plastic bag and put it in your pocket for lunch.

You walk back down the stairs to Ivory Tower's main entrance on Level 3. Levels 1 and 2 are somewhere further down, underwater, but you've never seen them. The polar ice caps melted and flooded the city before you were born.

From beside the bulletproof glass doors, a bored-looking guard looks up. "It's been quiet out there so far this morning," she tells you, as she checks a security camera screen. "But there was pirate trouble a few blocks north of the Wall last night. And those wild dogs are roaming around again too. Be careful, kid."

The doors grind open, just a crack, enough for you to squeeze through and out onto Nori Road. Well, everyone calls it a road, although the actual road surface is twenty feet under the murky water. Both sides of the so-called road have sidewalks of rusty girders and planks and bricks and other junk, bolted or welded or nailed to the buildings – none of it's too safe to walk on, but you know your way around.

Just below the worn steel plate at your feet, the water's calm. Everything looks quiet. No boats in sight. A few people are fishing out their windows. Fish for breakfast? Probably better than meatloaf.

Far over your head, a mag-lev train hums past on a rail bridge. Brine Street's only a few minutes away by train – for rich people living up in the over-city. Not you. Mac once told you that most over-city people never leave the sunny upper levels, and some of them don't even don't know the city's streets are flooded down here. Or don't care, anyway. Maybe that's why there are so many security fences between up there and down here, so that over-city people can pretend that under-city people like you don't exist.

There are fences down here too. To your left, in the distance, is Big Pig's Wall – a heavy steel mesh fence, decorated with spikes and barbed wire and the occasional skeleton. The same Wall surrounds you in every direction, blocking access above and below the waterline – and Brine Street's on the other side. The extra-dangerous side.

Big Pig's Wall wasn't built to keep people in – no, it's to keep pirates out.

The heavily guarded Tollgates are the only way in or out, and to go through them, everyone has to pay a toll to Big Pig's guards. A dollar per person, more for boats, all paid into big steel-bound boxes marked Donations. Big Pig has grown rich on those "donations". Not as rich as over-city people, but still richer than anyone else in this neighborhood. Some people grumble that Big Pig and his guards are really no better than the pirate gangs, but most locals think the tolls are a small price to pay for some peace and security.

Then again, you happen to know the Tollgates *aren't* the only way in and out – last week, you found a secret tunnel that leads through the Wall. No toll fees if you go that way – two dollars saved. You finger the coins in your pocket.

It's time to make a decision. How will you get to Brine Street?
Do you:
Go the longer and safer route through a Tollgate? **P109**
Or
Save time and money, and try the secret tunnel? **P140**

Tollgate

You jog the four blocks to the nearest Tollgate. A surly Gate guard rattles a "donation" box, and you hand over a dollar toll fee.

The gate opens for a boat you know well – the *Rusty Rhino*, an ironclad cargo steamboat with a dozen crew. Looking out over its armored sides is Captain Abdu McCall, wearing his favorite battered red top hat. He waves at you. "Morning, kid. Want a ride? We're headed for Blemmish Market."

The market's only three blocks south of Brine Street – that will save you a lot of walking, and there's no safer way to travel the under-city than on an ironclad.

"Thanks, captain. Great hat."

He smiles, showing all five of his gold teeth. "Another pair of sharp young eyes will be welcome. Pirate trouble's been simmering this last week. Probably just the Kannibal Krew and the Piranhas fighting over their borders, but my left knee's been aching since I woke up this morning, and that's never a good sign."

You don't trust the captain's knee, but you do trust his instincts – he's captained the *Rhino* for years. Maybe this won't be such a safe journey after all. Any pirate gang would love to get their hands on an ironclad.

The *Rhino*'s steam engine chuffs into action, and a sailor hands you a long spear, the same as most of the crew carry. You've never used a spear, and aren't sure whether you could, even to save your own life. Anyway, the spears and other weapons are mostly to scare pirates away. So you stand at the *Rhino*'s side, peer between two armor plates, and try to look fierce.

"How is dear Miss Betty?" Captain Abdu asks. "Still as lovely as ever?"

"Lovely as ever," you agree, trying hard not to giggle. According to rumor, Captain Abdu fell madly in love with Miss Betty twenty years ago. Maybe back then she didn't scowl all the time.

Five minutes later, the *Rhino* passes under a bridge. The crew scan the bridge suspiciously – bridges are a favorite ambush spot for pirates.

Nothing.

"Eyes to port," warns Captain Abdu.

You can never remember the difference between port and starboard, but a red speedboat is approaching at low speed. The driver is a pirate in a skull mask – no, as the boat gets closer, you realize it's a skull tattoo covering his whole head. Next to him is a woman with a Mohawk haircut and a necklace of human teeth. No weapons – well, none in sight.

The speedboat passes the *Rhino*. The pirates wave, grinning unpleasantly.

"A good morning to you," calls Captain Abdu. "You slime-sucking Kannibal Krew scurvy maggots," he adds under his breath.

Surely this can't be an attack – even the Kannibal Krew aren't crazy enough to attack an ironclad with just two pirates – but these two could be scouting before attacking later with bigger numbers. Or maybe they're just going grocery shopping. Either way, the *Rhino*'s crew aren't taking any chances.

The pirate speedboat disappears down a side street. "Good riddance," Captain Abdu mutters.

Half an hour and seven bridges later, just as the *Rhino* turns a corner, the captain kills the engine and sighs.

More pirates? No, a couple of blocks ahead are the flashing blue lights of over-city police hovercraft and jet-skis. Must be something serious – the police never pay much attention to anything happening down here, not unless it affects the over-city too. News drones are buzzing around above crowds of people watching a grey building, as if waiting for something to happen.

"Danger. Please stand back," repeats a voice every few seconds, over a dozen loudspeakers.

The grey building trembles, sways, then collapses in slow motion, and the surrounding block disappears under a huge roaring cloud of dust. The crowd cheer and yell. Some, especially those who were a bit too close, scream and run.

"Wow," says Captain Abdu.

Wow is right. City buildings fall down every year or so – they weren't designed to be up to their ankles in water permanently – but you've never seen it happen before.

"Very entertaining, but now the street will be blocked for weeks while they clear the mess," the captain grumbles. He turns the Rhino and heads south, but the streets are already crowded with boats, barges, canoes and jet skis, some heading towards the blocked street and others headed away, and everyone getting in each other's way. He tries turning east, then west, and shouts and toots the Rhino's steam whistle, but everyone else is shouting and tooting too.

"Can't say when we'll reach Blemmish Market." He looks over at you. "Might be faster to walk to Brine Street. It's up to you."

He's right. It's time to make a decision. Do you:

Stay on the Rhino, even though it might be slower? **P112**

Or

Leave the Rhino, and walk to Brine Street?**P123**

Stay on the Rhino

"I'll stay, thanks," you tell Captain Abdu.

He doesn't notice – he's too busy yelling at someone in a rowboat to get out of the *Rhino*'s way.

Eventually the *Rhino* starts moving again, its steam whistle tooting. The captain shouts so much that he soon sounds hoarse. The *Rhino*'s so slow that you're tempted to leave and walk after all, but the sidewalks are crammed too. Might as well stay on board.

You can't imagine pirates attacking with these crowds around, and you stop checking every single passing boat and bridge, and start daydreaming about what to have for dinner tonight after you've been paid. That's why you don't notice people abseiling down from a bridge onto the *Rhino*'s deck. Black and white striped bandanas cover their lower faces – it's the Piranha gang, the most fearsome slavers in the city. You try to yell a warning to the crew, but you're so scared that only a squeak comes out of your mouth.

One of the Piranhas twirls a baseball bat around her head and steps towards you. Do you:

Use your spear to defend yourself? **P113**

Or

Jump over the side of the boat? **P122**

Defend Yourself

You point your spear at the Piranha, but she just laughs and knocks it out of your hands with her baseball bat. She swings it again, this time at your head, and...

Everything turns black **P114**

Boom-boom-boom-BOOM

An elephant's jumping up and down on your forehead – well, that's what it feels like. There must be a huge bruise, you can feel it throbbing in time with your pulse.

So, you're not dead after all. Phew. But your cap's gone. And your backpack and package. And your money.

Above you is a low ceiling of rust-streaked painted steel. You try to sit up, but now a dozen imaginary elephants start jumping up and down.

Captain Abdu looms over you. "Careful, kid, you've been out cold."

He's lost his red top hat. What's that around his wrists...handcuffs? Oh no. You're wearing them too. So is the crew.

"Where are we?" you croak.

"The cargo hold of the *Rusty Rhino*. The good news is we're all alive, so far. The bad news is we're prisoners on my own boat. Damned Piranhas." He helps you up.

You've never been down here before. The cargo hold has rows of benches bolted to the wooden deck, with an aisle between. The benches are lined up with rows of small holes on each side of the hull. You've seen those holes before from the outside, but never knew what they were – too small to be windows. The holes are no longer empty – each now has a long pole poking through it.

The captain notices your puzzled expression. "We've been drafted as rowing slaves."

Your heart sinks. Looking out the nearest hole, you see that yes, the pole is an oar, its blade high in the air. "Why does a steamboat have oars?"

"I love my dear *Rhino*, but her engine's older than I am, and sometimes we have to row our way home or out of trouble."

"But...I can hear the engine, so why do the Piranhas need us to row?"

He sighs. "We've been wondering the same thing. This isn't the Piranhas' usual way of doing things. They weren't interested in our cargo – threw most of it overboard." A clang and a splash from outside interrupts him. "Hear that? They've been tearing off the *Rhino*'s stern armor plates and tossing them overboard too. Why go to the trouble of hijacking an ironclad, then remove some of its armor, and keep its crew as rowers?"

You try to think, despite your aching head. "They want to lighten the Rhino, but keep its front armor, and they want it as fast as possible, so…so it can ram something, really hard?"

He nods grimly. "That's what we think too. But not if I have any say in the matter. The *Rhino* may be old, but she has some cunning features the Piranhas don't know about. Okay, crew, let's see what we can do." He walks up to the front bench and pokes his fingers under it, and the whole bench hinges up, revealing a box of weapons and tools.

One sailor laughs, but is silenced by the captain's glare.

"We're still outnumbered, outgunned, and locked in," he says in a low voice. "One false move and the Piranhas will slaughter us." He rummages for a tiny silver tool and hands it to a sailor with a droopy moustache. "Grawlix, you're our best lock picker – get these handcuffs unlocked. But don't take them off – we need to pretend we're still cuffed." He turns to a short brown woman with a tattooed chin. "Crumb, you have the best ears of any of us. Sit yourself by the hatchway and listen for anyone coming. Be ready to raise the alarm with one of your famous sing songs."

She grins.

Grawlix soon has everyone's handcuffs unlocked.

Wondering where the *Rhino* is headed, you watch out the oar hole. Looks like the north end of Beach Road. What's worth ramming around here?

Captain Abdu distributes weapons around the crew. Not to you though. "Sorry, kid, but you're no warrior."

You remember how useless you were with the spear. "I know. When there's trouble, I'm only good at running away."

"That's often the best way to deal with trouble. And we may have need for a fast runner, depending on where the Piranhas are taking the *Rhino*."

"We're on Beach Road. The north end – King Volt's territory. Why, I don't know."

He chews his lip. "Me neither. Money is the only thing the Piranhas care about, and there'd be no profit in ramming one of Volt's power turbines."

The engine noise changes, and the *Rhino* starts to turn.

Crumb bursts into song, in a terrible squeaky voice. Everyone dashes back to their benches, and checks their weapons are out of sight and their handcuffs in place. The captain sits beside you, on a bench on the left side of the boat.

Two sets of footsteps clatter down the stern hatchway.

You glance out the oar hole again. The *Rhino* has stopped, facing south. Due south.

Of course. "They're going to ram Big Pig's Tollgate at the south end of Beach Road," you whisper to the captain.

He raises his eyebrows then nods. "Yes, that could be very profitable," he whispers back, barely audible over Crumb's singing.

A huge woman emerges from the hatchway, followed by a short man wearing spikey shoulder pads and spike-covered gloves, like he's some kind of pirate porcupine. Both have Piranha black and white striped bandanas around their necks.

"Shut up!" the woman yells at Crumb, marches to the front, turns and scowls at everyone. She has muscles on her muscles, and scars galore, and carries a buzzing stun-gun and a mysterious black box. Somehow even her hair – braided with pink teddy-bear ribbons – is scary.

The porcupine man blocks the hatchway steps, the only way out.

"We should have thrown you lot overboard and let the sharks chew on your flabby flesh!" Scary Hair yells. "And maybe we still will. Pick up those oars, or die."

"My crew will follow my orders," Captain Abdu says calmly. "We will row."

You're pretty sure that's his sneaky way of telling the crew to play along for the meantime.

Everyone grabs the oars – even you, although you've never rowed anything bigger than a raft.

"Not as stupid as you look," Scary Hair sneers. "Time to learn my favorite song." She presses a button on the mysterious black box, and a drum beat starts: boom-boom-boom-BOOM-boom-boom-boom-BOOM. For one crazy moment, you think she's going to start dancing or singing, but then realize the 'music' is a rowing beat.

"Pathetic!" she yells at the crew's first rowing stroke. She's right, the timing was terrible – yours especially, losing your grip and hitting your nose on the oar. "Synchronize or suffer!" She points her stun-gun at Grawlix.

The next stroke is better, everyone pushing their oars at nearly the same time, and the third even better. This crew have obviously had plenty of rowing experience together.

Over the drum beat, the *Rhino*'s steam engine chugs at full speed.

Out the oar hole, you see Beach Road whizzing past, faster and faster. The steam whistle blasts warnings every few seconds. There's a scream and a horrible crunch, as someone's boat doesn't get out of the way fast enough, and the Rhino doesn't even slow down. At this rate, you'll be at the Tollgate in minutes.

"Better," Scary Hair barks, marching up and down the aisle. "Perhaps some of you deserve to live a little longer."

"You know the Pimple?" the captain whispers to you, when she's not looking.

You nod. It's a huge broken concrete column near the Tollgate – people call it the Pimple because of the way it sticks out into Beach Road.

"Our only chance is to ram it," he continues. "Tell me when we're about twenty yards away."

"Less yapping, more rowing!" Scary Hair shouts.

Ram the Pimple? That sounds dangerous, and you have no idea how he'll do it, but you nod anyway.

Out the oar hole, Beach Road races past. Mermaid Street, Ocean View Road, and, wait for it... Armpit Bridge, which means the Pimple's close.

"Now," you shout.

"Hard to port!" Captain Abdu yells.

The whole crew stands. Everyone on the right pushes their oars extra hard. Everyone on the left jams their oars into the water and pulls backwards, you joining in.

The Rhino swerves left. Time seems to slow down. Scary Hair turns and snarls, raising her stun-gun towards the captain. The porcupine man waves his spiked fists in the air. The captain and crew drop their handcuffs and crouch down. Grabbing their weapons? No, grabbing the benches. You do the same, not knowing why.

Crunch! The *Rhino* jolts to a stop, so suddenly that both pirates are thrown to the deck. The *Rhino* crew pile over them. Moments later, Scary Hair stares nervously at her own stun-gun, now pointed at her by Grawlix, and the porcupine man is stuck to the wooden deck by his spiky clothing and two oars.

"No time to waste," the captain tells you. "Run to the Tollgate and raise the alarm."

He and most of the crew swarm up the hatchway. You're close on their heels.

The Piranhas up here on the main deck are still getting back to their feet, with no idea why the *Rhino* crashed into the Pimple. The last thing they expect is for their rowing slaves to burst out of the hatchway, waving weapons.

You dodge a pirate sword, hop over the crushed bow onto the Pimple's concrete, leap down, and race along the Beach Road sidewalk, heading for the Tollgate. "Piranhas!" you yell at the top of your lungs. "Pirate attack! They hijacked the *Rhino* and kidnapped her crew!"

That gets everyone's attention, especially at the Tollgate. Dozens of Big Pig's soldiers dash past you towards the *Rhino*.

The *Rhino*'s crew and the soldiers soon take the Piranhas prisoner, to the delight of the locals – the Piranha gang isn't popular around here.

Captain Abdu, who's somehow found his red top hat again, grins and claps you on the shoulder. "You can't fight and you can't row, kid, but you're quick on your feet. How'd you like to join my crew? Oh, and we found this in the hold." He hands you your backpack. The package is still inside, looking a bit squashed but intact.

It's time to make a decision. Do you:

Join the Rusty Rhino crew? **P120**

Or

Stay a Deadline Delivery courier? **P121**

Join the Rusty Rhino Crew

"Thanks, captain," you say. "I'd love to work on the *Rusty Rhino*."

Of course, it's not quite that simple – the *Rhino*'s still jammed onto the Pimple, with its bow crumpled and leaking.

But word quickly spreads through the under-city about how Captain Abdu's crew outsmarted the Piranha gang and saved Big Pig's territory from invasion. An hour later, Big Pig sends out his best mechanics and boat builders to rescue the *Rhino*. A few weeks later, the boat's been fully repaired. Its new bow is painted with an angry pig logo, signaling to everyone that the boat gets free passage through Big Pig's Tollgates. Forever.

"It's not entirely good news," Captain Abdu admits to you. "When Big Pig does anyone a big favor, he always expects a big favor in return too. But still, we've been attacked by pirates a dozen times before and this time ended better than most. Okay, kid, tomorrow we start our next voyage, transporting rat skins, dried plankton, and jellied eels across the city. Get ready to learn to fight, row, swim, and anything else I can think of."

"Yes, sir!"

Congratulations, this part of your story is over. You have survived a pirate attack and started an exciting new life on board the Rusty Rhino. But things could have gone even better – or even worse. You could have gone up to the over-city, or down to the mysterious domain of the froggies. And there are other pirates down here beside the Piranhas to worry about, like those Kannibal Krew. Or the mysterious Shadows.

It's time to make a decision. Do you:

Go to the great big list of choices? **P377**

Or

Go back to the beginning and try another path? **P105**

Stay a Courier

"No, thanks, captain," you say. "I'm not really sailor material. But, um, do you have a spare dollar? I'm broke, dead broke, and can't even pay my toll fee to get back home."

He laughs and gives you twenty dollars. Twenty! Then he hugs you. Half the crew hug you too, until you're blushing.

You wave goodbye, and run to Brine Street – your package delivery is late, and Miss Betty will probably yell at you.

After delivering it, you return to the Tollgate and hold out your dollar toll fee.

"You're that kid," says the guard.

"Um," you say.

"Helped save us from attack by the Piranhas," she says. "Thanks."

"No problem."

"No charge." She waves you through the gate.

Wow, that's never happened before.

Today's turned out pretty well. Twenty bucks in your pocket – enough for dinner and new shoes. Well, not brand-new, but new-ish, the right size and with no holes. Luxury.

You might only be a courier, but life's definitely improving.

Congratulations, this part of your story is over. Even though Miss Betty won't be impressed, helping to defeat a pirate attack was quite an adventure. Although if you'd made different decisions, today could have gone even better – or worse. What if you'd never gone through the Tollgate and caught a ride on the Rusty Rhino at all? Or if you'd left the boat after that building collapsed?

It's time to make a decision. Do you:

Go to the great big list of choices? **P377**

Or

Go back to the beginning and try another path? **P105**

Jump Overboard

You run for the side of the *Rhino*, getting ready to jump for your life. But before you can clamber up over the armored side, something hits you on the head, and...

Everything turns black **P114**

Leave the Rhino and Walk to Brine Street

You wave goodbye to Captain Abdu and his crew. "Thanks for the ride."

"Good luck," he shouts, as the *Rusty Rhino* chugs away.

"You too."

Twelve blocks later, near a line of people queuing for who knows what, you find a dented steel door marked with 390 in peeling yellow paint. It doesn't look like much – in fact, you recheck your package's delivery address to be sure this is the address. Yep, 390.

Whatever this place is, they have a serious security system. Cameras watch you, and the door snaps open then shuts itself the moment you've walked through. Inside are white walls and long shelves, ceilings with humming tube lights, and a half-flower half-chemical smell that catches in the back of your throat.

Another smell too – dog, maybe?

A man in a white coat takes the package, scribbles an electronic signature on a data tablet, then walks away, arguing on his phone the whole time and barely looking at you.

Some customers are like that. You don't mind – the worst customers are the ones who blather about nothing for half an hour and make you late for your next job.

The security door lets you out then snaps shut behind you.

So, what now, walk back to Deadline Delivery and hope Miss Betty has another job for you? Unfortunately, that could mean waiting for hours in the dispatch office, watching her playing Bouncy Bunnies on her computer. But at least there's ten dollars waiting for you back there – that's better than some days.

As you start the long walk back to Nori Street, you have fun imagining the ways you're going to spend that money, starting with a delicious dinner tonight. Just thinking about it makes your stomach rumble happily. You're so busy daydreaming that you don't notice the shadows in an alley, not until they start moving. Too late, you realize they're not shadows but Shadows, the local pirate gang who dress in black from head to toe.

Before you can decide whether it's worth trying to run, something hits you from behind and everything goes dark.

You wake in the alley, with a throbbing headache. Surprised to be alive, surprised that you still have your clothes, even your cap. Your shoes are gone though. A few yards away is your backpack, slashed open – pointlessly, since it was empty anyway.

Oh. They found the coins in your pocket too, so now you're dead broke. Not even a dollar to get back through a Tollgate. What an awful day.

"Are you okay?" calls a voice.

You look around but can't see anyone.

"Up here."

From far above, an over-city boy looks down through a security fence.

"I called for an ambulance, but…they said they didn't service lower levels," he continues, sounding confused. "Security reasons, they said."

Stupid over-city kid. Ambulances never come down here, everyone knows that. "Go away," you tell him.

He doesn't. "And then I called the police," he continues. "But I don't think they believed me when I told them three ninjas attacked you."

Huh? "What are ninjas?"

He frowns. "Those guys in black."

"Those were pirates, from the Shadows gang."

He looks even more confused. "Pirates don't dress like that. Pirates wear eye patches and stripy t-shirts and old-timey captain hats. And they have cutlasses and flintlock pistols. And peg legs. And parrots on their shoulders. Well, not all at once, I suppose. And they say 'Arrrrrr!' and bury secret treasure and then find it again."

What on earth is he on about? "Go away," you repeat. "I have to walk across town to Nori Street in bare feet, and I'm tired of your stupid over-city babbling."

"Nori Street? That's near where I live. Why don't you catch a mag-lev train? It's only a five-minute ride."

"There aren't any trains down here, dummy. And even if there were, I don't have any money – the Shadows took everything."

"No, I meant the train up here. I'll pay for your ticket. Look here, there's a gap in the security fence where you could squeeze through."

You look up, ready to yell at him, but he's right – about the fence at least – he's flapping a loose section of steel mesh. Just maybe he's not completely crazy.

It's time to make a decision. Do you:

Go up to the over-city?**P126**

Or

No way, you're staying down here. **P133**

Up to the Over-City

"Okay, I'm coming up," you tell the over-city boy.

Easier said than done – you have to climb a slippery concrete wall, then shimmy along a creaking girder, in bare feet. The final part's the worst – clambering hand over hand across heavy steel mesh to where he is. One slip and the thirty-foot fall will probably kill you.

Just as you get there, he holds the mesh closed, blocking your way. "Are you a hooligan or a vagrant?" he asks.

"What?"

"My father says that under-city folk are hooligans and vagrants."

Stupid over-city dad, you want to say but don't, coz you're dangling over a thirty-foot drop, clutching rusty steel mesh that's already digging into your aching fingers. "See my cap? Deadline Delivery, that's the company I work for. I'm just a courier who got mugged by, um, nin joes, like you saw."

"Ninjas," he corrects, then holds the mesh open and lets you swing through. "Hi, I'm Albert."

"I'm, um…Rhino," you lie, trying to rub some feeling back into your sore fingers. No way is he getting your real name.

"Rhino? That's such a cool name, much better than 'Albert'." He points down through the mesh. "Rhino, are they hooligans and vagrants?"

Following his gaze, you see half a dozen people looking up. "Maybe some of them," you admit. Let's be honest, any route up to the over-city will attract some bad people before long.

Albert puts his thumb to his ear and talks into his little finger. "Hello, I'd like to report a broken security fence. Yes, sending a location-tagged photo now. Thank you." He puts his hand down and looks at you. "They're sending someone immediately."

"You have a phone inside your hand?"

He nods. "I got it for my birthday. I was always losing my phones or forgetting to charge them, this one's so much more convenient.

You should get one too, it'd be perfect for a courier."

You laugh. "Sure, after I find one of those pirate secret treasures you were talking about."

"C'mon, Rhino, the next train's in three minutes."

Rhino? Oh, right, he thinks that's your name. Stupid over-city kid.

Maybe it would be safer to leave him and travel alone. But looking around, you feel lost. Even though they're exactly the same streets and buildings, everything up here looks unfamiliar.

So you follow him, shading your eyes. It's so bright – for once there are no security fences between you and the sun. And everything's shiny and clean – buildings, people, everything. The under-city's an almost invisible shadow beneath security fences. No wonder that over-city people forget the under-city even exists.

A hover-van races past and stops where you came through the fence. Two people in overalls leap out, carrying tools.

Albert sighs. "Unbelievable. I report you being mugged down there and no one cares, but…I report a hole in the security fence and they turn up in three minutes flat. It's so unfair."

Maybe he's not so stupid after all. For an over-city boy.

He takes you down the street, past a building which has an entire wall showing a giant video ad for deodorant, to a line of seats which look like they're made of glass (although surely that's impossible). In front of the seats, a gleaming silvery rail continues in both directions down the street – the mag-lev track, and so this must be a train stop, you suppose, but are too embarrassed to ask.

A small train soon approaches. It's shiny and clean, of course, and looks like a spaceship. Albert somehow pays for tickets by wiggling his magic phone-hand again.

"What else can it do? Make coffee?" you ask.

Albert laughs.

From four rows away, two young women turn and glare at you, sniff, and then move further away. Do you stink or something? Yeah, okay, probably. Albert either doesn't notice or is too polite to mention it. He launches into a long story about pirates – his sort of pirates, not the real ones – which makes no sense. Something about walking on a plank and some guy named Jolly Roger.

"Nori Street," a computer voice announces five minutes later.

One block away is Ivory Tower, although you barely recognize it. This level of the building is covered in marble and chrome and glass, almost beautiful. For a moment, you think you're dreaming and this must be the wrong address. But when you peer down through the security fence, there are the grimy old under-city levels you know so well.

"What's wrong, Rhino?" Albert asks as you cross the street together, on a lacy golden bridge that plays tinkly notes with your every step. Musical bridges – is there anything they don't have up here?

"Just wondering how to get back to the under-city levels."

He frowns, confused again. "Why not use the elevators?"

"Ivory Tower has no elevators on our levels. And the stairwells are blocked, to stop us horrible hooligans and vagrants getting up here." Hmm, wait a minute. Surely the stairwells and elevators must have connected *all* the levels once, back when the building was built, before the city flooded. So…maybe some connections *weren't* blocked?

It's time to make a decision, and fast. Rolling towards you is a police robot, making a grumpy beep-boop-beep-boop noise. Do you:

Go into Ivory Tower? **P129**

Or

Run from the Grumpy Robot? **P131**

Ivory Tower

"I've just had an idea, Albert. It may not work, and it could get me in a lot of trouble, so…goodbye and thanks for all your help."

"Bye, Rhino. Hope I see you again one day." He bends down, takes off his shoes, and gives them to you. "Here, you'll need these, for running away from pirates."

"What?" They're great shoes, so great that you don't want to put them on your dirty feet. You feel a lump in your throat. "Thanks, Albert. They're the best present anyone's ever given me."

He shrugs. "They're just shoes. I've got dozens. Good luck, Rhino."

Clutching the shoes, you sprint up to Ivory Tower's front door before the police robot can catch you.

"Can I help you?" growls a doorman in a fancy uniform, glaring from your grimy bare feet to your dirty Deadline Delivery cap.

You smile at him. "Yes, please. I'm a poor under-city kid who needs to get back to the under-city levels as fast as possible. You want me out of here too, right? So–"

He grabs you by the collar and drags you inside. "How dare you smear your dirty feet over our nice clean floor," he shouts, then adds in a whisper, "Play along for the security cameras. I was born in the lower levels of this very building, and I remember Deadline Delivery. Is Miss Betty still there?" Before you can say a word, he drags you into an elevator and starts shouting again. "We don't want your sort up here, understand, kid?"

Why's he still yelling? Oh, the elevator has a security camera in the corner.

"You're a bunch of dirty, um…"

"Hooligans and vagrants?" you suggest.

"Precisely! Dirty vagrants and hooligans!"

The floor numbers blink down to "8", the doors open, and he pushes you out.

"And don't come back!" As the doors close, you see him wink.

The elevator doesn't even look like an elevator from out here – there are no control buttons, just two stainless steel panels that you know are really its doors. So, it's a one-way elevator – sneaky.

Yes, this really is Level 8 – there's the tattoo parlor at the other end of the corridor, and next to it, Deadline Delivery.

Miss Betty scowls at you, as usual. But she pays you the ten-dollar delivery fee, as promised.

The steel door squeaks and starts to close, and you hurry out. Miss Betty doesn't say goodbye. She never does.

Congratulations, this part of your story is over. You've seen the over-city, and met Albert, who's pretty cool for a crazy over-city kid, and now you have a great new pair of shoes and ten dollars – this is the best day you've had in months. Would things have worked out so well if you'd made different choices?

It's time to make a decision. Do you:

Go to the great big list of choices? **P377**

Or

Go back to the beginning and try another path? **P105**

Run from the Police Robot

"Goodbye and thanks for your help, Albert. I'd better get out of here before that police robot catches me."

"Wait a moment." He bends down, takes off his shoes, and gives them to you. "Here, you'll run faster in these."

"Really?" They're great shoes, so great that you don't want to put them on your dirty feet. "Thanks, Albert. They're the best present anyone's ever given me." You feel a lump in your throat.

He shrugs. "They're just shoes. I have lots. Good luck, Rhino."

Clutching the shoes, you run down Nori Road.

But the police robot accelerates. Halfway down the block, it catches up and clamps you around the neck with a metal hand. "You are unauthorized," it says, and grabs the shoes with two more hands – it has six hands, at least.

"They're mine, a gift – I didn't steal them," you protest.

"Correct," it says. A little TV screen on its body lights up, and there on screen is Albert giving you the shoes. "You are unauthorized," it repeats, and more pictures appear – you climbing through the security fence, you and Albert catching the train – you've been watched the whole time on security cameras. So much for sneaking around without being noticed.

The robot drags you down an alley, to a large cage labeled Trash.

"I'm not trash!"

"Correct. You are unauthorized," it says again. Robots aren't great conversationalists, that's for sure. It seals the shoes in a plastic bag, and hands them back to you. Huh? "Please hold your breath. Have a nice day." It pushes you into the cage, on top of piles of real trash, closes the door and pulls a lever.

The bottom of the cage swings open.

You fall, screaming.

Just as you hit the water, you remember to hold your breath, even though you can't swim.

But as you splash, you bounce on something. Somehow you're not drowning, you're in a huge rope net stretched over the water. Around you, people sift through all the trash that fell with you.

"Look, it's one of Miss Betty's Deadline Delivery kids," says a man with a dozen earrings.

"Dead?" asks a bald woman. "I know a guy who'll pay ten dollars for dead kids, so long as they're fresh."

"No, still breathing."

"What a shame. Never mind then."

Everyone laughs. You hope they're joking.

"Half a slice of pizza, and the cheese is still soft!" yells the bald woman, swallowing it with a huge smile.

"That's nothing, I found two apple cores!" the man shouts back

Lying beside you on the net is your Deadline Delivery cap. It's soaking wet, like the rest of your clothes (except for Albert's shoes, safe in their plastic bag), but you put it on anyway.

Back at Deadline Delivery, Miss Betty scowls at you, as usual. She pays you the ten-dollar delivery fee, as promised, but only after deducting two dollars as a Wet Uniform fee for your cap. So unfair. You scowl back at her silently.

The steel door squeaks and starts to close, and you hurry out. Miss Betty doesn't say goodbye. She never does.

Congratulations, this part of your story is over. You've seen the over-city, and met Albert, who's pretty cool for a crazy over-city kid.

Even that grumpy police robot was nice to you, in a way.

And now you have a great pair of shoes and eight dollars – this is the best day you've had in months. Would things have worked out so well if you'd stayed in the under-city?

It's time to make a decision. Do you:

Go to the list of choices and pick another part of the story? **P377**

Or

Go back to the beginning and try another path? **P105**

Stay in the Under-City

Did that over-city boy really expect you to trust him, a total stranger? Sure, a free train ride home would have been cool, but…he was probably only joking or trying to trick you or something, coz, well, over-city people are crazy. Everyone knows that.

You leave the alley. Where now – home? But how, with no shoes and no money?

Hmm, Beach Road is only a couple of blocks away, and has fairly good footpaths and a Tollgate at its south end. Yeah, heading that way makes sense. As for how to get through the Tollgate without a dollar toll fee…um, you'll think of something. Maybe try that secret tunnel you found on Krill Road last week, although that will mean a lot of climbing over rubble in bare feet.

Twenty minutes later, you've stubbed your toes three times, trodden in dog poop, come within an inch of stepping on a rusty nail, and been sniffed by a hungry-looking cat. Not too much further though – you can see the Beach Road Tollgate in the distance.

A steam engine chuffs behind you, and you turn and see the *Rusty Rhino* ironclad again. Maybe Captain Abdu will give you a ride, perhaps even loan you a dollar for the toll fee.

But…why is the *Rhino* going so fast, and using oars as well as its steam engine? And that's not Captain Abdu at the wheel, although he's wearing the captain's crumpled red top hat. Strange. The captain never ever lets anyone else wear that hat – it's his favorite. Just visible at the guy's neck is a black and white striped bandana – the uniform of the Piranha pirate gang. The *Rusty Rhino*'s been hijacked!

Where are Captain Abdu and his crew? Taken prisoner? Dead?

And where's the *Rhino* going in such a hurry?

You look further up Beach Road and see a line of speedboats are quietly following the *Rhino* at a distance.

You turn the other way and see the Tollgate in the distance. Why isn't the *Rhino* slowing down?

Oh. It isn't speeding *to* the Tollgate, it's going to ram its way *through* the Tollgate. The Piranhas are invading Big Pig's territory!

It's time to make a decision. Do you:

Run to the Tollgate and warn them? **P135**

Or

No, ignore the Rhino. The Tollgate can defend itself. **P138**

Run to the Tollgate

Is this really a good idea? Outrun a steamboat, in bare feet?

It's not impossible, you tell yourself. The *Rusty Rhino*'s just a slow old cargo boat, even when helped along by oars.

So you start jogging towards the Tollgate.

For the first block, you easily outpace the boat. But then you trip on a loose sidewalk plank and fall, stubbing your toe yet again and scraping your knee.

Ignoring the pain, you get up and carry on running. The *Rhino*'s close on your heels.

Faster.

The Tollgate's just three blocks away.

Two.

One block. The *Rhino*'s catching up.

"Pirate attack!" you yell at the top of your voice. "The Piranhas have hijacked the *Rusty Rhino*!"

Can the guards at the Tollgate hear you yet?

Maybe not, but the people on the street around you can. The locals hate pirates, and hate the slave-selling Piranhas most of all. Some people run off, and others start throwing things at the *Rhino* – stones, bricks, rotten food. Someone even fires an arrow. Not that any of that will do much against an ironclad boat.

The *Rhino*'s chugging alongside you now, and getting faster, or you're slowing down, or both. Onboard, a Piranha glares at you over an armor plate. "I hate loud-mouthed kids," he shouts, and levels a pistol at you. Before he can pull the trigger, a flying brick hits him and he falls, cursing.

Exhausted and out of breath, you stagger to a stop near Armpit Bridge, and shout "Piranha attack!" one last time at the top of your voice.

Just ahead is a huge concrete column, locally known as the Pimple because of the way it sticks out into Beach Road. To your amazement, the oars on the *Rhino*'s left side suddenly jam into the water, and the oars on its right side push extra hard. The boat swerves left, bouncing hard off the Pimple and snapping lots of oars.

How did that happen? It was no accident, you suspect.

The impact has damaged the *Rhino*, and slowed but not stopped it. Its engine's still going and it's speeding up again.

Somehow you find a second wind and dash the rest of the way to the Tollgate, passing the *Rhino* again and hoping no one else takes a pot shot at you. "Pirate attack!"

"Yeah, we heard you the first time, kid," mutters a guard from behind the heavy steel mesh. "Stand back and enjoy the show. Now!" He raises an assault rifle.

You duck into a nearby doorway, wincing at your bruised and bleeding feet, then turn to watch the approaching *Rhino*.

Something whirs and clanks, and five enormous spikes emerge from the water in front of the gate. People on the *Rhino* shout at each other, and the boat tries to turn away. Too late – with a shriek like a dying dinosaur, it collides with the spikes, gouging long holes in its side. Soldiers run out from the Tollgate, and there's more shouting from the *Rhino*.

Only a few shots are fired. Five minutes later, a line of unhappy pirates are sitting handcuffed on the sidewalk outside the Tollgate.

"Look what those damned Piranhas have done to my poor old boat," says a familiar voice.

It's Captain Abdu on the *Rhino*'s deck, looking down at her ripped and crumpled side. He's reclaimed his red top hat, and that's more ripped and crumpled than usual too.

"Are you and your crew okay, captain?" you ask.

He gives a sad smile. "Thought it was you I heard earlier, shouting pirate attack warnings – thanks for that. We were imprisoned in our own cargo hold, forced to be rowing slaves. A couple of broken bones and a stab wound, but we're all alive and grateful to be so. Could be worse, could be far worse. But I fear the *Rusty Rhino* has made her last voyage."

To everyone's surprise, the captain's wrong.

Big Pig takes the Piranhas' attack on his territory very personally, and has the *Rhino* recovered and repaired, at his own expense. He orders its bow painted with an angry pig logo, signaling to everyone that the boat gets free passage through the Tollgates.

Captain Abdu isn't completely happy about this. "Big Pig just wants to look good to the locals – he'll expect me to pay him back, one way or another. But at least I have my dear old *Rhino* shipshape again."

Somehow Big Pig hears about you too, and orders you to have an angry pig logo tattooed on your hand – that gives you free passage through the Tollgates too. You secretly hate the tattoo, but hey, no more Tollgate fees ever? – that sounds great. Life's definitely improving.

Congratulations, this part of your story is over. You're a hero to most people, except the local pirates. And Miss Betty, who doesn't care about anything except packages being delivered on time, but you don't care about that.

What might have happened if you hadn't raised the alarm about the pirate attack? Or what if you'd never gone up to the over-city at all?

It's time to make a decision. Do you:

Go to the great big list of choices? **P377**

Or

Go back to the beginning and try another path? **P105**

Ignore the Rhino

The *Rusty Rhino* steams (and rows) past you, followed by half a dozen speedboats, each crowded with people. No weapons are visible, but you spot several black and white striped Piranha bandanas beneath shirts and jackets. Definitely a surprise pirate attack.

Part of you feels guilty, wishing you could do something to warn the Tollgate. But still – outrun a steamboat in bare feet? No way!

Too late now anyway. The pirate fleet has already passed.

Limping, you carry on down Beach Road, watching where you're stepping with your sore bare feet.

There's a huge bang in the distance – either at the Tollgate or close to it – then lots of little bangs. Gunfire? A haze of smoke or dust hides whatever's happening. You keep walking.

Your left foot's bleeding and your right foot has a blister, but you soon forget that as you get closer to the Tollgate – the whole gate's been smashed open. There's no sign of the guards. A body lies face down in the water, and blood stains a sidewalk.

You sneak through the wreckage (not that there's anyone around to hide from) and walk back to Nori Road, detouring each time you hear screams, gunfire, and revving speedboats. There's no other sign of life, except occasional frightened faces peering out from barred windows.

Hearing a throbbing engine, you take cover behind a smashed crate. A cargo boat goes by, laden with weeping handcuffed people, guarded by grinning Piranhas.

An over-city fire control hovercraft whooshes past. It sprays water over a smoldering boat, then disappears, ignoring you and the slave boat. Typical. Over-city people only care about stopping fires spreading upwards – they couldn't care less what happens to anyone down here.

Getting back to Ivory Tower unseen takes half an hour. You hammer on the bulletproof glass doors. "Let me in!" You can see someone's shadow moving inside, but the doors don't open. "Let me in! I work here."

Someone grabs you around the neck.

"Not any more you don't, kid," a Piranha sneers, and handcuffs you.

I'm sorry, this part of your story is over. You're now a slave of the Piranhas, being herded with dozens of others into a long boat, on your way to...who knows where. If you'd made different choices, things might have worked out better. Or even worse...

It's time to make a decision. Do you:

Go to the list of choices and read another part of the story? **P377**

Or

Go back to the beginning and try another path? **P105**

Secret Tunnel

You climb a creaking fire escape and clamber over the roof of a flooded car salesroom. Through holes in broken skylights, you can sometimes see car skeletons rusting under the water.

You cross a rickety rope suspension bridge, down an alley close to the Wall, and into a small building that everyone ignores because it's covered in bird poop and smells even worse. Then up a staircase with half of its steps missing, then under a broken door. You stop and wait, listening and watching through a hole in a wall, in case anyone's followed you. No point in having a secret tunnel if it doesn't stay secret.

After five minutes, you decide you're alone. There are dog and rat footprints on the dusty floor, but no shoe prints except your own. No other people have been here in a long time. You only found this place last week, completely by accident, while looking for shelter during a rainstorm.

You carry on, through a room lined with shelves of rat-eaten books (and rat nests, judging by the rustling and squeaking) then past a concrete-walled room full of cables, pipes, vents, spider webs and a wall of giant fans.

After swinging out the rightmost fan from its frame, you duck into the tunnel behind.

It's only an air duct, and so low you have to crawl on your hands and knees, your backpack scraping along the roof. With every move, the metal walls groan and creak and wobble like they're about to collapse. Don't think about that, keep going, it's worth it, because…

…when you get to the other end, and peer out through a jumble of torn girders, below you is Krill Road. You're through the Wall.

You wait again, watching, listening. Big Pig would be very unhappy if he knew this tunnel existed, and bad things happen to anyone who makes Big Pig unhappy.

Over there, under that floating tangle of blue plastic wrap – is that a pair of eyes looking back at you? No, don't be so paranoid.

Climbing down onto Krill Road, you're watched by a large three-legged ginger cat, but apparently no one and nothing else. The tunnel exit is invisible from here, just a shadow beneath an old upside-down sign advertising hot dogs. Why did people in the olden days always eat their dog sausages in bread rolls?

Everything's quiet. Maybe too quiet. That's always the problem with Krill Road. Long, wide and straight, with good sidewalks and three solid bridges. A great way to get across the city, for people or boats. And the reason pirate gangs like it too.

A line of ducks swims past. Must be safe, right? The ducks seem to think so, and barely glance up as you jog along the top of a crumbling concrete wall on Krill Road's left side.

Suddenly the ducks burst into panicked quacking and take off.

You turn to see a dozen wild dogs trailing you, led by a huge German Shepherd with a ripped left ear.

You know a dog that looks a lot like that. It knows you too, sometimes it even stops and says a doggy hello and you scratch behind its ears. But the dog you know doesn't have a ripped ear. Maybe this is the same dog and it's been in a fight recently, or maybe it isn't the same dog, and you're about to get your throat ripped out. Wild dogs eat almost anything, including kids.

Don't panic. Not yet. Avoiding any sudden movements, you look around, but don't see any ladders or other escape routes where a dog couldn't follow you.

Around a corner chugs a wooden boat loaded high with cabbages. At the boat's center, sitting on a box behind a small steering wheel, is an old woman. There's a sawed-off double-barreled shotgun by her feet.

She smiles toothlessly and slows down. "Jump on, dearie," she says. "You don't look like a cabbage thief. If I see you being eaten alive by dogs, I'll lose my appetite for lunch."

The dogs are getting closer.

It's time to make a decision. Do you:

Accept her offer of a ride? **P143**

Or

Decide not to trust her? **P155**

Cabbage Boat Ride

"Thank you." You climb down into the boat and sit behind the old woman, carefully avoiding cabbages, coiled ropes and an oar.

She revs the engine and the boat burbles off, to howls of disappointment from the dogs.

Something splashes nearby. No, not a dog, just a huge rat swimming past, perhaps escaping the dogs too. Another splash, a flicker of too many teeth, and the rat's gone, leaving only ripples. A shark? People claim there are crocodiles and giant octopuses prowling the flooded streets too. Or maybe it was froggies – the green-skinned mutant people who live underwater and snatch at anything and anyone on the surface. Not that you've ever seen a froggy, but everyone says it's true.

The dogs are soon out of earshot, but a few minutes later something else can be heard over the engine's burbling – a high-pitched roar, getting louder. Looking back, you see a blood-red speedboat approaching. On both sides of the road, people disappear behind doors and slam windows shut.

"Pirates!" yells the old woman, glancing back too. "Looks like the Kannibal Krew. So sorry, dearie." Everyone knows the Kannibal Krew really are cannibals.

"Not your fault." You grab the oar and start paddling. Every little bit helps, right?

She laughs sadly. "That's very sweet of you, dearie, but this old tub can't outrun a speedboat."

You scan both sides of the road, looking for somewhere safe to leap out.

The cabbage boat swerves around a corner, and the old woman cuts the engine.

"What are you doing? This is a dead end!"

She points her sawed-off shotgun at you. "Yes, I know, dearie. Drop the oar. Like I said, I'm so sorry, but the Kannibal Krew and I have an arrangement – I hand over any passengers to them, and in return they don't eat me."

"That's not fair!"

"Not for you, perhaps, but it's a pretty good deal for me. And you should know not to accept lifts from strangers."

"Look behind you. We're going to crash."

She sneers. "I'm not falling for that old trick – do you think I was born yesterday?"

The drifting boat really is about to collide with the side of the road. You have seconds to make a decision. Do you:

Jump out of the cabbage boat? **P145**

Or

Stay on the boat, jumping looks too dangerous? **P153**

Jump out of the Boat

With a bang, the cabbage boat hits a brick pillar on the side of the road, tipping the old woman onto the cabbages. Before she has time to recover, you leap off the boat and scramble onto the sidewalk, dodging from side to side to spoil her aim.

She yells some very rude words. Her shotgun blasts, and something stings your back.

It hurts, but you're still alive, so you keep running, and flee up a flight of worn steps that lead you don't know where. You randomly turn left and right half a dozen times, then fall in a heap behind a low wall, exhausted and gasping for breath and completely lost.

But safe. For the moment.

You check your stinging back. Just two shotgun pellet wounds and a little blood – you were lucky, very lucky. You can feel one pellet under your fingertips and dig it out, wincing in pain. The other's in too deep and hurts too much. Worry about it later.

Your backpack was hit too. What about the package inside? Pulling it out, you see three small holes and hear broken glass tinkling. Oh no. Miss Betty won't be pleased. Although…why isn't the package leaking more? A large broken bottle would be dripping everywhere, but this, there's just a little dampness and a weird sour smell. Not booze – that's a relief, you'd hate to have risked your life just so some rich person can get drunk.

You peer over the low wall. Carefully, in case any old women with shotguns are looking for you. Or pirates. Or anyone else.

Several blocks to the north is a tall green building you recognize – it's only a block from Brine Street, so you're closer than you'd expected. Maybe that old woman did you a favor after all.

Things are peaceful enough – people hanging washing from lines at windows, small children playing and arguing.

You make your way down to the street, ignoring two yapping skinny puppies. There's no sign of pirates or cabbage boats, so you jog north.

Two blocks later, you find a market you've never seen before, spread over the roof of a low building. Rows of stallholders are selling oily engine parts, electrical junk, toys, weapons, food, and all sorts of stuff. None of it's any good to you, not with only a dollar in your pocket. Ignoring the delicious smell of barbequed rat, you carry on.

Brine Street, at last. Most of the addresses aren't numbered, and it takes you a while to find the steel door marked 390 in peeling yellow paint. There's a long line of people queuing along the sidewalk, you don't know why – they're definitely not queuing for 390. Some of them pretty scary-looking. Nearly as scary as the three security guards, stomping around and keeping order with stun-guns.

You try to edge past the crowd, towards 390.

A man yells at you – maybe he thinks you're queue-jumping – and someone else joins in, and suddenly everyone's pushing and shoving and shouting. Then just as suddenly, everyone stops and backs away and pretends you're not there.

A security guard looms over you, his buzzing stun-gun in hand. "Where do you think you're going, kid? You steal that cap?"

"No, sir, I have a delivery for 390 Brine Street," you squeak, unzipping your backpack.

Without asking, he grabs the package and stares at it, then drags you over to the yellow door, hands you back the package, bangs on the door and walks away.

Huh?

A security cam swivels down at you. The door rolls open, then snaps shut the moment you're through.

What is this place? Lots of white walls and shelves, suspiciously clean, ceilings with quietly humming tube lights, and a half-flower half-chemical smell that catches in the back of your throat.

A huge grey dog shuffles towards you. He has no back legs, just two wheels held on with a frame of metal rods and leather straps. But even so, you're pretty sure he could eat you alive if he wanted to.

"Nice doggy," you stammer.

He sniffs at you suspiciously, and says, "Wuff."

A tired-looking woman in a white coat and a bulletproof vest marches through a doorway and snatches the package from you. She slices the plastic wrapping with a scalpel, revealing a Styrofoam box full of finger-sized bottles. "What happened?" she asks, holding up a broken bottle.

Oh no. Miss Betty deducts fees for any breakages, no matter whose fault they are.

"Shotgun blast. A couple of pellets hit me too."

"Show me," she orders.

None of her business, but she's still holding that scalpel and it looks really sharp, so you show her the two small bloody patches on your back.

She grunts, as if reluctantly believing you.

"What's in those tiny bottles?" you ask, even though it's none of your business – if she can ask nosey questions, then so can you, right?

"Drugs."

You choke. "I'm a drug smuggler?"

She laughs. "*Medical* drugs. To be precise, antibiotics, one week past their expiry date. They were donated to us by a wealthy over-city hospital across town – we need all the help we can get. I'm Doctor Hurst, and this is the Brine Street Community Medical Clinic. A shame that one bottle got broken, but there's enough left to treat half of the people queuing outside our main entrance next door. You want me to fix up those shotgun wounds?"

Is this really a medical clinic? The closest to a clinic you've ever seen is old Charlie on Level 6 of Ivory Tower – he charges a bottle of moonshine whiskey to stitch up any wounds, uses half of it to sterilize the wounds and drinks the other half while he's stitching. He's better than nothing, but not much.

"Um, okay," you say, deciding to trust Doctor Hurst. Well, she does look…doctory. And doesn't smell of whiskey.

It only takes her a few minutes to dig out the other shotgun pellet –
which hurts, but not too badly. The dog sniffs you again, and licks
your hand. Maybe it's being nice, or maybe it's tasting you.

The doctor dabs something purple on both wounds. "You were
lucky, they're just flesh wounds. Keep them clean and dry and they'll
heal fine." She walks over to a desk and types on a computer
keyboard. The Deadline Delivery web site appears on screen, and she
presses the green Delivery Received icon. "I won't mention the one
broken bottle."

"Thank you. Thanks so much."

The doctor looks you up and down, and frowns. "How much do
you make for a delivery like this?"

Another nosy question, but you answer anyway. "Ten dollars."

"No wonder you're so skinny. That's terrible – we pay the delivery
companies far more than that, but you kids take the risks. Wait a
minute, I've got an idea." She leaves through a door.

You can hear her arguing with someone, but not what they're
saying.

"Wuff," says the dog, sniffing your trousers.

"Nice doggy," you repeat nervously.

He grins, showing lots of teeth and a long tongue, and says, "Wuff"
again.

Oh, he can smell your leftover meatloaf from breakfast. You'd
planned to keep it for lunch, but...never mind. You pull the plastic
bag from your pocket, and share the meatloaf with him.

He swallows it in one bite, then licks your face. "Wuff, woof."

"You're welcome." You scratch behind his ears.

A few minutes later, Doctor Hurst returns. "How'd you like a
permanent job as our clinic courier? It'll be hard work, and dangerous,
but no more than what you do now, and you'll be better paid. And
better fed."

No more working for Miss Betty? Hmm, that sounds good...but
what do you really know about the Brine Street Community Medical

Clinic?

It's time to make a decision. Do you:

Take the job? **P193**

Or

Think about it and decide later? **P150**

Decide Later

"Um," you say. "Can I think about it?"

"Sure, no rush," says Doctor Hurst. "Where are you going now?"

"Back to Deadline Delivery in Nori Road for my next delivery job."

"That's a rough neighborhood," she says.

"Yeah, but so is Brine Street."

She grins. "True. How'd you like an easy delivery job on your way back? 157 Nori Road. Twenty dollars, in advance."

"Okay," you say, before she can change her mind. Twenty dollars is heaps, and 157 is inside the Wall, only a block away from Ivory Tower. Easy money.

She hands you a small heavy box and the money.

You say goodbye to her and the two-legged dog, and leave.

Outside, the queue of clinic patients is even longer than before. Most of the people ignore you – you're just some boring courier coming out a boring yellow door – but a few stare, including a scary-looking woman with a Mohawk haircut and a necklace of teeth. A pirate, maybe? She's carrying a baby, and the baby stares at you too.

You pretend to ignore them, but the woman turns and whispers to an old man with his beard in dreadlocks and red beads.

Trouble?

That's the problem with wearing a Deadline Delivery cap – every few months, someone tries to rob you, even though the stuff you carry is hardly worth stealing. But Miss Betty insists all her couriers have to wear the stupid caps, and somehow she knows if anyone doesn't.

At the end of the block, you glance back ever so casually, and sure enough, the old man's following you, his red beaded beard glinting in the sun.

You're not worried. Not yet. You know this part of the under-city well. At the next alley, you turn left, still walking slowly. As soon as you're hidden by the building walls, you dash down the alley, turn left through an archway, and keep running. You dodge through the second-right doorway, down another alley, up a ladder, along the top of a wall, then jump down the other side and back onto the road, and stop, out of breath.

Hiding your cap in your backpack, you check in both directions. No sign of the old man.

Okay, back to Nori Road.

Easier said than done. Four blocks later, you turn left and find the whole road ahead blocked by a collapsed building. Must have just happened – there are still clouds of dust everywhere. Over-city police hovercraft and ambulances and news drones buzz around, a team of giant rescue robots lift girders and concrete beams, and of course a zillion people are watching. You'll never get through this way, not for hours, perhaps days.

So you turn right and detour around several blocks, hiding or changing direction whenever you spot suspicious people or boats.

Unfortunately, that all takes time, and hours pass before the Wall comes into view again. Your feet ache, and so do your shotgun wounds.

There's the hot dog sign up ahead. Not far now.

You stop. Something's different.

Oh. The sign – before, it was upside-down, but now it's more…sideways.

Has someone else found the secret tunnel?

Staying out of sight as much as possible, you get closer.

A hand clamps down on your shoulder. It's the old man with the dreadlocked beard. "You're a sneaky dodgy twisty-turny wee thing, that's for sure. Dragging me halfway across the city, when all I want is a nice wee chat. Young people today – so rude. Now, I can't help but notice your interest in this here wall of junk." He smiles, revealing shiny metal teeth. "That seems a remarkable coincidence, because I hear that just a few hours ago some of Big Pig's crew were also terribly interested in this very same wall. Spent two hours hammering and welding, they did, and then went away, without a word of explanation.

Quite a puzzle. Although by another remarkable coincidence, we're right by the Wall, aren't we? And what with you being a courier, and needing to get through the Wall so often…ah yes, I see by your eyes that I guessed right. Well now, losing that wee secret door is a shame for both of us, to be sure. We in the Kannibal Krew are also fond of having a few hush-hush ways of getting from here to there and there to here, yes, indeed." His smile widens, as though this is some huge joke.

A blood-red speedboat approaches, driven by the woman with the Mohawk. Next to her is a bald man with a skull tattoo covering his head. He's holding the same baby you saw outside the clinic. It stares right at you, same as before. Eying you up as lunch, perhaps.

"Let's go for a wee trip," the old man says, and nudges you towards the boat. For a moment, his grip on your shoulder weakens.

This could be your only chance. Do you:

Try to run from the Kannibals? **P194**

Or

Follow the old man's orders? **P196**

Stay on the Boat

The collision rocks the cabbage boat to one side, and the old woman overbalances, her shotgun waving wildly. You dive flat onto the hull – not that a pile of cabbages will protect you. The shotgun blasts over your head, so close that you're amazed to still be alive.

Looking up, you glare at her. "I told you we were going to crash."

She snorts and spits into the water. "Right little smarty-pants, aren't you, dearie? Fat lot of good it's done you – or will do, for what's left of the rest of your short life."

You sit up – slowly, because she's pointing the shotgun at you again. The side of your head hurts, and something's dripping down your face. Blood. You take off your *Deadline Delivery* cap and see two small bloody holes.

"Don't cry," she says with a sneer. "You won't bleed to death. Well, not from that."

Huh? Oh, of course, the pirates. The red speedboat swirls to a stop in front of the cabbage boat, blocking the road and your last hope of escape.

In the speedboat are two pirates – a bald man with a skull tattoo covering his head, and a woman with a Mohawk haircut. Both wear necklaces of human teeth.

"Lunch!" they roar, grinning at you. They're not talking about the cabbages.

The man leaps onto the cabbage boat, giggling and waving a huge machete.

You scream. The last thing you ever see is that machete, glinting in the sun as it whooshes down towards you.

I'm sorry, this part of your story is over. You weren't careful enough in this dangerous city, so you died.

Perhaps things would have gone better if you'd made some different decisions… and lucky you, you can try again.

It's time to make a decision. Do you:

Go to the great big list of choices? **P377**

Or

Go back to the beginning and try another path? **P105**

No Cabbage Boat Ride

"No, thank you," you tell the old woman politely, keeping an eye on her hands. You know better than to trust a free ride from just anyone in the under-city.

Sure enough, she reaches down for her sawed-off shotgun.

You run, heading for the only nearby cover, a collapsed brick wall. Just as you duck around a doorway, the shotgun booms and the top of the doorframe disintegrates into splinters.

She yells some very rude words – well, some of them you haven't heard before, but they definitely sound rude. The shotgun booms again and you're showered in brick dust. She knows where you're hiding, and there are no easy ways out of here.

At least the gunshots have scared those wild dogs away.

You hear a speedboat approaching, then the woman arguing with someone. Sneaking a glance around the doorway, you see a blood-red speedboat with two pirates on it. Kannibal Krew, most likely – one is bald, with a skull tattoo over his whole head, and the other has a Mohawk haircut. Both wear strings of teeth around their necks.

"There!" the old woman yells, pointing straight at you.

Whoops. No time to lose, no time even to think. The only thing that matters is getting away, and fast. You run, ducking and dodging from side to side, not knowing where you're going.

Another shotgun blast, but nothing hits you. Hopefully you're out of range.

The pirates are a bigger worry than the old woman. No way can you outrun a pirate speedboat – your only hope is to go somewhere they can't follow.

You sprint towards an open door, but someone slams it shut and locks it before you get there. Can't blame them – everyone's scared of the Kannibal Krew.

Racing around a corner, you look for a half-remembered alleyway, but it's not there – oh, right, you're thinking of a different road, three blocks away. No useful doorways, ladders, or stairways are in sight. The speedboat revs, getting closer. The pirates have spotted you.

You dash over a bridge and around another corner. The water's covered in floating trash here, and it's nearly low tide. Soon, some of these streets will be little more than deep sticky mud. Enough to clog a speedboat engine or strand the whole boat.

Apparently the pirates think the same – their speedboat slows, and the tattooed man clambers up to the bow and pokes a long pole into the floating trash, probably checking whether it's water or mud underneath. But the boat's still moving, still getting closer. From behind its wheel, the Mohawked woman waves at you and laughs like a hyena.

Through a broken wall, you spot a concrete stairwell leading upwards. No idea where it goes, but it's got to be safer than here. You run up the stairs – as quietly as possible, in case the Kannibals give chase.

At the top of two long flights of stairs is another level with broken walls. A pathway's been cleared through the rubble, to a narrow footbridge stretching over the street. Just what you need, except a group of people are blocking the way – they're crouched by a nearby wall, peering down at the street below. They're wearing black and white striped bandanas – the uniform of the Piranha pirate gang, the worst slavers in the city.

Heart pounding, you duck behind a pillar, hoping they haven't noticed you.

No, they're too busy watching the street and arguing.

"How about that boat there?" one grumbles, pointing down. "An adorable family with four little kids and no weapons. Easy pickings. Little kids sell for fifty bucks at the moment – more if they're cute."

"No, we don't want no adorable families, not today. The boss wants an ironclad boat," says another.

"Don't see why. Ironclads have heaps of armed guards. Risky target, very risky. What's he want an ironclad for?"

"How would I know? Sunday afternoon visits to his dear old mum, maybe. Some new special sneaky plan, that's all I've heard. I just do what I'm told, and so should you."

From the shadow of the pillar, you take a longer look. Six Piranhas, wearing harnesses, and with coils of rope at their feet – they must be planning on attacking a boat by abseiling down from the bridge.

The grumbly pirate has a good point – why go to the trouble of attacking an ironclad boat? The only ironclad you know is the *Rusty Rhino*, a cargo steamboat with a well-armed crew who'd have no trouble fighting off half a dozen Piranhas.

From behind you, clattering up the staircase, come two sets of footsteps – probably the Kannibal Krew searching for you.

Pirates in front, pirates behind. Big trouble. Then again, the Kannibal Krew and Piranhas hate each other – that could help you.

It's time to make a decision. Do you:

Make a run for the bridge? **P158**

Or

Stay where you are, and hope the pirates fight each other? **P172**

Make a Run for the Bridge

"Kannibal Krew! Help!" you yell, running towards the footbridge.

Not that you expect the Piranhas to help you on purpose. And they don't – exactly as you'd hoped, they charge at the surprised-looking Kannibals instead.

Perfect. You dash over the narrow bridge, feeling clever.

But as you reach the other side, a foot stretches out and sends you sprawling across a dusty floor.

A dozen more Piranhas surround you. Oh, of course, they were hiding on *both* sides of the bridge. And you've spoiled their ambush. No wonder they're angry.

One of them knocks your Deadline Delivery cap to the floor, and rips your backpack off. "A courier?" He grins nastily. "You're lost, kid. Dangerously lost. This is a bad part of town."

"Grinder's signaling us," says a scarred woman, looking over the bridge. "They got Kannibal Krew trouble."

Most of the Piranhas lose interest in you and dash over the bridge, yelling and waving weapons.

"Kill the kid. We don't want no witnesses," the scarred woman says to the man rummaging in your backpack, then sprints after the others.

The man pulls out the package and reads the label. His nasty grin turns…almost nice. "390 Brine Street? They've sewed me up often enough. It's your lucky day, kid – I won't kill you this time. Get out of here before I change my mind." He tosses you your backpack and package and disappears over the bridge, leaving you alone and confused. Who sewed him up? What's at 390 Brine Street?

Whatever. Those Piranhas could return at any moment, so you run out the door in the opposite wall.

This building's stairwells are mostly blocked or missing, so finding another way out is hard work. Eventually you decide to squeeze through a broken window, trying not to break any more of its jagged glass in case the noise attracts attention.

You make it through with just one long scratch, then notice a bloodstained green plastic card on a lanyard, lying amongst the broken glass on the floor. Looks familiar – where have you seen those cards before? Oh yeah, it's a security pass for day workers going up to the over-city.

On its other side is the name Ortopa Baskirl, whoever he or she is. Or was – that's probably Ortopa Baskirl's blood on it.

You're soon back down on the streets and on the way to Brine Street again, but you keep looking up at the over-city and fingering Ortopa Baskirl's security pass in your pocket. Could you use it yourself? You've always wanted to see the over-city with your own eyes, not just from through a security fence or on television.

Ten minutes later, you're at 390 Brine Street, and deliver the package to some grumpy guy who's in too much of a hurry (or too snooty) to say "hello" or "thank you". You hardly notice, still thinking about the over-city.

A couple of blocks away, you pass one of the long ladders which go up to the over-city. They're fenced off and guarded, of course – over-city people don't want under-city people sneaking up there and getting up to no good. A dozen day workers queue at the ladder's bottom, wearing green security passes just like the one in your pocket.

It's time to make a decision. Do you:

Pretend the security pass is yours, and join the queue of day workers? **P160**

Or

Try to return the security pass? **P169**

Pretend the Security Pass is Yours

You stuff your Deadline Delivery cap into your backpack, slip the security pass lanyard around your neck, and join the line of day workers. A couple of them glance at you, but don't say anything.

As each worker reaches a steel gate at the front of the queue, they swipe their pass past a glowing green light, and the gate says "hello" and the person's name in a cheerful computerized voice, and then lets that person through.

When it's your turn, you swipe your pass the same way, ready to run if alarm bells ring, but the gate just cheerfully says, "Hello, Ortopa Baskirl," and opens. More people are already queuing behind you, so you go through the gate, keeping your head down.

Stairs. Hundreds of stairs, all the way up to the over-city. And at the top, there's another queue at another security gate.

"You're not Ortopa Baskirl," says a voice behind you.

Uh-oh. You turn and see an olive-skinned man with no eyebrows.

"Ortopa's sick today, so I'm doing his job for him," you say. Not a very convincing lie, but it's the best you can think of.

Mister No-Eyebrows raises his non-existent eyebrows. "Really? Strange, coz Ortopa's a woman – we work together. I don't know or care who you are, kid, but you'd better be a hard worker, or else."

"I am a hard worker. Um, working at what?"

He doesn't answer.

The security gate lets you through, and you get your first proper view of the over-city. Everything's shiny and clean, and so bright it hurts your eyes, although maybe that's just because up here the sunlight doesn't have to filter down though security fences. All the over-city people look shiny and clean too, just like on television. They ignore you and the other day workers, as if you're invisible.

Mister No-Eyebrows leads you a few blocks away to a tall building, and you both enter through a narrow side door, after swiping your passes again. He pushes you down a carpeted corridor and through several more doors (swiping passes each time) then into a room full of mirrors and tiles. He hands you a pair of purple gloves and a bucket full of plastic bottles and clean rags. "Okay, show me how hard you can work."

Looking around, you realize this must be a bathroom, although nothing like any in the under-city – down there, you hold your breath and get out as fast as possible, hoping there aren't too many cockroaches and rats in there with you. If you can find a bathroom. This bathroom…well, those shiny things must be taps, but why are there five of them? And why does this place need cleaning anyway? – it's the cleanest room you've ever seen. But he's watching you, so you put on the gloves, then mop and scrub and wipe and polish everything in sight.

"Mmm," he says, unsmiling. "A bit slow, but not bad for a first try. Next."

Next what?

He leads you along a corridor to…another bathroom, like the first except this one is pale pink and has gold taps. Solid gold? Who knows – over-city people are crazy.

"Well, what are you waiting for?" he asks. "We've got eighty-three more to do today."

Eighty-three? Sighing, you pick up your sponge again.

This time he helps, showing you a faster way to mop the floor, and a trick for polishing taps.

Eighty-two to go. The next one is pale blue, with butterflies painted across the ceiling. Pretty, although not much fun to clean.

And so on, bathroom after bathroom after bathroom, with just one short lunch break, hours later – thankfully not in a bathroom.

Mister No-Eyebrows never tells you his name, and calls you "Fake Ortopa". The only things he ever talks about are cleaning-related – stain removal, the best way to polish mirrors, and unblocking clogged drains.

By the end of the day, your hands ache, your back hurts, and you've got a weird itchy rash on your left wrist. Today wasn't what you'd expected from your first visit to the over-city – you now know more than you ever wanted to about fancy bathrooms. All you saw of the rest of the over-city was a few glances out windows.

"Good work today, Fake Ortopa," Mister No-Eyebrows says, as you return to the over-city street level together. "You scrub toilets better than the real Ortopa, and that's what matters to me. Back tomorrow?" He swipes his card.

"Maybe." Is scrubbing toilets better than working as a courier? Depends – are you going to get paid for today, and how much? Or does he love cleaning so much that he does it for free, and expects you do the same?

You swipe your card, the door opens and you walk out, straight into the arms of a burly security guard. "Ortopa Baskirl?" she asks, grabbing your security pass lanyard and almost choking you with it.

"Um, yeah?" you squeak.

She grins like a shark. "Really? Ortopa Baskirl was found floating face-down in an under-city street this morning." She turns to Mister No-Eyebrows. "You. Scram!"

He does.

"I found Ortopa's pass by accident," you babble to the guard. "I don't know anything about her, or her death. It was probably the Piranha gang, but…"

"Shut up." She drags you over to a gleaming dark green luxury car hovering a few inches in the air.

From its open rear window, a well-dressed man smiles at you. "You're in a lot of trouble, kid. Trespassing, possession of stolen property, identity fraud, interfering with murder evidence," he says, counting each point on his fingers. Then he opens the car door. "Or this could be the best day of the rest of your life."

Who is this guy? No matter how much trouble you're in, you don't trust him one bit. No way do you want to get in this car – but the guard just picks you up, tosses you inside then slams the door.

The guard gets into the front seat and the car glides away so silently you wouldn't know it was moving if the street outside wasn't sliding past.

"Relax, kid, enjoy the ride," the man says, still smiling. "I'm Bradley Lime, recruitment specialist for the Avocado Corporation – I'm sure you've heard of us." You shake your head but he doesn't notice and keeps talking. "I've been watching you on security camera footage, deciding what to do with you. Naturally, under-city people try to sneak up here every day. Most of them want to steal something or smash something or hurt someone, or all three. Can't have that now, can we? No, the nice folks up here want peace and quiet, law and order, not a bunch of dirty under-city hooligans running around. But you, you sneaked up here and ...spent the day cleaning bathrooms. Interesting."

Wasn't my idea, you feel like saying, but don't.

Bradley's still smiling like a toothpaste ad. "The Avocado Corporation thinks disadvantaged kids deserve a chance for a successful life here in the over-city, so we're offering you a job as trainee manager. All expenses paid, including food, accommodation, and uniform."

The car stops, next to a forest building – a skyscraper covered in plants and trees and flowers. You've seen them before, looking up from the under-city, but never up close like this.

"You'd be working here, at Avocado Corporation Urban Organic Farm number 29," he continues. "What do you say, kid?"

You don't understand half of what he's said. Some sort of job here in the over-city. That sounds good, but...what's an urban farm? And what does a trainee manager do, and what do they get paid?

It's time to make a decision. Do you:

Take the job, because it has to be better than being a courier? **P164** Or

Say no, and get away from this crazy guy as soon as you can? **P167**

Avocado Corporation

"Okay," you say to Bradley Lime, and try to smile.

But you can't compete with his grin, which just got even wider. "Best of luck, kid."

The guard takes you into the "urban farm" building, through a door labeled *Management Only*, and slams the door shut, leaving you inside. You try the door, but it's locked.

It's a strange room, hot and humid. The walls are thousands of small panes of glass, and through them is nothing but green – endless rows of plants and trees. Oh, the whole building must be full of plants. Yeah, an urban farm, that makes sense now. Places like this must be where farmers grow food for over-city people.

"What do you want?" asks a voice behind you.

Turning, you see a sweaty young woman in a green Avocado Corporation t-shirt.

"Um, hi, I'm your new trainee manager," you say.

"No one tells me anything." She sighs and taps on a tablet computer. "Oh, right. Lucky you. Hi, I'm Marcie, junior assistant manager, welcome to your exciting new career at the Avocado Corporation." Marcie sure doesn't sound excited. "Follow me. I'll get you a t-shirt – they must be worn at all times. Corporate policy. And you'd better watch the New Employees video. Corporate policy."

Over the next few hours, you hear "corporate policy" about a million times from Marcie. Apparently the Avocado Corporation has rules for absolutely everything.

Then it's dinnertime in the Avocado Corporation staff cafeteria. There's plenty of food and it tastes okay, and you eat until you're stuffed. But you don't enjoy it much – sitting at the same table are eleven other trainee managers, and they're the glummest people ever. So far, the only happy Avocado Corporation employee you've met was Bradley Lime. Maybe he wasn't really smiling, maybe he was just showing his teeth. Or maybe it's against corporate policy for trainee managers to smile or laugh.

Marcie looks at her watch. "Evening shift starts in three minutes. Follow me," she tells you.

Maybe now you'll finally find out what a trainee manager does around here.

She takes you up and down stairs and along glass-walled corridors, stopping now and then to check numbers on computer screens – humidity, temperature and so on. Despite the zillion plants on the other side of the glass, you haven't touched one leaf yet. Who's doing the weeding and planting and harvesting? Robots?

Then you see movement through the glass – people trudging along, carrying trowels and baskets. They look even sadder than the trainee managers, and aren't wearing Avocado Corporation t-shirts. Hey, one of them is Mac, the owner of Mac's Greasy Spoon back at Ivory Tower! What's he doing here? Behind them swaggers a man wearing a Piranha black and white striped bandana and carrying a stun-gun in his meaty hand.

All of a sudden, everything makes horrible sense. "They're slave workers, aren't they? The Piranha gang supplies the Avocado Corporation with slaves to do the farm work."

Marcie rolls her eyes. "Duh! This farm has to supply nine thousand lettuces and three thousand cucumbers by 4 am tomorrow morning. Who do you think's going to do all that work? Better them than us. Behave yourself, or you'll end up as one of them – that's corporate policy."

I'm sorry, this part of your story is over. You've made it up to the over-city, discovered the Avocado Corporation's terrible secret and what happens to the Piranha gang's slaves.

Working as a trainee manager is going to be awful, no matter how much they feed you and pay you – you don't want to have anything to do with slavery.

Life was so much simpler back in the under-city – if only you hadn't taken that security pass...

It's time to make a decision. Do you:

Go to the great big list of choices? **P377**

Or

Go back to the beginning and try another path? **P105**

Get Away from Bradley Lime

"Thanks anyway, but I don't think I'd be a good trainee manager," you tell Bradley politely.

His smile disappears. "I guess you're not so smart after all."

The guard opens the car door, and she drags you over to the urban farm building. You struggle, but she's too strong. Without a word, she shoves you through a door labeled *Staff Only*, then slams it shut, leaving you inside.

You try the door, but it's locked.

What is this place? There are plants absolutely everywhere, in pots and on racks along the walls. Some are vegetables and fruits, but others you don't recognize. The air is hot and humid. Bright too – the walls are thousands of small panes of frosted glass. Above, instead of a ceiling, there's a layer of steel mesh, and above that, more plants. Hmm, maybe the whole building's nothing but plants on every level? Yeah, an urban farm, that makes sense now. Places like this must be where farmers grow food for over-city people.

But why did the guard put you here? Will you be forced to become a trainee manager after all?

From behind a tree walks Mac, the owner of Mac's Greasy Spoon back at Ivory Tower. You stare at each other in surprise.

"So they got you too, huh?" he asks. "At least you're alive – we lost some good people today."

"What are you talking about? What are you doing up here, Mac?"

"What are *you* talking about?"

"What?"

"Stop saying 'what'. How did you get here, kid? Weren't you caught in the raid with the rest of us?"

"What raid?"

"You really don't know?" He sighs. "The Piranhas hijacked an ironclad boat and rammed one of Big Pig's Tollgates. They grabbed a hundred or so people, killing anyone who resisted, then brought us back here."

Oh no. You overheard those Piranhas talking about hijacking an ironclad – they must have wanted it for the raid.

He frowns. "So how did you end up here?"

"Um, well, pirates were involved, but…it's a long story. Believe it or not, I've spent most of today cleaning over-city toilets."

"Back to work, lazy scum," yells a sour-faced woman holding a whip. She has a black and white striped bandana around her neck.

"What are Piranhas doing up here in the over-city?" you whisper to Mac as you follow him down a long tree-lined passage.

"The Piranhas supply slave labor to the Avocado Corporation, of course. You don't think over-city people dirty their own fingers weeding lettuces and picking tomatoes, do you?"

"Maybe we could smash a window and escape?"

He snorts. "Look at those little windows, surrounded by those solid steel window frames. This is a prison, and there's no escape. We're slaves, kid. For the rest of our lives."

I'm sorry, this part of your story is over. Trusting Bradley Lime was a big mistake – clearly, the over-city's just as dangerous as back in the under-city. What might have happened if you'd stayed down there? Or escaped the pirates earlier? Or not gone through the secret tunnel at all?

It's time to make a decision. Do you:

Go to the great big list of choices? **P377**

Or

Go back to the beginning and try another path? **P105**

Return the Security Pass

You walk up to the queuing people, holding up the green security pass. "Excuse me, does anyone know Ortopa Baskirl?"

Most of them ignore you, except an olive-skinned man with no eyebrows, who grabs the security pass. "Where'd you nick this from?"

What? "I didn't, I found it."

"Where's Ortopa?"

"How would I know?"

He turns to at the queue of people. "Anyone seen Ortopa today?"

While he's distracted, you run, ignoring his yelling and swearing, hoping he doesn't chase after you. Luckily, he doesn't. He probably doesn't want to be late for work – workers at the front of the queue have started climbing the ladder up to the over-city.

Okay, that's far too much excitement for one day – time to head back to Deadline Delivery for your next delivery job.

A few blocks from the Tollgate, you realize someone's following you. Two someones, in fact. Big guys. Maybe pirates, maybe muggers.

You stop, take off your backpack, turn it upside down and shake it to show there's nothing inside, hoping they'll give up once they know you're not carrying anything worth stealing.

Doesn't work – they're still following you.

At the next corner, you clatter over a bridge of floating oil drums and run for a nearby alley.

They follow. As you emerge on the street at the other end of the alley, you can see the Tollgate in the distance. Safety. Except that between you and the Tollgate is a speedboat, which roars into life when the crew see you. Muggers, slavers, or cannibals, whoever they are – you're surrounded.

Your only hope is to cross the road, and get to that brick building on the other side of the water. It has a narrow hole in its side wall, too tight for most adults to get through – a great escape route. If you can get to it.

Unfortunately, there are no bridges on this block, and you can't swim, even your dog-paddling is terrible. The speedboat will be here in a minute, tops.

Just as you think things can't get worse, there's barking and growling behind you.

It's those wild dogs again, only a few yards away, and leading them is the huge German Shepherd with a ripped left ear. The two guys in the alley see the dogs, stop and keep their distance.

And that's when you remember the wrapped slice of meatloaf in your pocket, left over from breakfast. You toss it to the German Shepherd, which gobbles it down then licks your face while you scratch behind its ears.

"Help me?" you beg. "Over the road? Please?"

It's a smart dog – it's already spotted the speedboat, and the men in the alley. But is it smart enough to understand you? And does it want to help you?

"Help!" you yell, leap into the water, and dog-paddle for your life. You swallow water and choke, expecting to drown. But suddenly there's wet fur under your hands, and the big dog is towing you through the water to the other side of the street.

"Thank you," you say, as you squeeze through the hole in the brick wall, with seconds to spare.

The dogs and the people on the boat growl at each other for a few seconds, then the boat roars away.

"Thank you," you repeat, reaching back through the hole and patting the German Shepherd. "Double, no, triple meatloaf for you tomorrow."

Congratulations, this part of your story is over. You're wet and tired and late getting back to Deadline delivery, but you've survived a dangerous day.

What might have happened up in the over-city? Or if you'd done things differently around the Kannibal Krew and the Piranhas?

It's time to make a decision. Do you:

Go to the great big list of choices? **P377**

Or

Go back to the beginning and try another path? **P105**

Hope the Pirates Fight Each Other

The two Kannibal Krew reach the top of the stairs and run past the pillar you're hiding behind. Then they see the Piranhas, and stop so quickly that one crashes into the other. The Piranhas turn, equally surprised.

While both groups of pirates yell at each other, you sneak back down the way you came, unnoticed.

Brilliant.

But you soon hear running and raised voices behind you. Oh, of course, the outnumbered Kannibals are trying to escape down the same stairs you're on, and the Piranhas are chasing them.

Not so brilliant.

You leap down the stairs, two at a time, and slip, landing heavily at the bottom. Limping, you stagger past the Kannibals' red speedboat and hide behind an ancient fridge half-covered in broken bricks. Not much of a hiding place, but hopefully the pirates are more interested in each other than you. In the distance, the old woman's cabbage boat chugs away as fast as it can.

Seconds later, the two Kannibals dash out and leap onto their speedboat. The skull-faced man pushes the boat out into the water with a pole, while the Mohawked woman starts the engine. Or tries to – there's a whirring noise but nothing more. The man tries to start the engine too, but still nothing. They loudly blame each other. Hmm, you can see something they can't – wet handprints on the boat's stern, as if someone's been there in the last few minutes. Maybe they did something to the engine? But who?

Piranhas run out onto the sidewalk and screech to a halt – the boat is now several yards away from the sidewalk edge, probably too far to jump. One Piranha tries anyway, but instead lands in the muddy water with a huge splash. He coughs and curses, then dogpaddles through the floating trash towards the boat.

Abruptly, he vanishes under the surface. Didn't look like a dive, more like he was pulled down. By what? Froggies? The pirates stare at the water, as mystified as you are. Then they start yelling threats and throwing things at each other again.

Fine. So long as they're not yelling and throwing things at you.

Your left foot hurts, but you limp away.

Ahead is a rickety wooden sidewalk, its planks partially covered with flattened cardboard cartons. Or so you think, until you step straight through cardboard into thin air, and fall into the dirty water below. Weighed down by your backpack, shoes and clothes, you slowly sink.

An octopus swims through the murk and pulls off your backpack. No, impossible. Must be a hallucination – you remember reading somewhere that people see all sorts of impossible things when they're close to dying. The octopus somehow grows two brown arms and a body with green webbed feet. No, it's an octopus eating someone head first. No, that doesn't make sense either.

The creature drags you away, then pushes you up to the surface. You gasp for breath, coughing and spluttering and holding onto what feels like a rotting plank. Thick mud squishes between your knees, and there's nothing under your feet. The only light comes from one side. Where is this?

You cough again, and retch.

"Shut up," says the octopus. Oh, it's a girl, wearing a rubbery octopus mask over her head. She must be a froggy, yeah, that would explain the webbed feet too. Drowning would have been preferable, if half the stories about froggies are true. Worse than cannibals, people say.

She holds your plastic-wrapped package. With her other hand, she points a rusty harpoon at you. "Hate you." She points towards the light. "Hate them more."

You peer out, and realize you're under a sidewalk – the same sidewalk you were standing on before. On the other side of the street, the pirates are still shouting, but no longer at each other.

Grappling hooks and ropes have capsized the red speedboat. The Mohawked woman is shrieking and splashing somewhere in the water. There's no sign of the skull-faced man. Two Piranhas have ropes lassoed around their bodies and are being slowly pulled into the water, despite the other Piranhas trying to pull them back or cut the ropes. Some Piranhas are throwing bricks and rubble into the water, as if desperately hoping to hit someone or something.

As you watch, a nearby patch of floating trash rises a few inches above the surface and makes a kerchink noise. Something shoots out and hits a Piranha, who screams and falls to the sidewalk, next to the unmoving body of another pirate.

You hate pirates too, but not as much as these froggies do.

Out of the water next to you rises another pile of trash, with a man's mustachioed face underneath. (Unless it's a woman with a moustache – you're not going to ask.) He and the octopus girl peer at your delivery package and argue in loud whispers, glancing at you now and then. "Dry skins not for fungus deciding," he insists. "Verdigris afterwards delivery. Now fungus."

Or something like that – apparently froggies talk a special froggy language, and in a special froggy accent.

The mustachioed man disappears back under the water.

The octopus girl sighs, mutters to herself, and turns towards you. She's still holding that harpoon – and your package.

"That's not yours," you protest.

"Not yours either," she snarls, and shoves it back at you. Then she swims away, dragging you along by your shirt collar.

"I can't swim," you splutter, flopping around on your back, trying to breathe, trying to hold on to the package.

"True that." She takes you mostly under the shadow of sidewalks and buildings, and sometimes under piles of floating trash to cross streets. And once through a dark tunnel that seems to go right under a building from one street to the next. You try to keep track of the passing streets but are soon completely lost – the whole city looks different from down here.

At last she stops, by a steel ladder. The water's only waist-deep here, so you stand up. Above is a thick metal grate, with "390" scrawled next to it in orange spray-paint. Through the grate you can see part of a fluorescent light tube and a white ceiling.

"Hello, Chopper," she calls up.

A huge grey dog – presumably Chopper – looks down through the grate, and barks until a woman comes over and looks down too. She's wearing a white coat, a bulletproof vest, and a puzzled look.

"Delivery, 390 Brine," says the octopus girl.

This is Brine Street? You hold up the package, hoping the plastic wrapping hasn't leaked.

The woman frowns, looking at your cap. "Miss Betty's hiring froggies now?"

"I'm not a froggy," you protest.

"True that," agrees the girl.

The woman shrugs, unlocks the grate and swings it open. The girl pushes you up the ladder.

At the top is the whitest, cleanest room you've ever seen. What's that half-flower half-chemical smell?

Chopper stares at you, growling softly. He has no back legs, just two wheels held on with a frame of rods and straps. Even so, you're pretty sure he could still eat you alive if he wanted to, so you stay on the ladder, ready to drop back down if necessary.

The woman takes the package, slits it open and pulls out some finger-sized bottles. What would anyone put in bottles that small?

Chopper sniffs your trousers. Oh, your leftover meatloaf from breakfast. You pull the sodden bag from your pocket. What a yucky mess. "It's all yours, Chopper."

He swallows the lot in seconds, licks the bag, then licks your face.

"Okay, that's fine, thanks." The woman shows you a tablet screen displaying the Deadline Delivery web site, and presses the green Delivery Received icon. "Bye."

Just as you're wondering whether to try to escape up here, the octopus girl grabs your ankle and motions you back down with her harpoon.

"Um, bye." As you clamber down the ladder, the grate's closed and locked above you. "What is that place?" you ask the girl.

"Medical clinic. Obvious. No more nice – I save you only for package. Clinic good to froggies."

Huh? She saved you from drowning only because the package was for this clinic? If the package is that important, why not kill you and deliver it herself?

"Now verdigris," she says, grabs you by your shirt collar again and swims away again.

Verdigris? The mustachioed man said something about that too. Isn't verdigris the bluey-greeny stain you see on old copper and brass? What on earth is she talking about? Stupid froggies.

Perhaps ten minutes later, you arrive at a huge gloomy room with white tiled walls, balconies of seats on both sides and strange tall ladders at one end…oh, it's an indoor swimming pool, like you've seen in photos from the olden days. Why people back then needed a special room just for swimming, you don't know.

No-one's been swimming here since the city flooded. The tiles are lined with grimy horizontal tide marks – this whole room must flood every high tide. The pool is half-full of muddy water, and its far end has a large jagged hole, with daylight streaming in through it. More murky light filters in through dirty frosted glass windows along the room's walls.

Hundreds of froggies crowd the balconies above. To your surprise, none of them have claws, or fangs, or green skin, or webbed feet, like in the stories – they're just ordinary people. Except for their clothes, which are made from recycled…stuff, everything from plastic bags to metal bits to electrical cables. Lots of them wear hats or masks covered in trash – as disguises, presumably – and some wear goggles and web-toed flippers, also made from trash.

They all talk weird, like the octopus girl. But by listening hard, you realize some important stuff. Queen Verdigris is the name of their boss, a tall pale woman sitting on a deckchair on a tiny platform at the top of the tallest ladder, wearing a brass helmet from an old-fashioned diving suit. Fungus is the name of the girl in the octopus mask. "Dry-skins" is what they call anyone who isn't a froggy – under-city people, pirates, over-city people, even you. Not that you're dry at the moment.

Most importantly, the froggies are arguing about you. About whether to kill you.

"Dry-skin has seen too much froggy secrets," says one, and lots of froggies nod.

"Dry-skin run from pirates, just like us, sympathy," another says, and lots of froggies nod at that too.

"Dry-skin deliver for Brine Street clinic," Fungus points out. Is she trying to help you?

After a while, Queen Verdigris bangs on her ladder. Everyone quietens down and looks up at her expectantly. "Crocodile Doom," she announces in a gravelly voice.

A few people grumble, including Fungus, but most of them nod and shout, "Crocodile Doom!"

They're going to feed you to crocodiles? Is this their idea of fun? Maybe they don't have television down here.

Fungus shakes her head and mutters to herself, then pushes you into the pool.

The water's less than waist-deep, and not too cold. Too muddy to see what's below. As you stand, something crunches under your left foot and something else wriggles under your right foot.

Now what? Froggies with long spears are watching you from the pool edges, so clearly there's no point in trying to climb out of the pool. Try to escape out the hole in the far end of the pool? Seems too easy. Maybe it's a trap, and a hundred hungry crocodiles are hiding under the water, waiting. Or maybe this is all some stupid froggy joke, and someone wearing a crocodile mask will jump out and yell "Boo!"

and everyone will laugh. Probably not though.

"Doom!" chant the froggies. "Doom! Doom!" Over and over again.

Something moves under the water, creating a line of ripples heading in your direction.

The froggies see the ripples too, and cheer.

"Doom! Doom!" chant a line of little froggy kids at the front row of a balcony, stomping their feet.

You're scared, but staying here and waiting to die seems pointless. So you start wading across the pool, trying not to trip on the slimy debris under your feet, and trying not to splash too much. Doesn't work though – the ripples change direction to follow you. For just a moment, something long and scaly breaks the surface then submerges again.

Above, the shouting and stomping get louder and louder. Then something heavy screeches and snaps, someone screams, and the froggies start shouting and pointing. You look up and see a balcony's partly collapsed, probably from all that foot stomping. From a broken guard rail, a little froggy kid is dangling down over the pool.

It's time to make a decision, and fast. Do you:

Run for the hole in the far wall while everyone's distracted? **P198**

Or

Help the froggy kid? **P179**

Help the Froggy Kid

Trying to ignore the ripple from the approaching crocodile, you splash over to the broken balcony, and are just in time to catch the froggy kid as he screams and falls.

Ropes wrap around you both and you're dragged up into the air together. Just in time – moments later, a huge crocodile bursts out of the water, its long jaws snapping inches from your feet.

Hands pull you both up to a safer part of the balcony. Around you, dozens of voices yell and give advice and bicker all at the same time.

"Shut up!" Fungus shouts.

Everyone does. There's silence, except for the crocodile still snapping its jaws and thrashing around below, probably wondering where its lunch has gone, and the little froggy kid, crying in Fungus's arms.

"Why?" she demands, glaring at you. "Why help my bro Bucket?"

That's her little brother? What sort of name's Bucket? Although admittedly, it's no weirder than the name Fungus.

"I couldn't…do nothing and let a little kid get eaten alive," you say.

Bucket leans over and hugs you.

Queen Verdigris bangs on her ladder, and points at you. "Froggy friend," she announces.

Everyone cheers, and starts chanting, "Froggy friend," over and over. These froggies sure do like their chanting. There's no more foot stomping though, and everyone's keeping away from the balcony edges.

What "froggy friend" means, you're not sure, but it must be something good, coz everyone's smiling and no one's trying to feed you to crocodiles any more.

"Lunch," Queen Verdigris announces.

Everyone cheers again. For a horrible moment, you think maybe she means that you'll *be* their lunch, but they take you to a nearby room full of long tables and wonderful foody smells, and the queen insists you sit next to her. Fungus and Bucket sit on your other side, and Bucket gives you lots of shy smiles.

The food is…weird, like everything else down here, but it tastes as good as it smells, even if you can't tell what some of it is.

"Good, yes?" Queen Verdigris asks.

"It's the best meal I've had in months, your majesty," you say, and she looks pleased.

You gradually get used to their odd accent and language. They're talking about ordinary things – fishing, growing vegetables, recycling, playing sport, keeping safe, finding clean water and food. Sounds like life is even tougher for froggies than people like you, because absolutely everyone picks on froggies – not just pirates, but most under-city people too. You feel guilty, remembering the horrible gossip you'd heard and believed about froggies – almost none of it was true.

To be honest, now that the froggies have stopped trying to feed you to the crocodiles, they seem nicer than most under-city people you've known. They're like one huge family, all looking after each other. Not like most dry-skins.

"You froggy friend now," says Queen Verdigris. "We like you. So stay, be one of us, yes?"

Is she serious? "Become a froggy? Forever?" Part of their family?

She nods. Fungus and Bucket gaze at you, grinning.

It's time to make a decision. Do you:

Become a froggy? **P181**

Or

Stay a courier, and return to Deadline Delivery? **P191**

Become a Froggy

"Yes, I want to be a froggy." Your voice shakes a little. You won't be sorry to never see Deadline Delivery again (even though Miss Betty owes you ten dollars for the Brine Street clinic delivery), but giving up your old life is scary. What if this is a terrible mistake?

Froggies hug you and shake your hand.

"Fungus, find new froggy a job," Queen Verdigris orders.

Fungus nods. So does Bucket, even though no one asked him.

After lunch, they take you along dozens of gloomy tunnels and passageways, sometimes walking or wading, sometimes swimming and towing you. "Careful not get lost," Fungus says. "Tide rising now, some tunnels soon flood."

"I'm already lost, and I can't swim."

"We teach you," Bucket says, and Fungus nods.

Eventually they stop, in a huge hall that smells like a giant fart. There are tanks and pipes everywhere, and pulleys and pistons turning enormous wheels, and dozens of froggies busy on a long raised platform.

"Crabb Street sewage treatment plant," Fungus says proudly. "Filter sewer for city south suburbs."

"Mmm," you reply, trying to hold your breath.

"Stinky water down from over-city," Bucket explains, pointing to a row of pipes. "Clean water up to over-city." He points to another row of pipes.

They take you over to the long raised platform, where froggies are pushing giant sieves through a long tank of what Bucket calls "stinky water", and occasionally pulling out things like bottles and rags and rusty cans.

"Recycling," Fungus says. "Many things found, sometimes valuable – jewelry, phones, coins. We sell back to over-city."

You hope they wash the recycled stuff really, really well.

"And sell stinky sludge back to over-city for fertilizer," adds

Bucket, who seems to be an expert on stinky stuff.

Perhaps they can see you're not too impressed by sewage. They take you up and down more tunnels and corridors and streets for what seems like an hour. The farty smell is replaced by a fishy smell, getting stronger.

In the distance, at the end of a wide tunnel, you see bright light and water. Lots of water. More water than you've ever seen before. And the fishiest smell you've ever smelled before.

You reach the end of the tunnel, stop on a large platform and gaze out at the sea. Obviously, this is exactly the same sea which flows through the city streets. But you've never seen it like this before, with no buildings or security fences in the way, just endless waves, all the way to the horizon, under the biggest, emptiest sky ever.

To one side of the platform is a long boat full of glittering fish. On board is a golden-skinned woman with tiger stripe tattoos on her face. She frowns up at you.

"Move," snarls a voice beside you. Four froggies push trolleys with crates full of fish past you and down the tunnel. That looks like hard work.

Fungus turns to you and crosses her arms. Bucket copies her. "Which job? Sewage or fish?" she asks.

Not much of a choice. What about exciting jobs, like feeding the crocodiles, or ambushing pirates? Anyway, it's time to make a decision. Do you:

Work at the sewage treatment plant? **P183**

Or

Work at the fishery? **P186**

Sewage Treatment

"Sewage," you say glumly. You're not looking forward to working in that stinky sewage treatment plant, but you feel unsafe here by the sea – there's just…too much water.

After a few days working at the sewage treatment plant, you hardly notice the smell any more. Or maybe your nose has stopped working.

Anyway, the work's okay. One day you find seven one-dollar coins in your sludge sieve – it's amazing what over-city people lose down drains.

There's more to the job than just sieving sludge. You also learn how to clean tanks and pipes, to oil pistons and scrape filters, and to shovel dried sludge (which luckily smells better than wet sludge) into sacks labeled "All-Natural Organic Fertilizer".

At night, whenever the tide is right, you join groups of froggies outside, walking through the watery streets on long stilts, to collect recyclable bottles, cans and plastic. At first, you feel silly disguising yourself in a trash suit and hiding in the water whenever dry-skins walk by, but you soon start enjoying being a sneaky froggy. And it's fun helping the others scare away any dry-skins who get too close to the maze of froggy tunnels.

Fungus and Bucket teach you to swim. You're still terrible at it, but less terrible than before, and getting better every day – or so they claim.

Fog, the sewage treatment plant manager, says you're getting better at sieving sludge too.

Two weeks later, you spot something glinting in the sludge tank. Jewelry perhaps? Someone found a wedding ring down here last month. You grab at the glint with your sieve.

Wow. It's jewelry alright – a golden necklace, glittering with sparkly gemstones.

"Shiny," says everyone.

It sure is. But is it real gold and real gems?

Fog washes the necklace, examines it carefully, and then makes half a dozen phone calls. "Real," he tells you. "Worth fortune. Over-city owner offering return reward. Huge reward. Take now to Queen Verdigris."

You do.

"So pretty," the queen says with a sigh, holding the necklace up to the light. "Shame we can't keep."

"Yes, your majesty." You know the froggies never keep found valuables – that would be stealing, and would make froggies no better than pirates. But there's nothing wrong with claiming a reward. Even a huge reward.

"What to do with shiny reward? What you think?"

"Me, your majesty?"

"Yes, you find, so what you think, what to do? Maybe I agree, maybe not, but tell me even so."

"Well, um, I've only been a froggy for a few weeks, but, um, I was wondering…"

"Yes, yes?"

"Why don't we start a froggy courier business? We know a million routes around the city that dry-skins don't, and I reckon we could deliver stuff faster than anyone else. We'd make money, and…well, people might start treating froggies better if they knew we weren't monsters, just ordinary people making an honest living."

"Hmm," she says. "Hmm, hmm, hmm."

That afternoon, there's a meeting in the swimming pool room, and everyone else says "hmm" and argues and complains and disagrees. After an hour or so, they mostly agree that a froggy courier business is a good idea.

There's only one problem – other than you, no one's brave enough to be a courier.

But then Fungus stands up. "I be courier too." She turns to you. "If you teach me."

"And me," Bucket insists, sticking his bottom lip out.

He's far too young, you almost say. But then again, he's a far better swimmer than you, and can run faster than a hungry rat, so why not?

"Sure," you say. "Let's do it."

Congratulations, this part of your story is over. You've survived pirates and crocodiles and found a new life for yourself. And now, starting a courier business could change the lives of your new froggy family.

Things could have turned out very differently if you'd made different decisions. Maybe better, maybe worse.

It's time to make a decision. Do you:

Go to the great big list of choices? **P377**

Or

Go back to the beginning and try another path? **P105**

Fish

"Fish," you say glumly. All those fish smell really…fishy, but working here sounds (and smells) better than stinky sewage.

"New worker for you, Tiger Lily," Fungus tells the woman with tiger-stripe tattoos, then she and Bucket just walk off and leave you there.

From the fishing boat, Tiger Lily frowns at you again. "Can you swim, kid?" She has a strange accent.

"Not really, ma'am. Not yet."

"Call me captain, not ma'am. Can you catch fish?"

"No, captain. Well, I once found a small fish in my shirt after falling into the water – does that count?"

She rolls her eyes. "Can you push a trolley?"

"Not far, if it's full of crates of fish."

"Ever been to sea?"

"This is the first time I've even seen the open sea."

Some of the fishing boat's crew snigger.

Captain Tiger Lily rolls her eyes and gives a loud sigh. "Alright, get down here and help unload these fish."

"Captain, why don't you talk funny like the other froggies?"

More sniggering from the crew.

The captain glares at you. "What a nosy child. This is how everyone talked back in the over-city, where I was born."

"You left the over-city to become a froggy? Why?"

"Less talking and lift that fish crate, kid."

"Yes, captain."

After the crates have been unloaded and sent down the tunnel on trolleys, the crew do mysterious things with ropes and nets and sails, while you try to stay out of their way. Then the boat starts swaying and rocking and you realize it's moving, heading out to sea. Looking back, the city gets smaller and smaller. Will you ever see it again?

A wrinkled crewman claps you on the shoulder. "Feeling seasick yet, kid?" he asks cheerfully. "I still remember my first boat trip – I spent the whole time leaning over the railing, throwing up and groaning and wanting to die." He looks around at the other crew with a grin. "Two dollars says the kid will throw up in the next ten minutes!"

The crew laugh, and make complicated bets on how soon you'll throw up and how often.

The captain doesn't join in the laughter or the gambling, but she is watching you carefully.

This must be a test – if you fail, she'll probably send you to the sewage treatment plant. So you clutch a handrail, trying to ignore your lurching stomach, and wishing you hadn't eaten so much lunch. Closing your eyes doesn't help, and looking at the boat's deck makes it worse. Staring at the horizon helps you feel a little better.

Perhaps half an hour later, the sails are lowered, and the boat slows and stops in the middle of empty sea. To everyone's surprise, especially yours, you haven't thrown up even once.

"Well done, kid," says the wrinkled crewman, grinning even though he's lost his bet. "Perhaps we'll make a sailor out of you after all."

Lots of money changes hands. No one seems annoyed at you.

You spot fins approaching the boat. "Sharks!" you shout.

Everyone roars with laughter.

Even the captain smiles. "They're dolphins, our fishing partners."

Several dolphins stick their heads out of the water and they laugh at you too – well, not really, but that's what it looks and sounds like.

The captain whistles at the dolphins. They click and whistle back – they're talking! – then race away.

She shouts orders to the crew.

In the distance, the dolphins are returning.

"Wait," orders the captain, watching them through binoculars. "Wait…wait…ready…now!"

The crew launch a huge spring-powered net over the waves. It falls just in front of the dolphins, and the water fills with furious splashing from fish caught in the net.

As the captain shouts orders, everyone hauls the net in, even you. Dozens of ropes have to be pulled and tightened in just the right order. At just the wrong moment, you pull on the wrong rope and hundreds of fish spill from the net. The dolphins snap them up.

The captain bares her teeth and growls at you, looking more like a tiger than ever.

"Sorry," you mumble.

"The dolphins deserve their share," she snaps. "But not quite that much."

Desperate not to make any more mistakes, you watch and listen carefully, and do whatever anyone tells you. It's especially hard because the bits of the boat have such weird names, like the halyard – the line that raises and lowers the sail. And the boom – the horizontal pole at the bottom of the sail, that's nearly knocked you on the head twice already.

On the voyage back to the city, you don't make any more embarrassing mistakes or throw up. Sailing's cooler than you'd expected.

But during unloading back at the dock, you drop and nearly spill a crate of fish.

Captain Tiger Lily glares at you again. "See you tomorrow, 6AM," is all she says.

Tomorrow? So she wants you back, and you won't be sent to the sewage treatment plant? Yay!

Weeks go by. You go out fishing most days. Soon you can name all the boat's weird bits, know how to tie half a dozen different knots, can tack and jibe and trim as well as any of the crew, and duck under a swinging boom without even thinking about it. Sailing's hard work, even harder than being a courier, but the best fun ever.

Except for fish. Not the smell, you're used to that. But they're so slimy and slippery and wiggly and...fishy. You're always dropping them, or stepping on them, or tangling the fishing net, or doing something wrong. Every time, the captain rolls her eyes. Or sighs. Or both.

Most evenings, you're exhausted, but go for swimming lessons with Fungus and Bucket whenever they offer – a real sailor needs to be able to swim.

One morning at the dock, you see the captain talking with Queen Verdigris. They see you watching them, and turn away. If the queen's involved, this must be something serious. What if she decides you can't be a sailor anymore? Or worse, what if you can't even be a froggy?

They're walking over to you. Uh-oh.

"Would you like to hear a secret?" Tiger Lily asks you. "I hate fish. I hate catching them, hate their smell, don't even like eating them. Well, except for Swab's fish curry, but Swab can make anything taste good. So then why, you may ask, did I leave the over-city to come down here and captain a smelly old fishing boat?"

Good question, but you stay quiet, hoping she'll say more.

"Because I love sailboats," she continues. "I've loved them since I was a small child, staring out to the sea from the window in our thirty-ninth floor apartment." She points up to the over-city towers. "I gave up everything to sail. But even so, I wish there was more to froggy sailing than fishing. Don't you?"

You nod. "Sailing's like flying on the water."

She grins. "Yeah, you get it too. I could see that on your first day. Ever heard of Oasis?"

"The magical island where there's no over-city and no pirates, and froggies can live in peace and safety? That's Bucket's favorite bedtime story."

Queen Verdigris gives a mysterious smile. "More than bedtime story."

"What? Oasis is real?"

"Maybe," Tiger Lily says. "I've collected all the Oasis stories I've ever heard, and half of them contradict each other. But still, I reckon

Oasis is worth looking for. And if it doesn't exist, perhaps we'll find another island to turn into Oasis. So, I'm looking for brave sailors to join my crew."

"Me?"

Queen Verdigris laughs. "Yes, you. Why else we talking, huh?"

"It'll be dangerous," Tiger Lily warns you. "We may never return."

"Living here's dangerous too. I'm in."

It's not quite that simple. Queen Verdigris has bought Tiger Lily a boat – the Seahorse, named after an olden-days animal that could run underwater, or so Fungus say – but the Seahorse is old and leaks and needs lots of repairs. There are a dozen more crew to choose, and food and water and tools and weapons and a million other things to organize for the voyage.

But somehow everything gets done. A month later, you and Tiger Lily and the rest of the crew board the Seahorse, watched by nearly every froggy in the city. Bucket's crying because he wanted to come on the voyage too. You wave goodbye to everyone, knowing you'll miss them, wondering if you'll ever see them again. Or the city.

"Cast off. Make sail," orders Tiger Lily.

"Aye, captain." Blinking back tears, you turn to face the oncoming sea, and adventure.

Congratulations, this part of your story is over – who knows what the future will hold? And what might have happened if you'd made different decisions? Could you have ended up in the over-city? Or in the clutches of pirates?

It's time to make a decision. Do you:

Go to the great big list of choices? **P377**

Or

Go back to the beginning and try another path? **P105**

Return to Deadline Delivery

"Thanks, but I have to get back to my job," you tell Queen Verdigris. Not that it's much of a job. "But…I'd really like to visit again some time. If you'll let me."

She smiles. "You froggy friend forever."

After lunch, Fungus and Bucket tow you back to Nori Road near Ivory Tower, using a special secret froggy route that goes right under Big Pig's Wall – no toll fee to pay, yay!

Bucket's only half your age, but he can swim like…um, a frog.

"I wish I could swim," you tell him. Working as a courier would be so much easier if you could use secret froggy routes.

"We teach you," Bucket says, and Fungus nods.

You all say goodbye. A few minutes later, you're back at Deadline Delivery.

Miss Betty scowls at you. "You're late."

Late? "I was attacked by Kannibal Krew, Piranhas, and a crocodile!" And by froggies too, sort of…but not really. You're not going to say anything bad about the froggies.

"No excuses!" She counts out eight one-dollar coins.

"Eight? You said the job paid ten dollars."

She gives a sour grin and points to your dripping cap. "Minus two dollars – Wet Uniform fee."

So unfair. Maybe you should've become a froggy. Bet no one makes them wear stupid caps or pay stupid fees.

Miss Betty drops a long blue box on the counter. "Urgent delivery, Crabb Street. Pays nine bucks."

You sigh, nod, and take the box.

The steel door squeaks and starts to close, and you hurry out. Miss Betty doesn't say goodbye. She never does.

Congratulations, this part of your story is over. You have learned the truth about the froggies, and made new friends. Things could have happened very differently – you might have ended up in the over-city, or as a pirate slave, or rich, or broke, or with a different job. Or eaten by crocodiles.

It's time to make a decision. Do you:

Go to the great big list of choices? **P377**

Or

Go back to the beginning and try another path? **P105**

Become the Clinic Courier

Doctor Hurst was right – working as courier for Community Medical Clinic has been really hard work, and some days it's just as dangerous as your old job. But every day, you're thankful there's no more Deadline Delivery and no more Miss Betty. Never again.

The clinic feeds you, and pays you – pays you well. And they give you free treatment for gun wounds, rat bites, and plague mold.

On the downside, they also make you shower every single week, whether you need it or not.

You don't mind…too much.

Congratulations, this part of your story is over. You have a brand new life, and who knows where it might lead. What might have happened if you'd never taken that ride on the cabbage boat? Or not gone through the secret tunnel at all?

It's time to make a decision. Do you:

Go to the great big list of choices and pick a chapter? **P377**
Or
Go back to the beginning and try another path? **P105**

Run from the Kannibals

You twist out of the old man's grasp and sprint past the slowing speedboat.

You'll be a goner as soon as that speedboat has time to change direction and follow you, but maybe you can get out of sight before that happens, and before the old man can chase you down.

Diving through the next doorway, you race down a short alley, then up a tall fire escape ladder.

Bad mistake. Every footstep clangs on the steel. Now he'll know exactly where you are.

Sure enough, you soon hear him at the bottom of the ladder, grunting and swearing.

At the top of the ladder is a mossy brick wall with a small window, its glass long gone.

No other exit, except a thirty-foot drop onto concrete. You're trapped. Unless you can squeeze through the window? Yeah, the pirates are bigger than you and won't be able to follow. Unless they send that scary baby in after you, ha ha.

You push your backpack through the window, then follow it. Your head and shoulders get through ok, just, but then your hips get stuck. The old man's footsteps on the ladder are getting louder – he must be close to the top. No way do you want to die halfway through a window, pirates eating you from the toes up.

Desperately, you wiggle your hips. Something rips and you're through. Back on your feet, you grab the backpack and run, run, run, ignoring the old man yelling that you're a "crazy kid".

You keep running, sometimes aiming for Tollgate and safety, but mostly at random, until your lungs shudder and legs shake and you fall to the floor of a moldy-walled walkway.

Lying there, gasping, you suddenly realize what ripped earlier – your trouser pocket with all your money. It's all gone. Every last coin.

How will you get through Tollgate now?

Once you get your breath back, you work out where you are – four blocks from Tollgate – and carefully make your way there, because maybe you're still being followed. But the sidewalks are more crowded with people around here, and there's safety in numbers – or at least a better chance of someone raising the alarm if pirates are spotted.

And then you wait.

Hoping you'll see someone you know, someone who'll loan you a dollar.

You don't.

Hoping someone will feel sorry for your sad face, ripped clothes and bandaged shotgun wounds.

Fat chance.

Hoping a soft-hearted Gate guard is on duty.

No such thing.

The sun sets, and you're still stuck outside the Wall. Everyone's heard the stories about things which come out to hunt the streets at night. Things even worse than pirates and froggies. Just stories to frighten little kids, you tell yourself.

In what's left of the twilight, you find a hidey-hole between a collapsed wall and a sheet of rusty corrugated iron. Your dinner is the last crumbs from the meatloaf plastic bag in your pocket. You hug your knees to stay warm, and try to sleep, hoping something nasty won't find you in the middle of the night, hoping that tomorrow will be better.

This part of your story is over. Today was a disaster, but at least you're still alive. Would things have gone better if you'd taken that clinic courier job? Or stayed away from that old woman and her cabbage boat?

It's time to make a decision. Do you:

Go to the great big list of choices? **P377**

Or

Go back to the beginning and try another path? **P105**

Follow the Old Man's Orders

The Mohawk woman laughs at you, and the baby joins in. The bald man with the huge skull tattoo twists his mouth into either a smile or a snarl, it's hard to tell.

"What's so funny?" growls the old man.

"Your face," the woman tells him.

"Baa!" says the baby.

"Crazy kid," the old man tells you.

"What?" you say, completely confused. And surprised to still be alive.

"We know you're a courier, cap or no cap," he continues. "We saw you back at the clinic."

This is a robbery? They want Doctor Hurst's package, whatever it is?

"We do what we can to help the clinic, so we got you a present," the woman says. She tosses something to you.

You flinch, expecting something horrible.

The old man grabs it from mid-air and waves it in front of you. It's a necklace – alternating yellow and black plastic bottle tops and half a dozen human teeth on a long black string. Horrible, but not quite as horrible as you'd expected.

He places the necklace around your neck. "Any time you're in Kannibal Krew territory, just show this and no Kannibal will bother you."

"Um," you say, still confused.

The skull tattoo man frowns at you. "Well? Say thank you!"

"Thank you," you say. "I mean it. Thank you. Really."

The old man grunts. "You're welcome." He hops down into the boat and it roars off before you can say another word.

You hide the necklace under your shirt, put your Deadline Delivery cap back on, and walk the six blocks back to Tollgate, thinking hard. Safe passage through Kannibal Krew territory, forever? A necklace like this is worth its weight in gold, to any courier.

After paying your toll, you jog to Nori Road and deliver Doctor Hurst's package to 157, then return to Ivory Tower and Deadline Delivery.

Miss Betty scowls at you. As usual. But pays you the ten-dollar delivery fee, as promised. That's thirty-two dollars in your pocket – you're rich! Well, a lot richer than usual.

The steel door squeaks and starts to close, and you hurry out. Miss Betty doesn't say goodbye. She never does.

This part of your story is over. Today turned out pretty well, and who knows where tomorrow might lead. But things could have turned out differently – you might have ended up in the clutches of much nastier pirates, or gone to the over-city, or been captured by froggies, or eaten by crocodiles.

It's time to make a decision. Do you:

Go to the great big list of choices? **P377**

Or

Go back to the beginning and try another path? **P105**

Run for the Hole

You wade as fast as you can to the other end of the pool.

The mysterious ripple doesn't follow you. As far as you can tell. It's hard to be sure, what with the other ripples from you, and from bits falling from the balcony.

The froggies rescue the dangling kid before it can fall in the water. Good on them. But then they remember you, and all the "Doom" chanting starts up again, sounding even angrier than before. Someone throws something at you, and it lands in the water just a couple of yards away.

You run out through the jagged hole.

But it's not an exit after all, just a smallish room with one wall of glass bricks.

Two doorways.

One's blocked by a fallen concrete beam.

The other's on the far side of a raised platform occupied by a family of crocodiles. They stare at you. Two of them hiss then slip into the water.

You turn and look out the hole, only to see that ripple again, heading straight for you. At the front of the ripple, a crocodilian snout and eyes appear. The last thing you ever see is its jaw opening wide.

I'm sorry, this part of your story is over. You escaped pirates and the crazy old cabbage boat woman, but you were foolish to think you could escape the froggies and their Crocodile Doom.

It's time to make a decision. Do you:

Go to the great big list of choices? **P377**

Or

Go back to the beginning and try another path? **P105**

DRAGONS REALM

By Eileen Mueller

A Bad Start

"Hey, Fart-face!"

Uh oh. The Thomson twins are lounging against a fence as you leave the corner store – Bart, Becks, and Bax. They're actually the Thomson triplets, but they're not so good at counting, so they call themselves twins. Nobody has dared tell them different.

They stare at you. Bart, big as an ox. Becks, smaller but meaner. And Bax, the muscle. As if they need it.

Bart grins like an actor in a toothpaste commercial. "What have you got?" He swaggers towards you.

Becks sneers, stepping out with Bax close behind. "Come on, squirt, hand it over," she calls, her meaty hands bunching into fists.

Your backpack is heavy with goodies. Ten chocolate bars and two cans of tuna fish for five bucks – how could you resist? And now you could lose it all.

The twins form a human wall, blocking the sidewalk. There's no way around them.

Seriously? All this fuss over chocolate? Not again! They've been bullying you and your friends for way too long. There's still time to outsmart them before the bus leaves for the school picnic.

A girl walks between you and the twins. You make your move, sprinting off towards the park next to school. Your backpack is heavy, but you've gained a head start on those numbskulls.

Becks roars.

"Charge," yells Bax.

"Get the snot-head," Bart bellows. Their feet pound behind you as you make it around the corner through the park gate. Now to find a hiding place.

On your right is a thick grove of trees. They'll never find you in there, not without missing the bus to the picnic.

To your left is a sports field. Behind the bleachers, there's a hole in the fence. If you can make it through that hole, you're safe. They're much too big to follow.

Their pounding footsteps are getting closer. They'll be around the corner soon.

It's time to make a decision. Do you:

Race across the park to the hole in the fence? **P201**

Or

Hide from the Thomson twins in the trees? **P202**

You have decided to race across the park to the hole in the fence

You race across the grass.

Bart Thomson chases you, shouting, "Onto the field. Follow me."

Energized by fear, you pick up speed. The bleachers loom in front of you. You're nearly there. Racing around the back, you skid to a halt. In the air in front of you is an oval, swirling with colors, like a bubble shimmering in the sunlight.

A faint voice comes from the glimmering air. *"Help! Help me!"*

The twins' feet pound on the grass. Their breath rasps behind you.

Without thinking, you dive through the whirling colors.

The park is gone. The Thomson twins are nowhere to be seen. You're in a forest beside a river. Deep water rushes past you, gurgling past sharp rocks and disappearing around a bend.

The shimmering air you fell through shrinks and pops like a bubble.

You're stuck here, for now. You'll miss the school picnic, but at least you're safe from Bart, Becks and Bax.

Searching for a signpost or a clue to where you are, you glimpse an enormous flying creature with a long lizard-like tail in the sky. A dragon? Before you can be sure, it disappears behind a mountain peak.

Even though the river is loud, you hear that same faint voice again, *"Help me. Hurry."*

You can't tell where it's coming from. There's a trail leading into the forest and another trail along the riverbank.

It's time to make a decision. Do you:

Follow the trail into the forest? **P204**

Or

Take the trail along the riverbank? **P212**

You have decided to hide from the Thomson twins in the trees

You race among the trees, ducking branches and scrambling around bushes. Soon you're deep in the foliage. The twins' colored shirts flash like the stripes of prowling tigers.

"Over here, in the trees," yells Becks, "I see footprints."

"We'll find the rat in no time," shouts Bart. "Follow me."

They crash through the grove, breaking branches and startling birds.

You drop to your knees and shove your backpack under a large bush with lots of undergrowth, scrambling in behind it. Scattering dry leaves, you cover your tracks and tug the grass to conceal your hiding place. Heart pounding, you freeze. Barely breathing. Listening.

The Thomsons' rough voices bellow. They stomp through the grove and thrash around in the bushes, making a racket.

"Can't find the brat," calls Bax. His voice is so close, you twitch.

"I don't want to miss the picnic," Becks whines.

"Yeah, let's go to the bus," Bart says.

Bart's the ringleader. They'll follow him. You listen to them moving away from your hiding place. Everything goes quiet. The birds start to chirp again.

Heartbeat slowing, your breath whooshes out of you. You're about to relax and crawl out of your hidey-hole, when you hear a twig snap. You freeze.

Soft footfalls sneak among the trees. The Thomsons are still there!

It was a close call. They nearly had you fooled. But they won't wait forever. They're much too impatient to hang around here all day.

Time passes. Is that them you hear? Are they leaving? Soon you'll miss the bus. Cautiously, you crawl out.

"Got you!" Bart leaps out from behind a tree, a malicious grin on his face.

You're doomed! You squeak out a useless, "Help!"

But then something crazy happens. The air around you shimmers, and a swirling colored hole appears.

"*Help is on its way!*" booms a majestic voice.

Bart looks just as surprised as you.

A blue scaly arm reaches through the hole, and scoops you up with long fingerlike talons. Bart stands with his jaw hanging open and Bax and Becks stare wide-eyed, as they come out from the trees. Then you're yanked through the hole into a cloudless summer sky.

You're hanging beneath a brilliant-blue dragon, flying over a valley filled with farms, rivers and forests. The dragon's wings are spread in flight above you, blocking out the sun. Its underbelly is pale, with a broad leather strap around it, and its strong limbs are bluer than the deepest lake. Gripped in the beast's sharp talons, your heart pounds.

The dragon could be dangerous and want to harm you. Perhaps you should struggle and get free of its grasp? Or it may be friendly — after all, it did save you from the Thomson twins.

It's time to make a decision. Do you:

Stay still because you trust the dragon? **P218**

Or

Wriggle to get free of the dragon's grasp? **P221**

You have decided to follow the trail into the forest

The trail into the forest winds between massive trees with gray trunks wider than trucks. The mysterious voice is still calling, but you can't really hear it with your ears, just in your mind. Are you going crazy?

"Help me. Please."

The voice sounds desperate. Walking swiftly, you enter the trees, the tuna fish cans clanking in your backpack. You've only gone a short way when a boy, about the same age as you, steps out from behind one of the gray trees.

To your surprise, he bows. "I saw you appear out of midair. Are you a wizard?"

"A wizard?" you say. "Of course not."

"Who are you, then? I haven't seen you around before." He glances at your feet. "You've got weird shoes. Are you sure you're not a wizard?"

He looks like an urchin, with sturdy old-fashioned boots, rough-spun clothes and tangled blond hair. A sack is slung over his shoulder, and he has rope around his waist to keep his pants up.

"Um, I've just come here for a visit," you say, unsure how to explain how you got here when you don't understand it yourself.

His face lights up. "I know who you are! You're Zeebongi the Great. The old ones foretold of your coming. You came through a world gate, just like they said."

A world gate? Is that some sort of portal between worlds? "Um, I don't know how I got here."

"They said you'd say that. I'm Wil," he says, eyes shining. He bows again. "It's great to meet you, Zeebongi the Magnificent."

"I'm not Zeebongi," you protest.

"The prophecies said you'd say that too."

"My name's not Zeebongi."

"Oh, I know you have other titles," he says. "Which should I use? Wondrous One? All-knowing One? Highly Esteemed Gracious

Master? Perhaps I could just call you–"

"My name is–"

"The prophecies said you'd be modest and humble," Wil interrupts, "but this is ridiculous!" He shakes his head. "I should just call you by your real name."

"Exactly." At last he's talking sense. "My real name is–"

"I know, I know!" Wil shakes his head in frustration. "Zeebongi the Greatly-Esteemed Wise and Honorable One. But I prefer Zeebongi the Magnificent. Which do you like best?"

You sigh. You're never going to get through to this guy. "Zeebongi will do." At least Zeebongi is better than the other names. Although it sounds like some sort of kid's toy you get with a burger.

"I'm on my way to Dragons' Hold to become a dragon rider," says Wil. "Where are you going, Zeebongi?"

Dragons' Hold? A dragon rider? Maybe that *was* a dragon you saw in the sky. Scratching your head, you say, "Actually, I heard a peculiar cry for help coming from along the trail and thought I'd see who it was."

"Help." The voice sounds fainter, as if the owner is exhausted.

"There it is again," you say.

"I didn't hear anything, but I will aid you in your great quest, Zeebongi." Wil bows. "I am ever at your service."

A whimper comes from deeper in the forest.

"I heard that," says Wil.

Of course he did. That whimper wasn't in your head – and it was loud. "Come on, we have to go."

You run along the narrow trail with Wil close behind. He's fit and keeps up easily as you pelt through the woods, following the voice. Ducking around a bush, you startle a hare. Birds warble strange songs. Wherever this place is, it's not somewhere you've been before.

"Help, please." The voice in your head sounds closer. You stop and look around. "Wil, it's coming from somewhere nearby." You wave your hand to the right. "I think we need to search here."

Wil tilts his head. "Now it's stopped whimpering, I can't hear anything." He steps off the track towards where you motioned.

You follow him, scanning the ground in front of you and looking through the trees. Stumbling over a tree root, you land face-first on the ground, near a bush.

"*Watch out!*" the voice pipes up. "*You nearly squashed me.*"

"You're amazing," says Wil, his eyes glazing over with adoration, "that was the perfect dive."

You ignore him. Turning your head, you see a glimmer of purple under the bush. Two yellow eyes stare back at you. It's some weird creature that you don't have at home.

"*I knew you'd help me,*" its voice sounds in your head.

Scrambling to your knees, you push the foliage back. Your eyes nearly fall out of your head. On the leaf litter, under the scrub, is a purple dragon about as long as your forearm!

"A dragonet!" Wil exclaims over your shoulder.

Although you've seen dragons in books, you'd never thought they were real. Heart hammering, you slowly stretch out your hand.

"*I'm Aria,*" the dragon says. "*Thank you for coming.*" She zips out from under the bush and clambers onto your forearm, wrapping her tail around your elbow. She's trembling.

"Aria." You stroke her back and she lets out a throaty rumble, but keeps shaking.

Wil jumps back, shocked. "You heard a dragonet talk?"

You nod.

"It called you?" he asks.

You nod again.

"You mind-melded with a dragonet, *without touching it*. And you tried to tell me you weren't Zeebongi." He sighs. "I wish I had dragonet-finding powers too. All my life I've wanted to ride a dragon. That's why I'm going to Dragons' Hold."

"I don't have dragonet-finding powers," you say.

"Then how did you find it?" Wil frowns.

"I just heard her calling me."

"Her?" Wil looks at you as if you've gone mad.

Perhaps you have. It's been a very weird day. "Her name's Aria," you tell Wil. "She told me so."

Aria whimpers. *"I'm lost. I fell out of my mother's saddlebag and landed here. I'm lonely and hungry and need to go home."*

You stroke her again. "You're hungry, are you? Poor girl."

"You're so lucky, Zeebongi," says Wil. "I've always wanted to ride a dragon, and now you have a dragonet riding on you." His eyes shine with excitement. "If she's hungry, let's feed her."

You set the trembling dragonet down, and open your backpack. "Um, Wil, what do dragons eat?"

"You're testing me, aren't you, Zeebongi?" Wil laughs. "Meat, of course. But I only have bread and cheese. Do you have any meat?"

Aria, sitting among the flowers, opens her jaws, then snaps them shut.

"See that?" says Wil. "I know almost as much about dragons as you, Zeebongi."

What's he talking about? You stare at Aria, who snaps her jaws again.

"She's practicing to make fire, even though she's too young to flame yet." Wil beams proudly, as if he's just passed a school test with a perfect score.

"I'll be old enough to make flames soon," Aria says in your head, reminding you of little kids at school.

You chuckle and tip out the contents of your backpack to search through all that chocolate for the cans of tuna fish.

Wil stares at the shiny chocolate bars. "What are they? Is that metal?" He picks one up.

"Be careful," you say, "it bites."

He yanks his hand away.

You laugh. "I was only joking!"

He looks relieved. "I didn't think I could see any teeth. But then, I wasn't sure." He stares at the contents of your pack suspiciously.

"I have some fish in this metal box." You show him the can of tuna fish. "But it's pretty hot. I'm not sure if Aria will want it."

"How can it be hot?" asks Wil. "Is there a fire inside?"

"No, just some chili."

"Chilly? You mean that it's cold?"

"No, where I come from, chili is a type of pepper." You pull the tab on the tuna fish can and show him.

He wrinkles his nose, then pokes at the chocolate wrapper again. "You're sure it doesn't have teeth?"

"I'm sure." You open the chocolate and hold it out to him. "Here, have a smell."

Wil takes a deep sniff and his face lights up. "This smells great." He licks his lips.

You break off a piece of chocolate and give it to him. "It's called chocolate."

Wil pops the chocolate into his mouth. His eyebrows nearly hop off his head in surprise. He gives you a chocolatey grin. "This is good."

Aria perks up, nostrils twitching. *"Can I have some too?"* She stares at the chocolate. *"I'm so hungry."*

"No, Aria, that isn't for you." You're not sure if you should feed a baby dragon chili. But tuna fish has got to be better for her than chocolate.

You take a spoon out of your lunch box and carefully select a chunk of tuna fish without too much chili on it. Holding the spoon out towards Aria, you coax her towards you.

"Aria, come and have something to eat. I have some fish for you."

"Strange fish," she replies, taking a few tentative steps towards you.

She sniffs the spoon and sneezes. Will she reject it? Suddenly she gulps everything off the spoon, then leaps over to the can, and gobbles up the lot – tuna fish, chili and all.

"Wow, that was fast," you mutter.

Aria's body goes stiff. Her eyes spin. She roars. Flames shoot out of her tiny maw, blasting past Wil. She takes off, streaking along the path, leaving a scorched trail of grass behind her. Grabbing your water bottle, you douse a patch of flame. Aria shoots straight up in the air. She somersaults, her flames die, and she lands in the grass.

You and Wil rush over to the tiny creature, whose sides are heaving. Glancing at Wil, you start to laugh.

"What is it?" he asks.

"Your face is sooty."

"So is yours."

You wipe the back of your hand across your face. It comes away black. "I thought you said she couldn't breathe flame yet?"

"She shouldn't be able to until she's much bigger." Wil's eyes are large. "It must be that magic pepper-fish you gave her."

"It's not magic, Wil."

"Then what is it?"

It's no use, he's not going to believe you if you tell him about fishing boats, canning factories and chili plantations.

"That was fun," says Aria. *"Have you got any more?"* She burps loudly. Her belly is round, distended with food.

"I think you've had enough for today, Aria."

"I agree," says Wil, wiping his face with his sleeve. "But perhaps I can have another piece of that choklick?"

"Can I try some too?" Aria rolls her eyes, looking cute, but you shake your head.

"No way. If that's what chili does to you, I'm not about to give you a sugar rush!"

While you and Wil have some of his cheese in thick slabs of his homemade bread, you face the next problem.

"Wil, Aria said she's lost her mother and needs to get home, but I have no idea where her home is."

"That's easy," Wil speaks around his mouthful. "All dragons live at Dragons' Hold. That's where I'm going. I can take you both with me."

You hesitate. What about going home? "Wil, how can I find another portal?"

"A what?"

"That shimmering air that I came through."

"Oh, you mean a world gate?" He squints at Aria. "My ma says dragons have something to do with world gates, but my da says it's wizards who create them."

Aria ignores him, staring at you. *"You have to come too,"* she says, stamping her foot. *"I made a world gate to save you from those horrible bullies, now it's your turn to help me."*

She's right. She did help. Now it's your turn. "Alright, Wil. Aria and I will come with you. Where is Dragons' Hold?"

Before Wil can answer, Aria pipes up, *"Here, inside Dragon's Teeth."*

A ring of ragged mountains appear in your mind, as if you're flying over them. You swoop over the jagged peaks and down over a basin, flying over wilderness, forests, a silver lake, and farmlands. Dragons speck the sky, riders on their backs. Others sit on ledges, up the mountainside at one end of the valley. People dot the fields, and work in fruit orchards. *"This is Dragons' Hold."*

Wil is talking, "... so we'll just have to decide whether we stop for supplies on the way or not."

"Sorry, Wil. I missed most of that. Aria was showing me Dragons' Hold."

"You're so lucky, Zeebongi. I wish I had a dragon." Wil sighs. "I will, soon. I was planning to walk to Montanara, to get a few supplies, and then go on to the blue guards."

"Blue guards? Do they have blue skin?" Anything could be possible in this world.

Wil laughs. "No, they ride the blue dragons who take folk into Dragons' Hold. That's the only way in, and if you want to be a rider, you need to see them. But now you're here, we might have enough supplies to bypass Montanara and go straight to the blue guards." Wil eyes your backpack.

You open your pack again. Inside are the chocolate bars, four cookies, a mini-pack of potato chips, some dried fruit, and one more can of chili tuna fish.

Wil pokes at the potato chips and leaps back when the foil packet crinkles, shaking his head. You laugh, and he grins. "No teeth either!" he says.

He opens his bag and shows you half a loaf of bread and a small round of cheese, wrapped in cloth.

"Do you think we have enough?" he asks. "It's half a day's walk to Montanara, but if we get bad weather or run into trouble, it could take us days. Perhaps we should go for supplies. Wise Zeebongi, it is up to you."

Aria pipes up. *"I want to go straight to the blue guards. Their dragons are my mother's friends. They'll help us get to Dragons' Hold faster."*

Wil thinks you should go for supplies, but Aria wants to go straight to the blue guards. If you go straight there, you may not need supplies, but if you are delayed, you might not have enough food.

It's time to make a decision. Do you:

Go to Montanara for supplies? **P246**

Or

Go straight to the blue guards? **P262**

You have decided to take the trail along the riverbank

The trail follows the river then heads across a meadow into the trees. As you reach the tree line, a girl steps out, holding a bow with an arrow aimed straight at your chest. Was hers the voice you heard?

"Halt!" she calls.

No, it definitely wasn't her voice. You raise your arms in the air, mentally groaning. You've fled from three bullies, just to confront an archer.

The girl is a little taller than you, dressed in brown and green old-fashioned clothing with a dark green cape. Her hair is in braids and she's wearing hand-stitched boots. She narrows her eyes and looks you up and down. "What is that strange garb you're wearing? And where are you from?"

"What do you mean, *strange garb?*" you ask. "You look pretty strange to me. Are you on your way to a costume party or something?" But her arrowhead looks sharp enough. She's a real archer, alright.

She beams. "This is my new apprentice cloak." She's obviously proud of it.

"It's the nicest apprentice cloak I've ever seen." It's the only one you've ever seen, but you don't tell her that.

She looks you up and down again and lowers her arrow slightly, but still keeps it nocked. "Because you've been so polite, I won't shoot you straight away. Come with me. My master will want to meet you."

"Your master? Who's that?"

Her eyes glint. "It's obvious you're not from Dragons' Realm or you'd know Master Giddi. Now, take that strange rucksack off."

Dragons' Realm? Nowhere near your neighborhood, then. You drop your backpack, wishing you'd taken time to eat some of your picnic when you'd first landed on the grass.

She gestures with her arrow towards the trees. "Step away, over there."

You move back to lean against an enormous tree, as wide as a car.

The bark is smooth and gray, harder than any tree at home, and warm from the sun.

The girl drops her bow for a split second. A moment later she's wearing your backpack, her bow and arrow trained on you again. She's fast. You have no chance against her, unless you can distract her.

"Walk," she barks, "just in front of me. And no tricks. My arrow's trained on you."

You gulp, and go further along the trail. One false move and you'll have an arrow through your back. Perhaps you were better off with the Thomson twins.

"What's your name?" you ask.

"Mia," she snaps. "Keep walking."

Your attempts to chat with her go nowhere, so you walk in silence, passing many more of the huge trees. You step past plants you've never seen before – bushes with vivid orange and yellow flowers shaped like parrot beaks, others with long thorns, and ferns towering above your head. Where are you? What is this weird place with odd flying creatures, unusual plants and strangely-dressed people? Perhaps it's a movie set. Or some sort of virtual reality show. Or maybe it's real. Maybe you should've followed the trail into the forest, then you might have found out who called you through the portal into this strange place – at least you wouldn't have a mad archer following you.

Thwack! You jump as an arrow flies past you, thudding into a tree. Brown muck splatters your cheek. Was Mia aiming for you, or for something really dangerous – a snake or poisonous scorpion? You can't tell from the remains pinned to the tree, but it must be pretty dangerous because she's gone pale.

"What was it?"

"March!" she barks, tugging her arrow out of the tree and cleaning it on the ground.

You keep going. An arrow whooshes past your head, nearly piercing your ear. Another arrow flies into the undergrowth. She yanks it out before you can see what she's hit.

No doubt, some dangerous creature. Swallowing hard, you stutter, "Th-thank y-you for protecting me." Your heart pounds as she continues to march you down the trail, her bow up, ready for more perilous beasts.

Wump! What an awesome shot! Her arrow hits a trunk right in front of you, piercing the body of a hairy spider. Its legs struggle then flop still. She grunts and retrieves her arrow.

Why would she shoot a spider?

Suspicious, you ask her, "Are you scared of—"

"Keep walking," she snaps.

A few minutes later, she calls, "Halt! Use that large stick and clear the path." Her arrow gestures to the trail ahead.

"There's nothing there," you say.

"Do as I say," she barks. Her bow is shaking.

Why is she so scared? Walking forwards, you see fine gossamer threads in a beautiful pattern, blocking the way. It's a spider's web.

You glance back at Mia's pale face. "Are you scared of spiders? And their webs? Have you been shooting spiders the whole time?"

"Of course not." Mia glares.

You stifle a laugh. Yeah right! No wonder you didn't see what she'd been shooting. Her enemies were so small! You bite your cheeks in an attempt to not laugh, but a snigger escapes you.

"It's not funny." Mia blushes.

Her bow stops shaking as you break down the spider web with the stick, and clear the path. By the time you're finished, you're laughing out loud. "I thought you were killing scorpions or venomous snakes, or poison dart frogs – not spiders."

She laughs too. "No wonder you were looking so worried!"

"Look, Mia, I don't want you killing every spider in this forest, so I'll just move them out the way with my stick."

"But—" She sighs. "Oh, alright, then."

As you walk, you flick spiders out of the way, sending them flying into the undergrowth. It's a relief that Mia's arrows are no longer whizzing past your head, although you can't believe such a brave archer is so terrified of tiny spiders.

Finally you come to a clearing in the woods. A small cabin is nestled on the edge, a faint wisp of green smoke rising from its chimney. Green smoke? Now you know you're nowhere on earth.

Before Mia can march you up to the cabin, the door bursts open and a man appears. He reminds you of a toilet brush, tall and thin with bristly hair that sticks up. He's dressed similarly to Mia, but his cloak is longer, nearly touching the ground, and is a weird shade that flickers from green to brown and back again.

His dark eyes flash and his laughter booms across the clearing. "Aha, Mia, so I was right! There *was* a disturbance by the river." He looks you up and down. "A world gate, by the look of things. Let's see who it's delivered."

Without warning, the man raises his hand. Sparks shoot from his fingertips. Halfway across the clearing, they burst into green flame.

You duck. The flames narrowly miss your ear, leaving a warm glow as they pass.

He waves his hand again and a ball of green flame rushes towards you, aimed at your chest. You try to duck, but can't move fast enough. In panic you raise your hands. A flash of light shoots from your palms, extinguishing the fireball.

The cloaked man's deep laughter bounces across the clearing.

You stare at your palms as if they are aliens. What just happened? They've never emitted light before. After a moment you look up at the chuckling man. "Um, … Mister Giddi?"

"Master Giddi," he says, bowing.

"Head of the Wizard Council," Mia adds.

A wizard? This place is really odd. You move closer to the trees for protection. Glancing at Mia, you remember she's his apprentice. Her arrows were probably the least of your problems.

Master Giddi stares at you for a moment. "You showed good mettle just now, not running when I sparked you, and some raw talent, defending yourself with a flash-shield."

A flash-shield? Is that what just happened? Self-consciously, you glance at your hands again, wondering when the next blast of light will shoot from them.

Master Giddi's eyes rove over you, as if he's measuring you and memorizing his calculations. After what seems like forever, he says, "I'm looking for a few more apprentices. Would you like to learn magic?" He snaps his fingers and a fireball hovers in front of him. Waving his hand up and down, he bounces it in the air, then flings his arm outwards. The fireball shoots across the clearing, heading straight for a nearby tree. Master Giddi snaps his fingers again and it extinguishes.

That's awesome. You have a chance to learn magic. To control fire!

Before you can answer, your hair and the nearby leaves are stirred by a strong breeze. A whooshing noise comes from overhead. A huge bronze dragon spirals down and lands in the clearing. Its scales gleam in the sunlight. You've never seen such an awesome creature.

A soft "wow," escapes your lips as you duck behind a tree.

A young man – dressed in a hooded brown jacket, tight-fitting trousers and boots – swings down from the dragon's saddle. He strides over to Master Giddi and claps him on the shoulder. "Hello, Master Giddi." He nods at Mia. "Handel and I are heading to Horseshoe Bend to pick up some arrowheads from the blacksmith. Do you need any supplies?"

You can't see anyone else. Handel must be his dragon.

"Great to see you, Hans," says Master Giddi. "We're fine, but we do have a visitor…"

You step out from under the trees. Hans stares at your sneakers and jeans, frowning. "Such colorful shoes and strange clothes," he says. "Did this person come through a world gate?"

"I suspect so." Master Giddi nods to Hans, then his dark eyes rest upon your face. "You could go to Horseshoe Bend with Hans and Handel if you prefer not be my apprentice."

"Fine with me," says Hans, "but we'll need to go. I have to be back at Dragons' Hold soon." He walks towards Handel, and climbs up into the saddle.

What a choice! If you stay with Master Giddi, you'll learn to summon fireballs and use your flash-shield. Maybe Mia can teach you some archery. But if you go to Horseshoe Bend, you'll ride a magnificent bronze dragon and see more of this strange land of Dragons' Realm.

It's time to make a decision. Do you:

Stay with Master Giddi and become an apprentice wizard? **P223**
Or

Go with Hans on his dragon, Handel, to Horseshoe Bend? **P230**

You have decided to stay still because you trust the dragon

Mountains ring the valley with their vicious jagged peaks. A cold breeze bites into you, tugging at your clothes, trying to sneak inside. Wrapping your arms around the dragon's forelegs, you snuggle against its warm skin to break the wind. You'd expected its scales to be cool and rough, not comforting, like soft worn leather.

The dragon roars and a rumble courses through its body, making your skin tingle with excitement. Rushing towards you are dozens of dragons of all colors, frolicking in the air. Their riders' shouts echo off the mountainsides, bouncing around you in a strange medley of whoops and hollers.

In front of you, the air shimmers – another portal. Your chest tightens. Surely you're not going back already? Your adventure has only just begun. The portal warps as a blue dragon appears, clutching someone in its talons.

"Put me down, you monster!" It's Bart Thomson, a terrified grimace on his face. "Take me back. I want to go home."

Another blue dragon pops through the portal holding Bax in its talons. "Yahoo!" yells Bax, grinning. His dragon swoops. "Yeehar," cries Bax. "This is fun!"

Becks comes through the portal grasped by yet another blue dragon. There are dragons of all colors wheeling in the sky around you. Most of them have riders, but only the blue ones are carrying people in their talons. In fact, as you look more carefully, you realize that all of the blue dragons are holding people – all about your age. The blue dragons fly to a vast ledge outside an enormous cavern halfway up a mountainside. Your dragon swoops, depositing you there.

Awaiting you is a tall woman with dark hair. Like the other dragon riders, she is dressed in brown trousers and a thick jacket. Behind her, at the mouth of the cavern, is a silver dragon.

"Welcome to Dragons' Hold. I'm Marlies," the woman says. She has extraordinary turquoise eyes. "These are our imprinting grounds. The young dragons will be here soon, and if you're lucky, you'll form a lifelong bond with a dragon and it will choose you as a rider."

"Wow," you murmur. "I could imprint with a dragon? And become a dragon rider?" You've heard of imprinting, the special bond forged between animals and humans. It would be awesome to fly a dragon through the skies.

The dragon holding Bax drops him to the ground and he rolls to his feet. "That was great," he says, coming over to you. "Where are we?"

Although you don't trust Bax, you figure he won't hurt you in front of a dragon rider. "Dragons' Hold. This is Marlies." You gesture at the woman. "And this is Bax."

"Dragons are cool," says Bax. "Flying with that dragon is the best thing I've ever done."

"Welcome, Bax." Marlies smiles, her turquoise eyes lighting up like sun on a lake. "Come and meet my dragon, Liesar."

Bax eagerly follows Marlies into the cavern at the back of the ledge to meet the silver dragon.

You wander to the front of the ledge. Blue dragons swoop past you, setting people down. The blue dragon with Becks arrives. She rushes over to join Bax in the cavern.

The dragon holding Bart swoops in to land. Bart struggles to get loose and falls out of the dragon's clutches too early. His foot hits the edge of the ledge. He stumbles, losing his balance. Bart flies over the edge, saving himself by grabbing a rocky outcrop. The blue dragon bats its wings and lunges at Bart, but rocks are in the way so it can't get hold of him.

"Help," cries Bart. "Help me up."

Memories flash into your mind – Bart teasing you, tripping you, stealing your lunch money, cheating on tests and getting your friends into trouble. Becks and Bax always joined in, but he was the ringleader. You look down the steep cliff side at the valley far below. If you do nothing, Bart will die. He'll never bother you at school again. You're all here in Dragons' Realm, miles away from home. No one will ever know.

But your family has taught you to be kind to others, even if they aren't kind to you.

It's time to make a decision. Do you:

Save Bart? **P342**

Or

Do nothing and let Bart die? **P334**

You have decided to wriggle to get free of the dragon's grasp

The dragon roars and a jet of flame shoots from its maw. Not sure that you want to be in the clutches of such a ferocious beast any longer, you wriggle and try to squirm your way free, but it's clutching you too tight. It's probably just as well, you're way too high to survive a fall.

As if the dragon can read your mind, it tucks its wings alongside its body and plunges into a headlong dive towards a forest below. You gulp! Hard! Has the dragon rescued you from the Thomson twins just to dash you against the treetops?

Water streams from your eyes as the air rushes past, but you're too petrified to blink. The trees rush ever closer. You cling to the dragon. Just when you think you're about to be impaled upon the spike of a dead tree, the dragon lets out a rumbling chuckle and swoops upwards, then down over the edge of the forest towards a river.

Perhaps the river is a better place to be dropped. The water may cushion you. Nope, on closer inspection that's a roaring river, deep with a strong current. The dragon goes lower. Its grip loosens and you ready yourself for the cold wet plunge.

The dragon's talons start to open. You take one last breath.

The dragon flings you up and over the river. Oh, no! Your fall will not be cushioned by water. You're going to fall on land. Unable to help it, you squeeze your eyes shut, then open them as you land on your back in an enormous haystack.

Hay is much harder than you thought. But much better than drowning in a swift river, being dashed on treetops or plummeting onto land. The dragon circles you twice. From the haystack you see that the strap around the dragon's belly was to hold a saddle in place, and there is a rider astride the brilliant blue beast.

The rider waves, and calls, "Good Luck." It is the same deep booming voice that you heard through the portal.

The dragon roars, belching forth a blast of flame, and takes off over the forest leaving a smoking trail behind it.

Now that you have time to think, you understand the dragon probably wasn't going to harm you. It rescued you from the Thomson twins, and when it knew you didn't want to stay in its talons, it dropped you in the safest place possible.

The haystack is on the edge of a narrow field that runs alongside the river. Still wearing your backpack, you slide to the ground and brush the hay off your clothes.

There is a dense forest to the rear of the field and a track leading from the field along the river. You have no idea where you are, or how to get home, but maybe the trail leads to a cottage or a village where you can ask for help. As you're trying to decide what to do, you hear a faint voice calling, but you can't tell where from. Was it the dragon rider again? There's nobody in the sky. Perhaps it was just the water you heard?

Striding across the field, you walk to the river's edge. Water chuckles over jagged rocks lining the riverbanks. You're glad the dragon didn't drop you on those. A rotting jetty sticks out into the river, with a slimy raft tied to it. A pole lies under a sign that says: *Use at Your Own Risk*.

You could use the raft and see if you can find anyone along the river. Or you could walk along the trail by the riverbank.

It's time to make a decision. Do you:

Take the raft and go down the river? **P290**

Or

Take the trail along the riverbank? **P212**

You have decided to stay with Master Giddi and become an apprentice wizard

By the time Hans and Handel have left, you're ravenous, so you open your backpack and pass Mia a peanut butter sandwich, which she frowns at and sniffs.

"How did you cut the bread so thin?"

"We just buy it like that," you tell her as you munch your sandwich.

Her frown turns to a smile as she tastes peanut butter for the first time.

You take out two bars of chocolate, open one, and give a piece to Master Giddi.

"Smells delectable," he says, flicking his fingers at the chocolate on his palm. It floats into the air and hovers in front of his mouth for a moment before he snaps his teeth over it. "Delicious."

Mia agrees. "If I'd known you had this stuff in your rucksack, I would've taken it back at the river, before Master Giddi got any of it." She waves her finger and a piece of chocolate hovers above her mouth. A flame ignites from her forefinger, melting the chocolate so it drizzles over her tongue.

"It's called chocolate." You slide another bar into your pocket.

"I don't mind what it's called," says Mia, "just keep feeding it to me."

"Time for training." Master Giddi leaps to his feet.

Mia pokes a chocolatey tongue out at him. "Oh, alright."

Master Giddi laughs then addresses you. "Let's get your fingers sparking before nightfall." One of Master Giddi's bushy eyebrows rises. "Mia, the first step is… ?"

Mia sighs and gets up. This is obviously basic stuff for her. "To sense the energy around you."

"Alright." Master Giddi waves his arm at you. "Stand with your eyes closed and breathe deeply. Listen to your heart beating. Feel how it pounds, sending blood around your body. Now feel how your life energy pulses outward into the world. Feel your roots to the earth flowing out of your feet, down deep into the ground. Sense how everything connects."

The birds chirp in the trees. The sun is warm on your face, but you can't feel any roots sprouting from your feet. You stand forever, waiting for something to happen.

"Eyes shut," Master Giddi snaps.

How did he know you were about to open them?

"Focus!" he says. "Feel your pulse throbbing to nature's beat. Sense yourself in harmony with the world. Sense the trees, their energy, each of them part of one great—"

This isn't working. You open your eyes. "I can't feel anything. Just me."

"It takes time, close your eyes again."

Master Giddi repeats his instructions over and over. Each time, you feel nothing, no surges of energy. None of the stuff he's talking about.

Finally, the master wizard touches the tip of your pinkie with his forefinger. "Try this." As Giddi raises his finger, your pinkie is pulled upwards, and you feel connected. In fact, you feel a whole lot more.

Your fingertip pulses. You feel the stretch of your nail growing, and the blood coursing through your hand. The sensation grows stronger, flowing down your arm and into your chest cavity. Life force pulsates through you.

Leaping into the air, you cry, "It's true. It's true."

Mia rolls her eyes. "Don't get too excited," she says, "you haven't even made a spark yet." Casually, she flicks a few green flames across the clearing. They land in a pail of water next to the cottage, sizzling.

"That's a good start," Master Giddi nods at you. "But you need to learn to feel the energy yourself, all the time. We need to test you under pressure and see what you sense then."

Mia steps forward. "Master Giddi, I have just the trick." She winks at him and picks up her arrow and quiver. "May I?"

Master Giddi smiles. "Why not? I'll see you both at sunset for supper." He passes you a small knife in a sheath. "Mia will protect you, but you can't go into the forest unarmed." You slip the knife into your pocket.

Mia dons her bow and quiver, and motions for you to follow her into the forest.

"Where are we going?"

"A place where you can focus." Her grin makes you think that she's about to play a prank on you, but Master Giddi said you should go, so you follow her, holding a stick to ward off any spiders.

You come to a grove of the same large gray-barked trees that were near the river.

"These are strongwood trees," says Mia. "You need to hug one."

"What? I'm not a tree-hugger!" You shake your head. "No way, Mia, you can pull your prank on someone else."

Mia sighs. "Listen, it's part of your training. Giddi made me do the same. I felt ridiculous, but it works. If you want to create flames and fireballs, strongwood trees are the fastest way to access environmental magic."

You'll have to trust her, so you make your way to the nearest strongwood tree. Tentatively, you stretch your arms around it and lean your cheek against the smooth bark. The tree is warm, just like the one near the river, even though this one is in the shade. Closing your eyes, you focus on your pulse, feeling the blood running through your veins. This time it's easier to feel your connection with the earth and this tree.

Something thuds into the trunk next to your face. Your eyes fly open. An arrow is embedded in the tree, just in front of your nose. You whirl, jumping back.

"You nearly killed me!" you yell.

"No, I didn't." She looks bored. "Actually, I could've pierced your nose if I chose to, but I was aiming for the tree. You'll notice I hit it." She sighs. "I bet you lost your focus. You really should concentrate better."

You open your mouth to protest, but she's right.
It's time to make a decision. Do you:
Stay with Mia and continue training?**P227**
Or
Dash into the forest? **P305**

You have decided to stay with Mia and continue training

"Can you still sense the tree?" Mia asks.

"No, but…"

"Look if you're going to be any use in battle, you need to stay focused."

"In battle?" You gulp.

"It's just theoretical, most tharuks don't come too close to our clearing, but you never know…" she says.

"Tharuk? What's a tharuk?"

"You don't know what a tharuk is?" Mia shakes her head. "They're monsters."

Real monsters? The sooner you learn magic, the better. "Let's get on with this."

Something skitters across dead leaves. It's loud. "What's that?" you ask. "Could it be a tharuk?"

"No, it's nothing," Mia says. "Let's get on with training. Go and stand over there."

A dog-sized spider runs out from the trees. Its body is brown with yellow stripes and it has huge fangs. No wonder Mia is terrified of them. You wave your stick at it, and yell, "Mia, quick, your bow and arrow."

"What for?' she says, as cool as cucumber.

"The spider!"

The spider skitters over to Mia, and she pats its head. "Off you go," she says. The huge arachnid scuttles off into the forest. "It's only the small ones you have to worry about," she says. "They're still poisonous when they're little. By the time they get to this size, you can reason with them."

She's mad! Your knees are still shaking. You glance around nervously. "But–"

"Let's get on with it. You can face me, or you can hug the tree," she says. "Which do you prefer?"

"I'll face you." That way you might see the arrows coming.

Mia tugs a round red fruit out of her pocket. "Sit against the tree." You cross your legs and lean back against the trunk. She places the fruit on your head. "Now close your eyes and focus. Tell me when you sense the energy of the tree and of the forest."

The tree thrums against your spine. "I feel it," you call.

"Keep concentrating," she says, "and keep the pomegranate on your head."

An arrow thuds into the tree above you. And another.

Sitting straight, you balance the pomegranate, not moving your head, as the arrows whiz past you. Soon they come closer, disturbing the air near your cheek. Mia had better be careful or she'll hit you. You feel the energy around you building, the thrum of the tree growing stronger.

The next arrow stirs your hair. Hopefully she's just about finished with this stupid game.

Then an arrow hits the pomegranate, shattering it. Sticky fluid sprays over your head and face. Your eyes fly open, stinging as juice dribbles into them. Red seeds are splattered all over your T-shirt, jeans and hands. That's enough, you've had it. Mia is going to pay for this.

Furious, you stand, and point at her. "Mia, you're such a—" Sparks flit from your fingertip. You stare at them. How did they get there? The thrumming inside you builds, and a tiny flame bursts from your fingernail. Your jaw drops.

Mia laughs. "You did it! You harnessed environmental energy, that's great!" She drops her bow and runs towards you, grinning, her nimble feet dashing over dry leaves. Suddenly, the leaves swirl. A net yanks Mia into the air, suspending her from a strongwood tree. A bell on the net rings out.

"Tharuk trap," Mia calls from the net, her face pale. "The monsters will be here any minute. Quick, run for Master Giddi."

Ominous snorts come from the trees. It's too late. The monsters are nearly here.

"Hide in the trees," hisses Mia.

Scaling the strongwood tree that Mia's net is suspended from, you hide among the foliage.

A furry creature sneaks around the tree, edging towards Mia. It walks on two legs and has clothing, like a person, but has tusks like a warthog's, and beady red eyes. It swipes long claws through the air in a vicious slash, narrowly missing the net.

Mia stretches her fingers between the woven ropes, flinging flames at it.

The fur on the creature's chest catches fire. The tharuk bats at the fire, howling, and snarls at Mia. "I'll be back soon, weakling," it spits, "then we'll see who's stronger."

Mia shoots a tiny fireball after the retreating beast.

"Hurry up, do something." Mia says. "We've no time to get Master Giddi. You have to get me out of here."

What can you do? Desperately, you ferret in your pockets and pull out two items. A chocolate bar and the knife Master Giddi gave you. If the knife was bigger, you could slash Mia out of the net in a moment. But it isn't. It will take ages to free her with such a small blade.

Perhaps, if you offer the tharuks chocolate, you may be able to tame them.

"Hurry," calls Mia, "they'll be back soon."

It's time to make a decision. Do you:

Cut Mia out of the net with your knife? **P270**

Or

Offer the tharuks your chocolate? **P274**

You have decided to go with Hans on his dragon, Handel, to Horseshoe Bend

"Climb up," says Hans, reaching down towards you from Handel's back.

A moment later you're upon Handel, in the saddle behind Hans, who waves to Giddi and Mia. The pungent smell of leather fills your nostrils. The dragon's huge bronze wings unfurl and you feel the power in its muscles as its legs bunch. Then you're airborne, heading for the trees.

You duck to avoid being hit by branches, but the mighty creature flicks its tail downwards and flaps its wings so you clear the treetops. Below you, Mia and Giddi wave. You let go with one hand to wave back, then Handel swoops, speeding up. You grab Hans around the waist so you don't fall off.

The sun glints off Handel's bronze-scaled wings. The forest is a carpet of blurred green below. Far in the distance, a range of snowy mountains glisten in the sun. You gasp in awe at the amazing view.

Hans pries your fingers off his belt and guides your hands to clasp each other around his waist. "Loosen up there, I need to breathe." He chuckles. "First dragon ride, is it?"

"Sure is." You flex your cramped fingers. "It's awesome." Far behind you is a river winding between the trees and further beyond, vast plains. Here and there, threads of smoke wind up through the trees, perhaps solitary cottages like Giddi's. "I can see so far, see everything."

"It's quite different to being on the ground, isn't it?" calls Hans, the wind whipping his words past your ears. "I don't think I could ever go back to living without Handel."

The dragon rumbles, its body resonating beneath you, and looks back, shooting a tiny spurt of flame from its maw.

"Dragons and their riders can mind meld." Hans says. "It's even better riding a dragon when you know what it's about to do. Hold on tight!"

Hans leans forward and you squeeze his waist. A village is tucked among the trees, tendrils of smoke rising up to greet you before dissipating. Handel pulls his wings into his sides, flicks his tail up and dives head-first towards a grassy clearing. Wind rushes into your face, whipping your hair back, and making your eyes water. Your heart pounds. How can Handel stop in time?

Just when you think you're about to crash into the treetops, Handel swoops and circles the clearing, slowing as he descends, then landing gently on the grass. Breath shudders out of you, half in relief, half in excitement.

Hans laughs. "Handel, you cheeky monster, that may have been a bit too much for our guest." He slides out of the saddle and helps you down, leading you around to Handel's head. "I think Handel should apologize." Hans places your hand on Handel's forehead.

A voice rumbles in your mind. *"It was a pleasure giving you your first ride. I can sense you enjoyed it. Let me know any time you'd like another."*

WOW! A dragon spoke to you using telepathy. You grin and nod. "I'd love another ride some time, Handel."

Hans laughs and scratches Handel's nose. "You rascal, that wasn't exactly an apology. I'll be back with the arrows soon." He takes you across the clearing to a trail that winds through the trees. "I guess you haven't been to Horseshoe Bend, given that you're new around here."

"Why is it called Horseshoe Bend?" you ask. "Do they have a lot of horses here?"

"Good guess. But, no, it's because the Spanglewood River has a huge bend in it, shaped like a horseshoe, south of here. This is the nearest settlement. Sturm, the local blacksmith, is one of the best – he crafts fine swords and good arrowheads." Hans gives you a shrewd glance. "He has a son about your age called Mickel. Perhaps you'd like to spend some time with him?"

"That would be great."

Between the trees, you glimpse crude cottages with thatched roofs, and hear pigs grunting. An overwhelming stink drifts on the wind, making you wrinkle your nose.

"Only the best entrance for dragon riders," says Hans, rolling his eyes, leading you past a rudimentary fence around the pig sty. "Just breathe through your mouth until we're upwind." He winks. "And smile at the settlers even though the pigs stink."

Stink is an understatement. You've never smelled such a pong – it's even worse than Bart Thomson's feet in gym class.

Settlers stare at you. Children dressed in simple clothing, often with rope for belts, run up to greet Hans and tug your brightly-colored T-shirt – a gift from your cousin before he went missing two months ago.

It's really weird having everyone stare at you and touch your clothes. You blush, wishing something would happen to make them stop staring – anything. Even a detention would be better than this.

As you pass the sty, a pig squeezes between the fence palings and breaks free, oinking and charging towards you. Startled, you freeze. The pig leaps up, puts its muddy forelegs on your jeans, and chews on your T-shirt.

Hans pushes the pig back down. "Out of here."

Something hits your butt. You spin and can't believe your eyes. A goat, thankfully hornless, is taking another run at you. Its head is down, hooves smacking the dirt. You jump to one side but, ow! The pig has joined in, charging at you too.

You take off, racing between the crude dwellings and run into a flock of chickens, which take to the air and follow you, squawking and pooping. Shrill oinking cuts through the chickens' squawking. Oh, no! A whole horde of pigs is charging at you, the T-shirt muncher in the lead.

The settlers laugh as you spin and take off in the other direction, trailed by chickens, a mad goat and a pog of pigs.

A boy with a broad chest and huge well-muscled arms runs towards you. "Just keep running," he says, "I've got this."

The settlers cheer. He dashes past you and suddenly a pig goes flying over your head and lands in the muddy sty. Another pig follows, flying through the air, squealing like a – well, like a stuck pig – before splatting into the mud, grinning. The pigs are having the time of their lives. You skid to a halt beside Hans. The boy is slinging pigs in a rapid blur. Then he shoos the chickens away and tucks the goat under his arm, striding towards you. The settlers applaud him, then turn and go about their business, as if tossing pigs is perfectly normal.

A couple of children can't resist one last tug on your T-shirt. You can't help wondering what your missing cousin would think of everyone tugging the shirt he gave you.

"Hi, I'm Mickel," the boy says, holding out his free hand for you to shake. Under his other arm, the goat bleats. "Welcome to Horseshoe Bend."

Shaking his hand, you say, "I never thought I'd see pigs fly." You pat the goat.

Hans laughs. "Neither did I! They flew nearly as far as Handel. Mickel is the blacksmith's son I mentioned earlier. I'll call by the smithy in a few hours and see how you're both doing." Hans waves and leaves you with the strange, but very strong, pig-flinger.

"Um… thanks for helping me." You can't help glancing at Mickel's bulging biceps as he absent-mindedly lifts the goat up and down in the air like a weightlifter.

"No problem." Mickel grins. Three small children form a queue next to him. Without a break in the conversation, he lifts a kid too, working out both arms. "You new around here? You look like one of those other-worlders."

"Um, yeah, just came through a world gate," you reply, trying to sound cool. He looks so ridiculous lifting a goat and a child.

"We had another other-worlder here for a while," says Mickel, "but he went off to Dragons' Hold with Hans."

"Dragons' Hold? What's that?"

The other two kids grab hold of Mickel's thighs – one each – and he does sumo squats, giving his legs a workout while keeping up his overhead presses. This is really over the top. Totally OTT. Utterly ridiculous.

Mickel answers you as if weightlifting three children and a goat is totally normal. Perhaps it is. "Dragons' Hold is where Hans and Handel live, with hundreds of other dragons and riders, including Zaarusha, the Dragon Queen, and Anakisha, the Queen's Rider."

"A Dragon Queen?"

"Didn't you think Handel was magnificent?" Mickel asks.

"Handel was awesome."

"Well, Zaarusha is even more beautiful. They say every one of her scales shimmers with the colors of the rainbow."

This place is incredible, so different from home. Your trip on Handel was amazing, one of the best experiences of your life, and now you've found out that there are hundreds of dragons, some even more beautiful.

"How did you get so strong?" you blurt out. "Uh, sorry, I didn't mean to be rude. It's just–"

Mickel winks. "I had problems with bullies and had to do something."

Your eyes fly open in amazement. "Bullies? *You* had problems with bullies?"

Mickel shrugs. "Yeah, everyone wanted to challenge the blacksmith's son to a fight. I used to lose, until I learned two things."

He's so open and friendly, you find yourself telling him things you'd normally never tell a stranger. "I get bullied by the Thomson twins, back at home."

Another child leaps onto Mickel's back, clinging to him like a backpack. He hardly seems to notice, and just keeps exercising. "I can teach you both of the things that helped me," he says. "What would you like to learn first – the secret to developing strength fast, or how to fight like a warrior?"

You frown. What would be most use against the Thomson twins?

"Can you tell me a little more?"

"Sure," says Mickel, putting down the goat, and shaking the children off his back and legs as if they were breadcrumbs. He's still holding one child. "Although I honestly think that most problems can be solved by talking."

"Not with the Thomson twins," you reply. "Bart Thomson has only one volume – yelling – and his vocabulary consists of a lot of grunting."

Mickel absent-mindedly keeps lifting the child to continue his overhead presses. The kid grins. "Giant John is the best fighter in Dragons' Realm. He lives in the woods near here and loves new students," Mickel says. "Or I can show you the secret to getting strong quickly." Mickel winks again.

"Well, I think I'd like to – ow!" The goat butts your bottom. Not again!

"Oops," says Mickel, "I put the wrong kid down."

He lets the child go and snatches up the goat again – then carries it to a nearby pen. "What do you want to do first?" asks Mickel.

Learning combat skills will definitely help you face Bart Thomson, but so would being stronger.

It's time to make a decision. Do you:

Learn Mickel's strength-building secret? **P236**

Or

Train with Mickel and Giant John? **P240**

You have decided to learn Mickel's strength-building secret

Being stronger will help you face the Thomson twins when you get home. "I think I should build my strength," you say.

"Great decision," says Mickel, approaching you. "Do you mind?"

Mind what? Perhaps he's going to whisper the strength-building secret in your ear. "Sure, no problem." You lean towards him and suddenly find yourself upside down as he hoists you into the air and throws you up on his back. You're sitting on his shoulders with your legs hanging down his chest, like a little kid.

"A shoulder ride? That's your secret? How can that make me strong?"

"This isn't my secret," he laughs, gripping your calves so you don't fall off. "This is just transport." Mickel takes off into the forest, jarring the bones in your bottom as he leaps over fallen tree trunks, scrambles up a hill and bounds through a river. You duck to avoid the branches whipping into your face.

What is with this guy? Does he just think he has the right to pick up anything or anyone and do whatever he likes with them?

"Hey, Mickel," you yell, "put me down!"

He stops near one of those huge gray trees, panting, and puts you on the ground.

"We're here." Despite his marathon effort, he's still smiling.

"Where?"

"Here." He points at the tree. "This is my secret."

"A tree?"

"A strongwood tree." Mickel is still grinning. "And this is the biggest in the whole Spanglewood forest. That's why I train here."

"Mickel, are you mad? First you use kids as human-dumbbells, then fling me onto your shoulders, race out here like a maniac, and now you're speaking gibberish."

Mickel just shrugs and says, "Give it a try."

Could the guy start making sense? "Give what a try?"

"Want to be as strong as me?"

Do you ever. You imagine lifting Bart, Becks or Bax like human-dumbbells, and can hardly stand still.

Mickel wipes his brow with his shirt. "If you exercise in the shade of the strongwood tree, you build your strength a hundred times faster than exercising anywhere else."

Is this a prank? He probably developed his strength at the blacksmith's forge. But maybe not. His eyes look earnest as he smiles to encourage you.

You step under the tree. You don't notice anything different until you try some push-ups. Energy surges through your body, like an electric eel, making your muscles tingle. You pump your body up and down effortlessly ... ten times ... twenty ... a hundred times. After two hundred push-ups, you stop. The feeling of strength stays with you. It's like you've eaten a whole field of spinach – without getting green teeth.

Standing up, you grin, shaking out your arms. "That's incredible."

Mickel nods. "Are you tired yet?"

"No. My arms are warm, but they're not tired. This is great."

"Um, there's something I didn't tell you," says Mickel.

Oh, no. There's a catch. What is it?

"You have to exercise every second day to keep your new strength," says Mickel. "It doesn't have to be under a strongwood, although if it is, your strength will keep increasing. But if you don't exercise for two days, all your extra strength disappears."

"If it's that easy, why doesn't everyone look like you?"

"Only a few people know the secret. Some started exercising, but now they can't be bothered." Mickel shrugs. "Come on, let's do more."

You train with Mickel, doing squats and lunges while holding heavy logs on your shoulders. Your muscles tingle with that same strange electric energy as before. Next you do pulls-ups on strongwood branches, then burpies, bicep curls, and overhead presses. Mickel makes you sprint on the spot. Although sweat pours off you, you still feel great.

Mickel takes you to a nearby stream for a drink. "That should be enough training. You're looking good."

Your arms do feel firmer, your legs feel like they could run a marathon.

"Now that you're stronger, let's test your new speed," says Mickel. "Race you to the settlement."

It's never been as easy to run.

Following Mickel, you race between the trees, jumping across the river in one bound, and leaping over logs. Mickel laughs and you do too. That strange electric eel feeling still courses through you.

Long before you get to the blacksmith, the metallic clank of a hammer hitting an anvil rings through the air. The forge is joined to a stone cottage, and has an opening running the length of the building, with a thatched roof overhanging it. A fire blazes in a hearth. A barrel-chested man with enormous arms swings a hammer onto a piece of glowing metal lying on an anvil. A broad-shouldered woman with well muscled-arms is holding the hot yellow-orange metal with a pair of long tongs.

"Ma, Pa," calls Mickel, "we have a visitor."

After placing the metal back into the glowing coals, Mickel's father and mother come outside. His ma smiles. "Welcome to our hearth. I'm Hanishka, and this is Sturm."

Sturm grasps your hand, squeezing your fingers in his strong grip. You're glad you've just trained under the strongwood tree, otherwise your poor fingers may not have survived. Mickel winks, obviously thinking the same.

"I see you've been training in Mickel's favorite spot, developing your strength," says Sturm, "You're welcome to stay with us and keep developing your skills. We have a spare bed."

Mickel grins even wider than he's been grinning all day.

Hans comes around the corner of the forge. "Sturm, I've got my—"

He sees you. "Oh, you're back. I have all my arrows. I just picked them up from the fletchers, now I'm ready to go."

Sturm says, "Hans and I have been talking. There was a lad that came through a world gate a while ago. He's now living at Dragons' Hold..."

Hans' piercing green eyes regard you. "You can come to Dragons' Hold with me and meet him if you like."

Dragons' Hold sounds great. Hundreds of dragons and riders, a dragon queen, and a person from your own world.

"Or you can stay here, with us," says Mickel, "and I'll show you all my smithy secrets." He winks as he says *secrets*. You know he can make you strong and help you beat Bart, Bax and Becks if you ever get home.

"Come on," says Mickel, "I'll walk you and Hans to the clearing while you think about it."

It's time to make a decision. Do you:

Stay with Mickel? **P301**

Or

Go to Dragons' Hold with Hans? **P278**

You have decided to train with Giant John

"I need to learn how to fight. The Thomsons broke Bobby McGraff's arm a while ago."

"That's awful," says Mickel. "Giant John's training would help you stand up to them."

You nod. "I wish I could do both – get strong quickly *and* train with Giant John."

"You can." Mickel grins and his eyes gleam. "But we'll have to be fast. Jump on my shoulders."

He hoists you up over his head to sit on his shoulders, then he takes off, tearing through the forest, at breakneck pace. Well, you hope he won't break his neck – or yours! Ducking the branches that whip back into your face, you hang on tight. Mickel clambers over boulders, leaps streams, races across a mossy log bridging a chasm, and stops under one of the huge gray trees you saw earlier.

He pants. "If you exercise in the shade of a strongwood tree, you will increase your strength one hundred times faster than exercising anywhere else."

"You're joking!"

"No, I'm not. Watch this."

Mickel swings you into the air, using you like a dumbbell to do overhead presses. The trees around you bounce like yo-yos, but it's you that's moving, not them.

"Alright! I believe you," you gasp.

"Great!" Mickel puts you down. "Let's start training."

You both drop to all fours to do push-ups. As soon as you start exercising, a jolt goes through you, like touching an electric fence, and your muscles buzz with energy. Instead of doing ten or twenty push-ups, you manage hundreds without feeling tired.

"This is amazing."

"To keep your new strength, you have to exercise every second day," says Mickel. "It doesn't have to be under a strongwood. If you don't exercise for two days, all your extra strength disappears."

"Sounds fair enough. Exercising daily will be easy with this extra strength."

Mickel grins. "I know. Come on, I'll teach you a quick trick before you meet Giant John. Then you can surprise him when he suggests you spar with him."

"Sounds good. What is it?"

"Push me," says Mickel.

You reach out to shove him. He grabs your arm and a moment later, you're on the ground. "Oof!" Air rushes out of you and you gasp for breath. "How did... you... do that?"

Mickel pulls you to stand. "Grab your opponent's arm with both hands, using the momentum of their push to pull them towards you, like this." He gestures for you to push him again, then yanks your arm, pulling you off-balance. "Next, trip them, and their body weight will do the rest – as long as you're quick enough to jump out of the way." He demonstrates.

Once again, you're eating dirt. Leaping up, you say, "Let me try."

You yank Mickel forward and trip him, but he lands on top of you. "Ow! You're heavier than you look!"

"You need to move faster," he says, dusting himself off. "As you trip them, duck out the way."

You try again. Mickel lands flat in the dirt!

"Wow! This is awesome!"

"Come on, you need to practice a few more times, then we have to get going."

A while later, you're sprinting through the forest at Mickel's side, soon arriving at a thatched cottage in the woods.

Thuds and yells ring through the air – the sound of people fighting. Mickel rolls his eyes. "There must be a better way to solve all this conflict. I get so sick of using my fists to solve problems. Perhaps we should see whether Giant John wants to teach us mediation?"

"Come on, Mickel," you say, yanking him towards the clearing.

"Alright," he says, "but remember to trick Giant John with those new moves."

You burst through the trees into a clearing. Four people are fighting, in pairs, with wooden staves.

"Giant John," Mickel calls out. "I have a new recruit."

An enormous guy is bashing staves with a familiar figure. It's Giant John fighting Bart Thomson. The other two are Bax and Becks, and they're going like crazy, whacking each other.

You groan. Now you'll have to fight them all, and they'll have a great reason to give you a solid thumping. What rotten luck!

Giant John drops his staff to come over, but Bart is quicker. Tossing his staff aside, he races towards you. "Hey, Fart-face, wondered where you got to."

Frozen, you stare at him. He looms above you, larger than life. Behind him, Bax and Becks rush over. Bart lunges, arm out to shove you.

Your reflexes snap into action, strongwood strength zinging through your muscles. Grabbing Bart's arm, you yank him forward, trip him and twist out of the way. You're stronger than you think. Bart flips over your head and sails through the air. He lands on his back in the middle of an ant nest. Insects swarm over him.

What were you thinking? Now Bax and Becks are going to pulverize you. Your muscles are tight with tension.

Bax swings a punch. You grab his arm and a moment later he lands, dazed, against a tree trunk. A squirrel hops onto his chest, and bites his nose, as if it were a nut. "Hey!" yells Bax, then catches it, stroking its back.

Becks hangs back, frowning. "Something's changed," she says, scrutinizing you.

Bart rolls around to squash the ants, then clambers to his feet. His usual glower has been replaced with raised eyebrows. "You've been learning a few tricks." His eyes appraise Mickel, taking in his strong arms, and then flit back to you. He whistles, obviously impressed.

"Nice to meet you," says Bart, extending his hand to Mickel.

Your jaw drops. Bart is never polite. Ever.

Bart nods at you. "Well done, Fart-face. You bested me." He wanders back to the clearing to grab his staff.

You can hardly believe it.

Bax shakes your hand too, and strolls over to Bart, his new pet squirrel chittering on his shoulder.

Becks narrows her eyes, turns, and stalks off after her brothers.

Mickel raises an eyebrow. "Are these the Thomson twins?"

You nod.

"But there are three of them. They aren't twins, they're triplets."

"Shh," you whisper, "they can't count that well."

He laughs.

Giant John shakes your hand. "You've learned well." He shoots a shrewd glance at Mickel, who just grins. Giant John looks at you. "I gather you know my three newest pupils? It looks like they've been bullying you in your world. Is that right?"

"Um, yeah. This is the first time I've beaten them."

"Nothing like training under a strongwood tree, is there?" Above his dark beard, Giant John's eyes twinkle. "Let's forget learning staff, knife and bow techniques – that way they can't hurt anyone seriously." He scratches his beard. "That move you just did was one of my old wrestling tricks. How would you like to learn more?"

More cool moves to outwit Bart, Bax and Becks? That sounds great. Although, from the anxious looks Bart is shooting you, you may not need to learn many more tricks. Bart seems positively nervous. You try not to grin. You never thought you'd end up stronger than him.

Smiling at Giant John, you say, "Good idea. Can we start now?"

During the next hour, Giant John and Mickel take the four of you through basic wrestling techniques. Giant John stresses how important it is to obey the rules and be fair to those who are weaker. Much to your amazement, for the first time in their lives, Bart, Bax and Becks are model students – although Bart's feet still smell.

When Giant John is done, Mickel says, "Hans is expecting us back at the forge. Who wants a race?"

The Thomson twins yell in glee and take off after you and Mickel, dashing through the forest. Mickel takes a much more direct route home, a mad race through the trees and over a rickety bridge back to Horseshoe Bend. Much to the amazement of the Thomson twins, you run through the settlement with Mickel, flinging happy pigs into their sty, and weightlifting children and goats. The settlers laugh, greeting you both.

Bart, Becks and Bax are sweaty and panting as you reach the forge. You and Mickel are not even winded, as if you'd just taken a stroll.

The metallic clank of a hammer hitting an anvil rings through the air. The forge is joined to a stone cottage. A fire blazes in a hearth. A barrel-chested man with enormous arms swings a hammer onto glowing metal lying on an anvil. A broad-shouldered woman with well muscled-arms is holding the hot yellow-orange metal with a pair of long tongs. Hans is packing arrows into a sack.

Mickel points at the forge. "Those are my parents."

Hans steps outside the forge. He looks you over and raises his eyebrows, smiling. "Been training, have you? And found some more other-worlders. It's time to decide what you're doing next. All of you, come with me."

Hans leads you through the settlement, past grunting pigs and squawking chickens, to the clearing, where Handel is preening his bronze scales.

Bart Thomson looks startled. "Um…" He stares at Handel. "Is that thing safe?"

Hans chuckles.

"Bart's been terrified of animals since he was a kid," says Bax, earning himself a dirty look from Bart.

That's handy information. You file it away for when you get home.

"Handel wouldn't hurt a dragonfly," says Hans. "Unless it harmed one of his friends."

You walk over to Handel and put your hand on his nose. "Nice to see you, my *friend*," you say.

Your meaning isn't lost on Bart. "Um, nice d-dragon," he says.

Handel laughs in your mind. *"He's been a little annoying, has he? Let me know if he gives you more trouble, and I'll sort him out."*

Hans clears his throat. "I know you've enjoyed yourself here, but I think it would be best if you live with more other-worlders. There was a lad that came through a world gate a while ago. He's now living at Dragons' Hold. You can come with me to Dragons' Hold and meet him if you like."

Dragons' Hold sounds great.

Hans' piercing green eyes regard you. "Or you could go home. Handel can create a world gate for you to return, right now."

Bart blurts out. "Can we go home, please, now?"

He's just said *please*. Amazing. Handel must really impress him. You scratch Handel's nose. "If I go home, I'd love you to visit me on Earth, Handel," you say out loud, making sure Bart gets the message. "The more often, the better."

A rumble of pleasure courses through Handel and he spurts a tiny playful flame at you.

You swear Bart's knees are shaking. If you do go home, things are bound to be different from now on.

A whirling oval of shimmering colors appears in the air near Handel. Bart shoves Becks and Bax – squirrel and all – through the portal, then glances back nervously before he leaps through too.

It's time to make a decision. Do you:

Go home with the Thomson twins? **P326**

Or

Go to Dragons' Hold with Hans? **P278**

You have decided to go to Montanara for supplies

"We can't risk running out of food on the way," you say, walking along the trail. Aria wolfed down the tuna fish in such a hurry, you're sure she'll need more food soon.

"I want to see the blue guards and find my mother." Perched on your shoulder, Aria hides her head under her wing.

"I know," you reply, "but you don't want to go hungry."

A moment later she pulls her head out from under her wing and opens her jaws. Wil jumps back nervously as if she's about to scorch him, but no fire issues from her mouth, only sharp notes that trill through the trees in a crescendo.

Wil gapes at her. "Wow, I thought that I was going to get a pepper fish blast! But Aria's singing is beautiful."

Beautiful? The odd notes jangling in your ears are anything but that. You clamber over a fallen tree trunk. "Which way next?"

"Along there." Wil takes you along a narrow trail through the forest.

"What are those huge trees?" You point at the gray-barked trees that are dotted throughout the forest.

"Strongwood trees." Wil laughs. "The blacksmith's son in our village told me that if you exercise under their branches for longer than an hour, you get strong really quickly." He snorts. "But we all laughed at him."

"Was he strong?" You skirt a puddle on the track, Aria still screeching in your ears.

"Zeebongi, you don't have to keep testing me. Everyone knows that blacksmith's children are always strong." Wil pushes a low branch aside so you can pass.

You smile, even though this Zeebongi stuff is still annoying. "Did you ever try exercising under a strongwood tree?"

Wil just laughs.

Aria's singing is getting flatter with every step you take. Her notes are painful.

"Oh, great Zeebongi, isn't Aria's singing divine?" says Wil. "You were so clever to find her, and now you're training her to sing so beautifully."

Trying not to roll your eyes, you move Aria from your shoulder to your forearm to save your ears. "Aria, you look tired. Would you like to sleep?"

"Of course not!" she yawns. *"I'm calling my mother. Every dragon recognizes their dragonet's song. She should be here soon."*

She starts singing again, off-key and flatter than before. Even though you enjoy having a dragon, you've had enough of this terrible squawking. The sooner Aria's mother comes, the better.

Wil smiles. "I should've known she'd be a great singer. After all, her name is Aria."

Maybe Wil is tone deaf. Or can't hear at all. "Wil, you have such good taste in music!" you say. "Not," you mutter under your breath.

"Thanks," says Wil, missing your sarcasm.

"Wil," you ask, "have you heard a lot of music before?"

"Not much," he answers.

"That explains it."

"What?" says Wil.

"Ah, nothing." If you only had your MP3 player, you could teach him something about *real* music.

The longer you march, the worse Aria's singing gets. Finally, you have a brainwave. "Let's eat," you say. That way her mouth will be full and you won't have to hear her sing.

After the bread and cheese from Wil's sack are finished, you get out a chocolate bar. Wil's eyes light up, and so do Aria's. She snaps the chocolate out of your hand and gulps the whole bar in one swallow, wrapper and all, then gives a happy roar.

Wil beams. "Wow, Zeebongi, you're so clever! She liked that." Then his face falls. "But she didn't leave any for me. I wanted another piece."

"So did I!" But without the wrapper.

Aria's eyes spin faster and faster. She roars again, then scampers up your arm, and leaps onto Wil's head.

"Hey!" yells Wil.

Aria jumps into the air, flying off into the forest. She zips in and out of the trees, zigzagging around like a crazed chicken. You both watch her, grinning.

"She's gone crazy," mutters Wil, "absolutely crazy. I've never seen a dragonet acting like that."

"But I bet you've never seen a dragonet on chocolate before. Maybe they'll all be like that if we feed them chocolate."

Wil sighs. "I don't suppose you have any more choklick?" He licks his lips.

You wink. "I do, but don't tell Aria."

The dragonet roars and zooms out of the trees, crashing on your outstretched legs.

"That was fun," says Aria, *"but now I'm tired."* She burps and leaps onto your arm, only to start singing louder than before.

It's your fault. The chocolate rush is making her so loud. You grit your teeth, get to your feet and start walking. "Come on," you call to Wil, "let's get to Montanara."

Aria's raucous rasping scares away the bird life. Wil whistles along with her, also off key. Now you're certain he's tone deaf. After half an hour, Aria's voice fades and she falls asleep. Tiny snores rumble through her body, vibrating against your forearm.

"At last!" You sigh in relief, gazing down at her purple scales.

"Great, isn't it?" says Wil.

Nodding, you look up and realize he wasn't talking about Aria falling asleep. He thought you'd seen the large town ahead, visible through the last of the trees. You tuck Aria into your backpack, cushioning her with your jacket.

"Montanara," Wil says. "Our first stop is the market."

Fertile farmland stretches between the edge of the forest and

Montanara. You wander along the road, past fields of wheat waving in the breeze, and reach the outskirts of the town. The thatched cottages are densely-packed, lining winding streets full of people, horses and wagons.

"They're heading to market," says Wil. "It's the biggest one for miles around."

Nudging Wil, you ask, "Why are they staring?"

"They must recognize you, Zeebongi."

Sighing, you follow him past a huge wooden fence that reeks of manure. Snorts and whinnies come from behind the barricade.

"City stables," says Wil, "but I guess you knew that already, being the All-knowing One."

It's been a long day, and Wil's comments are getting tiresome, but you need him to help you reunite Aria with her mother, so you give him a tight smile, and don't say anything.

The market square is jam-packed with stalls. Over a fire, a tough-looking gigantic man is melting cheese and scraping it onto thick slabs of bread. Wil waves at him cheerily, calling, "Hi, Giant John."

Children munch roasted apples on sticks. Goats bleat as farmers milk them. Traders call out, selling their wares. Vegetables are piled high on tables and in the back of wagons, with horses tethered nearby. Brightly colored hats, shirts and cloth are for sale. You pass people haggling for the best price. With all the noise, you're surprised Aria hasn't woken yet.

You come to a stall piled high with pies and odd-shaped pastries with a spicy fragrance. Your mouth waters.

"Hey, Wil, before Aria wakes up, perhaps we should try one of those delicious-looking pastries."

"Sure, Zeebongi," says Wil. He pulls some copper coins out of his pocket.

"Zeebongi?" mutters a peasant woman next to you.

"Zeebongi!" says a farmer behind.

"Yes," exclaims Wil, "this is the Greatly-Esteemed Wise and

Honorable One.”

“Zeebongi!” someone calls. “Zeebongi!” Murmurs fill the busy market square.

Around you, people fall to their knees, their arms stretched up in worship. The haggling comes to a stop. Traders cease yelling mid-sentence. Children drop their apples as they fall to their knees. Even the animals go quiet.

“Hail,’ says Wil, jumping up onto the edge of a wagon. “Zeebongi the Magnificent will speak to you.”

You roll your eyes. He’s been wanting to use the *magnificent* title all day. After all, he admitted it was his favorite. “There’s no need for all this fuss,” you call. “Carry on as usual.”

Just then, Aria awakes and sticks her head out of your backpack. You open it and she climbs out, onto your shoulder, unfurling her wings.

“A dragonet!” someone calls.

The crowd murmurs.

Wil nudges you. “The prophecy said you’d be good with dragons.”

Above the crowd’s prostrate bodies, on the far side of the square between a stand of hats and a table piled high with vegetables, a large furry gray creature appears, dressed like a warrior. Black saliva drips from its tusks when it sees Aria.

“Tharuk!” The cry ripples through the crowd.

Someone hisses, “Fast, hide the baby dragon.”

Another furry creature appears behind the first, then a whole troop enter the market place. Beside you, Wil is pale. It’s the first time you’ve seen him without a grin. Those creatures must be bad.

“Dragonet!” bellows the first tharuk, pointing at Aria. “I’m hungry! Seize it, now!”

Still upon the wagon, Wil leaps into action, waving his hands at the crowd. “Stand up. Create chaos. Protect the Great Zeebongi and his dragonet.”

The crowd surge to their feet. Nearby, someone lets a cage of chickens loose and they flutter into the air around you, flapping their wings, clucking and squawking. Traders bellow at the top of their voices. Children dash between the stalls, shrieking.

Wil ducks a barrage of chicken poop. "Quick, Zeebongi! Do you want to hide here in the market or over in the stables?"

The market has many potential hiding places – any stall could provide cover – but the tharuks are already here, searching for you. You could give them the slip and go to the stables, but will other tharuks be waiting on the road outside the market square, ready to catch you?

It's time to make a decision. Do you:

Hide in the marketplace? **P320**

Or

Run to the stables to hide? **P252**

You have decided to run to the stables to hide

You snatch Aria off your shoulder and tuck her under your arm. "Quick! To the stables," you yell, dashing between the stalls, dodging children and horses. A few stray chickens are still flapping and cackling in the air, hopefully giving you cover. Around you, the bellows of monsters compete with shrieks and screams. Without time to glance back, you can only imagine the chaos.

Will leaps over a goat sitting in his path and leads the way to the road. You follow, racing down the cobbled streets. He wrenches the stable yard gates open and you sprint inside, only to come face to face with the Thomson twins.

Bart is shoveling a pile of horse manure. Becks is carrying a wooden pail of water and Bax is currying a horse, whistling. All three of them are wearing clothing similar to Wil's – simple brown trousers and shirts.

Bart looks up. "Fart-face?"

Wil puffs himself up, looking angry on your behalf. "That's no way to talk to the Great—"

Aria burps loudly, cutting Wil off before he can say *Zeebongi*. She winks at you. *"I thought that would stop him."*

Thankfully she was so quick. You don't want your whole school to call you Zeebongi when you get home – if you ever get home again.

"What are you doing here?" you ask.

"It's all Bart's fault." Becks scowls. "If he hadn't jumped through the portal and stolen some pies, we wouldn't have been forced to work here as punishment."

Bart sneezes. "And I'm allergic to horses."

The horse Bax is grooming snuffles in his pockets. "We're so glad to see you. You're the first normal person we've seen all day." Bax pats the horse's nose. "Wow, is that a dragon?"

"Yeah, her name's Aria. We need to hide. Tharuks want to eat her."

Behind you, Wil bolts the doors to the stable yard. "Are these your minions?" he asks.

Bart scowls.

"Wil, these are the Thomson twins. Bart, Bax and Becks, this is Wil."

"Great Zeebongi," whispers Wil, "I hate to disagree with you, but they're triplets, not twins."

"Ssh, don't tell them that!" you whisper back. "They can't count!"

Thumping sounds on the gates. "Open up," roars a throaty voice. Wil's face is panic-stricken.

"Quick," says Bax, "follow me." He runs to the stalls.

Aria flies after him. You follow with Wil. Bart and Becks go about their duties as if there weren't any monsters banging on the gates. The bashing on the gate gets louder.

Snorts and soft whinnies sound in the dim building. Horses shove their noses over stall doors to greet Bax.

"Always liked animals," says Bax, blushing. "Hurry, hide in the hay." He dashes back into the yard, and is soon whistling again.

Wil runs into a stall, and dives into a pile of dung-specked hay behind a brown horse. Wrinkling your nose at the manure, you race down the corridor to an empty stall, to find a fresh haystack. Burrowing your way inside, you make a peep hole so you can see. In the stall opposite you, Aria leaps into some hay to hide.

The gates creak as Bart opens them and greets someone. A moment later, the door to the stables is flung open.

"No, sir, there isn't anyone in here," says Bart. "Just a few horses, sir. See?"

"Think I'm fool enough to search filthy manure, do you?" Heavy stomps come along the corridor. "We all know humans are too pathetic to hide there. I'll check the clean stalls."

That's why Wil hid in that dirty hay! The stomping gets louder. The monster is coming closer.

Aria's voice pops into your head. *"I'm hiding, but I'm scared!"*

Aria's bottom is sticking out of the hay, her purple tail high in the air. Like a little child, she's only hidden her head and thinks no one can see her. It's too late to warn her. A tharuk steps into her stall.

The creature is quietly drawing its sword. You sneak out of your hiding place to save her, even though you're no match for a tharuk.

"*Oh, no!*" Aria says in your head. Her bottom twitches.

Rumbling shakes Aria's stall. A jet of brown gas and shredded streamers of blue-and-silver chocolate wrapper fly out of Aria's bottom. A pooey chocolatey stench overpowers the scent of horse. The tharuk stumbles back, clutching its nose as a shower of chocolate-wrapper-confetti rains down on its head.

You never knew dragon farts had such power!

Startled into action, you yell, "Aria, here!"

She zips into the air, hay trailing around her, and flies over the tharuk's head to your stall. Yanking your backpack open, you pull out the chili tuna fish and she gulps it down.

Roaring, the tharuk leaps up, snatching at Aria. Flames spurt from Aria's maw, straight at the tharuk's chest. Its clothing catches fire. The stink of burned fur fills the air. Again, the brave dragonet darts at the beast, flaming the monster's ears.

"Ow!" The tharuk clutches its ears and runs down the aisle.

Clank! Bart steps out of a stall and hits it on the head with his shovel. The beast crumples to the ground. Only then do you smell burning. A spark has caught the hay. It's frightening how fast the small flame is growing.

"Becks," you yell. "Water!"

Becks runs in with her pail and douses the fire. Wil clambers out of the filthy hay and joins you all, stomping on the steaming ashes.

The tharuk groans. He's coming around.

"We need to leave. He's got buddies." You cautiously open the stable door. There's no sign of the other tharuks. Yet.

An enormous wagon loaded with produce rumbles into the yard, horses snorting. Upon the seat is the giant you saw melting cheese in the marketplace. He leaps from the wagon and flips down the side, revealing a hidden compartment under the floor.

"Giant John!" cries Wil, still covered in strands of manure-coated hay. "Can you get us out of town?"

"Hop in," says Giant John, clapping Wil on the shoulder. "It'll be a squeeze, but I can hide you."

On the street outside you hear the roars of more tharuks.

It's time to make a decision. Do you:

Escape in Giant John's wagon? **P256**

Or

Stay in the stables and confront the tharuks? **P261**

You have decided to escape in Giant John's wagon

From his worn leather boots to the knife in his belt, Giant John looks exactly like the sort of person you shouldn't accept a lift from — especially in a hidden compartment in his wagon. As if picking up your thoughts, Wil nudges you towards the wagon.

"It's alright — I've known him all my life. You can trust him."

The tharuks are getting closer, their boots pounding the nearby street. It's a no-brainer really. Besides, Giant John looks tough — tough enough to handle a few tharuks, and the hidden compartment in his wagon is brilliant — much safer than fighting those beasts.

"Quick, jump in!" You gesture at the wagon and look at Wil.

Before Wil has a chance, Bart, Becks and Bax squeeze into the compartment, jamming themselves up against the far side. You let Wil go next, so you're not right next to the Thomsons, then you clamber in.

"Aria, come on."

She's trembling on the ground, eyes whirling. *"I hate tight spaces."*

"Come on, you'll be alright."

Giant John scoops her up, pops her in next to you, and snaps the side of the wagon shut. He thumps his way up onto the seat and the wagon rolls across the stable yards and out onto the cobbled street. Every cobble rattles through the metal-bound cartwheels, jarring your bones.

Bart groans softly. "No suspension," he whispers.

Roars surround the wagon. The guttural voice of a tharuk yells, "Halt. What have you there?"

"You want to buy something?" Giant John answers.

All five of you, and Aria, don't breathe, awaiting the monster's answer.

"Finest onions in Dragons' Realm, these are. How many do you want? Or how about some apples?" Giant John prompts.

Thuds sound above you.

"Here you go," calls Giant John.

Something thumps to the ground beside the wagon. Tharuks snarl. There's a rip, accompanied by slurping, crunching and more snarls. The pungent scent of onions drifts through the wagon. Then the wheels start to roll again.

Aria's voice sounds in your mind. *Giant John's so clever, distracting them with food.*

You nod, but don't dare answer in case the monsters hear you.

As you leave the town outskirts and get onto a softer dirt trail, the jarring stops, but with five of you and a dragonet jammed in together, it's getting warmer, and the smell of horse manure makes your nostrils twitch. Turning to whisper to Wil, a piece of hay stuck to his clothing tickles your face. The pong of horse dung is unmistakable.

"Poo!" you say. "I thought that was the horse, not you!"

Wil's teeth flash white in the dark. "Sorry, it was a good hiding place, even if it was mucky."

Perhaps you should've jumped in the wagon first, then you'd have the Thomsons between you and Wil's dung-smeared clothes.

Bart farts, loudly. A cloud of stink creeps through the wagon.

Becks giggles. "Bart, that's worse than Wil's horse poo!"

After a while, the stench mingles with the smell of sweaty socks and unbrushed teeth. You hold your nose, sweat trickling down your neck in the stuffy heat.

Aria squirms. *This is torture for a sensitive dragon nose.*

"And for normal noses," you mutter as Bart lets several more farts rip.

As the journey goes on, it gets cooler. Just when you think you can't stand being cramped up in a stinking box any longer, the wagon halts.

"Could be tharuks," whispers Wil.

You all freeze. Giant John thuds down to the ground. Your heart thumps in your chest. Aria is rigid with tension. The side of the wagon flies down. Sunlight floods the compartment, making you squint. You can't see anything.

Giant John laughs. "We're here! Look at you all, a sorry lot."

Aria explodes from the wagon so fast her wingtip hits your nose, making your eyes water. You stumble out, rubbing your legs. Wil falls onto the ground behind you. Bax shoves Becks and Bart on top of Wil in his eagerness to get into fresh air.

Bart clambers up and claps you on the shoulder. "I'm so glad you got us out of there. So glad. Thanks, buddy."

Buddy? This is Bart Thomson who has never said a kind word to anyone. You nod. "No problem."

"We're here," calls Aria, flitting around in the air. *"We're here!"*

"Where?"

You don't need an answer. Several blue dragons land near a long stone building, nestled at the foot of a steep mountain. Men and women in dark clothing are on huge leather saddles astride dragons. "The blue guards," you murmur.

The dragons' scales glint in the late afternoon sun, like dragonflies. Their powerful leg muscles ripple and bunch as they walk. Although all the dragons are blue, some have lighter-blue patches, different shaped tails, or more angular heads. No two dragons seem to have the same eye color, but all their scales gleam.

"Awesome!" says Wil, striding forward to touch a dragon.

Bax joins him. Becks and Bart hang back, not looking too keen.

A woman jumps down from a dragon and strides towards you, shaking Giant John's hand. "Welcome, John. You have passengers for us?"

He nods. "I can't smuggle them back into Montanara. My wagon may be searched. And this young dragonet needs to go to Dragons' Hold."

She nods and motions to you. "Climb aboard. Aria's mother has missed her."

Soon you're behind her on the back of a dragon, with Aria on your shoulder. Wil's eyes shine behind another dragon rider. Bax and Becks are doubled up, and Bart is grimacing, hanging onto another rider as they lift off into the sky.

A dragon! You're on a dragon! This beats the school picnic, any day!

Giant John becomes a tiny figure waving goodbye as you fly up the mountainside, leaving the forest and fields behind. Montanara is only a smudge in the distance. On your shoulder, Aria starts to sing.

Once more, she's hardly melodious. Your ears ring with flat notes. "Why are you singing?"

Aria stops to answer. *"To let my mother know I'm coming! Did you know these mountains are called Dragon's Teeth? Look how sharp they are."*

If you keep Aria speaking to you, she can't sing! "What's that?" you say, pointing to the tallest mountain.

"Fire Crag."

You soar over Fire Crag and find it's part of a ring of mountains. Aria's right. They do look like dragon fangs. Nestled in a valley inside the mountains are forests and a tangled wilderness at one end, and fields and orchards at the other. A lake glints silver, deep in the forest. And the sky is full of dragons. Dragons of all colors. The dragon you're riding roars.

Aria sings at the top of her voice, her shriek jolting through you like feedback from a microphone. From the other side of a valley, a purple shape is getting bigger. Its bellows ring across the valley above the din of the other dragons. Soon you make out a huge purple dragon, spitting fire, and charging towards you. Aria leaps off your shoulder, airborne.

You snatch at her, nearly falling out of the saddle, and just manage to snag her tail.

"Why are you stopping me?" Aria cries in your mind. *"That's my mother!"*

"That ferocious beast is your mother?"

"Yes!"

Aria wriggles from your grasp and, singing at the top of her voice, dives downwards. The purple dragon swoops through the air and opens its mouth. It's going to eat Aria! You scream in panic, but the dragon scoops Aria gently in her jaws, tosses her high and flings her into the arms of a rider on her back.

As you sigh in relief that Aria wasn't hurt, your rider shouts over her shoulder, "Great job, you reunited them!"

Her blue dragon roars and follows Aria's mother. Nearby, Wil whoops from another blue dragon. Bart sits behind his rider with his jaw clenched, knuckles white on the saddle. Bax and Becks are grinning from ear to ear as you all race behind the purple dragon towards a stony clearing.

Landing on the stones, the rider climbs down off Aria's mother. Aria flits to your arm. Her mother nuzzles you. Placing your hand on her snout, you hear her deep voice, rumbling through your mind.

"Thank you for bringing my daughter home to me. She's told me how you protected her. In return, I grant you permission to be her rider, when she is grown."

"Me? A dragon rider?"

The dragon nods.

"Awesome!"

But what about your family? If you stay here you may not see them, but if you leave, you won't get to ride Aria when she's bigger.

It's time to make a decision. Do you:

Stay at Dragons' Hold and ride Aria? **P340**

Or

Farewell Aria and return home? **P299**

You have decided to stay in the stables and confront the tharuks

"No thanks," you say to Giant John. "I'll be fine."

"You've got to be joking," say Bart, Bax and Becks.

"Oh great Zeebongi, I'll stay by your side." Wil looks longingly at the wagon. "But wouldn't you rather leave with my good friend Giant John?"

You shake your head.

"Are you sure?" says Giant John, raising an eyebrow at you. "The tharuks will probably kill you."

You gulp. Your family told you never to accept rides from people you don't know. But Wil knows Giant John. And your parents probably weren't considering a time when you were in another world, chased by crazy monsters that could kill you.

The roaring on the street is getting closer. You have one more chance to change your mind.

It's time to make a decision. Do you:

Escape in Giant John's wagon? **P256**

Or

Face the tharuks? **P292**

You have decided to go straight to the blue guards

"I think we have enough food, and Aria wants to get to the blue guards as soon as we can."

"I bow to your wisdom, Zeebongi," says Wil. "We need to take this trail." He pushes aside a giant fern and gestures towards a dense dark path.

You shiver as you enter the closely-packed trees. Not much sunlight filters through the treetops.

"*It's creepy in here,*" says Aria. "*I know just the thing to cheer us up.*" She opens her mouth and starts to sing. Her voice is shrill and scratchy and sounds off-key.

"Wow, that's beautiful," Wil says.

You stare at him as if he's nuts, but he doesn't seem to notice. How could he think Aria's screeching is beautiful? Stepping over a fallen tree trunk, you continue along the trail, Aria's discordant tunes jarring your ears.

Squelching through a marshy section of the trail, you take Aria off your shoulder to save your ears from splitting. Just as well, because her next tune is even more tuneless than the last. Mosquitoes nibble on the exposed parts of your skin. You slap them away, hoping this world doesn't have malaria or other mosquito-borne diseases. Dragonflies with blue, pink and green striped bodies flit in and out of the marsh grass.

Aria takes a break from singing to snap at a dragonfly.

"Aria," you scold, "can't you eat something nasty like these mosquitoes, instead of those beautiful dragonflies?"

Aria zips off your arm and snaps at the mosquitoes buzzing around you and Wil.

"What a shame she stopped singing," says Wil. "Her songs are so melodious and I do think she's getting better. It must be your fabulous training, great Zeebongi. You're whispering hints to her when I'm not listening, aren't you?"

The guy must be completely deaf. Aria has been getting worse, not better. You can't believe that he thinks she sounds good.

"You're joking, aren't you?" you ask.

"No, I wasn't, but I can tell you a joke if you'd like me to, Zeebongi." Wil's eager smile nearly has you rolling your eyes.

"No, it's fine. I don't feel like laughing." Avoiding a muddy spot, you grab a branch and swing out to land on firm ground.

Aria lands on your shoulder and burps. "Great mosquitoes," she says. "You're right. Those dragonflies are much too pretty to eat."

"And they're called *dragon*flies," you say. "It's almost like eating your cousins. You can't do that."

Aria hangs her head. "Sorry, I won't do it again."

"I tell you what, you must be hungry, let's stop soon and have something to eat. I have some more tasty food in my backpack."

Wil's eyes light up. "Any more choclick?"

You smile.

Luckily, Aria is distracted from singing. She chatters in your mind. *"See those big gray trees? They're strongwoods. People who exercise under them grow strong really fast."*

You run your hand over the smooth gray bark. It's warm and seems to thrum under your fingers. You raise an eyebrow and keep walking.

"In some parts of the forest, there are monsters called tharuks," says Aria brightly. *"They came through a world gate into Dragons' Realm. Sometimes they kill people and eat dragonets, but I'll be safe because I'm with you."*

You swallow, wishing you had as much confidence in your abilities as she and Wil do.

"See those bees?" says Aria. *"They make the best honey in the whole realm, my mother says. Oh I'd better keep singing so she hears me and comes to find me."* Aria opens her mouth to start singing.

"Wil, here's a good place to eat," you yell, suddenly sitting down near a puddle in the middle of the trail.

Wil frowns and gives you a concerned look. Then his face brightens. "Great Zeebongi—"

"Zeebongi will do," you snap, tired of his compliments and Aria's singing.

"Zeebongi, then," says Wil. "You should have told me you were so hungry that you couldn't wait!"

"Absolutely ravenous," you say. Your trick worked. Aria is staring at the backpack in your hands – not singing.

You pull out a packet of potato chips. Wil leaps as the wrapper crinkles.

"Remember, Wil, it won't bite."

He manages a small smile at your lame joke, but still stares at the foil as if it has a life of its own.

Aria nibbles a corner of the packet, before you can even get it open. You can't help smiling. With these two as companions, a snack will never be simple again. You pass them each a potato chip.

Aria snaps hers down in a single gulp.

Wil licks his and pulls a face. "It tastes so…"

"Salty?"

"What is salty?"

You scratch your head. "Um, salt comes from the sea."

Wil's face brightens. "I've heard of the sea. It's a long way from here."

How do you explain salt? "Well, it's um, … uh… do you like it?"

He licks his chip again. "Yes. It's very strong, but tasty."

"Wil, you're the clever one! You just explained salt perfectly."

He beams. "Me? Clever? Thank you, Zeebongi."

Aria leaps onto your arms, sticks her snout into the packet, and slurps every last chip out. When she jumps down, the packet is still stuck on her nose. *"Help me!"* she says, batting it with her forelegs.

You laugh.

She swipes at the packet with her talons, shredding it.

Wil laughs too. "What a shame. It was so colorful. I wanted it as a Zeebongi keepsake."

Perhaps it was good it got shredded. Next he'd be selling Zeebongi souvenirs. "Come on, we should get going."

A low growl comes from the forest.

You leap to your feet. "What was that?"

"A wolf." Wil's face is tense.

"Save me!" Aria leaps on top of your head.

"Zeebongi, what should we do?"

"How would I know? You're from Dragons' Realm, not me!"

The growls get louder. It sounds like more than one wolf.

"Stop being so humble, Zeebongi. Tell us what to do!"

"Quick, climb this tree!"

A pale wolf flashes through the undergrowth.

Aria flies into the tree. You and Wil scramble up after her, grabbing low branches to hoist yourselves up. A pack of wolves break through the underbrush. They surround the tree, snarling. One leaps up, just missing Wil's leg. He yanks it to safety. You both climb higher.

Your heart is pounding. Wil's hands are shaking. Aria sits very still, her eyes whirling.

"What do we do, now?" Wil asks. His voice trembles.

You have two ideas – both are crazy, but just might work. You could feed Aria chili tuna fish and see if she can flame the wolves to scare them off. Or you could ask Aria to sing to frighten the wolves away. You can't let her know that you think her singing is awful, so you'd have to ask nicely.

A wolf howls. Others leap up at the tree, snarling.

"Quick, Zeebongi!" yells Wil. "What should we do?"

It's time to make a decision. Do you:

Feed Aria chili tuna fish so she can flame the wolves? **P296**

Or

Make Aria sing to scare the wolves away? **P266**

You have decided to make Aria sing to scare the wolves away

The tree thuds as a wolf slams into the trunk, trying to shake you out. The other wolves copy it, slamming against the tree. Your branch shakes with each thud.

"Aria, I think if you sing, your lullaby may send the wolves to sleep. Would you like to try it?"

"*Really?*" says Aria. "*Is my singing that good?*"

"Great idea, Zeebongi," says Wil. "Her singing is so fantastic, it's sure to weave a magic spell over those rabid wolves."

Aria spreads her wings and puffs up her chest, as if she's an opera diva. Then she opens her mouth and screeches.

"Bravo," calls Wil.

"Louder!" you say. "Higher! More!"

She takes another breath and shrieks louder than you've ever heard her.

The thudding against the trunk stops. The wolves lie on the ground with their paws over their ears, whining.

Aria stops. "*Oh, they don't seem to like my song.*"

"They love your singing," you say. "See how they're joining in?"

"*It sounds like they're whining.*" Aria pouts, her lower lip sticking out like a sulky child's.

Well, she is a child, a dragon child. Now that she's stopped singing, the wolves jump up against the tree again, thudding against the trunk, nearly shaking you off the branch. You cling on. More wolves leap up, snapping under your legs. Wil keeps his on the branch. His knuckles are white where he grips the tree.

"Aria, they weren't whining. They were singing too," You tell her. "They're just not as good at it as you are."

Aria's mouth pulls back, showing her teeth in a strange grimace. It's a dragon smile, the first you've ever seen.

"Come on, Aria," says Wil. "You're my favorite singer."

By now you're sure he's deaf! But his cheerful words convince Aria to sing again. She bellows loudly, her eyes squeezed shut, her voice squealing higher and higher, until you think your eardrums will split. The wolves are all flat on the ground, their paws over their ears. One by one, they slink off into the forest, whimpering.

Long after they've gone, you let Aria keep singing, just in case they want to return. Finally, Aria stops, exhausted. She opens her eyes and gazes around.

"Where's my audience?" she says, peering out of the tree at the empty ground around the trunk. *"I thought they'd be asleep."*

"I think wolves are creatures of habit," you say. "They must have gone home to their dens to sleep. Your lullaby worked!"

Aria snorts, and looks at you doubtfully. Then she sniffs the air and looks skyward.

A roar echoes from above, shaking the branches. A mighty wind rustles the leaves. A purple dragon appears above the treetops.

"Mother! It's my mother!" Aria squeals in your mind. She sings again.

The purple dragon roars, and wheels away over the treetops.

"We need to follow her," Aria says.

Wil is staring into the sky at the disappearing dragon's tail. "Magnificent!" He's awestruck, clinging to the branch, unmoving.

"Come on, Wil, we have to follow her. It's Aria's mother!" you say.

"Great Zeebongi, you surely do have a way with dragons," he says. "She came to you."

"Actually, she came to Aria, because she sang," you tell him as you climb out of the tree.

"Oh, but that was your brilliant idea. Zeebongi, you truly are the All-knowing One, just like they said." He clambers down after you.

"Mother is in a clearing, a few minutes away," Aria says, flitting in front of you.

You scan the forest for stray wolves. The sooner you're near Aria's mother, the better, just in case the wolves decide earache isn't so bad after all. "Let's race," you suggest.

Wil is also glancing nervously into the forest. "Best idea you've had yet, Zeebongi."

You both run after Aria, whipping through the trees. The majestic purple dragon is waiting for you in a clearing. She has a leather saddle on her back, but no rider.

Aria flies straight to her mother, nearly hitting her nose in her enthusiasm to nuzzle her. She frolics in the air, turning somersaults and flapping around her mother's head in an excited frenzy. She's as small as a dragonfly compared to the fully-grown dragon. Her mother sits patiently, a quiet rumble coursing through her body, like an enormous cat purring, only ten times louder.

Sunlight glimmers off the dragon's scales. Its huge talons rake the grass in the clearing, like a cat kneading a cushion. Her eyes are bright green. When she turns her gaze on you, they draw you in, making it hard to look away. She seems to see through you in a glance, knowing your heart – your worst fears and your loftiest dreams.

You're filled with wonder. A dragon. A real live dragon. No one at school will ever believe this. Just as you think of school, two figures burst into the clearing.

"Watch it," shrieks Becks. "It's a dragon!"

"Wow," says Bax. "Awesome!"

"Hi," you ask. "Where's Bart?"

"Don't know," says Becks. "Last time we saw him, he was running away from a pack of whimpering wolves." She points at Aria's mother. "Aren't you scared of that monster?"

"Aria and her mother aren't monsters." You gesture at the dragon and her dragonet – now leapfrogging over her mother's spinal ridges. "They're my friends."

Bax's eyes shine. "Can you introduce me to them?"

"Depends how friendly you are." You draw yourself up to your full height and try to look as impressive as possible.

"You should both bow before my friend here," says Wil in a haughty tone. "It's not every day you meet someone so important."

You hope he won't call you Zeebongi in front of them.

"Important?" Becks screws up her nose.

"Of course," says Bax, bowing and elbowing Becks. He's obviously desperate to befriend a dragon.

"Yes," says Wil. "Very important – my friend here mind-speaks with dragons, foretells events and even scares away wolves. Those wolves you saw were scared away by us."

Becks look impressed. She bows too.

"Do you know these people?" asks Aria. *"Aren't they the ones that were mean to you in your world?"*

You nod, knowing no one else has heard her question.

Aria balances on her mother's tail. *"Then let's send them home."*

A portal opens right near Becks.

"Time to go home," says Becks, leaping through and yanking Bax after her.

"But," calls Bax as he tumbles through, "what are we going to tell Mom about Bart?"

Aria speaks to you. *"We're going to Dragons' Hold and taking Wil. Do you want to come too? Or do you want to go home?"*

It's time to make a decision. Do you:

Go with Wil and Aria to Dragons' Hold? **P307**

Or

Follow Bax and Becks home? **P294**

You have decided to cut Mia out of the net with your knife

The trap is suspended from the tree by two thick ropes. Lying on the branch, you reach down and grasp a rope with one hand to steady it. "Stop struggling, Mia, you're making the net swing."

"What do you expect me to do? Sit here and wait for you to free me?"

Flicking your knife open, you saw at the rope. "This should help."

"That puny little knife? Help? Fat chance!"

"You're right, but it's all I've got." It's slow work, cutting through the tough strands.

The branch lurches. You fumble, nearly dropping your knife. "Hey, are you mad? Quit moving around. You nearly knocked me out of the tree."

"Sorry, just trying to help. I should be able to reach now." Mia's arm pokes up through the net and sparks flit along the other rope.

You keep cutting, hand cramping from gripping the knife so tightly. The blade slowly frays the edge of the rope, but you're only about a quarter of the way through. Mia's rope is smoldering, wisps of smoke curling up from the brown fibers.

Grunting comes from the bushes. "They're coming!" whispers Mia. "Stay quiet. And keep cutting." A small flame bursts from her finger, setting the rope alight, but it dies out, only smoldering.

Three tharuks enter the clearing. The largest one sniffs. "Is that smoke?"

"Probably from her burning me before," says the beast with the singed chest.

Wisps of smoke from the rope curl around your face. Your nose starts to tickle. Oh, no! You're going to sneeze! The tharuks prod Mia through the net. She remains remarkably quiet. You struggle to contain the itching, but your nostrils can't stop twitching.

In an effort to keep your sneeze at bay, you remember your lessons on environmental magic and tune into the thrumming of the strongwood trees. Their energy buzzes through you, but it's no use.

"Aachoo!"

Your sneeze is so violent, you drop the knife right onto a tharuk's head. All three beasts stare up into the tree. You're cornered, trapped on a branch, with Mia stuck in a net and three monsters eying you.

It's time to make a decision. Do you:

Leap onto the tharuks' heads? **P272**

Or

Stay in the tree? **P303**

You have decided to leap onto the tharuks' heads

When dealing with the Thomson twins, you often found the element of surprise useful. With the echo of your gigantic sneeze still ringing among the trees, you bellow and leap down towards the largest monster, hands outstretched, ready to do some damage.

To your surprise, a flash of light bursts from your hands, striking a tharuk, knocking it over, and singeing the net.

"Ow," Mia yells. "You got me too."

You crash into the big tharuk. Another stands shocked, staring at you as the burned one writhes on the ground.

Mia flings flames around the clearing and at the ropes above the net. You scramble off the tharuk, but it grabs your shirt, shredding the back with its claws. Tugging away as the animal lumbers to its feet, you take a running leap and grab Mia's net, hanging on and swinging with it between the trees. The burned and half-cut ropes creak. You let go, flying past the tharuks, landing near a huge strongwood, and roll to your feet.

You duck as Mia's net swings back, her hands still flinging fire at the monsters. They snarl and swipe at her with their long claws, ducking her flames. The half-torn ropes groan under Mia's weight and give way. She crashes to the ground, knocking over a tharuk, and scrambles out of the ropes.

Spying her bow nearby, you snatch it up and dash to her, thrusting it into her hands. But before she can fire an arrow, the tharuks have recovered from their shock and have surrounded you both, snarling. Their small red eyes flick over you. Dark saliva dribbles off the end of their tusks.

Mia's eyes are wide with panic. You strain to feel the environmental magic around you, but your heart is pounding so loudly and your knees are shaking so badly, that you can't focus.

The tharuks leap towards you as a glowing oval of colored light shimmers nearby.

It's time to make a decision. Do you:
Take Mia through the portal? **P317**
Or
Stay and fight the tharuks? **P319**

You have decided to offer the tharuks your chocolate

Swallowing hard, you climb out of the tree to the sound of guttural grunts through the forest.

"Quick," hisses Mia. "Hide."

Ignoring her, you position yourself between Mia's net and the point where the burned tharuk disappeared into the trees.

"What are you doing?" Mia whispers. "Why aren't you hiding?"

Unwrapping the chocolate, you hold it out in front of you with a trembling hand. Your knees join in, shaking too.

"Now's not the time for a snack," Mia hisses. "Hurry up and hide."

The burned tharuk enters the clearing first, its nose twitching. Hopefully it likes the rich chocolatey scent emanating from your hand better than *your* scent. And, hopefully, its hungry – but not too hungry, you only want it to eat the chocolate!

The beast approaches, nostrils flared. "What's that?" it growls, staring at your chocolate bar.

Three more tharuks emerge from behind it, snarling and sniffing. Drops of dark saliva slide off their tusks.

"It's the best food you've ever tasted," you say, pretty sure it's true. "I'll give you a piece if you set my friend free."

The biggest tharuk snorts. "We'll take it off you anyway." It swipes its claws at you.

He's just like a scarier version of Bart Thomson – wanting to steal goodies from kids. You duck, dancing out of reach.

The beast lunges for you again, but a smaller tharuk yells, "Hey, stop that. It smells tastier than the putrid scraps Commander Zens feeds us. We should try some."

"I want some too, don't let the kid drop it," calls another tharuk.

"I'm troop leader," yells the burned tharuk. "I should get first bite. Stand down and let me deal with that human."

The large tharuk steps to one side and the burned tharuk approaches. The stench of singed fur clogs your nose, drowning out the aroma of chocolate. With nervous fingers, you break a piece of chocolate and hold it out to the monster. He spears it with a claw and pops it between his tusks into his mouth.

Roaring, his red eyes fly open and turn bright green. An enormous tusky smile breaks out over his furry face. "Delicious!" he yells. "Come on, troop, have some."

Breaking pieces off as fast as you can, you feed the other three tharuks a piece of chocolate each. They eagerly line up for more, green-eyed and beaming with delight.

Above you, Mia mutters, "What a waste of great food."

You don't have an endless supply. Thinking fast, you say, "First let the girl down, then I'll give you more chocolate."

"Let her down," the troop leader calls, mesmerized by the silver wrapper in your hand.

The other tharuks ease the net out of the tree, lower Mia to the ground, and open the net. Brushing herself off, Mia stalks over to the trees and snatches up her bow, then comes to stand beside you. "What will you do when you run out?" whispers Mia.

"Not sure," you whisper back. "Got any ideas?"

"You, troop leader," says Mia, "if we promise to feed you this delicious stuff, what will you do in return?"

Green eyes gleaming, the troop leader answers, "Anything."

"What's in that stuff?" hisses Mia. "Does it contain an obedience potion? These monsters are normally savage, but you've tamed them."

Could Mia be right? You decide to test her theory. "Um… jump up and down…"

The next minute they're all jumping on the spot.

"Great," says Mia. "Could you sing like dragons?"

They start to yowl, and one even flaps imaginary wings. Very weird. For them, chocolate is like some sort of wonder-drug. They'll do anything you say.

Mia keeps testing your theory, getting the monsters to dance and scratch their armpits.

This is great. You now have four monsters that will do anything you ask – for chocolate. You're just wondering how long the effect will last, when five more tharuks stumble out of the woods, snarling.

"What are you doing?" bellows the largest of the new arrivals. "And why are your eyes green?"

Snatching out your knife, you cut the chocolate into five smaller pieces, hoping little bits will still make tharuks obey. "Try this." You pass them each a piece.

Roaring, they stare at each other in amazement as their eyes turn green too.

Mia laughs with glee and soon has all nine of the tharuks doing as she wishes.

Suddenly the troop leader's eyes flash red and he growls a low threatening snarl. "You cast a spell on my troops! I'll get you." He lunges towards you, claws out and tusks aiming right at your face.

The air next to you shimmers, and you grab Mia's hand, ready to leap through the portal, but you can't! Something is falling out of the portal at your feet. Three somethings. The Thomson twins!

Bart falls straight onto the troop leader's back, pinning him to the ground. Becks and Bax land nearby.

"Stay there, Bart," you yell. "Keep it pinned."

The tharuk growls and snarls, but cannot move. For the first time in your life, you're grateful Bart is so big.

Becks whirls to face you. "W-w-what are these things?"

The eyes of two more tharuks turn red, and they snarl viciously.

"Tharuks," you reply.

Becks just stares at them, but Bart yells at the monsters, "We just came from that shiny swirling air." He points at the portal. "We have an army of a hundred men waiting on the other side. They'll come when I call, so back off." He grabs one of the troop leader's ears and twists it. "And if you come any closer, I'll rip his ear off."

"You heard him," barks the troop leader. "Stand down!"

Typical Bart, bluffing so convincingly – he's fooled you hundreds of times before. "Um, Bart," you say, "they love chocolate. Got any?"

Bart snaps, "Bax, deploy the stash."

Bax unzips the bag on Bart's back and chocolate bars spill out over the ground. The only place you've ever seen more chocolate is the aisle of a supermarket.

Snatching them up, you thrust one in the hands of every tharuk, and stow the rest in your backpack. The tharuks shovel the chocolate in their mouths greedily, tossing the wrappers on the ground. Hopefully, this bigger dose will last long enough to get them back to Master Giddi. Then they'll be his problem, not yours.

"Hey, you lot," yells Becks, "do you think this is some sort of barnyard? Pick up your litter!" She points at the wrappers. "You need to be tidy tharuks and care for the environment."

The monsters smile sheepishly and pass her their wrappers. "Sorry," mutters the troop leader.

Bart and Bax are standing next to the portal, as if they're thinking about leaving. Becks is scratching the tharuk troop leader behind the ears. "Just like a big kitty-cat," aren't you, she croons. "But lots meaner – I like that."

You have the tharuks under control, but it's only going to last as long as the chocolate supply. There may also be more tharuks in the forest, so you need to find a way to keep them supplied with chocolate too. The Thomson twins could do it. Perhaps you could convince them to bring you back chocolate regularly, to keep the tharuks under control. You stare at Becks. She seems to like tharuks. Maybe you could convince her to stay, so that Bart and Bax come to visit. Or perhaps you could use your magic to convince them.

The portal starts to shrink.

It's time to make a decision. Do you:

Convince Becks to stay with the tharuks? **P311**

Or

Use magic so Bart and Bax bring you chocolate? **P314**

You have decided to go to Dragons' Hold with Hans

"I'm going to Dragons' Hold," you tell Mickel. "Thanks for training me. I hope I get to repay you some day."

Mickel waves you farewell and leaves the clearing.

Gray clouds are gathering above the forest. "You'd better wear something warm," warns Hans, "and hang on tight."

You pull your rain jacket on over your T-shirt and climb up on Handel's back.

Handel rumbles, his body vibrating with a deep thrum, and takes off. The wind tugs at your jacket, trying to creep inside. Its icy bite easily nips through your jeans. Perhaps this ride isn't going to be as much fun as your last one with Handel.

Hans speaks, but the wind whips his words away before you can make out what he's said. Handel climbs into the sky. Your butt starts to slip in the saddle. You grab onto Hans. Then Hans throws his body forwards, holding onto purpose-built leather loops. Clinging to his waist, your head on Hans' back, you stop slipping.

The dragon climbs higher. Gray tendrils of cloud waft in front of your face, surrounding you. You can hardly see Handel, but the rough cloth of Hans' jerkin is still against your cheek.

It's spooky riding on a dragon you can't see, pressed up against a rider you can only feel, with murky gray all around. Dampness seeps through your jeans. Your hands are freezing cold. Even your socks feel wet through your sneakers. How much farther is Handel going?

Hands and butt numb, you cling on, not daring to let go, even to rub your cold nose. Rain lashes at you, driven sideways by bitter wind. Handel swerves, trying to counter the foul weather. Perhaps you should've stayed at Horseshoe Bend with Mickel. Then you'd be in the forge next to a warm fire.

The ride seems to take forever. Gradually the rain eases and the cloud thins. You gasp. Ahead is a sheer wall of snow, rock and ice.

Hans sits up straight. "Welcome to Dragon's Teeth, the guardians of Dragons' Hold."

Below, tiny fields reach the foot of the mountains, which rise into steep spiky tips, high above. "They do look like teeth, Hans." You try to keep the shiver out of your voice, but you're so cold you don't quite manage. "How much longer until we get there?" Hans reaches forward and opens an enormous saddlebag. There are two in front of him and two more behind you on Handel's haunches, four in all, but this is the only empty one.

"You could climb into this saddlebag to keep the wind off..." Hans pauses for a moment.

It's time to make a decision. Do you:

Stay in Handel's saddle behind Hans? **P285**

Or

Climb into Handel's saddlebag? **P280**

You have decided to climb into Handel's saddlebag

Getting into Handel's saddlebag sounds much warmer than sitting behind Hans, wet and freezing. Glancing at the houses dotted in the fields far below, you push down the fear clutching at your insides. If it was really risky, Hans wouldn't have suggested you move.

You scramble, bringing your knees up to kneel, then stand on the slippery wet leather saddle. Handel veers to the right. Your feet slip, throwing you off the dragon into the air.

"Help!" Flailing at a loose strap, you grab it with one hand, nearly jolting your shoulder socket from your body. "Hans, help!"

Hans looks down, obviously shocked. "Handel, quick! Rider overboard!"

Your hand slips down the wet strap, losing hold. Desperately, you grab for the leather with your other hand, but the wind whips the end out of reach. As you lose hold, the last thing you see are Handel's green eyes, whirling rapidly, beautiful against his bronze scales.

Plummeting through the cold air, the field below rapidly grows larger. Tiny beehives turn into cottage roofs. Small blobs of yellow become haystacks. Pale blue ribbons become rivers, with stones and dangerous-looking tree stumps along their banks.

Whump! With a roar, Handel clutches you in his talons and heads skywards. Relief washes over you as the river slowly becomes a ribbon once more and cottage roofs turn back into beehives.

Struggling to find your voice, you swallow. "Thank you, Handel."

Above you, the dragon shoots a lick of flames in reply.

"You alright?" calls Hans.

"Yeah." Cold and shivering, but alive – as far as you're concerned, that's alright.

Suddenly Handel drops you. You roll your eyes. Not again! Today you've done enough skydiving to last a lifetime. With a whoosh of wings, Handel dives under you and slaps you with his tail, bouncing you up into the saddle. You smack into Hans' back, your face mooshed into his shoulder.

"Oof."

"Um, sorry, Hans."

"No, I'm sorry. I was only joking about getting into the saddlebag," he says, "I thought you'd laugh, not take me seriously!"

Now he tells you! "Well, there aren't many dragons where I come from," you say through chattering teeth, "so all this is new."

"You handled that tail bounce pretty well for someone who is new to dragon riding. I'll think you'll make a fine rider." Hans reaches into the saddlebag, pulls out a green cloak, and passes it to you. "Put this on, over your damp gear."

Dubiously, you take the cloak. Your fingers instantly feel warm. Snuggling your face into the heavy material, your cheeks grow warm too. In front of you, Hans is also donning a similar cloak. You fling yours on.

"The cloak is wizard-wear," says Hans, "and contains a drying spell."

Copying Hans, you pull up the cloak's hood and feel your hair start to dry. Steam rises from Hans' hood. Soon you're warmer.

"We're nearly at Dragons' Hold," says Hans. "The home of hundreds of dragons and their riders."

"Hundreds of dragons?" you ask. "I can hardly wait."

Hans chuckles. "A few years ago, I was just like you and had never ridden a dragon, but Handel has changed my life. You'll love Dragons' Hold." He scratches Handel's neck and the dragon thrums.

Handel flies up over a jagged mountain peak. "These mountains are called Dragon's Teeth."

You're astounded. Dragon's Teeth are a ring of mountains, like an open dragon's maw. Hidden in the middle is a basin filled with farms, rivers, forests and a lake – sparkling silver in the sunlight. Dragons speck the sky, riders on their backs.

"Wow."

"Welcome to Dragons' Hold, home of Zaarusha, the Dragon

Queen, and Anakisha, Queen's Rider."

Descending, you see people in fields and orchards. Dragons are perched on mountainside ledges. A silver dragon flies towards you with a dark-haired young woman astride its back.

"Hans, who is your passenger?" she calls.

Her dragon flies alongside Handel. Both the dragon and woman have turquoise eyes. The dragon's silver scales shimmer in the evening sunlight.

"A visitor from a world gate," Hans calls.

"Welcome!"

Hans looks over his shoulder. "That's Marlies. See how well she flies?" His voice is tinged with admiration.

"You like her, don't you?" you ask.

The tips of Hans' ears go red. "Of course not," he says.

"Yeah, right!" You're pretty sure Hans is sweet on Marlies.

Hans clears his throat. "See how Liesar's scales glow in the sunlight?"

Her silver scales glint like diamonds in a jeweler's window. "Liesar's awesome." You grin, knowing he's deliberately changing the subject.

Liesar spurts a tiny flame towards Handel. Wings beating, both dragons race towards the end of the valley. Liesar's tail streams behind her. The air rushes past you, making your eyes water.

Handel skims the treetops.

Your heart pounds.

He swoops up into the air, making your belly drop, then shoots downward towards a lake. Handel flies over the lake, dragging his talons in the water. Fine spray shoots up on either side of the bronze dragon, covering the bottom of your jeans in droplets. Luckily you're still wearing the wizard cloak.

Hans laughs. "He's washing his toes!"

Far ahead of you, Liesar roars.

"Come on, Handel," says Hans. "They're winning!"

You thought Handel was going fast before, but now trees flash past you as he zooms across the fields. Workers wave below. Liesar swoops over a field. Children cry out below, chasing after her.

"Handel," calls Hans. "Let's show those kids some acrobatics." He glances back at you. "When I say, just jump, like you did before."

"Alright." Your stomach clenches into a tight knot.

Handel shoots up into the air.

"Get ready," calls Hans.

You crouch on the saddle, hanging onto his shoulders for balance.

"Jump! Now!"

Flinging yourself into mid-air, you wonder if you've gone crazy. A stony clearing rushes up towards you. Children shriek. If Handel doesn't catch–

"Oof!" he has you in his talons again, and speeds up into the sky, only to drop you.

To think you could've been having a picnic quietly with your school class.

Slap! Handel's tail sends you flying back into the saddle.

"Sorry," you mutter as you slam into Hans' back.

Hans laughs. "You're great! How would you like to become a dragon rider? You could join our acrobatic team. We're looking for riders who aren't afraid to try a few stunts."

You think of your family at home. Your friends. And the Thomson twins.

"How would I see my family?"

"Any dragon can create a world gate back to your world when you need one."

Handel lands in a stony area at the end of the valley. People rush out to meet you, most dressed in similar clothing to Hans. Dragon Riders – men and women of all ages, and a few young ones, about your age.

You could join them, become a dragon acrobat, and fly through the skies of Dragons' Realm on the back of your very own dragon, visiting your family when you want.

Or you could ask Handel to send you home now.

It's time to make a decision. Do you:

Become a dragon acrobat? **P324**

Or

Ask Handel to take you home? **P328**

You have decided to stay in Handel's saddle behind Hans

It would be an awkward clamber around Hans, over a damp saddle, on a slippery dragon to reach the saddlebag. Looking at the very hard ground far below, you say, "Um, thanks, Hans, but I, um…"

Hans laughs. "I was only teasing!" He reaches into the saddlebag, pulls out a green cloak, and passes it to you. "Put this on, over your damp gear."

Dubiously, you take the cloak. Your fingers instantly feel warm. Snuggling your face into the heavy material, your cheeks grow warm too. In front of you, Hans is also donning a similar cloak. You fling your cloak on.

"The cloak is wizard-wear," says Hans, "imbued with a drying spell."

Copying Hans, you pull up the cloak's hood and feel your hair start to dry. In front of you, steam rises from Hans' hood. Gradually you get warmer.

Handel is gliding alongside the mountain range, steadily getting higher. Now he's not flying vertically, it's much easier to hold on.

As Handel soars over a jagged mountain peak, you are amazed that Dragon's Teeth are a ring of mountains, like an open dragon's maw. In the middle is a basin filled with farms, rivers, forests and a lake – sparkling silver in the sunlight. Dragons speck the sky, riders on their backs.

"Wow."

"Welcome to Dragons' Hold, home of Zaarusha, the Dragon Queen, and Anakisha, Queen's Rider."

Handel descends over people working in fields and orchards. Dragons are perched on mountainside ledges at one end of the valley. Handel lands in a stony area below them.

People rush out to meet you, most dressed in similar clothing to Hans. Among them is a familiar figure wearing a faded baseball cap. You climb out of the saddle and run to meet him.

"Peter?" You can't believe it. Surely it can't be your cousin. Here? Of all places?

Peter grins and grabs you in a bear hug. He looks about four years older than when you last saw him. "Hey, you're still wearing that T-shirt I gave you!"

Hans waves the crowd away, leaving you and Peter to get reacquainted. "Peter," he says, "bring our visitor inside for dinner when you're ready."

Peter nods.

"How did you grow so fast?" you ask him. "You've only been gone two months."

Peter gapes at you. "Two months? I've been in Dragons' Realm nearly five years!"

"No, you haven't."

Peter looks you up and down. "You haven't grown much, although you do look a bit fitter." He points at your muscles. "Maybe time is different here. When did you get here?"

"This morning." You glance at your watch. "About eight hours ago. I was on my way to school for our annual picnic, but ended up here. Even if I do find a way back, I've missed the picnic by now."

Peter puts his arm around your shoulders. "Don't worry, we'll have some fun here instead." He frowns. "How are my mom and dad? Have they been worried about me?"

"Yeah, police searched your neighborhood, but never found a clue. There's still a reward out."

"I hate my family being so worried." Peter bites his lip. "Is Sarah okay?" He swipes at his eyes with the back of his hand.

Sarah is your other cousin, Peter's little sister. "Yeah. She still thinks you're alive and keeps telling your parents that she sees you in her dreams, flying."

Peter laughs. "She's right. Come and meet my best friend. She's a beauty."

"Have you got... um, ... a girlfriend?"

"Sort of…"

It feels odd. Peter was your age just two months ago, now he's five years older and likes girls. How weird.

Peter leads you away from the clearing towards a huge rocky outcrop, but before you go around the rock, a purple dragon swoops out of the sky and lands in front of you. Its yellow eyes flutter like a bird's as it gently butts Peter in the chest.

He scratches the dragon's head and grins. "Astera, this is my cousin." He gestures for you to put your hand on Astera's head.

Her scales are softer than you expected, and warm.

"Welcome to Dragons' Hold." Her voice thrums in your mind. *"Peter has spoken of you and his family often. He misses you all. Would you like to come for a ride?"*

"Wow, would I ever!" That'll be three dragon rides today. Luckily the weather at Dragons' Hold is sunny and warm, even though it'll soon be dark.

"Come on," says Peter. "Let's go."

Flipping Hans' cloak over your shoulders to keep it out of the way, you climb up onto Astera's saddle behind Peter. The dragon's huge legs bunch then spring high in the air, her wings flapping to power her ascent. She soars over fruit trees, roaring, startling workers returning from the orchard.

Laughing, Peter pats her side. "She's still young and a little playful. Hold on!"

Astera swoops low over a field then leap frogs up and down. Peter whoops with glee, and you hang on, laughing. This is much more fun than the ride you just had on Handel in the storm. After a while, Astera climbs above a forest until she's high above the lake.

In mid air, she twists her body, so she's head down. White-knuckled, arms around Peter, you grip his belt as Astera plummets headlong towards the lake. Her wings are tucked against her body and her tail streams out behind her. Your stomach drops. Tears stream from your eyes. Is Peter's mad dragon going to dive into the lake?

The setting sun reflects pink and orange on the water. Astera's reflection looms, a purple blob on the lake's surface that grows bigger by the minute. Heart pounding, you take a deep breath. Then Astera's wings flip out, breaking her descent and she slaps her tail down on the lake, sending a fine spray over you and Peter.

You feel Peter's ribs shaking. He's laughing! You slap his back, playfully. "That was a prank? You're mad!" Shaking your head, you have to admit it was a brilliant one.

Astera flies along the lake's surface, skimming the water with her talons. Roaring, she flips something silver from the lake with her talons, then swoops to catch it in her mouth.

"She's fishing," calls Peter.

Soon you're sitting by the lakeside, eating fish roasted by dragon fire, succulent juice running down your chin.

"This is the best thing I've ever tasted."

"Yeah, well I still miss Dad's cooking." Peter stares into the distance. "And chocolate."

"I have just the thing for you!"

"You haven't, have you?" His eyes fly wide open in anticipation.

You pull a chocolate bar out of your backpack.

Inhaling the scent, Peter groans and takes a bite. "This is awesome. Absolutely awesome," he says between mouthfuls.

You grin. "So is Astera's fish."

The dragon rumbles and nudges you with her nose, pulling her lips off her teeth, reminding you of a chimpanzee.

"Was that a dragon smile?"

"Sure was." Peter jumps to his feet. "We need to get back before the sun is gone, or Hans will send the dragon patrol out for us. Come on."

A while later, on dragon back, flying over the gravel clearing where you first landed, Peter turns his head to talk to you. "Although I love it here, I really do miss my family," he says. "Sometimes, I wish there was a way to go home."

You shrug. "I just assumed a dragon could open a portal when I needed it."

"I've never seen a portal again." Peter looks so sad. For a moment you wonder if either of you are ever going to see your families again. "You know, I wish–" Peter breaks off, pointing beyond Astera's head. "Look!"

A shimmering oval of swirling colors is right in front of you, barely visible against the sunset.

Peter turns to you. "I'm going. Want to come home?"

It's time to make a decision. Do you:

Go home with Peter? **P330**

Or

Stay at Dragons' Hold? **P332**

You have decided to take the raft and go down the river

You grab the pole and stride onto the jetty. It groans and creaks. A piece of rotten wood gives way. You crash onto the raft. Water splashes over the side, submerging one end. It looks dangerous, so you grab the tether rope to haul yourself back to the jetty. The rope rips free and you're adrift. Water seeps into your sneakers.

The edge of the river is slower moving, and you feel like a little adventure – after all it's not every day you travel through a portal into another world, and what could be worse than the trip you just took in the dragon's clutches?

Shoving hard with the pole, you push the raft out towards the centre of the river. You're not used to rafting, so your arms tire quickly. You relax and let the river do the hard work. Sitting on your backpack to avoid getting wet, you watch the forest and farms go by. Hungry, you reach into the pocket of your backpack for a sandwich and realize that your food is wet. Oh well, at least you can munch on chocolate and enjoy the scenery.

Ahead, the river narrows as the banks rise. The current snatches your raft and you start to move swiftly. That's easy to fix. You leap up and grab the pole, upsetting the raft slightly and letting more water on board. Plunging the pole into the water to slow the raft, you nearly fall off when the pole hits nothing. The water is too deep! You overbalance, stumbling to your knees. The pole floats away down the river.

The banks get higher, becoming steep cliffs on either side. The water rushes through a narrow channel, foaming and white where it hits jagged rocks. You have no choice but to cling to the raft through the surging water. About now, you wish another dragon would pluck you into the air.

Twice you are submerged, but your trusty raft pops back to the surface with you hanging tight. The cliffs open out and the river widens into a smooth-flowing broad expanse of water with a forest on one side and fields on the other.

Glad the rough part of your trip is over, you lie on the soggy raft, with even soggier clothing, hoping the sun will dry you out. Knuckles scraped and exhausted after your ordeal, you drift to sleep.

And awaken to an odd roaring noise. Your raft is still floating – barely. It's an inch or two under water and your back and legs are really wet. Cocking an ear, you listen. What's that roaring?

Heart pounding, you figure it out. It's a waterfall. The current picks up. The raft speeds along, far from the banks. You round a corner. And face churning white froth broken by dangerous rocks.

If only you had your pole, you could steer. Helpless, you hang on to the raft. It careens into a rock, splintering to pieces. Your chest slams into the rock, knocking the air out of you. Pushed under churning white water, you struggle to the surface, clinging to a piece of wood. Water hits your face, entering your mouth and stinging your eyes. You're swept over the edge of the falls.

The roar hurts your ears. Your belly drops. Pieces of raft debris slam into you. You cling to the wood, falling, still falling. It seems to take forever to get down the falls. Then, through the spray you see shimmering colors and wonder… could it be? It is!

A portal. It's a portal!

To reach it, you'd have to twist your body and let go of the wood. But if you hold onto the wood, you may be able to ride down the falls and have something to float on when you hit the bottom.

It's time to make a decision. Do you:

Hold the wood and ride down the falls? **P337**

Or

Dive through the portal? **P338**

You have decided to face the tharuks

"I'm staying," you say, "even if it's alone."

"Rather you than me," says Bart, and jumps into the wagon. Bax and Becks squeeze in after him.

"On second thoughts, I think you'll be fine on your own," Wil says nervously, jumping in the wagon too. "I'm sorry, Zeebongi. Good luck."

Aria wraps her tail around your neck and nuzzles your face. *Thank you for helping me, but I need to get back to my mother.* Jumping into the wagon, she snuggles up to Wil.

Giant John shakes his head. "Are you sure?"

You nod.

He slams the side of the wagon shut and leaps onto the seat. Snapping the reigns, he drives out the gate, leaving you alone.

Tharuks race into the stable yards, tusks dribbling dark saliva and red eyes gleaming. Their roaring stops. The stench of rotten flesh wafts on the breeze. Silently, they surround you, their claws at the ready. You gulp.

"Where's that delicious baby dragon?" barks one. "I know you had it."

"I d-don't know what you're talking about, I'm j-just a stable hand," you stutter.

"If we can't have dragonet dinner, we'll settle for stable hand stew," says another.

They laugh menacingly and close in.

Sorry, this part of your story is over. Staying to fight a troop of monsters when Giant John could have helped you to escape, may not have been the best choice. It's not too late, you can go back to your last decision and choose to go with Giant John.

Other adventures are waiting. You could go to Horseshoe Bend, be snatched by a dragon, train as a wizard, or find out what happens when you feed tharuks chocolate.

It's time to make a decision. Do you:

Go back to your last choice and escape in Giant John's wagon? **P256**

Or

Go to the great big list of choices? **P378**

Or

Go back to the beginning and try another path? **P199**

You have decided to follow Bax and Becks home

"Wil, Aria, I hope you understand, I have to go back to my world."
You shake hands with Wil.

Aria leaps on your shoulder and licks your face. You laugh.

"I'll come with you, just for a moment." says Aria, *"Jump."*

You leap through the portal, Aria's tail wrapped tightly around your
neck, and land on the grass in the park next to school. Bax and Becks
are standing nearby. Opening the last can of chili tuna fish, you feed it
to Aria.

A moment later, Bart lands on the grass. His clothing is tattered
and torn. Bax and Becks gape at Bart.

"We thought you were dog food!" says Bax. "Glad you're back!"

"Just escaped," says Bart, "but the wolves shredded my clothes."
He gestures at his torn shirt and ripped jeans.

Becks points at you. "It's your fault," she says. "You set the wolves
on him. That boy told us so."

You smile. "This is Aria," you say. "She's my friend too, just like
those wolves. And she'll be coming to visit me often."

"Now?" asks Aria in your mind.

You nod. Aria leaps into the air, and opens her tiny maw. A blast of
fire shoots past the Thomson twins, not harming anyone, but it's
enough to send them running.

Aria snorts. You laugh.

"Goodbye, Zeebongi!" says Aria, snorting again. *"What a ridiculous name
Wil gave you. I like your real one much better. Thank you for helping me to find
my mother. I'll see you soon."*

"Bye, my friend." You wave.

With a flip of her tail, Aria dives back through the portal.

Only a few minutes have passed since you left. In the distance the
bus motor is still running. Racing across the field, you are the last one
aboard. The only spare seats are down the back - with the Thomson
twins.

Everyone looks at you sympathetically, expecting you'll have to stand all the way.

"We saved you a seat," Bart calls out.

"We told them to wait," Becks adds, as you plop down next to Bax. There's shocked silence from the other students as the twins chat to you about how to beat wolves and how high you'd need to fly before there was no air to breathe.

The school picnic is great. The Thomson twins are kind to everyone all day, although you have to laugh when the teacher gives them a detention. She says they smell of smoke and won't believe them when they say they've never touched a cigarette in their lives. From that day on, they treat you respectfully.

Congratulations, you have rescued a baby dragonet and reunited her with her mother, outwitted wolves and made a happy truce with the Thomson twins. Now and then, Aria creates a portal allowing you back into Dragons' Realm so you can have more adventures.

There are many other adventures in Dragons' Realm. Perhaps you'll be snatched by a dragon, raft down a waterfall, train as a wizard, or face tharuks – the dangerous monsters in the forests of Dragons' Realm.

It's time to make a decision. Do you:

Go to the great big list of choices? **P378**

Or

Go back to the beginning and try another path? **P199**

You have decided to feed Aria chili tuna fish so she can flame the wolves

The tree thuds as a wolf slams into the trunk, trying to shake you out. The other wolves copy it, slamming against the tree. Your branch wiggles with each thud.

Legs clinging to the branch, you tear the can of chili tuna fish open. Aria gulps it and zips into the air, swooping down to blast a wolf with a jet of flame. It yelps and scampers off into the forest, its ears flat and tail between its hind legs.

Aria roars. Her purple body hurtles through the air towards another wolf, shooting flames at its face. Howling, it takes off into the trees. Another stubborn wolf is still leaping up at the tree, snapping. Whirling in midair, Aria swoops under a branch and flames its chest. The wolf lunges at Aria and grabs her tail in its jaws.

Aria's whine of pain slices through you.

Breaking off a branch, you drop it on the wolf's head. It growls, jaws flying open, and Aria scorches its nose, sending it scurrying. You snap off more branches, flinging them at the frenzied wolves. "Get out of here, you overgrown doggies," you yell. "Go and bother someone else."

Will applauds. "Go, Zeebongi! Scare those mangy mutts."

Breathing fire, zipping in and out among the wolves, Aria scares the rest away.

"Zeebongi! Aria! You are my absolute heroes!" Wil exclaims.

Aria's flames splutter and die.

Two people in modern clothing rush into the clearing, panting and gasping. Swinging out of the tree, you and Wil jump down to greet Bax and Becks.

"It's you two," you say, taken aback. "Wil, these are the Thomson twins."

Bax shakes his head. "We're not twins any more. There are only two of us now."

Wil nudges you, speaking softly. "Everyone knows two means twins. Even I can count better than them."

"We know that, but they don't!" you whisper, smiling at Wil. Then you ask Bax, "What happened to Bart?"

"He was eaten by an angry burned wolf." Becks leans against Bax, sobbing.

He puts his arm around her. "It's alright, Becks. Now he won't force us into bullying Fart-face anymore. Or anyone else."

Her face brightens. "That's true. I wasn't worried about Bart though. It's just that I got my best boots dirty!"

Bax laughs. "They'll scrub up fine."

"Why don't you come with us to Dragons' Hold?" Wil asks. "And train as dragon riders."

"Dragons?" Bax grins. "That would be cool!"

"Cold?" asks Wil. "I don't understand."

"It means he'll come," you explain. "Let's get to the blue guards."

A fierce downdraught rustles the leaves above you. Enormous blue and purple wings circle above the treetops.

"It's the blue guards," Wil says.

"And my mother!" calls Aria.

"Follow them," you shout.

Aria bursts into song. Bax and Becks clamp their hands over their ears to drown out Aria's singing. Racing after the flying dragons, you come to a clearing. The blue dragons land, tucking their magnificent wings against their bodies. A purple dragon trumpets and lands beside them.

Aria hurtles towards the purple dragon, shrieking at the top of her voice. Her mother sings too, her deep voice blending with Aria's to create a gorgeous harmony.

"That's beautiful," you murmur, surprised they sound so good together.

"Meet my mother," Aria says in your mind.

"Thank you for finding Aria," the female rider on the purple dragon calls. "We've been hunting for her everywhere. When we heard wolves were in the area, we came to check."

"You're welcome," says Wil, "but it was the Great Zeebongi who found Aria." He gestures at you.

"Zeebongi!" The rider smiles. "We'd like to invite you to Dragons' Hold so you can be Aria's rider when she's big enough."

You're so thrilled, you can't speak. Aria zips around, turning somersaults in excitement.

Wil answers for you. "That would be magnificent, but I'm afraid the Great Zeebongi will need all of us to come."

The dragon rider laughs, "Of course."

Bax and Becks frown and mouth *Zeebongi?* at each other, then shrug. You climb into the saddle behind the woman riding Aria's mother, admiring the dragon's glowing scales. Wil, Bax and Becks grin at you from their seats behind the blue guards.

Aria dives into her saddlebag, then pokes her nose out cheekily. *"I'm so glad you'll be my rider."*

"So am I," you say, grinning like an actor in a toothpaste commercial.

Congratulations, you have rescued a baby dragonet and reunited her with her mother. You have also outwitted vicious wolves and have no problems with Bax and Becks anymore. Aria grows at a rapid rate, and soon you are riding her. Now and then, she creates a portal so you can visit your family, always surprised at how little time has passed on earth. There are still many more adventures in Dragons' Realm.

If you choose again, you could face tharuks – the dangerous monsters in Dragons' Realm – imprint with your own dragon, or train as a wizard or dragon acrobat.

It's time to make a decision. Do you:

Go to the great big list of choices? **P378**

Or

Go back to the beginning and try another path? **P199**

You have decided to farewell Aria and return home

"I have to return to my family," you say, "or they'll be worried."

Wil hugs you. "Zeebongi, thank you for bringing me to Dragons' Realm. You're so clever. I'll always remember how you fed Aria the pepper fish so she could flame that tharuk. You're so wise."

You try not to wrinkle your nose – he still stinks of horse manure. Now that you're saying goodbye, Wil's compliments don't bother you so much. "Thanks, Wil. Have fun riding dragons."

Aria's mother lowers her head to your height. Her purple scales gleam in the early evening sun. You touch her head and her voice rumbles through your mind. *"You have my undying gratitude for returning my daughter. At last I can hear her sweet songs again."*

You smile. Aria's songs aren't exactly sweet, but that's okay with you.

A bundle of scales, energy and tail flaps into your chest, nearly bowling you over. You fling your arms around Aria, hugging her goodbye.

"Don't worry," she says, *"I won't tell Wil your name isn't really Zeebongi."*

"Thank you." You nuzzle against her. "I'm going to miss you."

Nearby, Bax sniffs. "It's sad to leave these dragons," he says.

Aria leaps out of your arms to her mother with a roar. *"Don't worry,"* she says. *"I'll make more world gates. You'll be back to visit in no time."*

The air in front of you shimmers. The twins leap through the portal. You swallow a lump in your throat, wave to Aria and Wil and dive through.

You land on the grass at the front of the school. The bus for the picnic is there and kids are just getting on board. It's like almost no time has passed. The Thomson twins are sprawled nearby.

"Phew, Bart," says Becks, waving her hand in front of her nose. "You still stink of horse poo."

"Who cares?" says Bart. He turns to you. "Hey, that was awesome!"

"Let's get to the picnic," says Bax.

You all race for the bus. Once on board, the teacher keeps checking everyone's shoes for poo, and when they all turn up clean, can't understand where the smell of dung is coming from.

At the picnic, your friends can't figure out how you made friends with the Thomson twins, and ask you, "Why do the Thomson twins call you the Great Zeebongi?"

"It's because Highly-esteemed Zeebongi the Magnificent is too tricky to pronounce!"

The Thomson twins laugh, and Bart says to your friends, "By the way, can't you count? We're not twins, we're triplets!"

You never have a problem with the Thomsons again. In fact, they stop bullying people, and you become friends, visiting Dragons' Realm together whenever Aria creates a portal.

Congratulations, this part of your story is over. You have reunited a dragonet with its mother and become a hero, escaped from tharuks and made friends with the Thomson twins.

You could also train as a wizard, give ravenous wolves earache, test the strongwood trees, or find out what happens when you feed tharuks chocolate.

It's time to make a decision. Do you:

Go to the great big list of choices? **P378**

Or

Go back to the beginning and try another path? **P199**

You have decided to stay with Mickel

"Hans, thank you for your offer, but I think I'll stay here with Mickel."

"I wish you many happy landings," says Hans, clapping you on the shoulder.

He climbs upon Handel. The dragon flexes his powerful back legs and lifts off into the sky, his bronze scales shining in the sun.

Mickel takes you back to the forge and shows you how to operate the bellows to keep the coals in the fire glowing. You pump the bellows, knowing the exercise will keep up your strength. You effortlessly lift a heavy sword from the fire and hold it still, while Mickel hammers it under Sturm's supervision.

Sturm shows you how to hammer out the metal blade of a spade. Your newly-developed muscles let you swing the heavy blacksmith's hammer with ease. It's obvious that Mickel's daily routine will help you stay in shape.

At the end of the day, after a fine dinner of fresh bread and vegetable soup, you fall, exhausted, into your new bed – a hard mattress stuffed with straw, on a rickety wooden frame.

After a few days, you're lifting toddlers above your head, as they shriek with delight, queuing to have a turn. A while later you're lifting bigger kids and easily helping Mickel with his heaviest duties.

By the end of the first week, you can fling the pigs back into the sty whenever they charge you. The wee porkers squeal with delight. They'd only been hoping to play!

Life is fun at Horseshoe Bend settlement.

One day while you're out for your training run with Mickel, the air near you starts to shimmer. You've seen this once before – it's a world gate! It's been so long since you saw your family and friends.

Mickel gasps. "It's beautiful. Look at all those spinning colors."

"Mickel." You clear your throat. "I have to go home. You'll always be my best friend, but I miss my family and my own bed."

Mickel nods sadly.

"Travel well, my friend. Good luck."

"Thank you, Mickel. You can have my rucksack and the things inside it, and you can have these too." Pulling off your sneakers, you pass them to him. He may as well use them on his runs. Going barefoot through these forests has to suck.

He hugs the shoes.

With a lump in your throat, you jump through the portal and land on the neatly-mown grass of the park next to school.

A bus is rumbling in the distance. The twins are exactly where you left them – it's like no time has passed at all.

"Oi, Fart-face!" Bart Thomson yells.

Standing straight, you face the three of them. Their eyes rove over you. "Yeah, what do you lot want?" You feel strong and confident – for the first time in years.

"Um…" Bart stares at your strong arms. "Um, the teacher wanted us to find you."

"Yeah," mumbles Becks. "Hope that's okay."

"What happened to your shoes?" Bax asks.

"Don't need them," you answer. "Tough feet."

"Tough everything," mutters Bart to Becks and Bax. "How did that happen so fast?"

Becks and Bax shrug.

You smile and sprint to the bus, leaving them to eat your dust.

Congratulations, you have had a ride on a dragon, grown very strong, and the Thomson twins won't be bothering you any time soon.

There are many more adventures. It's time to make a decision. Do you:

Go to the great big list of choices? **P378**

Or

Go back to the beginning and try another path? **P199**

EILEEN MUELLER

303

You have decided to stay in the tree

Two tharuks leap up and grab the base of your branch, shaking it so violently that your jaw rattles in your skull. Roaring, they climb the tree.

Mia yowls as a tharuk slashes at the net. "You got me, you brute." She spurts a flame at the beast who backs off, then runs and leaps up, swinging itself onto your branch.

The three tharuks swarm along the tree towards you, two on the trunk below, one on the branch in front of you. The air just below you shimmers, giving you an idea.

Diving into the portal, you hear Mia scream, "No, don't leave me!"

You land in the park on the lawn. The Thomson twins run towards you. Bart hollers, "Let's get Fart-face."

"Can't catch me," you call, diving back through the portal.

Bart bellows and follows you through, landing on the ground beside you. Becks and Bax thud to the ground too.

A tharuk roars and charges.

"Yay," yells Bart. "Fist fight!"

He swings into action, punching the monster on the nose. It howls and takes off. Becks trips another, then leaps on its back, tugging on his tender ears. The beast flees into the forest, whimpering. Bax and Bart gang up, attacking the last tharuk together. You and Mia help, flames flying from your fingers.

The remaining tharuk pleads for mercy, "Please, please, just let me go. I'll never bother humans again."

As the beast runs into the forest, you shoot flames at the ropes suspending Mia's net from the tree. The net lands on the ground, and Mia struggles out of it, snatching up her bow and training it on the Thomson twins.

"You could've caught me," she says, "instead of letting me fall."

Bart, Becks and Bax glance at the sparks trailing from your fingers, then at Mia's bow. "Um, all good, now, right?" asks Bart. "I mean, we did come and help you...," he says lamely.

You frown. "We'll see what the Master Wizard has to say." But inside you're smiling. The Thomson twins won't be bothering you again.

Congratulations, you have harnessed environmental magic, frightened away the tharuks and shown the Thomson twins that you won't be bullied again.

If you choose again you could ride a dragon, rescue a lost dragonet, encounter wolves or make it back home again.

It's time to make a decision. Do you:

Go to the great big list of choices? **P378**

Or

Go back to the beginning and try another path? **P199**

You have decided to dash into the forest

Upset that Mia has been using you for target practice, you dash into the forest – thrashing through ferns and undergrowth, and running between the trees – anywhere to get away from Mia's stupid arrows. She's so infuriating. She scared the pants off you. What an arrow-flinging, arrogant, unbearable–

What was that?

A snort! From the trees ahead. A gray-furred creature breaks through the ferns, looming in front of you. It walks on two legs and is dressed like a warrior. Its beady red eyes gleam and dark saliva runs down its stubby tusks. The stench of rotten meat wafts on the breeze, making you gag. More of the creatures step out from behind trees. Soon you're surrounded. The beasts start to growl, their claws extending and retracting.

The ferns and trees all look the same. Which direction did you come from? Your knees tremble. Why did you run off in a strange world without anyone to guide you?

Reaching into your pocket, you grasp Master Giddi's knife, but it's too small. It'll be useless against those beasts with their long cruel claws.

And you can't even harness any magic, because you didn't finish your lessons. Or can you? Raising your palms, you desperately try to summon a flash shield, a flame, a spark.

Nothing happens.

Snarling, the monsters close in, bringing the foul stink closer. Your stomach churns. You are about to die. Anything would have been better than this – even Mia's tree-hugging lessons. Even being pierced by one of her arrows. Even those giant spiders.

The monsters' snarls are the last thing you hear.

I'm sorry, this part of your story is over. Running off into the forest in a strange new world without paying any attention to where you were going, without learning magic and without a guide, was not the best choice. But don't worry, you can try again.

On your next adventure, perhaps you will be snatched by a dragon, encounter wolves, become a dragon acrobat or create chaos at the marketplace in Montanara.

It's time to make a decision. Do you:

Go back to your last choice and stay with Mia? **P227**

Or

Go to the great big list of choices? **P378**

Or

Go back to the beginning and try another path? **P199**

You have decided to go with Wil and Aria to Dragons' Hold

"I'd love to come to Dragons' Hold." You grin from ear to ear. "Wil says it's where dragons and riders live."

Aria leaps into one of her mother's saddlebags, then pops her head up with her snout sticking out. You and Wil swing up into the saddle. Within moments, you're airborne, the breeze rushing through your hair. Aria's mother's scales gleam in the sun. Atop her back you get a good look at the dragon's wings. Strong and ridged, they're nearly translucent in places, her muscles moving effortlessly to keep you in the air.

The trees are a vast tapestry of greens below you, leaves rustling in the downdraughts from the dragon's wingbeats as you pass. Mountains rise before you, with glistening snow-capped peaks above rocky faces. From so high, the world is silent, except for Wil's breathing, his excited gasps behind you – and the dragon's rhythmic flapping.

Thin trails of smoke rise from isolated cottages among the trees.

"Zeebongi," whispers Wil. "This is incredible. I can see for miles."

"Imagine riding a dragon every day," you reply.

"That's what I've always wanted to do," says Wil. "I've been training in archery for years. Shooting from dragon back will be challenging, but I'm keen to try."

Aria's mother climbs high along the steep mountain faces.

"Those are Dragon's Teeth," says Aria, *"sharp and pointy, just like mine."* She opens her maw to show you her fangs.

As you pop over the top of the mountain range, you can see why they're called Dragon's Teeth. The jagged peaks form a ring. Inside is a valley. Dragons fill the air, riders astride their backs.

"Home. We're home!" Aria sings, and her mother joins in. Somehow her mother's deep voice balances Aria's voice, the notes no longer jangling, but flowing over you in harmony.

Near you, a blue dragon trumpets. Bart is hanging onto the rider's back, his clothing in tatters.

Aria's mother roars in response and lands on the edge of a silver lake, edged by forest. Several other dragons alight nearby, their riders jumping down to meet you. Bart hangs back, watching.

It's like a home coming, with riders cheering and dragons roaring.

"Thank you for saving Aria."

"You saved our dragonet."

"She's home!"

"You hear us, you hear us."

"Zeebongi hears us!"

You think your mind will burst, so many voices sound in your head at once.

"The dragons say that I hear them. What does that mean?" you ask Wil.

"It's part of the prophecy. Zeebongi is the only one who can hear all the dragons. Most people can't hear any dragons at all, and riders only hear their own dragons, but you're special." He beams. "And you also rescued a dragonet – tharuk monsters often kill dragon babies or even eat them!"

A beautiful dragon strides towards you, every scale gleaming with the colors of the rainbow. Around you, riders bow. Wil falls to his knees with a look of awe on his face. You bow too. A regal-looking rider swings out of the saddle.

"My name is Anakisha," she says. "Rider of Zaarusha, the Dragon Queen of Dragons' Realm."

Zaarusha, the majestic dragon, bumps your shoulder with her snout. *"Thank you for saving Aria."*

"Zaarusha and I will grant you anything you want," says Anakisha. "What gift would you like, Zeebongi?"

"Name it. Name it," say the dragons.

"My friend Wil has a dream," you say. "Could he be a dragon rider?"

A smaller blue dragon comes forward and bows before Wil. He puts out his hand to touch her and you hear what he hears. *"Hello Wil,*

I'm Wilhemena, the dragon you were born to fly with."

Grinning, Wil hugs her. For the first time since you've known him, he's speechless.

You sigh, happy that Wil's dream has come true. You would enjoy it here too, if you didn't miss your family so much. "There's something else I'd like," you say.

"Whatever you want," Anakisha replies.

You point at Bart who is skulking around the edge of the crowd, glowering at you. "Bart was attacked by wolves. He needs new clothes and has to get home."

Bart's eyes fly wide open and he gapes at you. A rider passes him a tunic and trousers, and he ducks behind a dragon to get changed. When he reappears he claps you on the shoulder. "Thanks, buddy."

Bart has never, ever called anyone *buddy*. You nod. "No problem."

Zaarusha's voice rumbles through your mind. *"You've chosen a gift for Wil and Bart, but none for yourself, so we gift you the chance to become Aria's rider."*

Aria somersaults through the air to land on your chest, knocking you to the ground. She licks your face like a dog, then flaps her wings in glee. The air shimmers near you as a portal appears.

Aria's eyes whirl. *"I've opened a portal so you can go home. You'll still hear me from your world and I'll hear you. When I'm older, you can return to be my rider."*

You and Bart tumble through the portal and catch up to Becks and Bax who are running for the bus. The other kids love Bart's new rugged clothes, making him smile, instead of glowering at them like usual. From that day on, the Thomson twins are always on their best behavior, looking out for others, and begging you to take them back to Dragons' Realm. Sometimes you take them on your adventures.

Congratulations, you have become a hero in Dragons Realm, rescued a dragonet and made great new friends. The Thomson twins will never hassle you again, and one day soon, you'll return to ride Aria.

310

There are many more adventures in Dragons' Realm. You could train as a wizard, learn to wrestle, develop your strength or become a dragon acrobat.

It's time to make a decision. Do you:

Go to the great big list of choices? **P378**

Or

Go back to the beginning and try another path? **P199**

You have decided to convince Becks to stay with the tharuks

"Hey Becks," you say, "you have a real way with those tharuks. How would you like to stay here and be in charge of them?"

"Wow!" She grins. "You mean I'd boss them around all day?"

You nod.

"And they won't answer me back like my brothers do?"

"As long as we have enough chocolate."

"Oh that's easy," says Becks. "Hey, Bart, Bax…"

They turn to her, poised by the portal, about to jump through.

"You'll be back in an hour with a suitcase of chocolate!"

Bart wrinkles his nose. "You think we want to come back to this weird place?"

"Yeah, I do." Becks smiles wickedly. "Or Dad will find out Bax smashed the window on his Porsche. And Bart, Mom might just get a mysterious message mentioning who gave Bobby McGraff a broken arm."

Bart nods quickly, "A suitcase of chocolate in an hour? No problem."

"Make that two suitcases," says Bax. "We'll see you soon."

You focus on the energy around you and summon a blast of fire from your hands. "Real soon. Otherwise I'll be through the portal for you in no time."

"So will I," Mia pipes up, firing an arrow that flies with uncanny precision between Bax and Bart.

Bax stares at the arrow quivering in a tree trunk.

Bart gulps. "Back soon," he calls. They jump through the portal.

Becks strokes a tharuk's nose, making it purr, then pats another. "Follow me, my lovelies." She turns to you. "Where to?"

"This way," says Mia.

With your backpack half full of Bart's chocolate, you follow Mia, Becks and the tharuks. Mia leaves arrows in trees so Bart and Bax can find you.

By the time you get to Master Giddi's cottage, Becks has taught the tharuks her favorite boy-band hit. Their throaty voices echo through the forest in discord, but she doesn't seem to care that they're off-tune and out of beat.

"Oooh, baby, yeah, yeah, yeah!"

"Beautiful singing, my lovelies," she croons.

You roll your eyes and follow her into the clearing.

Master Giddi laughs and claps his hands. Their singing stops. "A green-eyed tame tharuk choir?"

"Hypnotized by chocolate," you mutter.

"Makes them submissive," says Mia.

Giddi's bushy eyebrows pull into a frown. "And who is this?"

"I'm boss of the tharuks," says Becks, "and sister of the chocolate suppliers."

Bart and Bax arrive, puffing, with two heavy suitcases. Bart walks straight into a mesmerized tharuk.

"Oof!" Bart says. "Got your chocolate. Plenty more where that came from."

"I see," says Master Giddi.

Secretly, you're not sure whether he does.

He clears his throat and continues speaking, "Well, it's good that you're here. I need some junior apprentices to serve under these two." He waves a hand towards you and Mia. "And make sure you do what they say, or I might just turn you into a tharuk."

Bart and Bax stare at the furry creatures sitting at Becks' feet and gulp.

You grin. Master Giddi does understand, after all.

Congratulations, you have harnessed environmental magic, tamed the tharuks and solved your problems with the Thomson twins.

Perhaps you'd also like to ride a dragon, learn to wrestle, rescue a dragonet or make it back home again.

There are many paths to try.

It's time to make a decision. Do you:

Go to the great big list of choices? **P378**

Or

Go back to the beginning and try another path? **P199**

You have decided to use magic so Bart and Bax bring you chocolate

Mia's eyes gleam as if she understands what you're about to do. She lifts her bow and points an arrow straight at Becks.

Raising your hands in the air, you summon a flash of fire, sending it flickering towards Bart and Bax. They leap back, eyes wide. Bart's hands are shaking and Bax's forehead beads with sweat. They flinch when you raise your hands again.

"Ok, you two. We have your sister hostage. You need to bring us back chocolate. Boxes full of it – if you want to see your sister alive."

"And what if we don't care whether we see her alive again?" Bart sneers.

Bax kicks him. "Ow!" And again. "Ow!" Bart holds his sore shin, hopping on the other foot and glaring at Bax.

Sparks drip from your hands as you approach them. "Oh, I'm sure you want to see your sister again, don't you?"

Becks pipes up. "Of course they do, or Mom and Dad might just find out about–"

Bart's face pales. "No problem. No problem at all. Five boxes of chocolate, is it?"

Five is way more than you expected. You tilt your head, as if their offer is stingy. "Make it six."

"Sure," says Bax. "Come on, Bart." They dive through the portal.

Mia giggles and puts her bow down.

Becks glowers at her. "Honestly, you didn't have to do that! I would've blackmailed them anyway." She absent-mindedly pats the arm of the tharuk standing next to her.

"But that was way more fun!" Mia laughs. "I'd do it again any day." Her laughter fades as a spider lands on her arm. Dropping the bow, she freezes, letting out a strangled cry.

Becks, too, has gone pale.

Laughing, you flick it away. It might come in handy knowing these two tough girls have the same weakness. A moment later, the air shimmers. Bax lands, clutching an empty carton, his mouth covered in chocolate stains.

"Um, sorry," he says, "couldn't resist. Peppermint is my favorite."

Next to Becks, a tharuk starts to get restless. Is the chocolate wearing off?

Becks pulls a cell phone out of her pocket and looks at Bax. You're not even sure if it will work between worlds, but you keep quiet.

"Mom or Dad?" she says, "Your choice."

"I'll be right back!" Bax leaps back through the portal. More tharuks start to stir. Some of them growl, deep in their throats.

"Hurry," you yell.

You duck as heavy cartons fly out of the portal, just missing Mia and Becks. Bart lands on the ground, grinning. "Chocolate for everyone," he calls. "Where's Bax?"

"The rotter ate the lot," Becks sneers, "but I fixed him." She waves up her cell phone. "And you'll keep bringing my lovely tharuks more chocolate every week, please, or Mom will be hearing about–"

"Sure, back soon with more," says Bart, leaping back through the portal as Bax passes him landing with a full box.

Becks grins at you and says, "That should keep them out of trouble."

Congratulations, you have harnessed environmental magic, tamed the tharuks and solved your problems with the Thomson twins. Eventually Bart and Bax figure out how to bring cocoa beans, palm seeds and sugar cane into Dragons' Realm. Master Giddi plants and harvests them and makes chocolate, keeping the tharuks under control. Becks sets up an earth-style café serving tharuks chocolate and teaching them circus tricks to keep the locals entertained. You become an excellent wizard and never need to be worried about being bullied, ever again.

Maybe you'd also like to ride a dragon, find a dragonet, develop your strength, or go back home again.

It's time to make a decision. Do you:

Go to the great big list of choices? **P378**

Or

Go back to the beginning and try another path? **P199**

You have decided to take Mia through the portal

You grab Mia's hand. "Come on," you yell, as the tharuks slash her cloak with their sharp claws, leaving it in tatters.

Another tharuk swipes at her head, but misses as you pull her to safety. Yanking Mia, you dive head-first through the portal.

"Oof!" You land face-first on the neatly-mown grass of the park near school.

Beside you, Mia lands nimbly on her feet.

Familiar voices holler, "Hey, Fart-face," and "Oi, you."

Not the Thomson twins! You thought you were rid of them. As you scramble to your feet, something zips past your ear. It's one of Mia's arrows.

Thwack! The hood of Bart's sweatshirt is pinned to a tree trunk by the arrow. Mia trains her bow on Bax and Becks. They hover near Bart, faces pale.

You raise an eyebrow at her. "Nice work."

She grins. "No one calls my friend Fart-face."

"Plee-ese, let us go," Becks whines.

"Quiet," says Mia, gesturing with her bow, "unless you want your nose pierced."

You grin, happy her arrows are no longer trained on you. Holding your hands high, you let sparks fly from your fingertips. The twins' eyes grow as huge as watermelons.

Bart unzips his sweatshirt and wriggles his arms out of the sleeves, his hood still pinned to the tree. The three of them take off, running.

"No more bullying," you call.

"Of course not," they answer, scampering across the park as fast as they can.

You and Mia laugh. She lowers her bow and places her arrow back in her quiver.

In the distance, a bus starts. You glance at your watch. Only a few earth minutes have passed since you left. "Hey, Mia, how would you like to go on a picnic?"

"What is *picnic*?"

"Trust me. I think you're going to love it." Together you run to catch the bus.

Congratulations, this part of your story is over. You have learned some environmental magic, seen a magnificent bronze dragon, and helped Mia escape from some formidable monsters. It also looks like the Thomson twins won't be bothering you again, and, if they do, a few stray sparks from your fingertips should sort them out.

Maybe you'd like to choose again so you can ride a dragon, discover whether tharuks like chocolate, go white-water rafting or visit Horseshoe Bend. Or perhaps you'd like to start the story over and find out what happens if you hide from the Thomson twins in the trees instead of behind the bleachers.

It's time to make a decision. Do you:

Go to the great big list of choices? **P378**

Or

Go back to the beginning and try another path? **P199**

You have decided to stay and fight the tharuks

"Remember your lessons," yells Mia.

Tuning into the environment, you hold up your hands and fling flames at the snarling monsters. They bat at their fur and advance. Nocking an arrow, Mia takes aim. Her face turns pale as a hairy spider on a silken thread drops out of a tree in front of her nose. Her legs shake and she drops her bow.

"No, Mia!" you yell. "Focus!"

Holding up a hand, you shoot a blast of flame at the spider, frying it instantly. "Grab your bow," you yell, ducking an angry swipe from tharuk claws.

Whirling, you fling flames at the beasts.

Mia, coming to her senses, snatches up her bow, and fires at a tharuk. It yelps and races into the forest. Her next arrow hits another tharuk's butt as it flees.

Your flames scare the last tharuks into the bushes.

You grin at Mia.

"Not bad," she says. "Not bad at all, for your first day of training." She grins, and you know, when you get home, you'll never have a problem with the Thomson twins again.

Congratulations, this part of your story is over. You have harnessed environmental magic and gained valuable fighting skills that will impress the Thomson twins when you get home.

There are many more adventures in Dragons' Realm. Maybe you could ride a dragon, go white-water rafting, develop your strength, or create chaos in the marketplace at Montanara.

It's time to make a decision. Do you:

Go to the great big list of choices? **P378**

Or

Go back to the beginning and try another path? **P199**

You have decided to hide in the marketplace

"Let's stay here," you say. "Quick, hide." You duck more chicken poo as the birds flap around your head.

Aria dives into a pile of hats, sending them toppling. She buries her head in a floppy red hat, her bottom and tail sticking high in the air.

"Aria, no, we can still see you." You run from a furry brute headed your way.

"Oh? I can't see you," Aria, replies.

Wil snatches Aria up like a football and leaps over a table, racing behind a wagon. You lose sight of them as a tharuk grabs your backpack. Shrugging it off your shoulders, you race away, leaving the monster rummaging through your bag.

Around you, people send livestock running through the square. Traders wave brightly colored fabric to distract them. Through the mayhem, more tharuks march three people into the square – the Thomson twins. They tie them to a wagon on the far side of the marketplace.

Ducking a tharuk and scrambling under a baker's stall, you make your way towards the Thomson twins. Even though they've bullied you and teased you, you can't leave them here with those monsters.

Bart looks up, surprised. "Why are you helping us?"

"You look a bit stuck." You grab a knife off a stand of tools and cut their ropes. "Create as much havoc as you can. We're trying to save the dragonet."

"Sure thing," Bart nods at Bax and Becks. "Come with me, you two." He runs over to a table laden with pastries. "Food fight!" Bart yells, and throws a pie straight into a tharuk's face.

Bax and Becks laugh and join in. Soon there are pies, pastries and cakes flying at the tharuks. People pelt them with vegetables, and someone joins in, throwing horse dung. Roaring in frustration, the beasts group on the far side of the market place.

You sigh in relief. But where are Wil and Aria?

Dashing around the wagon, you find Wil and Aria facing a tharuk. It has your backpack in its hands.

"Sing, Aria! Now!" you shout.

She opens her mouth and screeches. The tharuk claps its hands over its ears and drops your backpack.

Snatching it up, you pull the tab on the can of chili tuna fish and thrust it at Aria. She stops singing, gulping the tuna fish down in one swallow. Flames erupt from her maw and she flies after the tharuk, chasing it out of the square.

Wil grins. "You're so clever, Zeebongi the Magnificent."

Bart, Bax, Becks and the local people are still pelting the other monsters with food, but soon their supplies will run out. You run over to help them, picking up a huge pie and throwing it straight at the troop leader.

In midair, Aria flies at the pie-splattered tharuk leader and shoots a jet of flame at him.

"Fire!" he yells. "Disperse! Back to Commander Zens."

Ear-splitting roars sound above you. An enormous purple dragon is above the square, flanked by blue dragons.

"Mother!" Aria yells.

"The blue guards!" calls Wil, eyes shining.

The tharuks dash from the square, racing down the streets. The blue guards' dragons fly after them, roaring.

"Zeebongi! Zeebongi!" the people shout. You think your ears will pop with all the noise.

Someone rushes over and brings you and Wil chairs. Other folk scramble to give you the last of the pastries and pies.

Bart serves you cake. "Thanks for saving us."

Behind him Becks and Bax echo their thanks too. Becks tries on a hat.

Aria's mother lands nearby. Aria zips through the air, nuzzling her mother and purring like a cat.

"Mother wants to know if you'd like to come to Dragons' Hold with us," Aria

says in your mind.

"But my family…"

"Don't worry, I can make a portal for you to visit home, any time you want."

You smile. "Aria, I'd love to stay in Dragons' Realm. That would be awesome."

Wil hears you. "You're staying? Zeebongi, that's wonderful."

You turn to the Thomson twins. "Do you want to stay here or go?"

Becks grins. "I'd like to learn how to make these crazy hats."

"Go home and leave these delicious pastries behind?" Bart licks his fingers. "No way!"

"I love the dragons," says Bax.

"The blue guards will be back soon. I'm sure they'll take us all to Dragons' Hold, Zeebongi," says Wil.

"There's only one thing." Bart Thomson stares at you intensely. "Go on. Tell Wil your real name."

"Alright," you sigh. "My name is—"

"Zeebongi!" The Thomson twins chorus, interrupting you.

You know you'll never be able to use your real name again!

Congratulations, this part of your story is over. You have reunited a dragonet with its mother and become a hero, escaped from tharuks, and made friends with the Thomson twins.

Your new life at Dragons' Hold is full of adventure and everyone honors you as Zeebongi, even the Thomson twins, who never tell anyone your real name.

Aria and Wil become your best friends. Now and then, you go back through a portal to see your family, amazed at how little time has gone by on Earth. Who knows, maybe one day you'll convince them to come to Dragons' Realm too.

Perhaps you'd like another adventure, training as a wizard, going white-water rafting, or finding out what happens when you feed tharuks chocolate.

It's time to make a decision. Do you:

Go to the great big list of choices? **P378**

Or

Go back to the beginning and try another path? **P199**

You have decided to become a dragon acrobat

Riders crowd around as you climb out of the saddle, patting your back and congratulating you on your stunt jumps. Hans winks at you, and Handel nudges you with his snout.

Marlies comes over to shake your hand, smiling. "Now I can welcome you properly."

The crowd parts as a dragon lands nearby. You are awestruck. This dragon is even more beautiful than Handel and Liesar. It's larger, and each of its scales gleam with all the colors of the rainbow. The dragon's yellow eyes gaze at you. A middle-aged woman grabs a strap and swings out of the saddle, landing nimbly on her feet. Her piercing blue eyes stand out in her tanned face. Those eyes are turned on you as she walks over.

She glances at Hans, and he bows, then kisses her hand.

"Anakisha, Honored Rider of Queen Zaarusha." He introduces you to her.

You shake her hand, unsure what to do.

"You're a fine acrobat in the making." She smiles. "How would you like to become a dragon rider?"

Grinning, you answer, "Would I ever!"

The riders around you cheer. Marlies comes to stand beside you.

Hans puts an arm over your shoulders, and says, "We'll find you a dragon tomorrow."

Congratulations, this part of your story is over. You have confronted an archer, defended yourself with a magical flash-shield against a wizard, developed your strength and fitness, and performed stunts on a dragon. You absolutely love your own dragon, Zeebo, who is the perfect shade of green. Life at Dragons' Hold is full of adventure and every day you learn new riding stunts, gaining the respect of other dragon riders. Eventually your family join you in Dragons' Realm.

Maybe you'd like another adventure, giving vicious wolves earache, being snatched by a dragon, or feeding a dragonet chocolate.

It's time to make a decision. Do you:

Go to the great big list of choices? **P378**

Or

Go back to the beginning and try another path? **P199**

You have decided to go home with the Thomson twins

You face Mickel and Hans and say, "Thank you for looking after me and being my friends, but my family will be worried, and I miss them." The whirling portal is getting smaller. You don't have long. "I have to go home."

Handel rumbles. "We understand," says Hans. "Good luck."

"Remember to keep exercising," calls Mickel, as you jump through the swirling air. His voice drifts to you faintly. "And show those Thomson twins who's in charge."

You land on the grass in the park next to school. Bart, Becks and Bax are sprawled nearby. Bart jumps up and runs over to you, helping you to your feet.

"Ah, hope you're all right," he says gruffly.

A faint dragon roar floats through the portal. Bart twitches, staring at the shimmering air. When it closes with a pop, he looks relieved.

In the distance the bus motor is running. Hardly any time has passed.

"Come on," says Bart, taking your backpack for you. "Let's get to that picnic."

You all race to the bus together.

At the school picnic, Bart, Becks and Bax organize the other kids into a queue and get you to wrestle them. The sports teacher cocks an eyebrow, surprised when you win every match, and suggests that you form a school wrestling club.

Bart instantly nominates you as President. You appoint him as secretary and Becks and Bax as your advisors. Bax's squirrel becomes team mascot.

"Where did you learn to wrestle?" asks the teacher. "I've noticed you all use the same techniques."

Becks grins, "From a big family friend."

"Yeah," says Bax, "You could say he's a giant in the wrestling scene."

All the kids think he's joking. They jostle each other to wrestle you.

"Keep to the rules," calls Bart to the kids. "Wait your turn."

"No cheating," says Becks.

"Yeah," laughs Bax, "or I'll get a huge bronze dragon to eat you!"

Everyone laughs. Except Bart. He just looks nervous.

Congratulations you've developed your strength, been on a dragon, and formed a wrestling club with the Thomsons. Now and then, Handel opens a portal, letting you back into Dragons Realm, where Mickel and Giant John teach you more wrestling tricks so you can stay one step ahead of the Thomson twins. Although you don't ever become best friends with Bart, Becks and Bax, you do have an unusual bond due to your adventure. You tutor the Thomson twins in math, causing them to rename themselves the Thomson triplets.

This is the end of this set of choices but there are plenty more. Perhaps you'd like to train as a wizard, feed a dragonet chocolate or meet tharuks – the dangerous monsters lurking in the forests in Dragons Realm.

It's time to make a decision. Do you:

Go to the great big list of choices? **P378**

Or

Go back to the beginning and try another path? **P199**

You have decided to ask Handel to take you home

"Um…" You scrape the toe of your sneaker over the stony ground sheepishly. "Would you mind if I went home? I miss my family."

"Sure," says Hans. "Family is important." He puts his hand on your shoulder. "Would you like to go now?"

"Can I?"

Marlies shakes your hand. Dragon riders wave as you and Hans climb back into Handel's saddle and the great bronze dragon flies into the sky. In front of Handel, a shimmering oval appears in the air. You take one last glance at Dragon's Teeth, the fierce mountains that guard this beautiful valley.

Handel dives through the portal and lands on the grass in the park next to school. The Thomson twins run out of the trees and freeze, staring at Handel with their mouths hanging open. In the distance a bus is starting. Only a few minutes have passed since you left.

"Who are they?" asks Hans.

"The Thomson twins."

Hans frowns. "Don't you mean triplets?"

"Don't tell them," you whisper. "They can't count!"

Hans laughs. "Good luck. I hope to see you again soon."

Handel gives a dragon-y grin and blows a puff of smoke at the Thomsons. Then he and Hans leap through the portal.

Bart stares at the bronze tip of Handel's tail. "W-w-what was th-that?"

The portal closes with a pop.

"What?" You frown, pretending you're puzzled. "Oh, you mean Handel?"

Bart, Bax and Becks nod, their eyes wide.

"Just a friend of mine. He's always hanging around."

"Um, we'd better get to the bus before it leaves for the picnic," Bax says.

"You coming?" asks Becks.

"I can help you with your bag," says Bart.

"I'm fine, thanks," you say, trying not to smile.

You wonder what the teacher is going to say when she sees Handel's parting gift – the Thomson's soot-covered faces. She's never going to believe that a dragon blew smoke at them.

Congratulations, this part of your story is over. You have ridden a magnificent bronze dragon, met a wizard, developed your strength and fitness, and learned some dragon riding stunts. The teacher gives the Thomson twins a detention for playing with fire and warns them that arson is dangerous. They're too scared of Handel to ever trouble you again.

There are more exciting adventures in Dragons' Realm. Perhaps you'd like to tame a dragonet, find out what happens if you hide from the Thomson twins in the trees instead of behind the bleachers, or meet tharuks – the blood-thirsty monsters that roam Dragons' Realm.

It's time to make a decision. Do you:

Go to the great big list of choices? **P378**

Or

Go back to the beginning and try another path? **P199**

You have decided to go home with Peter

It would be good to see your family again. "Yeah, sure. Let's go."

"I'm so glad you're coming with me," Peter calls. "Go, Astera, jump through the world gate!"

The sunset and Dragons' Hold disappear. The icy peaks of Dragon's Teeth are gone. Astera lands on the neatly-mown grass at the park next to school, near the grove of trees and flower beds. It's still morning. In the distance the bus rumbles and the students chatter as they get on board.

Bart, Becks and Bax run out of the trees, and stop dead, staring.

Astera roars. You leap off her back, landing softly on the grass.

"What's that?" asks Becks, staring at Astera.

The purple dragon sends a small blast of flame towards the Thomson twins. They leap back, huddling together.

"I have to see my family and get Astera back before the portal closes," Peter calls.

You know he's right. "Good luck. See you soon."

Astera is a majestic sight flying across the park towards town, her purple scales gleaming in the sun. The twins gape at her speechless. You take off your cape and rain jacket and stow them in your backpack.

As Astera disappears, Bart, Becks and Bax turn to you. Standing tall, you look Bart directly in the eye.

Bart looks you up and down, obviously noticing your strong arms. His cheek twitches. "Um, I... uh... sorry for giving you a hard time this year." He scrapes the toe of his shoe in the grass and stares at his feet.

Becks looks like she'd rather be somewhere else.

Bax holds out a friendly hand so you can shake it. "Um, uh, want to sit next to me on the bus? It's time to go to the picnic."

You glance at your watch. Almost no time has passed since you went through the portal to Dragons' Realm. "Thanks, Bax, but I can manage getting to the bus." Striding away, you grin, reminding yourself to exercise your new muscles regularly as Mickel has taught you. Looking at your hands, you wonder if a little practice will help you to summon another magical flash-shield.

Your grin grows wider as the twins scamper after you, nearly tripping over themselves in an effort to be nice. Maybe you won't need that flash shield, after all.

Congratulations, this part of your story is over. You have confronted an archer, defended yourself with a magical flash-shield against a wizard, been dragon riding, developed your strength and fitness, weathered a terrible storm and found your missing cousin. And you won't have any more trouble from the Thomson twins, as long as you keep up the fitness routines Mickel has taught you.

Many more adventures await you. Perhaps you could rescue a dragonet, meet Giant John, go rafting, or train as a wizard.

It's time to make a decision. Do you:

Go to the great big list of choices? **P378**

Or

Go back to the beginning and try another path? **P199**

You have decided to stay at Dragons' Hold

"I'm going to stay here, Peter," you say.

"Then you'll have to jump," calls Peter. "Don't worry, Astera will catch you."

Peter stands in his stirrups to give you space. You gulp and awkwardly hoist a leg over the saddle.

"3, 2, 1, jump!" Peter yells.

Heart pounding, you fling yourself off the dragon. The wind snatches your cloak, and you plummet, feet first, towards the stony ground below. What were you thinking? You should've chosen to go home. If Astera's not quick, you'll be a human pancake.

"Oof!" The air smacks out of you as strong dragon forelegs grasp you in their talons. Astera deposits you gently on the gravel.

"Good luck!" You wave to Peter.

"You too," comes his faint reply.

Astera's tail disappears through the portal. The shimmering air shrinks and disappears.

"I'm glad you've decided to stay," says a voice behind you.

Whirling, you find Hans, his face glowing in the sunset. Above you, the snow-tipped mountains shine orange and pink.

Hans chuckles. "Peter's been here a long time. It's good for him to have a visit home." He places his arm across your shoulders. "But your adventure is only beginning. Let's find you a place to sleep and, in the morning, a dragon to ride. Before you know it, your dragon will be your new best buddy."

"A dragon of my own? That's amazing!"

Hans chuckles again. "I thought you'd say that."

Congratulations, this part of your story is over. You have confronted an archer, defended yourself with a magical flash-shield against a wizard, developed your strength and fitness, weathered a terrible storm and sent your missing cousin home.

Your new life at Dragons' Hold is full of adventure and your dragon becomes your best friend. Every day you practice the fitness routines Mickel has taught you. Now and then, you go back through a portal to see your family, amazed at how little time has gone by on Earth. Whenever you see the twins at home, they are always utterly respectful, which makes you smile. Sometimes Peter comes to Dragons' Hold and you race through the skies together. Who knows, maybe one day you'll convince your family to come too.

There are many more adventures. You could encounter ravenous wolves, rescue a dragonet, be snatched by a dragon, start a food fight, or meet Giant John.

It's time to make a decision. Do you:

Go to the great big list of choices? **P378**

Or

Go back to the beginning and try another path? **P199**

DRAGONS REALM

334

You have decided to do nothing and let Bart die

Bart's hands slip. "Please," he calls. "I'll never bully you again. And I'll make Becks and Bax stop too."

You watch him silently. The blue dragon he flew on scrabbles, trying to grip Bart, but rocks obstruct it. It roars. Bart's hands slip.

Someone shoves you aside and drops to the ground, reaching over the ledge. It's Marlies. She grabs one of Bart's hands as the other slips. His weight pulls her forward, but she hangs on tight to his arm with both of her hands. Her body slides towards the cliff edge.

Shocked that she could also die, you realize how foolish you've been and sit on her back, trying to prevent her from slipping. "Becks, Bax, help!"

They race from the back of the cavern. Bax grabs Marlies by the legs. In a flash of silver, Liesar lands on the edge of the ledge.

"A rope. In Liesar's saddlebag," cries Marlies.

Becks grabs the rope, passing Liesar one end. The silver dragon clamps it in her jaws.

Becks throws the other end down to Bart. He snatches it with his free hand and braces his legs against the cliff face, then Bart lets go of Marlies to grab the rope with his other hand.

You all scramble back from the edge, and Liesar slowly backs towards the cavern, helping Bart up onto the ledge.

Bart puffs and pants. He glares at you. "You were going to let me die."

"Is this true?" Marlies asks, her voice sharp.

You nod, staring at your shoes.

Bart glowers and mutters at you through gritted teeth. "Watch your back. I'm going to get you! Every day I'll be there, waiting for my chance."

"Yeah, Fart-face!" Bax says.

"Lousy coward!" yells Becks.

"Enough." Marlies holds up a hand. "The chance to become

dragon riders could help the four of you to change your relationship and become friends. But dragon riders must have the highest integrity."

"I'm sorry," you mumble, meeting her piercing gaze. "They've been bullying me for years."

"None of you have shown the maturity needed to overcome your grudges." She takes a deep breath, looking each of you in the eye. "I'm afraid you must all go home. Liesar, create a world gate."

The air in front of you shimmers.

"Goodbye," says Marlies, pushing you through the portal.

You land on the grass in the park next to school. Only a few minutes have passed since you left. In the distance, the bus is rumbling. It's about to leave for the picnic. Scrambling to your feet, you start to run.

A thud sounds behind you, then two more.

"Get Fart-face!" yells Bart.

"Right on," shouts Bax.

Becks lets out a whoop.

Their feet pound behind you. You spurt forward. Although you make it to the bus, the school picnic is miserable. The Thomson twins throw your lunch in the river, put beetles in your backpack, and shove you every time no adults are looking.

You apologize profusely, but know that Bart is never going to forgive you.

I'm sorry, this part of your story is over. Choosing to let Bart die means that you will not have a chance to become a dragon rider and that the Thomson twins will bully you for years. But don't worry, you can choose again.

More adventures await you. You could train as a wizard, imprint with a golden dragon, rescue a dragonet, or encounter tharuks – the dangerous monsters that prowl the forests of Dragons' Realm. You may want to try again.

It's time to make a decision. Do you:

Go back and save Bart to see what happens? **P342**

Or

Go back to the park and escape the Thomson twins through the hole in the fence? **P201**

Or

Go to the great big list of choices? **P378**

Or

Go back to the beginning and try another path? **P199**

You have decided to hold the wood and ride down the falls

Clinging onto the wood, you fly down the falls in stinging water, into a deep pool. The force of the water submerges you, turning you over and over until you no longer know which way is up.

As your breath starts to give out, you wonder what would have happened if you hadn't struggled with the dragon or you'd taken the trail along the river.

The wood you were holding flies towards you, hitting you on the head and everything goes black.

You are never found. Although Bart explains that a dragon was involved, no one ever believes him. But there is a positive ending to this story, because the Thomson twins never bully anyone again.

I'm sorry, this part of your story is over. Struggling with a dragon that came to your aid, taking a derelict raft, and not jumping back through the portal may not have been the best choices, but you can try again.

Perhaps you'd like to create chaos in a marketplace, ride a dragon, feed a dragonet chocolate, or encounter tharuks – the dangerous monsters that prowl the forests of Dragons' Realm.

It's time to make a decision. Do you:

Go back to your last choice and dive through the portal? **P333**
Or
Don't take the raft, explore the riverbank trail instead **P212**
Or
Go to the great big list of choices? **P378**
Or
Go back to the beginning and try another path? **P19**

You have decided to dive through the portal

You dive away from the spray, through the shimmering air. You land in a flower bed in the park next to school, hair and clothes dripping and water running into your eyes. Sinking back among the flowers, you breathe a sigh of relief. The nightmare is over.

Something soggy squelches beneath your back. Sitting up, you examine the remains of your shredded backpack. There isn't much left, except for the battered straps and a piece of torn fabric hanging off them. Your lunchbox, jacket and water bottle are gone. But you're still wearing your watch. It must've stopped a few minutes after you jumped through the portal.

Oh well, at least you're alive.

"Hey Fart-face!"

Not again. Bart Thomson rushes out of the trees towards you, Bax and Becks on his heels. After facing a dragon and an enormous waterfall, the Thomson twins are nothing. They loom over you.

Becks frowns at the water running down your face. "Crying 'coz we caught you?" she sneers.

"Hey, how did you get so wet?" says Bart.

"Just what I want to know!" says a teacher behind them.

The Thomsons whirl.

"It wasn't us!" cries Bax.

"We don't know what happened!" says Becks

"That's what they all say!" The teacher glares. "Look at that backpack. It's ruined." The teacher takes Bart's backpack off him and passes it to you. "I'm sorry they did this. You can have Bart's lunch. Run to the bus. You don't want to be late for the picnic."

Your watch hasn't stopped at all. Time is just different where you've been.

"We didn't do anything! It was a dragon," says Bart. "I saw it. I swear!"

"Bart Thomson. We've had enough of your bullying. And as for you two…," says the teacher leading the Thomson twins away.

You rush for the bus. Bart's backpack is heavy. You open it and discover all the snacks and money that Bart has stolen from other kids. When you give everybody their stuff back, they treat you like a hero. The school picnic is fun, but from that day on, you are careful around water, especially in rivers. You often wonder what would've happened if you hadn't wriggled and tried to get out of the dragon's grasp. Perhaps you would have had a completely different adventure altogether.

Congratulations, you made it back from Dragons' Realm alive. Your school mates think you're awesome for recovering their stuff. You survived the dragon carrying you in its talons and a crazy trip down a dangerous river on a derelict raft. Perhaps struggling in the dragon's grip may not have been the best decision. Perhaps you would have had a chance to meet dragon riders and ride a dragon yourself, if you hadn't struggled. Taking an old derelict raft from a rotting jetty also may have stopped you from having other exciting adventures.

Many more adventures await you, starting a food fight, giving wolves earache, becoming incredibly strong or rescuing a dragonet.

It's time to make a decision. Do you:

Go back and take the riverbank trail instead of the raft? **P212**
Or
Go back to your last choice and decide to hold the wood down the falls? **P337**
Or
Go to the great big list of choices? **P378**
Or
Go back to the beginning and try another path? **P199**

You have decided to stay at Dragons' Hold and ride Aria

A crowd of dragon riders come cheering from caves in the mountainside. More dragons land around you, roaring. Their riders clap you and Wil on the back, thanking you for bringing their dragonet home.

"This is the Great Zeebongi," calls Wil.

Around you, the crowd grows still. Then murmurs start.

"A feast," calls a man that looks like a Viking. "Tonight, we'll feast in Zeebongi's honor and to celebrate Aria's return."

The riders cheer. Wil grins. Bart, Bax and Beck whoop too, swept up in the midst of the celebration.

A woman with long dark hair and turquoise eyes approaches you. "Honored Zeebongi, my name is Marlies. I'll train you as a rider until Aria grows." She smiles, making you feel right at home. "And if you need to visit your family, Liesar can take you through a world gate any time you want." She gestures at her dragon.

The silver dragon lowers her head and nudges your shoulder. You stroke her nose. A hum thrums through her body. This is awesome. Yesterday you had no idea dragons existed, now they're your friends.

"Thank you, Marlies, I'd like that."

Wil grabs your arm. "I've always wanted to be a rider, and now we're here. We made it! I'm so happy."

As Wil starts questioning a dragon rider, Bart approaches you. "Um, thanks. You really aren't so bad after all." He smiles and gives you a friendly elbow in the ribs. "Thanks for bringing us to Dragons' Hold, Fart-face!"

People back home would find your tale of meeting dragons unlikely, but they'd *never* believe Bart Thomson was thanking you.

Your new life at Dragons' Hold is full of adventure and everyone honors you as Zeebongi, even the Thomson twins, who smile but don't tell anyone your real name. Aria and Wil become your best friends. Marlies trains you in archery, sword fighting and riding techniques. Aria grows quickly and is soon large enough for you to ride. You enjoy cruising through the skies on dragon back. Now and then, you go back through a portal to see your family, amazed at how little time has gone by on Earth. Who knows, maybe one day you'll convince them to come to Dragons' Realm too.

Congratulations, this part of your story is over. You have reunited a dragonet with its mother, escaped from tharuks and made friends with the Thomson twins.

More adventures await you. You could train as a wizard, test the strongwood trees, be snatched by a dragon, or find out what happens when you feed tharuks chocolate.

It's time to make a decision. Do you:

Go to the great big list of choices? **P378**

Or

Go back to the beginning and try another path? **P199**

You have decided to save Bart

You can't let Bart die. Lying on the rocky ledge, you reach over the edge and grab Bart's hand, hollering, "I've got you! Hold on!"

Bart's weight drags you forward and your body slips towards the edge of the cliff. The blue dragon roars. Two people thud onto your legs, stopping your slide forward.

"Gotcha!" shouts Bax, calling from your right leg.

"Hang in there, Bart," yells Becks, who's got your other leg.

Behind, the crowd murmurs. Boots appear beside your shoulder, at the edge of the ledge. "Don't worry," Marlies calls to Bart, tossing a rope around him.

Bart braces his feet against the cliff, and uses one hand at a time to get his arms through the rope so it's around his chest. When he's secure, the rope goes taut.

"You alright?" you ask.

Holding the rope, Bart grunts and starts pacing up the cliff face. He's heavy. How is Marlies holding him? Bax and Becks hop off you. You scramble to your feet. Liesar has the rope tight in her jaws, behind Marlies. The silver dragon backs towards the cavern, her powerful leg muscles flexing, hoisting Bart up onto the ledge. Everyone moves out of the way to make room for Liesar's massive body.

Puffing and panting, Bart lies on the ground for a moment. Becks and Bax haul him to his feet and hug him.

"Man, you're alive!" says Bax.

"Thanks to Fart-face," says Bart, coming over to you. He raises his hand.

You resist the impulse to flinch away. Surely he's not going to hit you.

Bart claps you on the shoulder. "You saved my life. I owe you. We'll never hassle you again." Behind him, Bax and Becks nod. Then Bart hugs you.

It comes as such a shock, you just stand there gaping. "Um, no problem."

"Well done," says Marlies. "Quick thinking is just the type of quality dragon riders need. Take a moment to relax, the dragons will be here soon."

"What dragons?" asks Bax.

Marlies explains, "Those just old enough to imprint. They need riders." She hands you strips of meat. "Once you've imprinted, feed your dragon. It will help establish a bond." Others crowd around her, taking meat too. She and Liesar usher everyone back to the cavern. "Leave space on the ledge for your dragons to land," Marlies says.

Bart puts an arm over your shoulder, and announces loudly. "You're my hero. I hope you get the best dragon."

The crowd murmurs, looking at you in awe.

Confetti-like specks appear in the sky on the other side of the valley. Soon a myriad of colors fill the air and the flurry of wingbeats announces the arrival of the dragons. They land on the ledge.

A pulse of energy thrills through you. Then another. Like a tide, the energy sweeps you forward, until you're eye to eye with a golden dragon. Your heart stands still as she regards you with her startling green eyes. Images and feelings wash through you – her wonder at breaking out of her egg, the thrill of her learning to fly, the joy she feels at meeting you.

A clear high voice sounds in your mind. *"At last, you've come. I've been to the imprinting grounds many times and never met my rider. I'm thrilled you're here. My name is Neronya."* The dragon winks at you. *"Hop on. Come fly with me."*

"Neronya. I can hear your thoughts – that's amazing." Your skin prickles with anticipation. Wonder fills you. She's the most beautiful creature you've ever seen. Her scales glimmer in the sun and her green eyes pierce you, taking your breath away with their intensity. You hold out the strips of meat Marlies gave you. Neronya delicately takes the meat from your hands, then licks your palms clean.

Around you, people and dragons are moving, but you hardly notice them. "You're really choosing me?"

"*Of course. You're the only one for me. Dragons choose their riders for life.*"

Touching the warm scales on her neck, you marvel. Although each scale is tough, her skin is supple and moves under your hand, giving it that soft leather feel. Her scent reminds you of warm summer days outside.

Marlies appears with a saddle, and shows you how to put it onto Neronya's back, then adjust it and fasten the straps.

Impatience grips you. Neronya snorts. You sense she's impatient too. She wants to fly with you. You clamber into the saddle. Her enormous legs tense, and she leaps off the ledge.

Airborne, you let out a whoop. The mountainside falls away. You shoot into the sky. Neronya's golden wings catch the light, shimmering in the sun. Your heart soars as Neronya ascends. Below you, dragons roar, their new riders shrieking with excitement. Neronya bellows in reply, her roar thrumming though her, resonating through your body.

Catching a thermal current, Neronya stops flapping and soars. You glide through the air, adrenaline rushing through you, the wind streaming into your face.

"Yahoo!" you cry.

A ripple of dragon laughter flits through your mind. "*Yahoo is about right, but your yahoos have only just begun.*" Neronya furls her wings, tucking them against her side, and dives headfirst towards the valley.

The other dragons are blurs of purple, green, red, blue and orange as you pass them, plummeting downwards. Snatches of sound whip into your ears, dragons roaring, people calling, but you can't make out their words.

The forest on the valley floor is getting closer. The trees, first a carpet of green, seem to rush up at you, suddenly becoming pointed treetops that could spear you.

"Neronya!" you squeal in panic, thighs tense, and hands tight on the saddle grips.

"*Relax, everything's under control.*" Neronya flips out her wings and breaks your rapid descent, flying over the forest towards a lake.

Your heart slows and you laugh. "That was incredible! Can we do it again?"

Neronya chuckles, a deep throaty sound that vibrates through her. *"I'm glad you enjoyed that. We have plenty of other tricks to try too."*

"I can't wait!"

A low horn peals throughout the valley.

"I'm afraid you'll have to wait. We've been summoned."

She lands in a grassy clearing near the edge of the lake. A dragon rider with dark curly hair and green eyes, astride a magnificent bronze dragon, much larger than Neronya, blows the horn again.

"That's Hans," says Neronya. *"He trains new riders."*

Dragons drop out of the sky onto the grass.

Bax is riding a red, Becks is on a green, and Bart has a purple dragon. They grin and wave at you. Other newly imprinted riders wave too. Everyone knows you, because they saw you save Bart.

"Liesar mind-melded and showed me how you saved that boy. You'll always be my hero too," says Neronya, raising her head proudly. *"You've saved me from being riderless and given me great joy."*

Your heart swells until you think it will burst. This is much better than a school picnic.

"Who is that boy you saved? And the other two?"

"The Thomson twins," you say. "They used to bully me."

"Even more noble of you to save him, then," Neronya says in your mind, sounding puzzled.

"What is it?" you ask.

"You called them twins, but there are three of them."

"Oh yes, they're actually triplets," you say. "But don't tell them that. They can't count!"

Congratulations, this part of your story is over. You have saved Bart's life, imprinted as a dragon rider and are about to start your training in earnest. Your new life at Dragons' Hold is full of adventure and

Neronya becomes your best friend. You know you'd never want to live without her. Bart's experience in falling off the ledge has changed him and he becomes your friend too, never bullying anyone again. Every day, you and the Thomson twins fly through the skies together, enjoying life in Dragons' Realm. Now and then, you go back through a portal to see your family, amazed at how little time has gone by on Earth. Although they miss you, they're thrilled that you're so happy. Who knows, maybe one day you'll convince your family to come to Dragons' Realm too.

Perhaps you'd like a longer adventure, starting a food fight, being caught by an archer, giving a dragonet chocolate or meeting tharuks – monsters roaming Dragons' Realm.

It's time to make a decision. Do you:

Go back to the park and escape the Thomson twins through the hole in the fence? **P210**

Go back to your last choice and let Bart Thomson die? **P334**

Go to the great big list of choices? **P378**

Or

Go back to the beginning and try another path? **P199**

CREEPY HOUSE

By DM Potter

The new house

Your family got a cheap deal on a bigger house, and the day you move in you find out why. Right next door is a creepy old place with ripped drapes and peeling paint. It looks like the set for a horror movie. Your family says it has character, but you think it might have rats. Or worse.

Your cat is safe in the spare room while the movers are going in and out so she doesn't get lost. The cat was a bribe from your family to make up for moving away from your friends. She's a little gray cat from the animal shelter. You thought of the perfect name for her: Ghost.

After the movers have gone and the doors are shut downstairs, you let Ghost out to explore her new home. She comes into your room as you are putting away the last of your books and jumps on your bed.

"Hello, Ghost. Do you like your new home?"

You settle down next to her with your book, but you are distracted by tapping at the window. That's odd, it's a second story window. You'd better take a look.

There's a tall tree just outside. You open the window and see that a branch is caught on some old wires. That must be causing the noise. You untangle the wires and then hear "Dinner's ready!" from downstairs. Your stomach growls. You don't need telling twice.

When you come back, Ghost isn't on your bed anymore, and you can feel a breeze from the open window. As you start to close it, you see your cat disappearing inside a window next door. She has climbed through the tree over to that creepy house.

"Ghost! Ghost! Puss, puss, puss!"

Through tattered drapes you can make out an old fashioned bed in the room over there. A movement catches your eye and makes you jump, and then you recognize yourself reflected in a long grimy mirror. You shiver a little. There's no sign of Ghost.

It's time to make a decision. Do you:

Go over to the house and try to get your cat back? **P354**

Or

Leave the window open and wait for her to return? **P349**

You have decided to wait for Ghost to return

You leave your bedroom window open hoping the cat will return. There is still no sign of her as you get into bed. As you drift off to sleep, you hear that tapping noise again. *It's just the tree*, you think.

In the middle of the night you wake with the feeling you aren't alone. You reach out for the bedside lamp, and flip the switch, but it hasn't been plugged in yet. The faint light coming in the window makes weird shadows on your wall. So what do you do?

Do you cross the floor in the dark to switch on the light? **P352**
Or
Stay in bed. It's too scary to move? **P350**

You have decided to stay in bed

You move a foot out from under the covers toward the floor. Why do people wear nothing on their feet in bed? You wish you had boots on. Your bare foot touches warm fur.

Please let it be Ghost. Please let it be Ghost, you think as your toes stroke something much bigger than Ghost. It's huge! A deep purring sound vibrates through the room. Too scared to stop in case it turns on you, you keep stroking the long, long, furry body. What is it?

"Meow."

The cry is from the tree outside your window and, before you can warn her, Ghost jumps through the window onto your bedroom floor. A sliver of starlight briefly illuminates her small silver body and then you can make out nothing. Beneath your foot the purring becomes a low deep growl and the creature rises from the floor beside you.

Your foot shrinks back under the covers. Ghost could just jump back out the window and stay safe, but she doesn't. Instead you hear a strong answering yowl. Doesn't she sense how big the thing is?

Amazingly, your intruder backs down. Its growls subside, and you sense that the two of them are meeting nose to nose. Your heart just about jumps out of your body as Ghost leaps onto your bed, and a minute later the other creature leaps up with her too. There is barely enough room for you. Both animals turn and tramp the bedclothes as they settle down for the night. Warm bodies wrap around you and you practically vibrate from their satisfied purring.

Too scared to contemplate moving out of the bed, you fall into an exhausted sleep. In the early morning you wake just in time to see the back of an enormous cat bounding out of your window.

When you go downstairs for breakfast, the TV is on in the kitchen.

"Shh!" your family says when you start telling them about your night. "Look at this."

The reporter on the morning news show is telling everyone to watch out because a tiger has escaped from a local wildlife park.

"Keep your kids safe inside their rooms," the reporter is saying.

There's a knock at the door, and Mr. Closeur, the realtor who sold the house, comes in. "Oh great, you've heard the news," he says.

Then Ghost walks in and lets out a friendly meow.

"Better keep the cat in again today, she'd never survive a meeting with a tiger," Mr. Closeur says.

You stroke Ghost. She might look like she wouldn't survive a meeting with a tiger, but you know different.

This part of the story is over. You've survived a night with a predator. It could have been worse, you could have been eaten! What would have happened if you'd made a different choice?

Do you want to:

Go back to the beginning of the story? **P347**

Or

Find out what would have happened if you'd switched on the light? **P352**

Switch on the light

Local Family Eaten By Wild Animal

A local family were eaten alive in their home on Saturday night. The police said that the murderous rampage started when one of them stupidly decided to turn on their bedroom light to find out what was under their bed.

"Everyone knows you don't do that," investigating Detective, Kahn Ivor, said. "You stay in bed and hope the boogie man moves on."

Wild life expert Terri Trimmings was stalking the tiger after it escaped from a local secret laboratory. "Some kid left their window open and the tiger has just slunk in there to hide. It would have been frightened and tired and disorientated. Oh, and drug-crazed too. It would have wanted a safe place to sleep off the injection we gave it and then head for the hills. Instead we got carnage and now people will want to put the animal down. The tiger is the real victim in all this."

Local realtor Mr Ford Closeur said he didn't think the accident would affect property prices on the street. "If anything, it's put our neighborhood on the map." He is handling the sale of the house and says the blood stains will easily come out of the carpet. Mr Closeur is new to the area himself after the mysterious disappearance of four realtors in the past two years. "They probably found themselves a bargain or two and retired. Being a realtor is an exciting job."

A memorial service for the family is likely to be canceled as they were new to the neighborhood and nobody knew them that well. "They didn't even come over and introduce themselves before they got killed," said local resident Ima Prodnoser. "Not great manners."

That's the end of this part of the story. Do you wish you'd stayed in bed?

Yes, stay in bed? **P350**

Or

Go back to the beginning and try another path? **P347**

Head next door to get the cat back

You grab a flashlight and go out into your yard. A wooden fence surrounds the house next door. An overgrown hedge has pushed the boards loose in places. The fence paint is weathered and flaking and even the graffiti has faded to gray.

You could probably crawl through, but you'd better go knock on the front door. Maybe, just maybe, somebody lives in this place. You come to a rusted iron gate between two fence posts. Through it you can see an overgrown path leading up to a rickety front porch.

It's starting to get dark. Are you sure you want to go next door?

Turn Back **P358**

Or

Keep Going **P355**

Keep going

The old gate creaks as it opens. You pick your way between the weeds growing through the broken path. Halfway between the road and the front door the gate shuts with a clang. There's no turning back now.

The front porch smells of decay – like a pile of rotting leaves. You can't see your own house next door through the overgrown trees. Your knees feel like jelly. Maybe you should have told someone where you were going.

You cautiously knock on the door, then look back towards the street. It's getting darker now. You put your hand up to your ear but can't hear anyone inside. Should you walk around the side of the house?

"Here, Ghost."

Suddenly, the door pops opens a crack. Maybe it was the force of your knocking?

You poke your head inside. "Hello?" you croak.

There's no reply.

"Ghost? Ghost. Come here, kitty, kitty."

Still no reply.

It's nearly dark. Nobody knows you're here. What should you do?

Turn back **P358**

Or

Step inside **P361**

You head into your house

Despite the overgrown lawn and battered old sign, this is your 'new' house. Maybe it's a joke. Your family is probably inside laughing right now.

The front door is locked and nobody comes when you knock. Perhaps the back door is open.

Nope, the back door is boarded shut.

Back out front you see the realtor your family bought the house from. He's just walking up the path with a new sign. He stops when he sees you.

"Hey kid. What are you doing here? This is private property."

"Yeah, I know," you say, "it's *my* family's property. Do you know what's going on?"

The realtor looks at you strangely. "Nobody has lived here for years. Get out of here."

OK, something really weird is happening. You go back out to the road. As soon as your foot hits the sidewalk, the spooky house looks spooky once more and your house seems fine. Relieved, you head to your house.

But when you step on your front path, everything changes again.

"I thought I told you to beat it, kid," the realtor says. "I don't want to have to call the police, but I will if I have to."

Argh, this is a nightmare!

You step back onto the sidewalk and again the house looks like the one you moved into. You try jumping quickly onto your property a few times but it's no use – the house switches on you and the realtor is getting more and more annoyed. He starts talking about calling child protection. You need to try something else.

"Meow."

In all the craziness you'd forgotten that Ghost was still next door. There she is now sitting on the porch, licking a paw and acting like she lives there. You trudge back over.

Next door's gate gives a shriek from its rusted hinges and you almost trip on a clump of weeds on the front path. You look up at the house. The illusion has slipped away. The house is once again a neglected ruin.

Ghost springs off the front porch and runs toward you, jumping weeds and rusted junk. She twines herself around your legs. You pick her up and stand there wondering what to do. On the second floor you can see your bedroom window. It's still open.

What if you could crawl across through the tree like Ghost did? What if you could get back to your house that way? As if in invitation the front door of the creepy house swings open.

Are you going to go inside? **P369**

Or

Are you going to chicken out? **P358**

You've chickened out

When you step back on your front lawn you stare. The neat grass you left a few minutes ago is wild and overgrown. There is a pile of newspapers on the front porch. The house looks like it's been empty for years. It looks like the creepy house and—

Whoah. When you glance at the creepy house next door, you do a double take. It looks perfect!

Its fence is straight and painted, the garden is manicured and flowers bloom in neat beds down the side of the path. That's not all.

A little gray cat is sitting on the porch next door. It's Ghost. Now you're conflicted. Should you:

Keep going to your new 'old' house? **P356**

Or

Go back to the spooky old 'new' house? **P369**

Trapdoor

As you pull the book from the shelf, the floor beneath you gives way and you slide down into waist deep water. There seem to be a lot of logs in the water. Oh, wait a minute. They aren't logs, they are aligaaaaaaaaaaaaaaaators!

Silly you.

Luckily, this is a 'you say which way' story and you can choose again:

This is the end of this part of the story. What do you do now?

Go back to the beginning and try a different path? **P347**

Go to the great big list of choices? **P380**

Or

Go back to the Library Room? **P370**

360

Get Tall and Slim Instantly

You've always wanted to be taller. You pull the book from the shelf. Perhaps this will be a bit like Alice in Wonderland.

It isn't.

As the book comes free, the ceiling starts to go upwards. The walls start to close in. Closer, closer, closer. You get it now. You'll be taller and much, much slimmer. Also a bit dead. You should have picked another book.

Your only hope is that this is a You Say Which Way and you can choose again:

What do you do?

Go back to the beginning and try another path? **P347**

Go to the great big list of choices? **P380**

Or

Go back to the library? **P370**

Keep Going (You're really, really going to go inside that house)

Drawing a deep breath, you push on toward the house. The very creepy house. The house that creepy things could happen in.

"Not helping," you mumble, as you try not to think about things that go bump in the night.

Bump.

"Oh, come on," you think, "not bumping. Not when I just thought of bumping. Note to self, don't think of anything worse than bumping."

Bump, bump, bump!

The bumping noise is coming from inside the house. You've just set your foot on the front porch when you hear it again.

Bump, bump!

Maybe it's Ghost trying to get out of there. You put another foot on the porch and reach for the front door.

Creeeeeeeeaaaaak. The front door swings opens by itself.

It's gloomy inside. Actual gloom that sucks up the light of the setting sun and makes it vampire-ready. Agh! Why did you just think about vampires? Think about happy bunnies. And lambs. Cute lambs running and bumping … oops, bumping.

Bump, bump, bump!

The noise is definitely coming from somewhere inside.

"Meow."

Is that Ghost? Maybe you won't have to go in if you can call Ghost outside. "Hello? Ghost? Puss, puss, puss. Here, kitty, kitty."

Nobody comes to the door. You push it open a little more.

C

R

E

A

K

Well, you won't be surprising anyone. It's weird how

opened, though. Maybe it was loose floorboards on the porch. Yeah, that had to be it.

Bump, bump, bump.

"Meow."

You take a step inside. You're in a long wood-paneled hallway that smells like dirty socks. There are stairs you could take to the next floor. Ghost might be up there because she got in upstairs through the tree outside your room.

"Ghost, here, kitty, kitty," you call, hoping you don't need to go any further.

Bump, bump, bump!

You could head down the hall. That could be where the bumping sound is coming from.

There's also a door to your left. Maybe you should check in there?

Which way do you go?

Go up the stairs. **P372**

Or

Go down the hall and find out what is bumping. **P363**

Find out what's bumping

There's a crack of light through a doorway at the end of the hall. You take a few cautious steps. Maybe Ghost is down there?

Bump, bump.

"Help!"

Whose voice is that? The bumping is directly ahead. So was the cry for help. You take a few more steps, then push the door open.

"Don't come in here!"

There's a guy wearing glasses and a striped t-shirt pinned against a boarded up back door. He's fighting off a huge washing machine that is taking up the walk space in a narrow laundry room and squashing against him.

Wait! A washing machine? You study the scene again, not quite believing your eyes.

Bump, bump.

Yup, a washing machine.

The man pushes the machine back a little and takes a deep breath. Then the washing machine kicks into the spin cycle and advances towards him once more. Bump, bump, bump.

"Arghhh, this thing is possessed! I'm getting tired. It's going to get me. Save yourself, kid."

He heaves the machine back so he has a little more room to breathe, but it looks like it's only a matter of time before he's flattened against the wall and squashed like a bug on a windscreen.

Bump, bump, bump!

The electric cord hangs out of the back of the haunted washing machine like a tail. Perhaps you can pull the plug out of the wall. You rush to the wall socket and yank on the plug. A blue arc shoots out of the wall narrowly missing your hand. The machine stops and stays stopped and the whir of the spin cycle stops too. In your hand, the cord starts to wiggle like a snake towards the outlet.

"Get out of there now!" you yell at the guy, who is standing there dumbly behind the machine. He gives the machine another push and manages to get himself free. In two strides he has joined you.

"Thanks I—"

He doesn't get to finish his sentence because the cord snaps out of your hand and back into the wall socket, and the washing machine turns abruptly and starts heading toward you both! You fling yourself back into the hall. The young guy lands next to you. When the machine gets to the doorway, it cuts out and retreats back into the laundry where it hunkers there perfectly innocently.

"Thanks for helping me. I thought I was a goner." He holds out his hand. "Harkness Keptic – ghost hunter."

"Ghost hunter?" you say. "Wasn't the ghost hunting you?"

"Wish I'd gotten some footage of that washer in there. Definitely emanating paranormal behavior."

"I think it was just an old machine with faulty wiring," you say. "There's probably a lot of faulty wiring in this house." You flick on your flashlight as you talk and play the light around the walls of the hall. "I came in here to find my lost cat. Do you think it's okay to look around?"

"Be quick. I'm going back to my office to get more equipment."

With that, the ghost hunter heads out the front door. Suddenly, you feel very alone. Okay you need to move on. What do you want to do?

Go up the stairs? **P372**

Or

Go back home? **P368**

Go up the stairs

Your left foot finds the first step, your right foot moves to the second. The hand rail wiggles when you grab it to steady yourself. It's a wonder this place is still standing.

The sound of your footsteps is almost as loud as your heart beat. Surely anyone or anything up here would hear you. You play the flashlight back and forth at the top of the stairs. There's a bathroom further down the landing. You can see right into that room because its door is lying on the floor. There is some kind of nest in the sink.

"Ghost?" you say softly. With all that has happened, you are seriously rethinking the name you gave your cat. Hopefully any actual ghosts up here don't think you want to chat.

"Here, kitty, kitty."

"Meow!"

"Ghost!"

Ghost's head peeks around the corner of a door on the right. You push it open far enough to get through. This is the bedroom opposite your own. There's the old bed you saw earlier. You walk over to the window and point the flashlight through the tree to your house. You can see your bed.

Clink. Clink.

Behind you there's a noise like metal on glass.

Clink, clink.

A sort of let-me-in noise. A shiver runs down your spine.

Clink, clink.

There it is again.

Turning, you are dazzled by a light pointing towards you.

Remembering the mirror you saw earlier, you relax, but then the hairs prickle at the back of your neck. You aren't pointing the light toward the mirror. Why is light pouring out of it?

Ghost growls as she stands between you and the mirror.

You slowly raise your own light. There in the mirror are *your* sneakers, *your* jeans, *your* t-shirt. And then you see *your* face. The reflection beckons you toward the mirror. It taps its flashlight against the glass and holds a hand up flat against the surface. Whatever is trapped in the mirror is trying to say something.

Clink, clink, clink.

Do you:

Run home? **P368**

Or

Touch your reflection? **P367**

Touch your reflection

You can't help reaching out your hand to touch your reflection. But when it makes contact with the mirror, coldness rushes through your body like you've fallen into freezing water.

You stumble forward into a weird room with icy walls. Behind you is the mirror. You look back through the mirror and see the tree and beyond it your own bedroom. Your reflection is in there too.

Then Ghost walks in. Your reflection bends to stroke her but Ghost puts up her back up and hisses.

You bang on the glass, but it's no use. You're trapped. The reflection looks up, sees you inside the mirror, waves, and then walks away.

THE END

Come on – you know that wasn't the best decision to make. It could have been worse – you might have been eaten by alligators. Maybe you want to be eaten by alligators? You do? Okay, well here's your chance, and a few others too.

Eaten by alligators. **P359**

Start the story over and try a different path. **P347**

Go to the great big list of choices. **P380**

Or if you want to go back in time to your previous choice:

Run Home! **P368**

Run Home!

"Let's go, Ghost," you yell. You streak past the mirror.

As you pass, the reflection scowls and tries to grab you. You swerve and rush out the door. Shining your flashlight down the stairs, you take them two at a time. Ghost bounds along ahead of you.

Downstairs, the front door is slowly closing. You reach it and slip through just before it shuts with a bang. Without looking back, you launch yourself off the porch and race to the gate. As you pass through the garden every shadow seems monstrous and threatening but in seconds you are wrenching the gate open and you're safely on the sidewalk. Your heart pounds. Ghost wraps herself around your legs and you bend down to pick her up.

You go back to your house and up to your room. You walk over to the window to shut it securely. Looking out, you can see the other bedroom. You catch sight of your reflection as you bend down and click the safety lock on your window. The reflection is doing everything you did, so for a second you think you imagined it. Then, as you stare, the reflection waves. It isn't a friendly wave. You draw the curtains and get onto your bed. Would anyone believe you if you told them? You doubt it.

THE END

(or one of them)

What now? Do you:

Start the story over and try another path? **P347**

Or

Go to the great big list of choices? **P380**

Enter the house with Ghost

Perhaps everything would return to normal if you went back to your house by climbing through the tree? Gulp. You'll have to go through the spooky house.

The front door swings open before you touch the handle. Why do you get the feeling the house has been waiting for you? You feel like a fly in a spider's web. You step inside with your heart pounding.

A light flickers on over the stairs. It's like the house is telling you to go up. The rest of the house is in darkness. Through the gloom, you can just make out a door to your left.

Maybe you should check it out instead? Are the stairs a trap?

Do you:

Try the door? **P370**

Or

Go up the stairs to the tree? **P372**

370

Open the gloomy door

As you step inside, a desk lamp flickers on. Resting in a pool of light on the desk top is a note. As the lamplight gets stronger, you see that the room is round and lined with shelves. There must be hundreds of books in here.

As you take another step toward the note, the shelves start moving. When you turn back to look at the door, it isn't there.

Uh oh.

You pick up the note.

> WATCH OUT FOR MOVING BOOK SHELVES.
> IF TRAPPED, READ YOURSELF FREE.

Well, great. If this note hadn't lured you into the middle of the room, you might not have triggered off the moving shelves in the first place.

You try pushing the wall where you think the door was, but nothing budges. Okay, the note said 'READ YOURSELF FREE'. Maybe there are books that can help you get out of here.

You'd better pick a book. You browse the titles of the closest shelf. But which one do you pick? A few seem familiar.

Trapped in a Library **P371**
Trapdoor to Alligator Holding Tank **P359**
Dragons Realm **P199**
Get Tall and Slim Instantly **P360**
Dinosaur Canyon **P1**
Deadline Delivery **P105**
Creepy House **P347**

Trapped in a Library

The shelves begin to move as you pull the book out. When you see the door appear, you grab the handle and leap back into the hallway. Ghost jumps silently after you and you slam the door.

Then you remember the note. Now it's too late. You left it back on the desk. You should have written a warning for the next person. Well, you know how to get out now. Smugly, you open the door and head towards the desk. Just like before, the shelves slide over the door.

When you pick up the note, you realize your mistake.

> NEVER GO BACK INTO A HAUNTED ROOM.
> DON'T YOU KNOW THE SAME STRATEGY WON'T
> WORK TWICE? HOPE YOU FIND THE DOOR
> BEFORE YOU FIND THE ALLIGATOR PIT!

You walk over to the shelf where you found the book that let you out before. But these aren't the same books! In fact the books aren't even written in English! You're going to have to pick randomly. Your hand hovers over the place where you got the right book last time.

You hold your breath as you pull it from the shelf....

THE END

Sorry about that. There wasn't a logical reason to explore this room and you weren't getting out alive. The creepy house won this round. Would you like to try again? Do you:

Start at the beginning and take a different path? **P347**

Go up the stairs to find the tree? **P372**

Or

Check out the great big list of choices? **P380**

Go up the stairs to the tree

The old stairs creak and groan. Half way up, your foot pushes through rotten timber. You grab the stair rail and sway. Remnants of the steps fall below, landing with a splash. You point your flashlight down into dark, glinting water. It must be the basement. Looks like it's flooded down there. You shudder, thinking about the stairs giving way and falling into the dark, murky water.

There's muffled thumping and bumping somewhere else in the house. That bumping can remain a mystery as far as you're concerned. You just want to climb out the window and through the tree back to your house. With luck, you'll be able to get back to your proper house and your family so long as your feet don't touch the ground.

Ghost pads next to you as you reach the top.

"Which way, Ghost?" Oh, you wish you hadn't said 'which' and 'ghost' out loud. Ghost mews and trots through the first doorway, so you follow. It's the room you saw from your bedroom earlier. Your window is still open and from here everything looks just as it should.

A movement brings your attention back to the room you are standing in. There's an old mirror in the corner. For a moment, it almost seems as if your reflection moved, but it can't have. You ignore the mirror and open the window. Ghost jumps out and scampers along a sturdy-looking branch. It will be tricky but you are pretty sure you can make it over the branch too.

You ease yourself out of the window, grabbing a high branch for balance while your feet find another. Carefully and slowly, you make your way to the trunk. Ghost mews encouragement. You don't need her to tell you not to look down.

Thump!

Not. Looking. Down.

Thump!

The whole tree shudders. Okay, you're going to have to look down.

Thump!

Swinging an ax, at the bottom of the tree, is the realtor.

"Hey!" you yell. "Stop that! I'm in the tree!"

The realtor looks up and smiles the least friendly smile you've ever seen, and then takes aim at the tree and swings again.

You're angry now. You know you've chosen the right path to get home and for some reason this realtor does not want you to succeed. And this beautiful tree is being wrecked and broken by him.

You stroke the bark and whisper to the tree, "I'm so sorry he's hurting you." You hurry across. Is it your imagination or is the path a little easier? The branch you are standing on feels thicker and it seems to be moving you toward your bedroom window. Ghost is nearly home. She stops and rubs her head against one of the branches and yowls down to the man with the ax below.

Thump!

Oh no, how long will the tree stand?

With the sound of cracking branches and twigs, a massive branch lowers itself to the ground and grabs the man in its giant wooden hand.

There is a scream as his ax falls to the ground.

Meanwhile, you are lifted to your bedroom window and gratefully scrabble inside. From the safety of your room, you watch the tree deposit the Realtor in the room you've just left. He shakes his fist defiantly at you, then turns to leave.

But the tree pushes the man toward the mirror instead.

You brace yourself, ready to hear shattering glass as the man nears the mirror, but it doesn't happen. The realtor is absorbed into the mirror and his reflection can be seen banging against the inside of the glass. After a moment, his image begins to fade and soon all you can see is yourself leaning out of your bedroom window

"Phew, that was close, Ghost."

Ghost rubs herself round your legs purring and meowing. You pick her up and turn back to the tree.

"Thank you," you say. The only reply is a thud of the window shutting in the old house.

It's going to be interesting living here.

THE END

(or one of them)

But have you tried all the paths?

It's time to make a decision. Do you:

Go back to the beginning and try another path? **P347**

Or

Go to the great big list of choices? **P380**

List of Choices

DINOSAUR CANYON

At the campsite 1

Go left into Gabriel's Gulch 5

Go right, towards the eroded hills 9

Climb the arch 12

Go back into the canyon 16

Go into the deserted mine shaft 20

Follow the trail further up the hill 23

Stay on the arch 28

Get off the arch 33

Follow the ridge 38

Head back to where your school group set up camp 42

Go exploring in Gabriel's Gulch 46

Try to explain the time travel to Mister J 52

Follow a dry watercourse to the canyon floor 58

Keep the time travel secret to yourself 63

Decide to time jump on your own 66

Tell Mister Jackson what happened 69

Go further into the mine 76

Dig your way out of the mine. 82

Try to disable the truck. 86

Rush back to camp 93

Animal Facts 97

Dinosaur Facts 99

DEADLINE DELIVERY

Dispatch Office 105

Tollgate 109

Stay on the Rhino 112

Defend Yourself 113

Boom-boom-boom-BOOM 114

Join the Rusty Rhino Crew 120

Stay a Courier 121

Jump Overboard 122

Leave the Rhino and Walk to Brine Street 123

Up to the Over-City 126

Ivory Tower 129

Run from the Police Robot 131

Stay in the Under-City 133

Run to the Tollgate 135

Ignore the Rhino 138

Secret Tunnel 140

Cabbage Boat Ride 143

Jump out of the Boat 145

Decide Later 150

Stay on the Boat 153

No Cabbage Boat Ride 155

Make a Run for the Bridge 158

Pretend the Security Pass is Yours 160

Avocado Corporation 164

Get Away from Bradley Lime 167

Return the Security Pass 169

Hope the Pirates Fight Each Other 172

Help the Froggy Kid 179

Become a Froggy 181

Sewage Treatment 183

Fish 186

Return to Deadline Delivery 191

Become the Clinic Courier 193

Run from the Kannibals 194

Follow the Old Man's Orders 196

Run for the Hole 198

DRAGONS REALM

A Bad Start 199

Race across the park to the hole in the fence 201

Hide from the Thomson twins in the trees 202

Follow the trail into the forest 204

Take the trail along the riverbank 212

Stay still because you trust the dragon 218

Wriggle to get free of the dragon's grasp 221

Stay with Master Giddi and become an apprentice wizard 223

Stay with Mia and continue training 227

Go with Hans on his dragon, Handel, to Horseshoe Bend 230

Learn Mickel's strength-building secret 236

Train with Giant John 240

Go to Montanara for supplies 246

Run to the stables to hide 252

Escape in Giant John's wagon 256

Stay in the stables and confront the tharuks 261

Go straight to the blue guards 262

Make Aria sing to scare the wolves away 266

Cut Mia out of the net with your knife 270

Leap onto the tharuks' heads 272

Offer the tharuks your chocolate 274

Go to Dragons' Hold with Hans 278

Climb into Handel's saddlebag 280

Stay in Handel's saddle behind Hans 285

Take the raft and go down the river 290

Face the tharuks 292

Follow Bax and Becks home 294

Feed Aria chili tuna fish so she can flame the wolves 296

380

Decide to farewell Aria and return home 299

Decide to stay with Mickel 301

Stay in the tree 303

Dash into the forest 305

Go with Wil and Aria to Dragons' Hold 307

Convince Becks to stay with the tharuks 311

Use magic so Bart and Bax bring you chocolate 314

Take Mia through the portal 317

Stay and fight the tharuks 319

Hide in the marketplace 320

Become a dragon acrobat 324

Go home with the Thomson twins 326

Ask Handel to take you home 328

Go home with Peter 330

Stay at Dragons' Hold 332

Do nothing and let Bart die 334

Hold the wood and ride down the falls 337

Dive through the portal 338

Stay at Dragons' Hold and ride Aria 340

Save Bart 342

CREEPY HOUSE

The new house 347

Wait for Ghost to return 349

Stay in bed 350

Switch on the light 352

Head next door to get the cat back 354

Keep going 355

You head into your house 356

You've chickened out 358

Trapdoor 359

Get Tall and Slim Instantly 360

Keep Going (You're really, really going inside that house) 361

Find out what is bumping 363

Go up the stairs 365

Touch your reflection 367

Run Home! 368

Enter the house with Ghost 369

Open the gloomy door 370

Go up the stairs to the tree 372

More 'you say which way' adventures

Pirate Island

In the Magician's House

Between The Stars

Danger on Dolphin Island

Lost in Lion Country

Once Upon An Island

Secrets of Glass Mountain

Volcano of Fire

The Sorcerer's Maze - Adventure Quiz

The Sorcerer's Maze - Jungle Trek

The Sorcerer's Maze - Time Machine

YouSayWhichWay.com

29279094R10238

Made in the USA
Lexington, KY
28 January 2019